A DEVIL'S
GOSPEL

ALSO BY KARL EL-KOURA

The *Father John* Trilogy

  Father John VS the Zombies

  Bishop John VS the Anitchrist

  Saint John VS Death (forthcoming)

The Last Adventure of Garrius Arilius

Ooter's Place and Other Stories of Fear, Faith, and Love

The Lost Stories: A Series of Cosmic Adventures

New Releases by the Author

Want to be among the first to know when new books by Karl El-Koura are published? Send an email to newsletter@ootersplace.com or visit http://www.ootersplace.com/newsletter/ to sign up.

KARL EL-KOURA

A DEVIL'S GOSPEL

A Devil's Gospel
© 2017 by Karl El-Koura

ISBN: 978-1-988798-00-4
Cover design by the author. Cover image from Pixabay.com.

For more information, visit:
www.ootersplace.com/ADevilsGospel

To my dad, the priest of our "little church"

Book One: Shadows

1	The First War	3
2	A Man and a Woman	15
3	A New War	23
4	A Man of Faith	35
5	A Man of Dreams	49
6	A Man Called Israel	63
7	A Prince	81
8	A Savior	95
9	A Line of Judges	111
10	A King	125
11	A Master Builder	139
12	The End	153

Book Two: Substance

1 The Son of God   165
2 The Tempted Man   171
3 The Lamb of God   179
4 The Mother of God   187
5 The Two Questions   195
6 The Divine Savior   203
7 The Incarnate God   213
8 The Problem   221
9 The Wonder   227
10 The Triumph   233
11 The Victory   243
12 The Eighth Day   253

Book One *Shadows*

Chapter One

The First War

IT all started with a man and a woman.

Did we think He-Who-Rules could do it, even after he'd failed so spectacularly? We all did, each of us for our own reasons: because we wanted the relief that his success brought, or because it was so much fun to torment them, or even because some of us came to really believe the lie he told us, that we could be victorious against Him after all.

Did the Enemy have this planned all along? That question tortures me above all else, tears me apart from one end of my being to the other, and is worse to me than anything He-Who-Rules can do. Did we ever have a chance? It's a silly question, isn't it? Some of the fallen ask this other silly question: can the Enemy create a stone so heavy that even He can't lift it? Before the First War, He-Who-Rules asked us something similar, and at the time it didn't seem silly but very serious.

We met in a hall I'd sung myself. I think that bit was on purpose, though I never thought of asking then or since, and now it's too late.

Few of us remember those days, but I've never been able to forget. I'd been reshaping an old castle I'd built long ago, singing it into a more rounded style that I thought was different and would please my friends, when suddenly I became aware that I was being watched.

"Lucifer sends me," Moloch said.

"God would like—?"

"I said Lucifer sent me," Moloch interrupted, smiling, "not God." He whispered a location in one of the lower dimensions, but it wasn't until I shifted there that I realized we stood in one of my old songs.

"Welcome, brethren." Lucifer shimmered the lightest blue, his glow more radiant than any angel I'd ever known, and yet duller than usual. To look at Lucifer was always an experience, but even then I noticed a difference—as if he stood behind a thin wall of smoke. The

3

Transformation had already begun, I just didn't know it yet.

His voice was as strong and commanding as ever, and it projected across the entire hall.

"I've called you together, brethren, to tell you a sad truth. We've been had, tricked by God Himself. We watched as He created a new dimensional space and like fools we cheered. We sang together and shouted for joy. We thought he was creating shiny stars and pretty planets. We didn't realize what he was actually making."

I didn't understand what was happening, or why we were meeting in secret, in a dimension I'd used to practice my songs. I didn't understand, but I didn't like the way it made me feel.

"Do you know what He was actually making, Enoch?"

I looked up, startled. The room was empty except for Lucifer and I; it was a trick he had and still has, to make you feel that he's speaking to you alone in a room full of people.

His eyes, green and luminous, bored into me. In those eyes I'd always read judgment and criticism, or perhaps I equated how intimidated Lucifer made me feel to the inadequacy that always accompanied it.

"What?" I said.

"He was making a home."

"So? He's made all sorts of things."

"This is different. It's a home for a new kind of creature, a creature also possessed of an intellect and will, but a creature not like us."

"How do you know all of this?"

"I've been offered dominion over their home."

"To rule over them?" I said, surprised.

Lucifer's eyes flashed a deep, fiery red. "To help them," he said, speaking slowly. "To guide them. In other words, to serve them."

I took a step back. "I don't know that we should be talking like this."

"Is that what you want, Enoch? To spend eternity in servitude?"

"We were created to serve."

"To serve God!" Lucifer's voice seemed to have turned to flame, and his words burned as they washed over me. "To serve the Ancient of Days, not his new pets. Not these new creatures with two natures."

"Two natures?"

He shrugged, his eyes glimmering green again. "I don't know that

I understand it; I do know that I don't understand why he's chosen to create these beings. Are we insufficient? Do you feel insufficient, Enoch?"

I did, but kept the thought to myself.

Suddenly the room was full again, packed with the other angels I'd seen before, angels whose eyes were fixed on Lucifer.

"Can God create a creature so powerful that even He can't stop him?"

I didn't know what he meant, but presumably the others did because they cheered.

"If we claim our right to be self-ruled, who will stop us? If we demand a dimension of our own, away from God and these new pet creatures, free to form it as we wish, free to rule it as we wish—who will stop us?"

As he spoke, the angels cried out their support and excitement.

"You're not with me, Enoch?"

Again I felt that we were alone and that the distance between us had collapsed. Lucifer stood so close that I could feel the sense of disappointment radiating from him.

"It's not that," I said. "It's just... I like it here."

"Because you get to make trifles?" Lucifer must have sensed my annoyance, because the tone of his voice suddenly changed, from a condescending to an appeasing one. "I've never known a better builder, Enoch. But what are you really doing, after all? You're taking pre-existing material and reshaping it, suggesting new forms and functions to things that already have a form and a function. Wouldn't you like to truly create something? To create it from nothing?"

"But that's not possible." I paused. "Is it?"

Lucifer smiled. "If you follow me, you won't ever feel the need to ask that question again."

The angels cheered once more. There were yells for Lucifer to waste no time in speaking to God and asking for a dimension of our own.

Lucifer put up his arms to silence them; his glow was angry, though he tried to restrain it.

"Brethren," he said, voice soft and gentle and betraying none of his annoyance, "do any of you know God better than I do? Is any one of you closer to Him than I am?" He paused to look around the room; the angels seemed suddenly subdued and their excited glows had dimmed. "And do I think that God will hand over the reins to a new kingdom for us to rule together just because we ask? He respects strength, force, and action; not cowardice and humility and pleading. If you want to continue being servants—go your way. But if you want to rule, as God rules—if you feel you deserve to exercise your powers and your will without interference—you need to demand it with force and not just with words!"

"Use force against God?" someone said. "We'll be destroyed!"

"He won't destroy you," Lucifer said, shimmering red so brightly that no one could have missed it. His glow was back to normal in the next moment. "God will give us what we want, if we give Him no other choice."

Looking around, it seemed to me that there were fewer angels now than when Lucifer had first welcomed us.

"You're either with me or you're against me," Lucifer said, and his appearance began to change. He grew, taller and taller, towering over us several-fold by the time he stopped. Of course now we would recognize it as the dragon, scaly and metallic and breathing fire, that has haunted the fantasies of the fallen, but at the time none of us had seen anything like it, and we were mesmerized.

"Enoch," the dragon said with Lucifer's voice, "sing us weapons."

I did it, of course, tearing apart the hall that I'd built and reshaping the broken pieces into one sword after another. I worked in a daze, so quickly that I didn't know how many weapons I'd already made and how many were left to make. At one point I noticed that most of the armed angels had been led away by the dragon. The remaining angels followed one at a time, leaving as soon as I handed them a sword. Much later, when the hall lay in ruins around me, and only a handful of angels were left, Moloch shifted in, looking haggard and pulsing a dull, pained glow.

"Come quick, all of you," he said. "Forget about weapons, just come! We are being laid to waste!"

Moloch was already starting to shift but I called out after him. "By God?"

"By Michael," Moloch said. "He's assembled his own army. We tried to take them by surprise, but they knew. They knew we were coming and they were ready for us. Now move!"

We followed Moloch, the handful of us who hadn't yet picked up a sword and probably weren't too keen on getting one anytime soon. We arrived in a higher dimension of Heaven to a scene of pure chaos. Sparks of lightning flew from swords as they crashed against each other; angels grappled and struck at other angels, causing bursts of fire to erupt when their fists made contact. Towering above all was the Lucifer-Dragon, swiping his tail and breathing fire in a mad, angry attempt to damage someone or something. Mesmerized, I watched Michael dodge the dragon's attacks. Beelzebub rushed at him, but one of Michael's troops—Gabriel, maybe, but it's so hard to remember now—dove between them and knocked Beelzebub to the ground, landing on top of him.

"Enoch, don't just stand there!"

I didn't know who spoke or even if it was one of Michael's angels or one of Lucifer's.

Beelzebub threw Gabriel off of him, then picked up his sword from the ground and swung. Gabriel stepped into the attack, grabbed his arm, and snapped it. In one motion, he grabbed the falling sword and plunged it into Beelzebub. His scream at that moment was like nothing I'd ever heard before. Squealing, desperate, pathetic, he yelled in pain and agony, then burst into flames. The sight and sound was horrible, and soon I saw and heard it repeated throughout the battlefield as more of Lucifer's angels were overthrown by Michael's soldiers.

Suddenly a sword was pressed into my hands. "Come on!"

It was Abaddon, and he was already charging at Michael. I ran after him to pull him off course—what was the point of this madness? We'd already lost, I knew; it was time to lay down weapons and suffer the consequences.

Abaddon cut down an angel on his way to Michael, but another appeared in his way. I was so focused on Abaddon that I didn't realize someone was standing in my way too; in my panic I struck with my sword, connected. Jegudiel fell back, but reached forward almost immediately and wrenched the sword from my hand. Before I could move, he plunged it into my chest.

The pain was so powerful that for a moment I didn't make a sound. Then I felt my entire body turn to fire and, unconscious of anything but the anguish and the terrifying feeling that my very existence was being consumed, I screamed. Slowly, although the pain didn't subside, I became conscious of something else: I was sinking, falling, as if the fire had burned away my substance and I was no longer solid enough to stand. Before I could have another thought, an explosion like lightning blinded my vision, but I didn't need to see to know what had happened; Lucifer was overcome, struck down by Michael's fiery sword.

I felt myself slipping further and tried to scramble to keep my footing. But it was impossible, and I fell through the dimensions, screaming in agony and convinced that I was being annihilated.

"Have mercy, Lord!" I cried, but I knew it was too late. It will infuriate Lucifer to learn that even in those first few moments of defeat, I begged for God's mercy, but I don't care. What more can he do to me now?

No one realizes, or at least no one remarks on how we have gradually come to use the words of the fallen to understand ourselves, even to understand and describe half-remembered events that occurred before the fallen were created. We've lived among them for so long now that their very concepts and images have become our own. I suppose we thought—certainly Lucifer thought—that influence and persuasion could flow in a line with a single direction from us to them. But can any of you listen to yourself speak for a moment and deny that they have influenced us just as much as we've tried to influence them?

I remember nothing of what happened next, nothing until I awoke some time later, feeling dazed and groggy, to borrow three more concepts from the fallen. I wasn't sure where I was, not because I couldn't see but because I saw everything as if through a fog. I stumbled to my feet. Shadows passed over me.

"Hello?" I said, and suddenly I became aware of the sound of wailing coming from all around.

I tripped over something and fell to the ground. The fog started to clear, or I grew accustomed to it. A creature crawled on the ground next to me.

"The pain," Beelzebub said, in a voice as different from his old voice as his appearance, dark and glob-like, was from his previous form and radiance. "Make it stop. The pain...the burning."

I kneeled beside him, not sure if touching him would provide comfort or agony, and especially not sure which sensation it would cause in me. "I'm sorry, I don't know what I can—"

There was no point in continuing to speak. Beelzebub had forgotten about my presence and returned to wailing and crawling, half-blind, searching like the others for something that would quench their agony and ignoring everything else, including one another.

Before us stretched plains of dark, craggy rock. As my vision cleared, I saw a lake on fire and walked toward it. The lake burned and bubbled, and as I stood on its shore, something reached out and grabbed my ankle, burning me with its excruciating touch.

"No!" I yelled, and struggled against the slithering fire that crept up my leg. "Let go!"

But suddenly a head emerged from the fire. The once-luminous angel of God used my body to pull himself out of the lake. Finally he stood before me, charred and ugly, not equal to the shadow of the creature he used to be—not that the creature he used to be had ever cast a shadow.

"Lucifer, I—"

"Don't call me that anymore," he said, his voice soft and distant and choked by pain. He looked past me, over my shoulder to the pathetic sight of the crying, crawling remains of his army.

"Silence!" he yelled suddenly. "Silence all of you!" They quieted down, probably as a reflexive response to his voice, which still carried the memory of the power and glory of the one he once commanded. "Gather around me."

The dark angels pulled themselves together and, one by one, walked or crawled toward Lucifer, who stood backlit by the small explosions of the fiery lake.

"You're scared," he said, spreading out his arms as if he wanted to embrace us all and make the fear disappear. "You're terrified because you think we've lost the war." His voice suddenly dropped in intensity, as if he were about to whisper a secret. "We haven't lost. We've won!" He spun his arms around. "What did we fight for? Independence, no? A home of our own, far from the Enemy? Look around, brethren!"

They looked around, and saw what Lucifer wanted them to see. In a loud and happy voice, he told us that the pain we currently felt was the Enemy's one parting shot; he told us to think about the agony He must be in to have lost his greatest angels; and when finally he said "We won, brethren! We won!" a great cheer went up, although it sounded more like screaming than cheering.

He turned to me. "Enoch, sing us a palace."

"A palace?"

Lucifer nodded, eyes burning with lust. "Make it the same as the

Enemy's."

I sang, but nothing happened. I sang again, more insistently, then more desperately, but still the rocks didn't respond.

The fire in Lucifer's eyes flickered for only a moment. "Brethren, it is as I suspected. This is the price of freedom! It is not a cost I hesitate to pay. Mammon, pick up that stone you're sitting on. Moloch, Agares, Sytri—knock down that cliff. Enoch, don't just stand there—show them what to do!"

I did my best, directing the dark angels like a colony of ants. Some pieces could be used as they were brought to me; others needed to be smoothed out in the fiery lake; still others could be combined by smashing them into one another. Soon I had everyone separated into groups of gatherers and smoothers and smashers. We worked in a frenzy while Lucifer watched with thinly veiled impatience. When construction was complete, we had a structure that looked nothing like the Enemy's palace, consisting entirely of a throne room that was barely worthy of the name.

"Behold your castle, brethren!" The brethren screamed their cheers. "Is it not wonderful?" Lucifer led everyone inside. "Is it not more glorious than anything you've ever seen?" He sat down on the rocky, jagged-topped throne. "We must elect a leader, brethren. Someone who will—"

"Lucifer!" Beelzebub yelled and the cry was taken up by others. "Lucifer!"

He held out his hands to quiet them. "I accept," he said, leaning forward. "I ask only one thing—call me Lucifer no longer. I am Satan, and I will oppose the Enemy and bring destruction on everyone He favors."

As the dark angels chanted the new name of their new leader, Satan sank back into the chair, looking comfortable and pleased with his throne and his castle.

Through thousands of years, we've rebuilt that chair, and the room, and the palace. We've added levels above and below, and rooms all around. And when Satan asked me to design and build a dungeon far beneath everything else, I carried out his order and had no idea that he was making me build the place where he planned to imprison me.

ONe day Satan found me walking along the shores of the fiery lake. "It doesn't end," I said. "I've shifted up and down the shore, every day going a little bit further before coming back. It just keeps going."

"You're not like the others, are you, Enoch? You still remember what it was like before."

I nodded.

"Many of them have mostly forgotten; the rest are forgetting more and more as time goes on. That's good—if they remembered what they were like before..." He let the unfinished sentence hang in the air. "They're better than when we first got here, don't you think?"

"I guess so, yes," I said, anxious for him to get to his point because I felt so uncomfortable speaking to Satan, especially alone.

"People trust you, Enoch. I need you to find out what they're saying about me."

"I can tell you right now," I said. "They're not happy. They're bored."

Satan kneeled over the lake and stared into it, as if it were a mystery he wanted to solve.

"Some of them still remember the war," I continued. "They say that we lost, despite your assertions to the contrary. You led us in an uprising against God—against the Enemy—and He is still in His High Country and we are in... this place."

Satan turned his head to look at me, his eyes burning. "Do you think I lost the war, Enoch?"

For a moment, I thought of lying. But I knew that eventually word would get back to Satan; I'd been the most vocal person reminding anyone foolish enough to repeat Satan's words that in fact we'd been defeated in a spectacular way, and that when the fearsome Lucifer-Dragon fell like a bolt of lightning, Michael was left standing. "Yes, we lost," I said.

"Don't look so scared, Enoch. Of course we lost—but that was only the first war."

"It was the only war," I said.

"So far." Satan stood and faced me. "Our brothers have forgotten the way things were, but they've also forgotten the way they themselves were. They've become impatient, restless, selfish. But I have a plan that will solve all of our problems."

"A plan for a second war?" I said.

Satan nodded.

I spoke my next words carefully. "A war against the Enemy?"

"Not exactly."

"Then who?"

"His new creatures."

"Oh," I said.

He motioned for me to follow him back to the castle. "Enoch, I may be gone for a while. Some of our brothers may be tempted to do something foolish in my absence. You understand of course how that would be bad for all of us?"

"What do you want from me?"

Satan stopped in mid-shift and put a hand on my shoulder. "You've spent a lot of time talking about how I've lost the first war," he said. "Now you will spend time explaining to our brothers that a new war is beginning."

I tried not to look into Satan's eyes. "God—the Enemy—will know you're coming."

"So much the better!" He stopped himself, then continued in a calmer voice, "But I'm not asking you to worry about the Enemy's plans, am I? I'm asking you to share with your brothers your excitement about the opportunities this new war will provide for all of us. Can I count on you to do that, Enoch?"

No longer able to avoid his eyes, I saw in them a vision of myself bound and thrown into the lake of fire, yelling from pain and shame as the dark angels stood on the shore and cackled with mirth. "Yes, I can do that."

The terrifying image cleared from Satan's eyes. "Good. Now follow me."

I followed his shift to the throne room. Satan called for his angels to gather; I don't think it was lost on him that they assembled more slowly than the last time he'd called them together, or that more of them were moaning with every step and that a few were even crawling again.

"Brethren," he said, "I am not blind to your suffering or deaf to your cries. Am I doing nothing, as some of you say? Do I sit on my throne all day, while you are in misery? Lies! Attend to my words. For your sake, I am leaving the safety of this palace. I am going on a mission, to visit these new creatures the Enemy has created. I go for you, to bring you relief from pain and respite from boredom."

With that, and without waiting for a response, he disappeared.

Some energy seemed to have flowed back into the assembly. The dark angels bombarded each other with questions and theories and suspicions. I was closed off to some of the conversations—as much as Satan believed that his angels trusted me, most of them also sensed that there was something different about me, which led to a certain degree of suspicion. I did my best with the conversations that were open to me, jumping in when the focus shifted to the first war and its failures, reminding my brothers that this was a new war and that it seemed to me Satan knew what he was doing. I have no idea how confident I sounded. The talk went on for a long time, but before any of the conversations had wound down, I became aware that Satan had reappeared, and was sitting on his throne, watching and listening.

He looked different; taller and fuller, but also darker than before. The little light that had still existed in him seemed to have been completely swallowed up. If he'd been fearsome before, he was terrifying now.

A few other dark angels became aware of his presence, then many more, then everyone and the silence was complete.

"Brethren," he said, "some of you had faith in my mission, whereas others are still questioning my leadership. I thank those of you who trusted in me; as for the others, I ask only that you listen to my next words and tell me if there is room for doubt left in your minds. *Today I have made the Enemy burn with fury.*"

A moment of shock elapsed, and then we shouted, together as if we were a single, deafening voice, "What happened?"

A now-familiar smile spread across Satan's face; a smile fueled not by humor or joy but by anger and lust; a smile whose only pleasure is the suffering of others.

"Brethren, I will be very pleased to tell you what happened." He leaned forward and waited for us to draw closer. "It all starts with a man and a woman."

Chapter Two

A Man and a Woman

I will tell you a story (Satan began), the likes of which you've never heard before. Brethren, I have seen things that will make you laugh in wonder; I have done things that will astound you; I have brought something completely new into the world, something the Enemy never planned for.

This new creation of the Enemy is not hard to find; it is a dimension unlike any of the others. It has weight; it has sub-dimensions! There is backward and forward; up and down; before you and behind you. And there is a strangeness of time, too. One moment follows another and precedes a third. Each moment, no matter how full or empty, feels exactly the same as every other.

It is disorienting to enter this new world, but enter it I did. I practiced moving in space and time, and after a while—listen to how I speak!—it came naturally enough. I traveled through the galaxies and saw wonders I could spend an eternity describing. But none interested me so much as a small garden on a small planet, where the Enemy had fashioned His new creatures of matter and spirit. These were His favored creatures, yet they were trapped in their spatial sub-dimensions and slaves to the tyranny of uncaring time. They were so pathetic I almost returned here without causing them any harm. But soon I realized that they weren't aware they were imprisoned. They were happy, and their joy was like a roaring fire, enveloping and tormenting me. Was it not because of them that we were exiled from the High Country?

My hatred for them grew the more I observed the way they went about their lives. There I stood, tortured by the presence of the Enemy—yes, brethren, don't you understand yet? All of our pain would be gone if we could find a place where He wasn't—but here were these two creatures, a man and a woman, this Adam and this Eve, and they'd never tasted any real suffering.

The question that I asked myself was how to injure a creature that had no capacity to feel pain; a creature so full of joy that no room was left for sadness. Soon I began to despair. These creatures had everything, and lived in perfect communion with the Enemy and His angels. (Should I tell you of what I suffered at their sight? But it wouldn't profit you to hear of it, and would only cause me pain in remembrance...there are more pleasant things to talk about).

Eventually I approached the problem from another angle. If these were truly free creatures, as the Enemy had said they were, then they must be free to choose. To obey because no other alternative is open to them would be cheating; therefore, I reasoned, there must be an option to disobey: a thought they couldn't have, a word they couldn't utter, a place they couldn't go.

The garden teemed with other creatures, pets for His pets, of all kinds and colors and shapes and sizes. One of these was a tall and thin creature, and although all the others kept their distance from me (how they sensed my presence, I don't know), this one didn't.

I looked into its eyes, and stared for so long that eventually I fancied that if I could just push hard enough with my mind, I could enter this creature and take control of its body. I kept staring, trying to force myself in, then suddenly the world shifted and I found myself staring *out* of the creature's eyes. It is an exhilarating experience, brethren!

I'd been watching the woman Eve as she dug with her hands into the soft ground, making little holes and then filling them again, patting the earth back into place with great satisfaction. I moved closer to her and she took no notice of me.

My dear Eve, I said, whispering into her mind. *I am curious about something. Is there a place in this garden where we're not supposed to go?*

Eve shook her head without looking at me or pausing in her work. "You may go wherever you please," she said.

Is there a word that is forbidden to say?

Eve trilled with laughter. "You are a silly creature! You may say whatever you please!"

Has your God made no commandments then? Is there nothing for you to obey?

Eve paused and looked at me thoughtfully. "Only the commandment about the tree, of course."

What tree? What commandment?

"The tree in that clearing; we are forbidden from eating its fruit. But we can eat the fruit of any of the other trees!"

The excitement was building up in me to a high pitch. How furious would the Enemy be when I convinced His new pets to choose me instead of Him, to listen to my words and ignore His?

And what's so special about that tree in the clearing?

I now had Eve's full attention; she'd completely forgotten about the seeds she'd been planting. "The fruit of that tree will teach you the difference between good and evil."

She said something else, but I was no longer listening. I left the serpent and flew to the tree—would the Enemy really have created a tree whose fruit could teach me about evil? But I saw the joke within the moment: it was a tree like any other, with fruit like any other fruit.

Immediately I returned to the serpent, furious but trying to control my anger. *That doesn't sound so bad, dear Eve. What's wrong with a little knowledge?*

"Oh no!" she said. "It's bad. In the very moment we eat of that tree, we will die."

Die? I said. *Did God tell you that?*

She nodded.

No, no. You won't die. God knows all about evil and when you eat from that tree, you will be just like Him.

Her gaze shifted to focus on the tree. I whispered more words along the same lines, and before she knew what she was doing, she had walked over and plucked two of its ripest fruit.

Would you look at that, I said. *Don't they look delicious? Give one to Adam and together you will eat the fruit and become equal to God.*

I followed her to her husband. Eve parroted my words, Adam parroted her reluctance, finally he gave in just as she had. I watched with delight as both bit into the fruit. Although I knew there was nothing magical about it, in that moment I almost doubted myself. Their eyes seemed to dim, and they looked around with a bit of confusion, as if they were seeing less of the world than they were used to and wondering where the rest had gone.

They threw away the fruit in their hands, and spat out the pieces in their mouths, but of course it was too late; the transformation was complete.

"I don't feel well," Adam said, and spoke the words as if he hardly knew what they meant.

I felt great; I could barely contain my mirth; although how I felt then was nothing compared to how I felt when the Enemy found out. He was shocked, betrayed, furious. Full of rage, He banished the man and woman from this garden He'd made for them, and promised them no end of trouble all the days of their lives! They will have descendants, giving birth to them in pain, all of whom will take up their own share of suffering. And every one of those countless lives will end in deterioration or destruction.

Do you understand what I'm saying to you, brethren? I have taken these pets of the Enemy and separated them from Him. As if that weren't enough, I have introduced something completely new into the world, a disease that these two creatures now carry within themselves, a disease they will pass on to their descendants, a disease called sin, a disease that ends in corruption and death.

WHen Satan finished speaking, half of the assembled angels deafened us with applause as the other half bombarded him with questions.

I was part of the second group, but I seemed alone in not being thrilled with the story or what it entailed. Wasn't our torment enough? What was the point of incurring the Enemy's wrath and risking further, perhaps more severe, punishment?

"Enoch," Satan said. "Speak." In his eyes, I saw a familiar image being replayed. This time Satan himself bound me and threw me into the lake, while his dark angels stood around and shrieked in pleasure.

"Your story was wonderful to hear," I said, and the image cleared from his eyes. "So wonderful that it makes me curious to know more."

"Ask your question."

"Did Go—did the Enemy not try to punish you?"

Satan shook his head and laughed. "He did not! Oh, He had some harsh things to say to the serpent. But for me? Not a single word! You know what that made me realize, brethren? The Enemy can do no more to us. This place is—"

"What did He say to the serpent?" I said.

Satan's eyes flashed with fire. "Words that are of no consequence to us. Does no one else have questions?"

Now that I'd broken the ice, almost all of them did. What did he mean by descendants and birthing? What did it mean for a human being to die? If Satan could control a serpent, did he think they could control one of these humans?

Satan answered each question with delight. He felt, or at least he wanted to project that he felt, that this second war had gotten off to the best possible start. He'd corrupted the new creatures (by this point he insisted we call them "the fallen"), sparked the wrath of the Enemy, and all without consequence to himself.

I would've agreed that it was the best possible start—except that I didn't believe him for a moment. I didn't believe that the Enemy would be angry, let alone as furious as Satan portrayed him. The Enemy put the tree in the garden—apparently He felt that obedience by choice was of more value than a forced submission. But if that were the case, He knew there was a possibility that Adam or Eve would break the commandment and eat the tree's fruit.

Even then, standing in the throne room and never having visited the fallen, I was convinced that there was another reason they'd been banished from the garden. In fact, I felt that if the Enemy was angry at anyone, it would be Satan. The others did what they did out of weakness, including the serpent that allowed Satan to take possession of its body. Satan himself acted out of strength, and used that strength to entice the new creatures to rebel against Him. Could I believe that Adam and Eve were sent into exile, the serpent chided for its role, but no punishment at all reserved for Satan?

"Obviously the fruit did have some power," Satan was saying in answer to one of the questions. "But I guess it only had power on the fallen, which is why I didn't see anything special about it."

"I don't think so," I said, speaking before thinking and without noticing right away how annoyed it made Satan to be contradicted, especially by me. "The fruit didn't give them any knowledge. It was the act of eating the fruit, the act of disobedience, that taught them what it meant to reject good and choose evil."

"That's interesting, Enoch. The act of disobedience is evil, is it? Do you think we are evil, then?"

He's leading me into a trap, I thought. "Yes," I said, and felt the angry attention of every angel in the room focus on me. "But I think evil is good."

The words were nonsensical at best, but they had the effect I'd hoped for. Their anger turned to laughter and cheers and even a chant that was taken up, repeating the phrase.

Riding the wave of my popularity, and desperate to confirm my two suspicions about Satan's story, I said, "Take us to the fallen! Let us see them for ourselves!"

Satan raised his arms to quiet the eruption of noise in support of this notion. "We don't know what dangers await us in that world, brethren." He raised his arms again and called for silence. "I can only be sure to protect one other, and since Enoch seems to have gained your favor, I will take him. Once we've both confirmed that the way is safe, I will take the rest of you."

I tried to suggest other options, but Satan was very persuasive and the dark angels shouted down my protests.

"Ready?" Satan said, rising from his throne.

I met his gaze, convinced that the way to this new world would not be safe for me, and not because of where I was going but who I was going with. Unable to see a way out, short of a direct confrontation with Satan, I nodded.

"Then follow," he said, and shifted.

I followed, but saw that Satan reversed course almost immediately. I wasn't ready for that and had to complete the movement. A bright object glowed before me, and with a shock I realized that this was one of the stars the Enemy had made. I'd never gotten a chance to see one up-close, and the experience was overwhelming. I turned away, or tried to turn away, and remembered what Satan had said about how disorienting this dimension was. I careened in place before I gained control again. When I came to a stop, I stared out at spinning planets and their circling satellites, and at asteroids and comets as they flew by me.

"Satan never said how beautiful this world is," I said, to no one. "I'd forgotten."

I spent a long while getting used to the concept of time, and to the idea of physical objects, and learning how to interact with them. More than a few times I sat on meteoroids, and rode them as the fiery rocks zipped through the air and exploded into the surface of different planets, sending up showers of pebbles and dust.

Did the thought occur to me to go back? I don't think it ever did, and not because I didn't want to confront Satan or risk a worse punishment than exile, but because I was... not happy or even content, but less tormented. For entire moments, I forgot the constant pain that enveloped me with its crushing arms. Novelty has a certain power to distract.

The thought of going back didn't cross my mind, at least, until I was called back. I was floating between two giant planets in a system I'd just discovered, staring at a star whose light reminded me a little of the High Country. I thought I heard my name being called from somewhere far away.

"Enoch!"

The insistence and annoyance forced my attention back to the present. Zephar stood to one side, looking at me as if he hardly recognized me.

"Enoch!"

"Zephar," I said, "what are you doing here?"

"What's the matter with you? You've been looking right through me. I called out your name a dozen times."

"Is everything okay?" I said. "Has something happened?"

"Everything's great!" Zephar said. "And everything's happened! I'll tell you all about it, but first you need to come back with me. He-Who-Rules asked us to find—"

"He-Who-Rules? God?" In an instant, I saw the whole story. We were restored to our former status, our rebellion forgiven; we would live once more in the High Country. In that instant, excitement and joy burned so hot inside me I didn't think I could contain it all.

In the next moment, I noticed that Zephar had retreated from me. "What did you say?"

"Nothing—I was making a joke."

Zephar didn't respond, but at least he wasn't retreating any further.

"Tell me what happened, Zephar."

"I will, but right now we need to go back."

"Tell me what happened, and we will."

Zephar seemed about to argue, but saw something in my expression and changed his mind. "What's happened? We've won, Enoch! Where do I start to tell you everything? The fallen invent new ways to sin every day; they are an intoxicating creature! Murder, rape, theft—corruption is everywhere! And now—now the Enemy has decided to destroy everything, to abandon them completely. Their souls fill Sheol."

"Start from the beginning, I can hardly follow what you're saying."

"The beginning? It started with a murder. The sons of—"

"The beginning, Zephar. What happened after Satan and I left the throne room?"

Chapter Three

A New War

WE grew tired of waiting (Zephar began), and wondered if we shouldn't follow you to Earth. Satan had said the new dimension wasn't hard to find, we remembered; but we also remembered his other words, that this new world may not be safe. Some of us were in favor of waiting, as Satan had asked us to do; others were anxious to leave Sheol and experience some of the elation he had described.

The arguments from the two camps increased in intensity and finally turned violent. The throne room erupted. Angels threw each other into and through the walls, causing enough damage that the ceiling started to crumble. At one point, Belial struck Moloch, who landed on Satan's throne and crushed it. As Moloch picked himself up and stood to his full height, Belial screamed for silence.

"Brethren!" he said. "Why are we fighting?"

Most of us, stopped cold in our struggles, couldn't remember. But Moloch supplied the answer almost immediately, "Because we despise the cowardice of you and yours, Belial."

He launched himself against him, and Belial, full of anger at the insult, met him half-way.

We would still be fighting now if Satan hadn't appeared and put a stop to it. A mighty hiss swept through the throne room. Mammon and I let go of each other almost immediately; the others did the same. I don't think anyone could hear that frightful sound and continue what they were doing.

Satan sat on what remained of his throne. "What has happened here? Who will speak?"

No one did at first; then finally Moloch said, "You tarried, brother, and we didn't know why. An argument arose among us. Some wanted to wait here like cowards; others wanted to follow you... and see if we could provide assistance."

At that there was another eruption of noise that verged on violence. Satan hissed again for silence. "No punishment will be meted out in this matter," he said, when we quieted down. "The first group was obeying my orders, the second was driven by concern for me to disobey them. But come, let us be divided no longer. We have much to accomplish."

"Where's Enoch?" I asked.

"I don't know. He didn't follow me."

"Shouldn't we find him? Who will rebuild our palace?"

"We will find him in due time," Satan said, speaking with impatience, "or he will find us. For now, you must attend to my words."

"Is something wrong?" Moloch said.

"Just the opposite. Everything is right. I have had success in the new world beyond anything I dreamed of."

"Tell us," Belial said.

"After I lost Enoch, and before I could go looking for him, I became distracted by the fallen. Adam and Eve lived outside the gates of Eden, where the Enemy had placed an angel, and not just an angel but a cherubim. I didn't wish to approach and give away my presence, but I imagine his orders were to cut down the fallen if they tried to force their way back into the garden.

"Their life was pathetic, especially compared to the ease and comfort they once enjoyed. All was suffering to them now; all work was hard work. They complained of aches in their bodies; their minds seemed always distracted and unfocused; survival was a constant struggle. Amid all of this activity to sustain their lives, they became purposeless. Once they had lived to serve the Enemy; now they seemed merely to exist.

"Things changed when Eve bore a child. Her pain was wonderful to behold, her shrieks so loud and tormented that it made me laugh with delight to hear them. And yet at the end of it all, she held this creature and in her eyes I saw a glimpse of the joy I thought I'd destroyed. Adam cradled mother and child in his own arms and in his eyes I saw it too, the return not only of purpose but of hope. Their foolishness angered me to the core—did they think they were saved simply because a child was born?

"They named the creature Cain, and from the beginning I set to work on him. I whispered in his ears of the blessed life his parents had once enjoyed in the garden beyond the angel with the fiery sword, and how because of them he now had to till the hard ground and make food grow by the sweat of his brow. Soon he became sullen, moody, angry—at his parents, yes, but mostly at the Enemy. Was he there when his father ate of the forbidden fruit? Was it fair to punish Cain for acts committed before he was even born?

"Focused as I was on the delightful Cain, I almost missed the birth of the second child. But even as a young boy, Abel was stubborn and narrow-minded. When through his older brother I spoke to him of the things which had fueled Cain's anger, Abel's reply was infuriating. 'What right do we have to speak of fairness, brother?' he said. 'Did we call ourselves into existence? From our parents we inherited life, and from them we inherited this condition. And what makes you think you would have chosen differently from Mother or Father? We are all in debt to God, for we all have disobedience in our hearts. But do not be afraid—God has not forsaken us, and one day we will be reunited with Him in Paradise.'

"With these and many other words Abel began to unravel my work in Cain. But then Abel made a big mistake, and paid for his life with it.

"One day after the end of the growing season, Cain and I came upon Abel and we watched him from afar. He picked out the best lambs in his flock and slaughtered them, which wasn't unusual in itself. But then he set aside the best parts and burned them. 'Your brother has gone mad,' I said.

"But of course Abel had plenty of words to justify his actions. 'The lamb was a sacrifice to God,' he said.

"'To erase this debt you feel you owe Him?' I had Cain say, in the condescending older-brother way we had perfected through the years.

"Abel ignored the tone and answered, 'It is a gift I offer to Him with a free heart; not of what He deserves, but of the very best that I have.'"

"Cain and I didn't understand this logic. 'Does he think shedding the blood of an innocent lamb will manipulate God into letting him back into Paradise?' I said to Cain. 'And what's the logic of giving a gift to God—doesn't He already have everything? Do you win accolades for depriving yourself of something God doesn't want or need? And if the point is to sacrifice something, why sacrifice the best of what He has given you? Why not set aside the worst parts, or those parts not suitable for food?'

"Cain misunderstood me, because he started gathering up some of his own harvest to offer as a sacrifice. I tried to convince him that this was a silly course of action, that he was aping his younger brother, but Cain had stopped listening again. Because I kept him away from his family, Cain often expressed his anger (never directed at me, of course) over how much time his parents spent with Abel and the other children. He saw this ridiculous ritual as yet another attempt to catch up to Abel. I stood back and watched as Cain set his carefully arranged pile of fruits and vegetables on fire, not sure what would happen next.

"The fire died. Cain relit his torch and again pressed it to the foot of his pile; the food again caught fire and again the fire died before consuming his sacrifice. The scene repeated itself a few more times, Cain becoming more frustrated with every attempt. Soon he was wild with fury and I pounced. 'Cain,' I said, 'this is Abel's doing. So long as he's around he will always be the favored one.'

"'I can't,' Cain said, but he'd never before responded to my suggestions when they went along these lines.

"'Of course you can,' I said. 'Spill his blood as he spilled the blood of the lamb. Offer him up as a sacrifice to God. Bring death upon him.'

"'I can't,' he said again, but I recognized the tone and backed off. Through the years I've learned that if one pushes the 'I can't,' one reinforces it. But give it room to breathe and the 'I can't' turns into 'I can't now,' which in fact means 'I will later.' This is an important lesson, brethren, one you will need to learn if you will be successful at the work I have planned for you. The fallen must be helped into committing these acts in their hearts first, as if in rehearsal; then they will be able to do things in actual fact that they never could have brought themselves to do otherwise.

"Not much later Cain took his brother to the field for a talk, far from everyone else. Abel was as unsuspecting as one of his sheep, and he let his older brother lead him where he would. It didn't take long for Cain to find Abel's preaching insufferable, and it didn't take much to suggest to Cain that here was the perfect opportunity to do what he thought he couldn't do, but knew that he must. He picked up the dried bone of an animal's carcass as if he wanted to inspect it, then turned that wonderful remnant of death into an instrument of death. One blow, swung with all of his mighty strength, and half of Abel's face peeled away and blood and teeth and bone sprayed Cain's arm.

Abel's body dropped to the ground, lifeless.

"In that instant, terror gripped Cain's heart. It was such a powerful transformation to behold, brethren, as the delicious fury that had pushed him into the act turned into even sweeter fear, the whole process fueled by guilt and shame.

"I found his terror so intoxicating that when Cain fled, I went with him, forgetting about Abel for the moment. When I returned, his spirit was gone. Too late I'd thought of how much fun it would be to drag Abel to this place; to bring he of such faith in the Enemy's mercy to Sheol. Where his spirit escaped to, I don't know. But we won't make that mistake again, will we, brethren?"

Satan stood. None of us made the slightest sound; we knew that what he said next would change everything, and we were in desperate need of change.

"There is no danger for us in this new world, brethren. There is only a herd of fallen creatures; weak, petty, greedy, selfish creatures; as easy to manipulate as if they had no wills of their own. Are you bored? Are you in pain? Do you want your suffering to end? Then follow me!"

He shifted and those of us quick enough to follow did so. We stormed the Earth, rolling through their cities like a choking fog. Where can I begin to tell you of those days, Enoch? We spent them in splendor. We honed our skills trying to outdo each other in the sins we could talk our creatures into committing. We made heroes out of them, mighty men who traveled in groups, gangs who could terrorize towns with the mere news that they were headed their way. Some committed suicide rather than wait to be raped by these great men; others tried to barter their sons and daughters in exchange for their own safety. Old people and young children escaped to underground tunnels, then looked long at each other when the food ran out. These great heroes tore through the world, taking what they wanted and ripping to shreds what they didn't, and when they had no one else to kill they turned on each other. Blood filled the streets and valleys, and the moaning of those who grieved for their lost loved ones rang through the air.

But I'm getting ahead of myself! When we first arrived on Earth, Satan wanted our help in an experiment: he would arrange for another murder, and we would stand around the dead body and try to catch the spirit before it could escape. He shouldn't have been so worried.

I've seen it happen thousands of times now, but it still gives me
pleasure to watch. The fallen are creatures who've given themselves
over to their physical natures so completely that when they find themselves as pure spirit they don't quite know what to do. It is as easy
as anything to drag these disoriented spirits to Sheol; they don't offer
any resistance until they see the lake of fire, and by then it's too late.

Some of the spirits are a mystery, though; we can't even see them
when they're wrenched from their bodies at death. Satan says that
these fallen don't have spirits, but I don't think that's quite right. The
spirits we can't see are always those of the fallen who didn't give us
much sport while they lived. Satan must've suspected this on some
level, because when he noticed that many of these were descendants
of Seth (the Enemy's line, Satan called them) he asked us to focus
our energies on them. Most of us didn't; the other creatures were
so much easier to be around—they weren't always calling on the Enemy's name, and offering sacrifices to Him, and driving us away. Reluctantly, Satan left us to the others and worked on the children of
Seth himself.

I would never say this if we weren't so far from him, Enoch, and
certainly I'll deny ever having said it at all, but I think Satan feared
them in some way. Or maybe it just angered him to see anyone so
devoted to the Enemy. Either way, he dedicated all of his time to
Seth's descendants. It fascinated me to watch, and because I love a
good challenge, I helped out when I'd had enough of the other fallen
for a while.

Was it my idea or Satan's? I don't remember, but I think I was
saying how hard it was for me to leave the people of Nod, who offered every pleasure one could desire, and how hard to be among the
descendants of Seth.

"Yes," Satan said, because I do think it was my idea. "We'll bring
these people to Nod, or bring the people of Nod to them."

Later Satan would say that it was a great lesson (you'll see that
he's a teacher now, full of important insights he wants us to remember). The Enemy's line were the Enemy's until they met the beautiful
and fascinating people of Nod. Of course, among those people the
Enemy was a fairy tale, tolerated as a concept to teach children obedience and threaten them with punishment, but not something to be
taken seriously by intelligent adults. Soon these sons and daughters

of God were marrying the sons and daughters of Nod, and then even Satan couldn't tell them apart. The Enemy's name was almost completely forgotten, and when it was used at all it was used as a curse.

"You can't be both a son of God and a son of man," Satan said to us, which was his lesson: the more attached one of the fallen became to the world they inhabited, the less mindful they would be of the Enemy and His world.

I wish you could've been there to see him, Enoch. The fall of the house of Seth energized Satan and filled him with ambition. He convinced politicians to conspire together to oppress their people and enrich themselves, then turned them against each other so their cities erupted in civil war. He planted seeds of selfishness and jealousy like a master gardener, then allowed us into the garden to taste of their fruits.

Violence was the law and the spirit, and nothing was done that wasn't done through violence. Blood-lust made the whole world crazy. Houses and schools and stores were falling apart, but instead of repairing them the fallen built arenas where warriors battled to the death and whoever they considered undesirable that year was ripped apart by wild, starved animals. One by one we dragged their spirits to Sheol, dipping them in the fiery lake or throwing them into a large pit we dug for the purpose, and laughing at their pathetic attempts to get out, often crawling over one another just to gain an inch.

Each spirit we took fueled Satan's ambition. The Earth groaned with suffering, and we watched in amazement at Satan's success in defeating the Enemy's creatures.

And then, as Satan gathered us together in the throne room, we learned that the most amazing thing of all was yet to come.

"The Enemy's plan is completely frustrated," Satan said. "The war is over, brethren, and we have won!

"The sea levels are rising, or haven't you noticed? There is a man who has spent the last seventy years building a barge, and when he's not building it he's trying to convince the others that unless they repent of their ways, the Enemy will drown the whole world. At first I thought this man was crazy, but I've seen the signs. A great deluge is coming, brethren; the Enemy will purify this world even if it means killing all the creatures on its surface."

He hissed for silence. "Now is not the time to celebrate," he said. "We have a lot of work to do, or all may yet be lost. This silly man

and his silly barge may still convince some of the fallen to turn back
to the Enemy, especially when the waters continue to rise and the
skies open and rain falls without cease. When the safety of their
towns and homes are washed away, then must we be there to ensure
that the Enemy isn't able to use that fear to save even one of these
creatures—bodies or spirits.

"As for this fool, I will take care of him myself. This is my promise—before he secures the final plank, he will renounce the Enemy
and retract all of his warnings about a coming flood. He will pro-
claim it a joke and a prank, even as rain falls on his head and water
swallows his ankles."

Satan again quieted down our cheering, then divided us into three
groups. The first he dispatched immediately, and their job was to
make sure none of the fallen were lost. "When they hear of disasters,"
Satan said before letting these angels go, "let the fallen be glad in
their hearts that they weren't affected and their possessions are still
in their hands. But when disaster comes to their door, let them forget
that tragedy has touched anyone else; let their hearts be full of self-
pity and anger."

The next group he sent to gather the spirits of the dead and bring
them to Sheol. When they were gone, only a handful of us remained.

"Our brother Enoch is lost somewhere in that world," Satan said
to us. "Find him and bring him to me. Soon this place will overflow
with the spirits of the dead; we need to build prisons to hold them
all."

Satan looked around. "And is it right for us to meet in this ruined
hall? I have made the Enemy sorry He ever created this world—should
I not rule from a worthy throne? Go, bring Enoch to me. Tell him He-
Who-Rules recalls him to his duty."

ZEphar didn't know how to shift back to Sheol from where we were,
but at least he remembered how to get back to Earth. On our
way there, I pictured what I expected to find: a dead world, or at
least a drowned world. What we actually saw when we arrived was
so shocking that neither Zephar nor I could communicate coherently
for a few moments.

"But—" he said.

"— doesn't make any—" I said.

"I don't—"

The Earth teemed with life. Human life and animal life; life in the sea, on the ground, and in the air. Amid the shock and confusion, I wondered if Zephar had told me the story accurately; and if he had, if Satan understood the Enemy's intention properly; and if he had, if the Enemy had different plans for the world than Satan had guessed. Did He drown the world only to raise it up again?

"We should go see He-Who-Rules," Zephar said.

I nodded and we shifted together. We arrived in the throne room, but I almost didn't recognize it. Someone had made an attempt to rebuild the walls, but they were placed at strange angles—in fact, it was more like they weren't placed at all but tossed and left where they landed. Satan's throne was even more ridiculous, and only the sight of Satan himself, sitting on that oddly-shaped mess and yet looking three times more imposing than I remembered, kept me from laughing.

He stood. "Enoch, finally."

"What happened up there?" Zephar said. "Did we fail?"

Satan looked past him for only a moment. In the next, Zephar was gone; two angels had come to take him away. Asmodeus and Mulciber moved too quickly at that moment for me to know who they were, but of course I've seen them work since, and recently I've had the misfortune of getting to know them better than anyone else has known them before—but all of that came later.

"I've been waiting a long time for you, Enoch," Satan said, as if Zephar hadn't been standing beside me only a few moments before. "No one around here can build anything without your direction. I want you to start by making me a new throne, and then restoring this room, then the rest of the palace. After that I want you to build prisons, all around, above ground and underground and in the air if you can. I want cells, millions of them. Make them just large enough for one of the creatures." He'd been stepping closer as he spoke and now he stood directly in front of me. "By the way, I discourage talk of 'down here' and 'up there.' That's fallen talk."

"Millions of cells?" I said, not able to think of anything else. "There are that many of them here?"

"With more coming all the time. You should probably get started."

With great effort I held back the questions I desperately wanted to ask. He-Who-Rules (soon anyone who called him Satan, although never formally corrected, would find themselves visited by Asmodeus and Mulciber) had definite plans for his new throne, much larger and more ornate than the one that had been destroyed, and plans just as grandiose for his new palace.

At first the dark angels cooperated as before, but soon they grew bored and forced the fallen to do their work. It took a while to build everything, especially because most of the fallen needed to be told to do something three or four times before they would understand; and when they finally did understand, they moved with agonizing slowness. But even then, sooner or later they'd forget what they were doing and fall to the ground, crying and screaming for relief because the pain was too much to bear. Although the other dark angels enjoyed this part the most, He-Who-Rules was impatient for his throne, and then his palace, and finally his millions of prison cells. I found that when the fallen got into that state of self-pity and clearer awareness of their suffering, no amount of yelling at them would help; torture was the only thing that could reach them and I became very good at using stones dipped in the lake of fire to motivate the fallen to take up their work again.

Part of what fueled my anger toward them was that no one could help me understand what had happened on Earth, either in the garden or before or after the flood. They claimed they didn't remember their lives back on Earth, although I've always felt that they were lying and they just didn't *want* to remember. Either way, no amount of torture could get them to tell me what I wanted to know and soon I gave up trying.

"This is good," He-Who-Rules said to me one day. He'd been very pleased with the throne and the new castle, and now he seemed equally happy with the first cells. "Funny how these fallen are helping to build the very prisons that will hold them captive, isn't it?"

"Yes," I said, although I didn't think it was that funny then and I certainly don't think it's funny now.

"You have a way with them, Enoch. I wonder if you could be of assistance to me on Earth."

"Wherever I can be of service." I paused and tried to get a sense of his mood before continuing; he seemed so pleased with the pace of construction that I forged ahead. "Can I ask you what happened up there?"

"We don't say 'up there,'" he said, but did so offhandedly, as if he'd already made the correction a thousand times that day. "Life goes on as usual—pain and suffering, murder and mayhem, birth and death."

"Forgive me, Master," I said. "My question is about what happened before. Zephar told me that the whole world was going to be destroyed."

"Yes, that was the Enemy's plan. But there was a crazy person—a fallen who knew of that plan and built a barge to save himself and his family."

"He was crazy?"

"Of course. He wouldn't listen to reason. He had no proof that a flood was coming, yet he spent his days building this boat and his evenings warning people of the supposed coming deluge. Plank after plank, he laid them down without allowing himself to consider the possibility that he was wasting his life building this thing; without caring that he was ridiculed everywhere for his prophecies of doom. He sold off more and more of his belongings until one day he'd sold everything and had nothing but the barge. And all because he thought he'd heard the voice of the Enemy. Does that sound like a sane person?"

"And his ship survived the storms?"

"Yes, he survived. So did the children he took with him. And if I couldn't find a way to move Noah, at least I was able to reach his son." He-Who-Rules paused, then waved off the topic. "That's all in the past now. There is another fallen, one perhaps even more dangerous than Noah. The Enemy is giving this man a lot of attention, which means we should be as well. But what do your brothers do? They're with the Canaanites and the Amorites, going after easy prey and leaving the hard and important work to me. The rest of them seem to forget that we're still at war. But you're not like them, Enoch. You have a sense of responsibility." He stepped closer. "Your work here is done. Asmodeus will take over—even he should be able to use the fallen to make copies of the cells you've built. I need you on Earth." He stepped even closer. "I want you to study this man; I want you to tell me why the Enemy speaks to him; I want you to tell me how we can break men like him, men of foolish faith."

After I'd given Asmodeus his instructions, He-Who-Rules led me back to Earth, to the largest tent in a large caravan of tents. There I encountered the first living fallen I'd ever met, an old man with wrinkled sunburnt skin and wispy gray hair where he had any at all.

"This is him?" I said.

"Don't underestimate this man. He left his father's house and his country, all because he thought the Enemy told him to. At that one command, he walked away from the safety and comfort of home to wander the wilderness and struggle for every peaceful night's rest. Nothing I said could convince him to do otherwise, and no amount of strife or suffering could make him go back to his own people. That is the kind of irrationality we need to understand if we will continue to have success against the Enemy. Do you understand the importance of this?"

I did understand; moreover, I understood that here was a man who could answer my questions. What had happened in the garden? If the Enemy was so displeased with them, why was He maintaining a relationship with the fallen? Why was there a stench of fear that seemed to be behind every move He-Who-Rules made? Was all of this part of some plan of the Enemy's—and if it were, where did I fit into that plan?

As I watched this old, tired, fallen man go about his daily work, a new question occurred to me. I'd never before felt the jealousy toward these creatures that He-Who-Rules and the dark angels did. But at that moment, watching this man who had a personal relationship with the Enemy—the Enemy who'd rejected and abandoned me—I felt all the rage I saw in the Master's eyes.

The new question bubbled up inside me with increasing intensity, and it wasn't so much a question as a challenge. All of my other concerns were soon consumed by this new one; all of my other thoughts faded away before its glow. Only it remained, and my energy became focused on understanding where this man's faith came from and on finding a solution to the task He-Who-Rules had set for me. How could I take that faith, I wondered, and smash it into a thousand pieces?

Chapter Four

A Man of Faith

"THe seed of the woman will crush your head, and you will bruise its heel."

The words I'd heard so often meant nothing to me until I mentioned them to He-Who-Rules in passing; then everything became clear. The fear that burned in his eyes was all the confirmation I needed—here was the answer I had once wanted so desperately to discover.

"Where did you hear that?"

I tried not to betray any of the contempt I felt at the Master's thinly veiled panic. "The man Abram," I said, "or Abraham, as he insists on calling himself now. He whispers the words all the time." I paused. "What do they mean?"

"They don't mean anything!" The throne room grew quiet at his outburst. He-Who-Rules looked around, then seemed to return to himself. "I don't know what they mean," he said, sitting back down. "I assume they mean nothing."

"Of course," I said, guessing the truth in that instant: these were the words the Enemy had spoken to Satan; this was the punishment for his part in the events in the garden. The Master would hurt and wound a son or daughter of Eve, but that child of hers—a fallen!—would do much worse to him. Here was the explanation for all the fear that motivated the Master's actions against Seth, and against Noah, and now against Abraham. He lived in terror of them and each of their descendants, hyper-vigilant and paranoid because any one of them might turn out to be the one the Enemy had promised the fallen.

I felt something close to pity for He-Who-Rules and in an attempt to placate him, I continued, "They probably don't mean anything. Abraham says all kinds of things I don't understand."

He hissed at me. "Fool, your job is to understand this man! How else will you break him?"

"Maybe I am a fool," I said. "Maybe I'm not the right person for the job."

"You like this assignment, Enoch. I can see it in your glow."

"Maybe I do. But I'm not making much progress. And I've had opportunities. When the Enemy destroyed—"

"Enough of that," the Master said. "Sodom and Gomorrah were a resort, a paradise, a return to the old ways, to the world before the deluge. But those cities are gone—and their souls are ours. Why has everyone lost sight of that fact?"

"I don't care about Sodom or Gomorrah," I said, perhaps a little too impatiently. "I never spent any time there anyway. I just meant that through their destruction I should have found a lever to move Abraham away from the Enemy."

"He's not dead yet."

"But meanwhile I'm last in the rankings." I regretted the words as soon as I said them, because I didn't know if He-Who-Rules was aware that the dark angels were keeping score; and I didn't know if he'd approve of them if he were aware; and I didn't want to be the one that let the secret out if the answer to both questions was no.

"The rankings?" he said, in a low voice. "I give you the most important mission of all, and you're distracted by a game?"

"You know about it?"

The Master was out of his chair and whispering in my ear: "I invented it."

"You did?"

"Your brothers need encouragement," he said, still whispering. "They tend toward laziness; I didn't want them to lap up whatever sins the fallen dreamed up for themselves." Disappointment flashed in his glow. "I never thought you'd be taken in, Enoch."

"It's not just a game," I said, my anger assuaged by his confiding in me and feeling the need to justify myself. "Baal, Moloch, and Beelzebub are at the top of the rankings, and each one is worshiped by the fallen."

"Is that what this is about?" the Master said, returning to his throne. "The fallen worship monkeys and cows. Are you jealous of them? Are you jealous of the sun and the moon—a piece of rock? What you're doing is much more important than any of that."

"This man is not like others."

"But he is a man; he can be broken."

"He has unshakeable faith in the Enemy, even more now than when you were working on him."

"Melchizedek?"

I nodded. While the Master was in Sheol inspecting my work on his new throne and castle, a Priest-King named Melchizedek visited Abraham. Whatever else happened during that meeting—and there was talk of a weird meal-sacrifice of bread and wine—Melchizedek left an imprint on Abraham's soul and his faith in the Enemy became stronger than ever before.

"Any progress on that front?" I said.

The Master shook his head. "I've been to see him myself; he's useless. He senses our presence and refuses to listen to anything we have to say. He just praises 'the Enemy Most High' and offers his silly sacrifices. It's infuriating." He shifted in his seat. "Find a way to break Abram, Enoch. Do something. Make him walk in on another man's wife while she's bathing, or—"

He stopped, fury blazing in his eyes.

"I'm sorry," I said. "I didn't mean to laugh. It's just... he's infatuated with Sarah. A person like that isn't susceptible to desiring another man's wife; he's too busy desiring his own."

I saw the Master was about to say something else, but I put up my hands to stop him. "Everything he touches turns to gold. In business, he's an unmatched negotiator—so skilled that no one walks out of the tent unsatisfied. In war, he's a brilliant strategist. He has great material wealth but isn't attached to any of it; at the slightest provocation he shakes off possessions as if he were shaking off dust from his feet. He takes strife in stride and doesn't think very much about the next day's troubles; 'today has troubles enough for today,' he likes to say, which I believe is another saying taught to him by that King of Righteousness and Prince of Peace."

"We should've been at that meeting," the Master said, not for the first time.

"The point is, how do you corrupt such a man? Except for that initial test of faith, the Enemy asks almost nothing of him—and grants him every blessing."

"Is there nothing he lacks?"

"A child by Sarah," I said. "The Enemy promises it to him but—"

"What?" The Master gripped the arms of his throne. "Why wasn't I told about this?"

"I didn't... it's not... they're both very old now, they're not going to—"

"Return to Earth!" I fell back at the ferocity in the Master's voice, half-afraid that he would launch out of his chair and attack me. "Why have you wasted all this time talking about rankings and missed opportunities? Even as we speak, it may be that a child is born—a child that will open up the path to victory. If Abram or Abraham or whatever he's calling himself—if he wants this child more than anything, he will love this child more than anything—more than the Enemy! Which means he will be ours. Unless you keep standing here staring at me!"

I shifted immediately, of course. And of course the Master was right—a child had been born. When I arrived, the boy was five or six but there was no doubt who his parents were. If the way they doted on him wasn't enough indication, Isaac's bright eyes couldn't be mistaken for anyone but Sarah's, and his set jaw and thin but warm smile were Abraham's to the smallest detail.

Abraham himself had changed. He'd always been joyful—I suppose it's hard to enjoy every professional success while married to the love of your life and not be full of joy—but now he seemed at peace as well. This was a deep, solid joy, a joy that didn't consume him and leave him exhausted with the effort—a joy that reminded me of the High Country. With the birth of Isaac, Abraham seemed to lose interest in everything else, except for the Enemy. He taught Isaac how to pray and how to offer sacrifices, and taught him that if he lived a life where he valued the Enemy above all else, no evil could ever touch him.

I tried my best to move Abraham, but all of my efforts were unsuccessful. Ironically, it was through those failed efforts that I learned the answers to questions that had once burned so hot within me; but at the time I was so focused on my task, and so conscious of my utter inability to reach this man, that although I heard the answers, it wasn't until much later that I actually thought about what they meant.

"If God loves you as much as your father says," I whispered in Isaac's ear one night after dinner, "why did He banish you from Eden?"

The child, now eight, put the question to his father. The old man, his wrinkled features lit by the flickering light of the fire, lay on his side, resting on one arm. He stared at his son with a strange look, as if he suspected the question had come from somewhere other than his child's own mind. But, after a pause to reposition himself, he said, "My son, the answer is in the question. What He did, He did out of love for mankind."

"Love?" I said. "Is that a joke? Is love quick to anger and anxious to exile its beloved? What kind of God banishes people He loves from His presence and condemns them to a life of pain and trouble?"

Ever the polite and obedient boy, Isaac ignored my questions and told his father that he didn't understand.

Abraham watched his son's serious face for a moment, then smiled. Abraham's smile was contagious for everyone, but for no one more than Isaac. He tried to struggle for a while but Isaac had never been able to resist before and this wasn't the exception; the same smile broke through on his young face.

Satisfied, Abraham said, "I will try to explain. When the Lord created man, He made him neither mortal nor immortal, but with the capacity to become one or the other. God's plan was for man to grow in spiritual maturity and, when he was ready, to eat from the Tree of Life and become immortal. That was the path of obedience, but the Lord didn't force man down this path. In His wisdom, He decided that if man were to be more than a camel—"

At the word, and the impression of a camel's face Abraham made by pursing his lips together, Isaac giggled.

"—man would have to be free to choose. It was a risk, of course. On the one hand, if man used that freedom to choose good (which is to say, to walk in the way of the Lord), the universe would be filled with a creature like Him, made in His image and spreading His light and love. Creation would be fulfilled, perfected. On the other hand, if man used that freedom to choose evil (that is, to reject the Lord), the universe would be filled with sin and death; the universe would be corrupted. The Lord decided that the risk was worth it—and lucky for you and I that He did, or we wouldn't be having this conversation. We'd be outside, chewing grass and—expelling gas."

Isaac, whose eyes had begun to droop, giggled again.

"When our ancestors listened to the Evil One and disobeyed the Lord, they became mortal. They bowed their heads to sin. But if they stayed in the garden and ate from the Tree of Life, they would have made that corruption permanent; bound themselves to sin with eternal shackles. The Lord has a plan to redeem us from the bondage we chose for ourselves, and the plan started with exile from the garden before we could make those bonds permanent ones."

Instantly I was over by Abraham's side and screaming in his ear. "He has a plan, does He? And where does this plan end? Tell me!"

Abraham grunted. I thought it was directed at me, then realized it was just the sounds that formed part of his getting-up routine now. It struck me as such a strange thing, the idea of growing old—to slowly start to lose the abilities one had perfected over a lifetime, to have one's body turn from a finely tuned instrument ready to carry out one's every command into a worn-out and rusty piece of equipment grumbling and complaining at the slightest demand put to it.

Abraham walked over to his son and covered him with a blanket. He bent over slowly and kissed Isaac on the forehead.

At the other end of the room, he pushed aside the curtain and walked through carefully, trying to step lightly.

"It's okay," Sarah said in the dark. "I'm awake."

Abraham sat down on the edge of the bed. "Did we keep you up? Were we loud?"

"Not at all," Sarah said, turning over, half-asleep. "Did you cover him?"

"He wanted to know why the Lord exiled us from Eden."

It took a moment for Sarah's sleeping mind to process the words. She seemed to shake the sleep off and sat up. "Did you explain?"

"I tried to. I did my best. It's not an easy thing for a young boy to understand."

"Or for an old woman."

"I believe the Lord wants us to return to Him, Sarah. I believe that one day He will show us the Tree of Life and that anyone who eats of its fruit will live forever with Him. I believe He has a plan."

"Not everyone has your faith," Sarah said, putting her hand on his back.

"How do you know He has a plan?" I screamed again, and again Abraham seemed not to hear me as he lay down beside his wife, hands behind his head and eyes open and staring at the ceiling of the large tent.

I watched him quietly, lost in my own thoughts; later I heard him murmur something as he drifted off to sleep, and though I couldn't be sure, I suspected that he was repeating the mantra taught him by the Priest-King.

As the months and years went by, the urge to shift back to Sheol grew strong, but I knew that He-Who-Rules had run out of patience with me. *Either I go back having beaten Abraham*, I thought, *or I go back with a strategy to beat people like him.* To go back with nothing more than a story of continued failure, I knew, wasn't a smart or safe choice.

I didn't shift, but I did wander a little. There was a man in particular, a citizen of Gerar, where I spent most of my time away from Abraham. His name was Ash and he was a merchant in the marketplace. During the day he sold potions and charms that were as effective as any colored water in flasks and drilled stones on strings can ever be; but he spent his evenings and nights trying to call on what he called "dark and insidious forces." Those dark and insidious forces toyed with him, and I often joined in.

One day I returned to Abraham's tents to find that he wasn't there, and neither was Isaac. Sarah sat by herself in a corner of her room, a drink of water held in her hand. Her lips were dry but she didn't bring the cup to them; and as she stared at the wall, she seemed to hardly blink. Trying to control my panic, I walked around from tent to tent, hoping to get some indication of where they'd gone. But I made the round of the camp twice, and didn't hear a single word about Abraham or Isaac.

This was it, I felt. This was the chance I'd been waiting for, this was the reason He-Who-Rules had stationed me in that place for all those years. *Did I miss it? Did I miss it because I'd abandoned my post to watch a few dark angels drive a fool mad?*

Without knowing when they'd left or which direction they'd taken, I decided to fly in widening circles around the camp. When I finally found them, at first I was sure it was another false alarm and almost didn't break off to approach and verify. But I did get closer and the two figures standing to either side of a strange central figure turned out to be two servants on either side of Isaac, who rode a donkey as if it were the noblest creature in creation. Looking further up, I spied a fourth figure closer to the mountain—Abraham, of course.

Abraham turned his head to look back at us, and on his face was an expression I'd never seen there before. His gaze was unblinking and staring, as if he and Sarah were looking into each other's eyes across all that distance. The rest of his features were set, determined, almost fierce. He looked like a warrior ready for his final battle, a soldier about to rush into a fray he knew he couldn't survive.

I shifted to stand beside him. "What are you doing here, son of Adam?" I said, but he didn't hear me.

The sound of Isaac laughing carried from fifty feet back. A spasm tore through Abraham's features; in the next moment, they were still and under control again.

Although I couldn't explain how I knew it, I was sure that Isaac rode the donkey to his death; and equally sure that Abraham would be his murderer.

In the shock and confusion of that thought, I did something that had never been tried before—I manifested myself to Abraham as an angel of light, as a bright and blinding messenger of the Enemy.

"Abraham!"

He stopped walking and shielded his eyes with the back of his hand. "Here I am," he said.

"What are you doing in this place?"

"The will of my Lord."

"The Lord does not will your son's death!"

"The Lord I know," Abraham said, dropping his hand, "but who are you?"

As I disappeared, he turned to face the approaching figures and waited for them to catch up. "Son, descend," he said, and Isaac immediately jumped off. "Give me the torch," Abraham told the servants. "My son and I will go up the mountain to worship and we'll return in a short while. Wait for us here."

"You can't do this, Abraham," I said in his ear. "This is your son, whom you love. This is the child of promise, given to you by the Lord Himself! Think of Sarah if nothing else can move you to compassion."

"Take up the wood," Abraham said to Isaac, "and follow me."

The boy did as his father commanded, slinging the pile over his shoulder.

I left Abraham and whispered into Isaac's ear: "Don't you see what's happening here? Your father is going to kill you. He's going to sacrifice you on the very wood you're carrying on your back. He thinks he's doing this for God, but he doesn't know what he's doing!"

Isaac was quiet for a while as they hiked up the side of the mountain. Finally he said, "We didn't bring a lamb for the sacrifice, Father."

Abraham didn't look back. "The Lord will provide a lamb."

Instantly I was at his ear. "This is not the will of the Lord, Abraham. You've gone mad." It didn't occur to me then to wonder if He-Who-Rules would be pleased or angry with me. On the one hand, I was trying to convince Abraham not to do what he believed the Enemy wanted him to do; on the other, I was only doing it to save him from committing an insane act.

"The Lord's will be done," he said, walking ahead of Isaac, speaking softly to himself. "From the moment I woke up three days ago I've known what I must do. And my son died in my heart, and he's been dead since. And I must kill him, this son in whom I am so pleased. But Isaac will not stay dead. The Lord has spoken; all the world will be blessed through him. My son will not stay dead."

Although the words were not intended for me, they convinced me. A few days earlier, the Enemy had asked Abraham to sacrifice Isaac.

"Did He give you this son only to take him away?" I screamed. "Is this the way of the Lord? Will only the shedding of innocent blood satisfy Him? Don't go through with this, Abraham. Let the boy live! This is not an act of faith. You are not Noah. This is not spending your life building a boat and preaching to a world that finds you ridiculous—this is the murder of your own flesh and blood!"

Abraham came to a stop, and I stopped speaking. He speared the handle of the torch in the ground, then took the bundle from Isaac's back and untied the wrapping. He placed the wood in a clearing, creating one strip the length of a man and a shorter strip across the first.

While Abraham worked, I whispered in Isaac's ear that he should escape, that his father would kill him otherwise and then spend the rest of his life regretting his mad and murderous act. But Isaac stood perfectly still throughout, and when Abraham was finally done and looked up at him, Isaac walked over to the altar and lay down on top of it as if he were going to sleep.

"There is still time to escape, Isaac," I said, raising my voice. Abraham tied one of his son's arms down to the wood. "Do you give up your life so easily?" Abraham tied down the other arm, then his feet. "Is this the God you worship?"

Abraham pulled out his knife, sharp and long-bladed with jewels on either side of the hilt.

"That knife spilled the blood of goats and lambs," I said, now yelling in Abraham's ear. "Will it spill the blood of your son? And by your own hand?" Then, louder than I'd ever yelled at a fallen, I yelled at Abraham, "This is not the will of the Lord!"

Abraham froze, looked startled, blurted out, "I'm here; I'm listening."

He's listening to me. After all this time, he's finally listening.

Abraham did seem to still be listening, but I wasn't talking. His grip on the knife loosened, almost fell to the ground. He looked over his shoulder, but I was too mesmerized to follow his gaze. Then he looked back at his son, bound and stretched out on the wooden altar, and his grip on the knife tightened.

"Abraham, no!" I screamed, but he had already swung. He swung again and then a third time.

"Arise, my son," he said.

Free from his bindings, Isaac sat up. "Look, Father," he said. "A ram is caught in that bush."

"Yes," Abraham said without looking.

In a daze, I watched him bind the ram to the wood and sacrifice it instead of Isaac. If earlier I thought I would lose my mind because Abraham was going to kill his own son, now I thought I would lose it because he hadn't. What stopped him? What changed his mind when all of my words had no more effect on him than if they were the chirping of crickets?

Father and son walked back down the mountain, as if they were returning from a hike and not a horror.

A part of my mind was always working on the task He-Who-Rules had set for me, and it was in that part that was born the idea, or the hope, that this experience could be used to turn Isaac against the Enemy and steep him in sin. But I realized immediately that that wouldn't happen—the boy bounded onto the donkey with unrestrained joy and laughed when he almost fell off.

Abraham looked like a man returned to life himself; years seemed to have fallen off of him, and he walked taller and with more energy. A mission, a burden almost too much to bear, had been set to him, but now his duty was done and the weight was lifted.

"Abraham can't be touched," I said to He-Who-Rules, not much later. Before the fury in his eyes could blaze any hotter, I said, "He will do anything for the Enemy. He was prepared to sacrifice his son. If the Enemy asked him to carve out his own heart and throw it away, he'd do it."

"Enough of this!" He-Who-Rules stood and spoke so that all of the dark angels around the throne room could hear. "You are a failure, Enoch. And I am tired of your excuses. I—"

"I didn't come here to offer excuses, Master," I said quickly. "You asked me to find a way to break Abraham or men of faith. The first I can't do; Abraham's faith is too strong. But I think I may have found a strategy that will work for others, something that I don't think anyone has ever thought of before."

"Is that so?"

"These people we hate," I said, choosing my words carefully to pacify him, "belong to the Enemy. So to defeat them, we must become like the Enemy."

He-Who-Rules sat back down. "I know you're afraid of me, Enoch. I can sense it every time we speak. So I believe you wouldn't say what you've just said unless you mean something very particular by it."

"I do, Master. We shouldn't try to convince these men and women of faith to hate the Enemy. What's the point? We should only try to convince them that we are the Enemy, and get them to do our will."

"How?"

"By appearing as angels of light; as the Enemy Himself if we think we can pull it off." He-Who-Rules seemed intrigued by the idea; the confidence that knowledge engendered loosened my tongue. "It would've worked with Abraham, but you gave him to me too late; he was already too familiar with the Enemy and His messengers."

"Careful, Enoch," he said, but in a distracted way, "you're making excuses again." After a short pause, he said, "At best Abraham is familiar with the Begotten; why didn't you manifest yourself as the Unbegotten or the Proceeding and explain the difference that way?"

I shook my head, but politely. "I don't think Abraham has any notion that the Enemy is triune. Anyway, I probably should've tried appearing to Abraham as one of his ancestors—Noah, maybe, or even Adam. That might have worked, at least to cast doubt on the Enemy's command to sacrifice his son. I just didn't think of it early enough."

He-Who-Rules was quiet, and by the concentration on his face I knew not to disturb his thoughts.

From outside the palace, I heard the screams of the tortured fallen and the happy screeching of the dark angels.

By then three ranks had formed and solidified, the same ranks we have now: the torturers who preferred to stay in Sheol; the tempters on Earth; and the officers who carried out the Master's will, often acting as messengers between him and the tempters. As I stood there watching him, I realized that it had been a long while since the Master had visited Earth.

How interesting, I thought. *There was a time when He-Who-Rules wouldn't take us to this new world, because it might be dangerous. Now he'll send everyone without pause, but won't go himself.*

"If what you say is true," the Master said, startling me, "then the Enemy is keeping this knowledge from the fallen. He has not revealed Himself to them, not fully. Why? What can it mean?"

He wasn't expecting an answer, and I didn't offer one.

"He's waiting for something? For someone?" The Master made a signal with his hand and one of the low officers went to fetch Sytri. When he arrived, He-Who-Rules said to him, "Dispatch a message to all of our field agents. Any fallen who refers to the Enemy as triune is to be reported to me immediately."

Sytri was a model of perfect obedience—I could see the order piqued his curiosity, but he nodded and turned away.

The Master looked back at me and seemed surprised that I was still there. "That is all, Enoch; you may go."

As much as I hated having the Master's attention focused on me, being dismissed made me feel even worse. "That's all?"

The Master nodded amiably; his anger toward me seemed to have cooled completely. "It never occurred to me that the fallen didn't grasp that the Enemy is triune." Something about the Master's behavior felt strange, but I couldn't pinpoint it just then. "I'm comforted by the thought that He has chosen to withhold that knowledge from them. What was there to fear of Seth or of Noah or even of Abraham? All along I've known more about the Enemy than they have." He-Who-Rules was speaking more to himself than to me, or I'm sure he never would have implied that he'd ever feared the fallen. "This also gives us something we've never had before, a sort of early warning system. Mark my words: the first fallen to know that the Enemy is three-in-one—that is the first fallen to be wary of."

"Do you want me to go back to Earth?" I said, but I felt sure that I already knew the answer.

"As you wish, Enoch."

"Can I approach the throne, please?"

The Master nodded, a little wearily. The goodwill I'd earned with my revelation was quickly being depleted.

"Isaac needs to be watched," I said. "He's dangerous."

He smiled. "Thanks for the warning, Enoch, but I'm not concerned. If it makes you feel better, though, I can pay him a visit."

"You? But I thought—" Then the seemingly separate thoughts bumped into each other; they fit, and I realized the truth. He-Who-Rules had been avoiding Earth. He'd sent me, supposedly to break Abraham; yet he didn't seem overly concerned about my failure to do so, and seemed ready to punish me (torture in the lake of fire, no doubt, and in front of the fallen, paraded out of their cells to be spectators so that the humiliation could be complete) only to make an example of me. But he did seem surprised that I'd done well, surprised that I'd given him knowledge he could use.

"It was me," I said, speaking in anger and without thought. "I was your early warning system, wasn't I? You never believed I could beat Abraham. You just wanted someone right in front of him, someone to take the first hit so you'd know the attack was coming. Did you do the same thing with others, feed them the same lines and position them throughout the fallen world? And all this time you've been hiding in this room, surrounded by these guards, too scared to return to Earth!"

I spoke not only without thought, but also without awareness; with my first few words, the Master's glow had turned a fiery red as dark as the lake, but I took no real notice and kept going.

When I finished speaking, I was surprised to find that I'd taken a few steps back—to get away from the heat of the Master's glow, I finally realized. I looked around the room grown suddenly quiet; every dark angel was staring at me. I looked back at the Master, saw that he'd crushed the arms of his throne.

"You should've left when you had the chance," he said, an ugly smile spreading across his face.

Chapter Five

A Man of Dreams

IN his own way of punishing transgressors without explanation until everyone figured out a newly-instilled rule, the Master banned anyone from talking about what happened that day.

He had stood, pieces of the throne still in his fist and crumbling into dust under the pressure of his anger.

I wasn't the first to point out that the Master's actions and tirades sometimes seemed motivated by fear. I wasn't the first to notice that no matter how much he assured us of eventual victory over the Enemy, his reaction to reports from Earth almost always went from desperation bordering on terror to relief, usually upon hearing that the fallen in question was now dead (nothing made the Master feel happier—feel safer—than learning that a fallen who served the Enemy had died). But the others had the intelligence to point out these interesting facts among themselves, in private and when they knew no one could overhear them, while I said them to the Master himself and—as if that wasn't self-destructive enough—I did it in front of the whole assembly of dark angels in the throne room.

Watching the dust fall from the Master's hands, two thoughts went through my mind: first, that even if he wasn't angry, I'd just put He-Who-Rules in a situation where he would have to make an example of me; and second, that he wasn't only angry but furious.

"You really should've left when you had the chance," he repeated, and he began to spread his arms—to what end I had no idea. I shifted, to the first place that came to mind: the mountain on which Abraham almost sacrificed Isaac.

Certain that He-Who-Rules, or Asmodeus, or Mulciber, was only one step behind, I prepared to shift again. But to where? Where could I go that the Master couldn't find me? I waited, tense as a harp string, ready to disappear as soon as He-Who-Rules or his enforcers appeared, frantically trying to think of a good place to hide.

In some ways, I'm glad I couldn't think of anywhere to go; I'd probably be there still, unwilling to stick my neck out for fear of being discovered by the Master or his minions. Then again, maybe that life in hiding would have been better for me than the one I have now.

Eventually I realized that I wasn't being followed; I accepted the fact without understanding it. *Maybe the Master has written me off*, I thought; *deciding, perhaps, that a coward who runs away isn't worth pursuing*. It would be a long time before I learned the real reason no one followed me that day.

I descended the mountain called Moriah and began searching for Isaac, mostly out of force of habit but also because I believed what I'd told the Master: Isaac was dangerous and needed to be watched. He-Who-Rules is fickle, but there's one good thing to say about the fickle: if they turn on you the moment you displease them, they're just as quick to welcome you back when you make them happy again. *If I can show the Master the danger Isaac presents*, I thought, *all may yet be forgiven*.

I'm not sure what I expected; the concept of linearity and the notion that the fallen age in time was still so strange to me. But when I found Isaac, I thought I'd found his father; and it came as a shock to learn the truth. Isaac lay propped up in bed, staring at nothing from eyes that had become useless with age. *Here is the young man I last saw leaping on a donkey and shouting with joy*, I thought; *here he is, ancient of bones and with wrinkled skin, blind and bed-ridden. So it goes—Abraham is dead and Isaac is dying. And so much for winning back the Master's favor.*

"Do you remember me, Isaac?" I said to him one night, when he was alone.

"I remember the voice," he said. "Yes."

"My name is Enoch. I'm an angel."

"Welcome, friend."

For only the briefest moment I thought of correcting him, telling him that in fact I wasn't a friend, that I was one of the bad angels. "You are a man of the—of God, Isaac. I know that. I've heard you speak of a plan; you say He has one. What is it?"

Isaac pulled himself up in bed. "A plan, yes. The Lord of my father will reconcile the world to Himself."

"How?"

Isaac smiled, pale and wrinkled lips pulling back to reveal a toothless mouth.

"I don't know," he said. "That is one of His mysteries; it will be revealed in the fullness of time. How I wish I could live to see it happen!"

"Grandfather?"

Neither one of us had noticed the child who had snuck into the tent, but Isaac recognized his voice right away. "What are you still doing awake, Joseph?"

The boy felt his way toward his grandfather's bed. "I had a bad dream."

"Dreams don't mean anything," I said to Isaac.

"You did, did you?" Isaac said. "Come, sit beside me. Tell me about your dream."

Joseph told him, but I stopped paying attention because a new thought had occurred to me: did the Master have any idea that Isaac was dying? Would he send someone to try to capture his spirit?

Amid the rising waves of panic and the deep desire to escape, a part of me tried to stay rational. He-Who-Rules wasn't going to send anyone for Isaac. Sheol was already overrun by spirits; he wasn't about to wrestle them away from the Enemy—we'd tried that and failed. Not that he or any of his dark angels could wrestle away a soul they couldn't find in the first place. *It's safe here, near Isaac*, I told myself; *probably safer than anywhere else on Earth.* And just then, I didn't want to shift to some far-off planet by myself; I wanted to continue speaking with Isaac and find out what else he knew about the Enemy and His plan.

I never got the chance. Isaac fell asleep with his grandson curled up in his arms. As dawn broke the next morning, Isaac whispered in Joseph's ear to run out and ask Jacob and Esau to come see him.

"You're dying," I said, when Joseph had left the tent.

Hardly able to speak anymore, Isaac moved his head in what I took to be a nod.

He was dead by nightfall; he spent his last day being hugged and kissed by a stream of sons and daughters and grandchildren, as one after another they came into his tent and thanked him for whatever it was he'd done for them in particular—made them laugh when they were feeling sad, or taught them how to ride a camel, or told them all about Father Adam and the Tree of Life, or Father Noah and the Flood, or Father Abraham and the Three Hundred and Eighteen Soldiers who saved Lot from the Four Kings. When he died,

I thought I saw something descend on his body, or ascend from his body—something like a shimmering sheet. I took a step closer and almost yelled in terror—the Master stood over Isaac's body.

His back was to me; he hadn't seen me. I retreated slowly, had another start as I saw that Abaddon stood beside him—but he wasn't looking my way either. Fear continued flooding into me, but I refused to shift. I backed away further, out of the tent; crouched low and tried to blend in with the shadows. *If the Master sees me*, I thought; *if he focuses on me for even a moment, I'm lost*. But I needed to know what he was doing there, or why they hadn't come after me right away, or whether the Master's presence on Earth and with Isaac meant he'd seen I was right after all and had forgiven me.

"I told you, didn't I?" He-Who-Rules said, his voice dripping with disdain. "There's no danger here; the fool was wrong. Isaac is dead."

"But his spirit—"

"—is of no concern to us; he's dead, that's all that matters. Jacob's the one to watch. Stay with Zephar. If it happens again, one of you come and tell me immediately. I expect regular—"

Without waiting for the Master to finish, I flew to the tent of Isaac's son Jacob. He sat at the entrance, his own son Joseph curled up in his lap, staring at the fire and not seeming to hear what his father and his father's brother Esau discussed in angry but restrained tones.

I found Zephar inside the tent.

"Enoch," he said, startled. "You shouldn't be here."

"What are *you* doing here, Zephar? Why are you watching this man?"

Zephar's glow dimmed. Outside someone shouted to Jacob that Isaac was dead.

"I don't have time for this!" I said. "Abaddon's on his way!"

Zephar distanced himself from me. "You need to get out of here, Enoch! If the Master finds you... and if I'm found talking to you... shift away! There's a price on your head—don't approach anyone. Stay away from Jacob, too—stay away from all of them. Leave!"

I was gone with his last word. His panic was infectious enough by itself, but my own terror was fueled by the constant certainty that Abaddon's hands were about to fall on my shoulders.

I went back to Mount Moriah. Although returning to it (twice, by then) was an act of instinct, I decided that it was as good a place as any—the mountain was deserted and afforded a view of the valley below, which made it easier to detect the intrusion of any living being, spiritual or physical; and it kept me close to Jacob and his family. I never even considered running away and hiding like Zephar had told me to do. I needed to find out why Jacob was suddenly so important, and how Zephar himself fit into any of this.

One day, about four years later, I saw two human figures in the distance accompanied by two spirits, all of whom I recognized immediately. Whenever I ventured near Jacob to see if I would find Zephar alone and learn what more I could from him, Abaddon's hulking frame and angry red glow had sent me right back to the mountain. Now both dark angels were headed in my direction, as were Jacob and Joseph and a donkey loaded down with sacks of food.

When they reached the foot of the mountain, Jacob tied up the animal to a tree, and he and Joseph and the dark angels started making their way up the path.

I hid, trying to blend into the shadow cast by one of the shrubs, but found it difficult to listen to both conversations at once.

"See, it's nothing," Zephar said to Abaddon.

"This is the place," Jacob said to Joseph.

"The kid just wants to see where—"

"—your great-grandfather—"

"You're wasting your time here. Nothing has happened since—"

"I don't either. Sometimes the ways of the Lord are—"

"The Master doesn't trust me? I'm the one who—"

"Your great-grandfather said they were the hardest three days—"

I didn't want to miss a word from the two conversations, but I wasn't getting anything from either one by trying to listen to both at once. I focused on the dark angels.

"No," Zephar said, "what I'd rather be doing is working on a way around the problem."

"Others are doing that," Abaddon said. "Everyone has their role."

"And what's my role? To shadow Jacob until the Enemy decides to go another round with him? And what's your role, Abaddon? To shadow me as I shadow him? To babysit me?"

I wasn't looking directly at them for fear they might sense me, but even so I could tell that Abaddon's glow intensified. "The Master

believes there's nothing more important than keeping an eye on this
creature. If what you said is true, and if the Enemy takes human
shape ever again, it may be our best chance at ending this war."

Jacob started to walk away, and the two dark angels followed him
almost reflexively, Zephar complaining that he'd grown bored of Jacob
and his people and their tents. Neither angel seemed to notice or care
that Joseph had stayed behind. When they were sufficiently far away,
I left my hiding place and approached him.

Joseph had gotten down on his knees, closed his eyes, and was
whispering.

"...frightens me so much," he said. "My own people—my own
brothers. They turn everything I say against me; they answer any
kindness I show them with suspicion or ridicule—but...can it be true?
Will they sell me for silver? Will my own brothers stand by while a
foreigner binds my hands together and puts shackles on my feet?"

A sob escaped him and his body slumped forward so that he had
to put out his hands to stop himself from falling onto the ground.
"Maybe I'm wrong, maybe I've misinterpreted the dream," he said, in
even lower but quicker tones. He shook his head. "Your will be done,
Lord."

He stood and, after a few moments of silence, started down the
path.

He and his father—and his father's dark escorts, of course—were
back the next year in the same season, and the year after. The following year, however, Jacob presumably decided that Joseph was old
enough to make the journey on his own.

What made me speak to him? Maybe it was listening to him confess to the Enemy year after year—maybe I felt that I knew him well
by knowing the dreams and visions he'd had. Or maybe after all that
time alone, I just needed another creature to talk to. Either way,
when I saw that he approached by himself on his donkey, and that
both Zephar and Abaddon had stayed behind with Jacob, I felt a great
sense of relief for not having to hide and worry that I'd be discovered.
When he reached the top of the mountain and knelt down, I spoke to
Joseph.

"Who are you?" he said, scrambling back to his feet and looking
around.

"I'm an angel," I said, taking shape beside him.

He took another step back, his robe fluttering in the wind, the jewels embedded along its bright purple cloth reflecting sunlight so he seemed almost like an angel himself. "You're not my angel," he said.

"No," I said, wondering if he saw through the disguise, if he saw my true nature behind the image I projected. "But I mean you no harm."

"What do you want with me?"

"I need to ask you some questions, Joseph."

He finally relaxed, and a small smile broke out on his lips. "An angel of the Lord wishes to ask me questions?"

"I need to ask you about your father," I said, delighted at the assumption he'd made. "Did anything happen to him, before your grandfather died? Something big?"

Joseph's lips pursed in thought. "You mean his vision?"

"Tell me about it."

"He saw a ladder that joined Heaven and Earth," Joseph said, and spoke as if he could see it himself. "At the top of the ladder stood the Lord; and the Lord spoke to him, telling him that through his seed all the people of the Earth will be blessed."

I'd be lying if I said I thought the vision was significant at the time. In fact, I thought the exact opposite, taking it as simply another example of Joseph's monomania, his obsession with dreams and visions.

"Anything else? Something really big? Something. . . cosmic? Something involving the Enemy?"

"The Adversary?" Joseph said, and too late I realized my mistake and was thankful that Joseph hadn't picked up on it. "No, nothing I'm aware of."

"What about the Lord?"

Joseph shrugged again. "You mean when the Lord tested my father's strength and resolve? You already know about that, don't you?"

"Tell me anyway. Tell me the story the way you know it."

"The Lord tested my father by taking the shape of a man and wrestling with him throughout the night. When day broke and the Lord saw that my father still refused to give up, He blessed him and called his name Israel."

This is it, I thought, remembering Abaddon's words: "If the Enemy takes human shape ever again, it may be our best chance at ending this war." But that wasn't the whole story, of course; Abaddon had started with the words "If what you said is true." Some of what had happened began to be clear to me. Zephar had been following Jacob, either on his own initiative or on the Master's orders. He'd seen Jacob wrestle the Enemy and—sometime between when I escaped the throne room and when I descended the mountain to see Isaac—he'd reported in to He-Who-Rules; and something about his report caused the Master to forget about chasing me.

Over the next several months, I thought about how I might get time alone with Zephar. I wanted to speak to him, to fill in the gaps, to understand what Zephar had seen that made the event so important to the Master.

By springtime, I had still not come up with a very good plan for separating Zephar and Abaddon, but something happened that changed my priorities. Joseph never returned to the mountain. As the days changed into nights and back again, I became increasingly convinced that something horrible had happened and was so worried about him that I decided to go back to Canaan.

Jacob confirmed every fear I had. I watched from hiding because Abaddon still lurked around him, but I didn't need to get closer: Jacob walked with slumped shoulders, his gaze hardly leaving the ground in front of him, and at night when he thought no one was watching he cried and prayed for Joseph's spirit.

Not for a moment did I believe Joseph was dead; I remembered the vision he'd had of his brothers selling him into captivity. I went from tent to tent until I found one of them who still tossed and turned, someone who was more racked by his conscience than the others. Into Reuben's ears I whispered Joseph's name over and over, hoping that he'd wake up in the morning and confess everything to Jacob. Instead, he awoke, sat up in bed, and looked around the room. "Who are you?" he said, his voice so panicked and high that I worried he might attract others into his tent. "Why are you troubling me?"

"Peace," I said, trying to speak softly. "I am an angel, and it is your heart that will trouble you unless you confess your sins."

"What sins?"

"Joseph," I whispered again into his ear, and he started to weep.

After a while, when his sobs had quieted down, he said, "We were tending to our cattle near Dothan and my father sent Joseph to check up on us. When we saw him approaching, some of us wanted to kill him. But I told them not to shed his blood. I pointed to a well that had gone dry and told them to push him into it."

"Why?"

"I thought that later I could double-back and save him."

"I mean, why did you want to harm Joseph at all?"

Reuben reached across to a small table near his bed and picked up a cup of water. He held it in his hand but didn't drink from it. "I don't know—jealousy, I guess. My father... worried about Joseph more than the rest of us, forgave him quicker, laughed more with him... he loved him more than he loved us. That might not have been enough by itself, but Joseph didn't help matters. He spoke endlessly of his dreams and visions; in one, we all bowed down to him, as if he were a king. When we threw him in the pit, Dan said, 'Who's bowing down, Joseph?' I guess those words explain our feelings best."

"What happened? Did you go back and rescue him?"

Reuben shook his head. "When he was still in the pit, Judah noticed some merchants passing by and he told the others that they should sell Joseph to them. I wasn't there. When I got back, the deal with the Ishmaelite merchants was already done, and my brothers had already pulled Joseph out of the well and handed him to them."

"Sold for silver," I said. "And his brothers stood by while foreigners bound his hands together and put shackles on his feet."

Reuben nodded, brought the cup to his lips but still didn't drink.

"Where did they take him?"

"To the south. To Egypt."

For a moment, I thought of saying something to make Reuben feel better. *But he shouldn't feel better*, I thought; *not only for everything that he did or allowed his brothers to do in the heat of the moment, but for keeping the truth from his father after he'd seen how much Jacob suffered over Joseph.* I left without saying a word; I could hear that Reuben still spoke, but he offered his excuses and pleadings to an empty room.

Egypt wasn't hard to find; shortly after heading out, I saw that trains of merchants all seemed to be headed toward a certain point in the distance, while others seemed to be headed away from there. When I arrived in Egypt, its grandeur and beauty made me forget all about Joseph for a while.

Pyramids of startling symmetry soared into the sky like arrows fired from the center of the earth, and stone palaces and temples towered over the wooden homes of commoners. *This is a far cry from the tents of Abraham's people*, I thought, amazed at the genius of the fallen that could create such structures, and with nothing more than stone and wood and mud.

A few days later, as I stood in the hall of one of the smaller palaces, studying in wonder the intricate pictures carved into the walls, I heard a familiar voice bellowing orders. I followed the sound, and found Joseph running through the halls, yelling commands to the house servants.

That night after the party, I appeared to him. "Well-loved of the Lord," I said, "who is sold into slavery but becomes head of a household."

Joseph smiled. "My master Potiphar has been very good to me."

"You're good for Potiphar and his house, I think. I saw the way you ran things tonight. And I've heard what people say of you. The Captain has put all of his money and investments into your care, and since that day his whole house has prospered."

A few weeks later, the Captain showed that he wasn't very good to Joseph after all. I had been staying away from Potiphar's wife because she always had a dark angel with her and I didn't want to risk being noticed. But I realized that was a mistake when Potiphar sent his guards to arrest Joseph.

Too scared of being discovered, I stayed in place as Joseph was dragged away, bound and shackled once again. When Joseph was thrown into prison a short while later, I found out that Potiphar's wife had accused him of trying to seduce her.

"Why didn't you defend yourself?" I screamed at Joseph, raising my voice although he'd been whispering. He flinched, but I continued in the same tone. "You're innocent! Potiphar must have known it too, or he would have had you executed! If you'd just said something, anything—you could've saved yourself!"

I was disgusted with Joseph, and infuriated with the injustice of the situation and of his life as a whole. "You were born to a father who loved you more than anything," I said, forcing myself to speak in a normal tone, "and one would expect your life to be easy and happy. But then your brothers turned on you and sold you into slavery. Somehow you kept from despair and proved yourself a trustworthy and capable servant to your master, and he raised you up and put everything into your care. Did you do a bad job? In fact, you're in jail now because of your innocence—because you refused to give in to that harlot. Where is the justice in that, Joseph? Where is the—where is God? How can He let someone who is innocent suffer like this?"

Joseph smiled as gently and widely as ever before, even though he now had nothing more in his possession than the clothes he wore, and his home was a small cell he shared with several other prisoners. "Some people ask how we can say the Lord is good if He allows the innocent to suffer. But the truth is that innocent people often suffer much more than guilty ones. It seems to me that those closest to the Lord have been made to suffer the most by the world, because they are far from the world."

"And you think that's fair?"

"It's not about fairness," he said. "The Lord allowed all of this to happen to me; He has a reason."

"And what reason might that be?"

Joseph yawned, then turned over on his side. "The fullness of time," he mumbled, among other words.

It struck me then, as it has many times since, how odd it is that the fallen need to shut down every sixteen hours or so, and how annoying it must be to interrupt an activity or a conversation or a thought just to give in to the need for sleep. But then again, we don't have dreams or visions, do we?

A few weeks later, during which Joseph wasted his energy keeping up the spirits of his fellow captives, two of them had dreams that kept them awake most of the night. When Joseph asked what was wrong the next morning, they told him.

Something struck me about the dreams that I wouldn't have noticed had they not happened on the same night and been recounted one after the other. The first dream was about bread and the other wine, as if the shadow of Melchizedek had followed me even into Egypt. What was the significance? I didn't know, but Joseph at least thought he knew the meaning of the dreams themselves. To Pharaoh's chief butler, who dreamed of pressing grapes on three vines into wine, Joseph gave the good news that Pharaoh would set him free in three days. To Pharaoh's chief baker, who dreamed of birds eating through three baskets of bread, Joseph gave bad news: Pharaoh would have him executed in that many days.

When the butler and the baker were taken away, I told Joseph, "Tell them not to forget their good friend if they're set free." Joseph said the words only to the butler, even though I thought it more prudent to say them to both in case his interpretations were wrong. But he wasn't wrong then or any other time—the baker was led to his death and the butler to freedom.

Despite Joseph's plea, the butler forgot all about the man who comforted him in prison, and served him, and defended him to the warden. I've seen the pattern repeated countless times with the fallen. In a desperate and pitiful situation, they crave the smallest degree of comfort and hope, and rivers of gratitude flow when it's offered to them. But once out of that dire situation, the rivers dry up and they can't find a drop of gratitude or a single thought to spare on those who helped them through it. I must've whispered Joseph's name in his ear a thousand times over the next couple of years, but the butler didn't give him a second thought.

When he finally did remember Joseph, the butler did so only because it served his purposes. Pharaoh had had dreams that troubled him; he was convinced that a message was hidden inside the visions, a message he'd ignore at his own peril. But no one could interpret the dreams to Pharaoh's satisfaction.

"Joseph will know," I whispered in the chief butler's ear. "Bring him to Pharaoh and your reward will be great."

No sooner than the last word was out of my mouth but the chief butler was speaking of the imprisoned Hebrew who had an amazing ability to interpret dreams. Pharaoh called for him to come immediately.

I returned to Joseph because I wanted to be there when he got the good news. The warden came down, looking crestfallen, telling Joseph to shave and change his clothes because he was called to an audience with Pharaoh.

I was amazed at how collected Joseph seemed as the warden escorted him into the presence of the king of Egypt.

"I'm told that you have a special talent for interpreting dreams," Pharaoh said.

"No, I don't," Joseph said, remaining calm even though I was screaming at him.

Pharaoh waited, one eyebrow lifted expectantly.

"God will provide the answers you seek," Joseph said.

Pharaoh smiled, then told him about his dreams.

As he heard them described, Joseph's eyes grew wide. Almost before Pharaoh was done speaking, he said, "God has revealed these things to you because they will happen, and they will happen soon. Seven years of plenty will be followed by seven years of famine. You must store up enough food in the first seven years to last through the next seven. Otherwise your people will starve and your country will become a wasteland."

On that day, Joseph was not only set free from prison, he was put in charge of all of Egypt, second only to the king himself. In the first seven years, Joseph took a fifth of the harvest throughout the land and held it in reserve, storing the food in the cities closest to each growing field. The crop was so abundant that soon he couldn't keep track of it all.

When the famine struck in the eighth year, the people—from Egypt and from the neighboring lands—came to Joseph and he gave them bread.

"Dear angel," he said to me one night, "you once whispered in my ears that the Lord had abandoned me; you asked me where was the Lord when my brothers sold me into slavery, and where was the Lord when Potiphar threw me into prison. But now I understand how you were testing me; now I see that you asked me those questions to help me be patient. From the depths of the dungeons I was lifted up to the right hand of the king, and people all over the world are saved from starvation because I was sold into slavery."

One day an amazing thing happened: his brothers came to buy grain from Pharaoh. Not recognizing him in his makeup and jewelry, they bowed down to Joseph.

"Your dream!" I said. "Your words have come true: your brothers bow down before you. They honor the man they ridiculed and sold into slavery, so blinded by your new brilliance that they don't recognize the one for the other!"

At first I thought he and I were thinking along the same lines and that Joseph would use his position to exact revenge for everything they'd done to him. But it turned out he wasn't interested in revenge. I could barely watch as a weeping Joseph revealed himself to his brothers.

Disgusted, I left Joseph for a few days and wandered through Egypt, trying but failing to understand how someone could suffer at the hands of his own people, then turn around and save them. Because I wasn't there, I didn't hear Joseph ask his brothers to depart

and bring back Jacob and all the Israelites to live with him. When I
did hear the news, a familiar terror seized me. So far the dark angels in Egypt had been easy to avoid. Most had been on Earth so
long that they didn't recognize me at a passing glance, which is all I
allowed them; some were too busy with the fallen to pay any attention to another spirit; and the rest couldn't be bothered to confront
me, I presumed, so they pretended they didn't notice or recognize me.
But if Jacob is coming, I thought, *Abaddon will come with him*. And
Abaddon, I knew, would recognize me, and would confront me happily, and wouldn't hesitate to drag me in front of the Master to collect
his reward.

I hated to leave Joseph, even if I couldn't understand why he'd
thrown away the opportunities the Enemy had given him. I hated
to return to my lonely hiding spot—of course now I'd welcome the
mountain with open arms, but at that point I wanted to stay with
Joseph and his children. I waited as long as I could, watching every
day for the return of Pharaoh's carts. When they did return, I scanned
the horizon, past the fallen and their livestock, hoping that Abaddon
and even Zephar had given up on Jacob. At first I didn't see either
one, then suddenly I saw both at once, flying directly toward me.

Did they see me? Was it too late for me to shift away unnoticed?

The questions froze me in place for a moment, but with an effort I
shook them off and shifted away, convincing myself that they hadn't
seen me, that they wouldn't notice an angel they had no reason to
expect to find in Egypt, and that in any case they couldn't possibly
know where I was escaping to. Not much later I found out I was
wrong on all counts.

Chapter Six

A Man Called Israel

"How did you find me?" I said, as Zephar appeared on the mountain. I kept my distance, not sure if Abaddon was a step behind or if Zephar thought he alone could drag me back to Sheol and collect the reward for himself.

Zephar had changed; his glow was different, deeper and darker. *All that time with Abaddon has been good for you*, I thought.

"I saw you when we came up here with Jacob that first time," he said. "I didn't say anything because Abaddon was with me. When you left Egypt, I figured that this is where you'd return."

"Abaddon didn't see me?"

"Relax, Enoch. I'm not here to harm you."

"Why not?"

Zephar's glow lightened slightly. "Because I think you can help me."

I backed away, ready to shift if this were a trap, if he were there to distract me so that Abaddon could take me without a fight. "Help you how?"

"You're so tense, Enoch."

"Where's Abaddon?"

"In Egypt where I left him."

I stopped moving away. "Jacob's dead?"

"No. But he's as old as the world. He won't be wrestling with the Enemy or anyone else. Enoch, I'm asking you again to relax. Abaddon isn't coming; he doesn't even know I'm here."

"What did you tell him?"

"That I needed to check on something, at the place where Jacob had struggled with the Enemy. You see? He has to stay with Jacob, so you're safe. And even if he or someone else tries to find me, this is the last place they'd think to look."

I tried to project a calmness I didn't feel.

If Zephar saw through it, he encouraged me anyway by saying, "There, that's better."

Although there were a dozen questions I wanted answered, I forced myself to be patient, not wanting to upset Zephar. "What do you need my help with?"

A sound like a laugh escaped from Zephar. "You should ask me the question you really want to ask, the one you asked me when we last met."

"I don't remember," I lied.

"You asked me why I was watching Jacob. I'll tell you—because He-Who-Rules asked me to keep an eye out, to watch for things."

"To spy on me, you mean."

"Not at all. My orders were to leave Abraham to you but to keep a lookout for anyone else who might be suspicious. When Jacob left for—but I should begin at the beginning, shouldn't I?"

IT was never my intention to interfere with you (Zephar said). In fact, I think you'll see that in all things I went out of my way to stay out of yours.

I chose Lot to start with, who was close to Abraham in blood but distant from him in space. I caught up with Lot in Sodom, and there I saw the first hint of the main problem we face. I listened as he spoke with no one at all, like a madman, then watched as he and his wife and daughters were led—practically dragged, I'd say—by a hand I couldn't see right out of the burning city. Are you starting to understand, Enoch?

Anyway, I earned some points for coaching Lot's wife to turn back to Sodom; and although I had nothing to do with it, I received points when his daughters got him drunk in the cave and seduced their father. But I felt like I was spitting in the sea; I wanted to do more, to impress the Master with something big; I didn't want a few points here and a few there—I wanted to bring him something so spectacular that the Master himself would award me all the points in Sheol.

I grew tired of Lot and went back to Abraham, and was amazed to find that he was alone. I worried every minute that you'd come back and complain to He-Who-Rules that I was interfering with your work, so when Isaac was born and Ishmael and his mother were sent away, I saw my chance. I spent years with them in the desert, trying as hard as I could to stoke resentment and anger against Abraham in Ishmael's heart; and when that didn't work, I tried to make him jealous of Isaac. "Will you stand for this, Ishmael? Will you allow the second to overthrow the first, the elder to be rejected and set aside in favor of the younger?"

When I was finally convinced that neither Ishmael nor Hagar had any interest in going back to Canaan, I returned by myself, saw that Sarah was dead and that Abraham was still alone. I know now that you had gone to Sheol to speak with He-Who-Rules; I didn't know that then. Not wishing to be perceived as violating the Master's orders, I stayed away from Abraham and focused on his son.

Rebekah bore twin sons for Isaac, first Esau then Jacob. . . but once again the younger would be blessed over the elder. Although Abraham died and was buried and still there was no sign of you, when Jacob was sent away to Mesopotamia to find a wife, I decided to follow.

Right away I knew I'd made the right decision. Jacob had a dream that affected him in a great way; in it, he saw a ladder that united the High Country and the Earth. At the time I thought it was simply interesting, but would you believe that I got more points for reporting Jacob's dream than for everything to do with Lot combined? The Master believes—or worries, perhaps—that this ladder is real. He has sent angels to look for it all over the Earth—and beyond, now that we're sure that if the ladder does in fact exist, it isn't on this planet.

When he reached the land of his mother's brother, Jacob met a young woman named Rachel and he fell in love. Not much could be done with him at that point, of course—it was real love and not lust, unfortunately. Jacob worked in her father's house for fourteen years to earn her hand in marriage; to me they were long, but Jacob went about his tasks as if they were fourteen days or fourteen hours. That is the real problem with love, isn't it? It makes their hearts light, but it is only heavy hearts that we have any chance of reaching.

As year followed year, at least once a day I seriously considered abandoning Jacob and finding someone else, someone more fruitful. I hadn't yet reported Jacob's vision of the ladder; and I'm glad I didn't or I might have given up on Jacob completely. But not having reported it, and not yet having been laughed at by Arakiel, I still believed it was important and interesting, and I was afraid that if I left Jacob, I might miss another vision.

Twenty years after he arrived in Mesopotamia, Jacob decided to return to Canaan. I didn't welcome this news. Although Jacob and Esau didn't get along—and few things are more fruitful than brothers who dislike each other—I worried that Isaac was still alive and that you were watching him as you'd watched his father. I worried that I'd have to find someone else, return to Ishmael and his descendants maybe, and miss whatever other opportunities I'd have through Jacob.

He packed up his family and possessions and headed back to the land of his fathers. I decided to go in front of them, to see what the situation was while there might still be a chance to return to Jacob and change his mind. I didn't find you in Canaan, but Arakiel found me.

"We've been looking for you," he said.

"I was following one of the fallen, like the Master asked me."

"You haven't checked in for a while," he said, with more than a little disapproval in his voice, and ignoring my subtle reminder that my orders came directly from He-Who-Rules.

"I've been waiting to have more to report," I said.

"Well, Sytri has new orders. You must alert us immediately if any fallen displays knowledge that the Enemy is triune. Do you understand?"

I nodded, though I wasn't really sure what he meant. "I do have something to report, actually. It's about a dream Jacob had. In it, he saw—"

"Is this a joke?" Arakiel said, interrupting. "We don't award points for dreams, Zephar."

"And you have the authority to make that decision, do you?"

After a pause, Arakiel said, "I have to go," although he looked like he wanted to launch himself at me much more than he wanted to go. "My orders are to deliver the new instruction to as many angels as quickly as possible. I have a list of them who've decided that it isn't worth their time to report back to Sheol as they're supposed to." He paused, his glow intensifying. "But maybe when I'm finished with my list, I'll come back and we can finish this conversation."

He didn't shift away immediately, but I decided to keep quiet until he did. Once he was gone, I wondered if I should shift back to Sheol and appeal to Sytri or even to the Master himself.

Afraid that I'd be laughed at by them as well, I decided to stay; and not knowing where else to go, I backtracked and returned to Jacob, more despondent than ever.

It was nighttime, but Jacob wasn't with Rachel; and he wasn't with Leah; and he wasn't with any of their handmaidens; and when I found him, he wasn't alone.

From a distance, it looked like he was struggling with a man. But a step closer and a glimpse longer, and it was obvious as the sun—this wasn't a man at all, this was the Enemy, this was the Begotten in human form! Can you imagine anything more ridiculous, Enoch? Did you ever think the Enemy was capable of something so stupid?

I marveled at the sight. If He wanted to enter this world He created, and even if He wanted to take human shape, why not appear as a roaring, raging superman, like the heroes the world saw before the flood? Why appear as a weakling, struggling with this old man, begging him to let go when day broke?

Jacob himself didn't seem to care about the Enemy's motives; he just wanted His blessing. So even with a dislocated hip, he refused to let go until he received it.

In shock I watched the Enemy bless him and change his name to Israel, but what happened next surprised me even more. The Enemy shed the foolish shape of a man, and I turned away because He was too bright, but before I did so I caught a glimpse of other bright lights around him—Michael, I think, and Gabriel. I don't know—there may have been others, too, but they were gone by the time I looked back, only a moment later.

Immediately I shifted to the throne room—it was so quiet that my arrival was noticed by everyone. The Master stood at the front, his arms outstretched as if he were about to launch himself at someone and rip them apart, disbelief emanating from him.

After a moment, the Master dropped his arms and began to yell orders. "All of you!" he screamed, the disbelief completely swallowed up in anger now. "All of you and all of the angels in Sheol—go! To Earth, to every planet in the universe—go to every place an angel can hide. Bring the coward back to me!"

"Master, wait!" I said, not quite sure what I was doing but certain that I better do it quickly before I lost my nerve.

When He-Who-Rules turned on me, he did so with such ferocity that I found I couldn't speak a single word.

"Zephar," he said, sitting down and speaking slowly and deliberately. "Do you know that you have chosen the absolutely worst moment to come into my throne room? And you've chosen to yell at me, which is not a good decision even in the best of times. Probably you think I'm about to drag you around Sheol like one of the fallen, for all to witness your humiliation, then tie a rock around your neck and drown you in the lake of fire, where for the rest of eternity you can contemplate your poor timing and judgment. But I'll do what you asked, I'll wait a few seconds more—I'm curious what you have to say that you've risked so much punishment to say it."

At first I thought I might not be able to find my words, but the way the Master's eyes bored into me encouraged me to speak. Don't look so surprised, Enoch—I would've done anything in my power to get him to stop looking at me like that. "It's about Jacob," I said.

"Jacob who?"

"The son of Isaac, the son of Abraham. I just witnessed him wrestling with the Enemy. Hear me out, please! He wrestled all night with the Begotten, who had taken—"

"The Begotten?" the Master said, almost angrily. "Did he know it was the Begotten?"

The question threw me at first, then I remembered what Arakiel had told me and I was quick to answer. "If Jacob knows the Enemy is triune, he's never displayed that knowledge, no. But it was the Begotten I saw him wrestling with, the Begotten who'd taken human form."

"Start over," He-Who-Rules said, but he no longer looked at me like he was contemplating the different ways he could torment me. "Start at the beginning."

I explained everything, how I'd stayed away from Abraham and then Isaac; how I'd followed Ishmael to no avail and then decided to follow Jacob. I told the Master about Jacob's vision, and when I saw that the dream interested him greatly, I told him about trying to report it to Arakiel. Then I told the Master about Jacob's return to Canaan and how he'd wrestled with the Begotten, and how for the briefest moment I thought I saw Michael or Gabriel or maybe both.

"This is the problem we're facing," I said. "We're fighting an enemy we can't see. His angels must be everywhere on the face of the Earth. We wonder why we can't capture the spirits we really want; now we know. The Enemy's angels are taking them first, wrapping them in their wings so we can't even see them. They're stealing all these spirits without a single fight!"

The Master turned to Abaddon, but I wasn't worried. "You and Zephar go to Jacob right away," he said. "Report back regularly. Shift back immediately if the Enemy takes human shape again."

"You think it might be easier to attack him in human form?" I said.

"I don't know," He-Who-Rules said. "But I'd like to try."

I nodded. "What about not being able to see the Enemy's angels?"

"Others will worry about that. And I'll send some of my angels to look for this ladder Jacob saw, in case it exists. You've done well, Zephar—you'll not only get the points you earned yourself, you'll also get half of Arakiel's points, as a punishment to him for not bringing me this information. Once I've had a chance to review things, Arakiel himself will personally deliver your new score to you."

Before we shifted away, Abaddon said, "What about Enoch?"

"If he crosses your path," the Master said, smashing down on his throne in anger, "bring him to me. Otherwise forget about the coward; we have more important things to attend to."

We left to find Jacob and almost immediately we heard that Isaac was close to death. Because you were so adamant that Isaac was such a danger, Abaddon shifted back to tell the Master; and soon enough you yourself appeared in Jacob's tent.

Now you know everything, and I think you can see how you can help.

BEfore Zephar finished speaking, two thoughts clearly fixed themselves in my mind. The first was that he was lying; and the second was that I suspected I knew the solution to the problem he'd uncovered.

"Just so we're perfectly clear," I said, "what you want is for me to find a way for us to see the angels of the Enemy, right? And you want me to tell it to you so you can tell it to the Master."

Annoyance flared in Zephar's glow, but he pushed it away quickly. "Don't you feel you owe me, Enoch, at least a little? How many times have I saved you?" He raised his arms in a crude approximation of a shrug. "And it's not exactly like you can walk into the throne room yourself to collect, is it?"

"All right," I said, "I'll try to figure it out. How can I be in touch with you?"

"Don't leave this mountain. I'll come and see you regularly—once a week, or more often if I can do it without raising suspicion."

Although I was convinced that Zephar was holding something back from me, I didn't know what it was or why he was lying. I was sure, for example, that the Master wouldn't smash down on his throne in anger, yet say to forget about me. That part at least was a lie—but in which direction? Did the Master forget all about me in his eagerness to explore the new paths Zephar had opened up for him? Or did he add me as a fourth item, and just as there were angels looking for Jacob's ladder, other angels were coming after me?

Trying to put that thought out of my mind, I descended the mountain to test out my hypothesis. I found the experiment more painful than I thought it would be, and yet I couldn't see any of the Enemy's angels—either because my theory was wrong or because they weren't there to be seen, I didn't know.

I wandered further than I intended, so focused was I on finding the angels of light. Night turned into day and back again and I hardly noticed; I just wanted to find them, to prove to myself that I was right and to redeem myself in front of the Master.

One day at dusk, I thought I saw something on the horizon. The translucent dot was smaller and dimmer than I imagined the Enemy's angels to be, but I blamed it on the distance between us. The glimpse filling me with excitement, I shifted beside the figure, the possibility that this could be a dark angel not occurring to me until I saw that it was Belial.

He looked sharply at me as I tried in panic to reverse my shift. He said, "Oh, it's you."

I started to shift away, then the words caught up to me and I stopped.

"You're acting strange," Belial said, distractedly. Leaves rustled from some nearby shrubs, capturing his attention.

I stared at him. "I'm acting strange? Is this a trick, Belial? There's an order by the Master to attack me on sight."

"No," he said. "Zephar gave He-Who-Rules too much to think about for him to worry about you. Apparently the angels of—"

"I know all about that!" I said. "But after Zephar told him those things, Abaddon asked him, 'What about Enoch?' and the Master said—"

"The Master said to Zephar, 'Tell him to put his creative mind to work on our problem. You'll run into the coward no doubt; he likes to hang around the Circumcised Ones.'"

"He said that?"

Belial paused to whisper in the ears of one of the fallen in the bushes, then looked back up at me. "He said that, yes. He also said that if you came up with the answer, you could go to the throne room and tell him yourself. He said he needed a new throne anyway."

"All that hiding," I started but had the rest of the thought in silence. Had Abaddon or the Master himself seen me in Isaac's tent, and just ignored my hiding as eccentric behavior? Did Abaddon sense or see me on the mountain, as Zephar had? And all the dark angels in Egypt I'd avoided and snuck around—had they noticed me and wondered why I was acting strange, like Belial had said? "This is so embarrassing," I finished.

The two fallen rose from the bushes; they readjusted their clothing, avoiding one another's eyes.

"See that, Enoch?" Belial said, and he spoke harshly to me for the first time. "That's embarrassment—it's a fallen emotion, understand? It's not becoming for us to speak like that about ourselves."

"But why didn't anyone tell me?"

"Arakiel said you knew. I wasn't there anyway; I heard all of this from him. He said he went to give Zephar his updated score—he's nearly top-ranked now, did you know that?—and Zephar said he'd run into you in Jacob's tent and that he'd told you everything."

"He left a few things out," I said, turning away, resisting the urge to shift to Egypt and drag Zephar to Sheol, tie a stone around his neck and drown him in the lake, and do to him all the other things the Master had threatened. But I needed to be patient, I knew; without a proven way to see the Enemy's angels, I was worth much less to the Master than Zephar.

Heading back in the general direction of the mountain, burning in fury at Zephar, a new suspicion came into my head—what if Zephar had told the truth and it was Belial who was lying? Or Arakiel, who'd told Belial everything Belial had told me, and maybe told the lie to lots of other angels who weren't there, hoping it would get back to me? Zephar would lie so he could take credit for my ideas. But Belial or Arakiel might lie out of sport, to have a good laugh when I shifted into Sheol and casually marched into the throne room, only to have all of the Master's angels descend on me.

Fear clouded my mind so that I couldn't discern who might be telling the truth. But I had to know—could I trust the dark angels on Earth, or should I avoid them? Was Zephar lying and using me, or was he taking a risk by protecting me, if only because he planned to benefit from me ultimately?

After a long time, I made up my mind: I would shift to Sheol, as far away from the palace as possible, where I would confirm one story or the other with a lower dark angel who wouldn't have a reason to lie.

Within moments of arriving in Sheol, however, I felt myself grabbed under the wings, picked up, carried forward toward the palace.

"Stop," I begged, not even able to see who was carrying me. "Let me go."

We landed in front of the castle doors; Asmodeus pushed me through them and into the throne room.

"Ah, Enoch," the Master said, and the look he turned on me filled me with terror and made me regret ever having thought I could return to Sheol safely.

"Master—" I began, but couldn't think of anything to say. Asmodeus kept a hand on my shoulder, presumably so I wouldn't get far from him if I tried to shift away again.

"Bring him closer," the Master said to Asmodeus, then waited until he'd done so. "Well, Enoch?"

Does he want me to beg for mercy? I thought. *Does he think I'm that stupid?*

He-Who-Rules stood. "Enoch, have words finally failed you? Speak. We are all waiting to hear it."

"To hear what, Master?" *I won't beg for mercy,* I told myself; *that will only delight him and everyone else and will probably only increase my punishment.*

The Master took a step down, then another. "To hear how we can see the Enemy's angels, of course. I can't believe even you'd be so self-destructive as to come here without that information."

Relief swept through me like a tide, washing away the fear that threatened to choke me. *Belial was telling the truth!* But then the relief was gone and a single fear was left behind: I didn't have the answer the Master was seeking, did I?

"No, of course not," I said, trying to project confidence. "I have a theory."

"A theory?" the Master hissed. "You came here with nothing more than a theory?"

"I came as soon as I thought of it, Master, not wanting to waste any time. I need volunteers to test it out—it isn't pleasant to try, and of course it may be dangerous."

An ugly smile spread across his face. "Brethren, herein lies a lesson—a coward once is a coward always. Go ahead, Enoch, tell me this theory."

I ignored the scorn that still emanated from the dark angels around the room and said, "I believe that our inability to see the angels of the Enemy is like a man who can't see anything above him because he won't lift his head."

"What does that even mean, Enoch?"

"It means that we must fix our thoughts on the Enemy. Once we focus on Him, I believe our minds will shift to a place from where we'll be able to see His angels. It's as if the man lifted his head from the ground."

The Master emitted a low, long hiss. "You make me regret ever putting my trust in you, Enoch," he said, motioning to Asmodeus to take me away. "First you want us to pretend we are the Enemy, now you want us to fill our thoughts with Him?"

"Wait," I said, struggling against Asmodeus's grip. "Master, listen. Zephar saw the Enemy's angels because he'd just been thinking about the Enemy, right? You saw a cherubim guarding the way back to Eden, but you'd just been terr—you'd just been with the Enemy, and you'd just spent some time talking to us about the Enemy and how you'd foiled his plans. Right?"

Asmodeus was still dragging me away. "Test it out," I yelled. "What do you have to lose?"

"Stop," He-Who-Rules said. "Bring me Sytri." While they went to fetch him, the Master said to me, but loud enough for everyone to hear, "We'll test your theory, Enoch. If you're right, you'll have earned your freedom from the punishment you deserve—let no one say I'm not fair and more than fair. But if you're wrong, no amount of punishment will suffice. Do you understand?"

Sytri arrived and I begged to explain things myself, which the Master allowed. "I can't stress enough," I said after telling him what

I'd told He-Who-Rules, "that we must think about the Enemy, or at least the High Country—no matter how unpleasant it might be. If we force our thoughts along those lines, we'll be able to see the Enemy's angels."

When Sytri left, He-Who-Rules turned to other business but Asmodeus didn't. His hand on my shoulder felt heavy, and seemed heavier with every moment that passed.

It will work, I told myself; *it makes sense. It will—*

A new fear interrupted the flow of positive thinking—what if Zephar was the first to hear of this? What if, discovering that I'd gone behind his back, he decided to come to Sheol himself, and tell the Master that he'd tried out my theory but that it didn't work? Of course, once my punishment was complete, he could always return and say that he'd decided to try it again and this time it had worked—and probably he'd be rewarded for his thoroughness.

What's keeping Sytri? I wondered, shrugging my shoulders a little. Asmodeus gripped me tighter.

What if Sytri didn't impress on his officers the importance of thinking hard about the Enemy, I thought, despite the pain? Or—worst fear of all—what if I were wrong? What if my idea just plain didn't work?

When Sytri finally appeared, he didn't even glance at me. He walked up to the throne and whispered in the Master's ear; I couldn't tell if he brought good news or bad.

He-Who-Rules nodded, then said, "Bring him here."

Sytri shifted away, then almost immediately returned—with Zephar.

Of course he'd go to Zephar; and probably he thought he was giving my theory the best possible chance to be proved right by going to the last person who'd seen the angels of light.

Before my fear forced me into a crazed act like trying to shift away even as Asmodeus held me down with his vice-like grip, the Master said, "You're sure it worked?"

Zephar looked over at me for a moment, then nodded. "I saw them. More than once—I wanted to make sure before coming to you. Most recently I saw them comforting the spirit of a child who had died of an illness, and leading her into the higher dimensions."

"So you were right," the Master said, but he spoke to Zephar. "The reason we couldn't see some spirits is that the enemy angels were hiding them from us." He was quiet for a moment, looking through everyone and everything in that way he has when his mind is integrating new knowledge and formulating a new plan. "You've done good work," he said after a while, and again he spoke to Zephar. "Jacob still lives?"

"For now," Zephar said.

"Return to him," the Master said.

Zephar looked at me one more time—it seemed he was trying to communicate something, but I found it hard to figure out exactly what that was, and whether he intended to attack me or beg my forgiveness the next time we met alone. He shifted away.

"Enoch, approach." Asmodeus pushed me forward. "Zephar has done the hard work of testing your theory, but I think you'll agree that now it's time for you to contribute something concrete, wouldn't you?"

"I—" I said, not knowing how to even begin to respond. "That isn't exactly—" I stopped, the fire in the Master's eyes goading me into making another mistake. "Yes," I said, "I would like that opportunity, Master."

"Good." He-Who-Rules smiled, his ugly smile of victory. "Find a way to liberate these spirits from the enemy angels. Do that and you will be forgiven for your past foolishness."

Again I stuttered in my response and again I forced myself to say what I knew he wanted to hear. "I'll do my best, Master."

He-Who-Rules nodded to Asmodeus, who finally let me go.

"In the meantime," the Master said, "you can build me a new throne."

"If I may, Master," I said, needing to win some victory, no matter how small, against him, "I'd like to be with Jacob when he dies—I think I can learn a lot from the experience, now that we've figured out how to see the Enemy's angels. Can I rebuild your throne after he dies?"

If the Master suspected what I was doing, he didn't show it. "Go," he said. "But send Abaddon back to me."

I shifted to Egypt and quickly found Zephar and Abaddon watching over Jacob and his family. I approached carefully, making sure Abaddon had received the latest news and wouldn't attack me; and when he didn't, I told him that I would stay with Zephar and he should return to the Master to receive his new orders. Abaddon showed the same restraint as Sytri, the same unquestioning willingness to follow an order or course of action without understanding it. He shifted away, I had no doubt to check with He-Who-Rules if these instructions came from him; and upon finding that they did, he didn't return.

"We're even, right?" Zephar said, watching me warily.

"Are we?"

"Sytri came to me first with your idea; I could've lied."

"You would've been found out."

"Eventually. Too late for it to do you any good. The point is, Enoch, you need all the friends you can get right now."

Zephar's words made me think of a phrase Joseph liked to say when negotiating and someone claimed they were only willing to give him a certain deal because of their friendship. "With a friend like you," Joseph would say, "all of my enemies can go on holiday."

"So you saw them?" I said. "The angels of the Enemy?"

Zephar nodded, shrugged. I sensed he was holding something back, and I thought I could guess what it was. Several months later, when I saw the angels of light leading away Jacob's spirit, I was sure of it.

"Did they see you?" the Master asked, after we reported in.

Zephar spoke first; I'd let him take the lead on everything so far, because I was sure that he'd missed two things that had happened before Jacob died, things I knew the Master would find interesting. "I don't think they did, no," he said.

The Master looked at me; that was the sequence so far, He-Who-Rules would ask a question, Zephar would jump to answer it, then the Master would turn to me for confirmation.

Did they see us? Zephar was right; I was pretty sure they hadn't. But I was more sure that they didn't care to see us. It was easy to forget about the Transformation most of the time, but impossible to put it out of your mind on a day when you'd seen one of the Enemy's angels. They were bright and beautiful and graceful; we were clumsy and deformed and dark, like a misshapen shadow.

"They didn't see us," I said.

"Anything else?" the Master said.

Zephar said what I hoped he would: "That's everything we need to bother you with, Master."

He-Who-Rules looked at me.

I glanced at Zephar. "Yes," I said, faking hesitancy. "Yes, I think there are two other items we should bother you with, actually."

Before we'd shifted to Sheol, Zephar wanted to get our story straight. "Jacob died," I had said, "and really bright angels carried him off. What's to get straight?"

Zephar stared at me for only a moment, with a mix of incredulity and understanding in his glow, then turned his attention back to the Master. I kept staring at Zephar, as if begging him to explain to me why he wasn't giving a full report to the Master.

On his throne, He-Who-Rules hissed impatiently.

"I'm sorry, Master," I said quickly. "It's probably nothing"—I glanced back at Zephar, then quickly away—"still, I think you should know." I paused, pretended to steel myself to go on. "As he lay in bed dying, Jacob blessed Joseph's sons, Manasseh and Ephraim. Now normally he would bless the elder with his right hand and the younger with his left; in fact, Joseph made this easy for him by placing the children in the correct position. But this half-blind old man in his half-dead body went to the trouble of crossing his arms—and did so with so much solemnity that you would've thought he was offering a sacrifice and not putting one arm over the other—and blessed the younger over the elder."

The angry red glow from Zephar faded away as I talked, which is what I'd expected and why I'd decided to report the blessing first.

"Is that true?" the Master said, turning to Zephar.

Zephar looked like he wanted to say that sure it was true, but so what? He didn't; *perhaps he's learned from poor Arakiel*, I thought, disappointed. "Yes, it's true," he said, looking around without meaning to, as if he expected Asmodeus and Mulciber to descend on him. "I understand how busy you are, and I wanted to gather more information before coming to you with this."

The glow of annoyance from He-Who-Rules was subtle but unmistakable.

I said, "This isn't the first time we've seen this sort of thing—"

"— from the Circumcised Ones," the Master said. "That's what I was thinking."

"Jacob himself was blessed over Esau," I said. "And before him, Ishmael was set aside so that Isaac could receive the inheritance."

The Master stood, descended the steps, approached me. "You don't think we need to worry about the firstborn, is that what you're saying?" he whispered.

"That's not what I'm saying," I whispered back. "Abraham was first-born and he was as dangerous as any fallen before or since."

"So what are you saying?"

"There's a message here," I said. "I don't understand it yet, but the firstborn is so important to these favored ones of the Enemy, and this type of thing has happened too many times for it not to be significant somehow."

The Master returned to his throne. "Figure out the significance, Enoch—quickly."

"There's one more thing," I said. "Perhaps the most important thing of all. Jacob also blessed his own children, and he spoke prophecies to each, telling them what would happen in the last days."

"The last days of what?" the Master said.

"Their new nation, the world—who knows? But this is what I wanted to tell you: Jacob promised Judah that from his children would come the rulers of this new nation Israel. He said that the scepter wouldn't pass from Judah's children until the Peacemaker comes, under whom all nations would be gathered."

"And you're saying that it's this Peacemaker that..."

"... that we need to watch," I finished. "Yes, that's what I'm saying. He will be a child of Judah's, I'm sure of it."

"All because a fallen said so?" Zephar said, his sulkiness overwhelming his good sense.

"A fallen who wrestled with the Enemy and received His blessing," I said. "Or did you forget?" I turned back to the Master. "There's something else he said to Judah, something I don't understand but that seemed important to Jacob. He said that Judah, or one of his children, would bow down, and sleep, and be woken up... but he said it as a question. 'Who shall wake him up?'—as if the who in that question was very important."

"Stay with Judah," He-Who-Rules said, but he spoke to Zephar. "If anything happens, report it to Enoch immediately; Enoch will also send someone to receive regular updates."

Zephar looked like he was about to explode, but he took a moment to calm himself, then shifted away without even a glance at me.

"You don't want me watching Judah myself?" I said, when he was gone.

"I need you working on other things."

"A new throne, to begin with," I said.

"Yes. And a way to steal spirits from the Enemy before they reach the High Country—if that's where they're being taken."

Over the next weeks and months, I built the Master a large new throne, even more intricately ornamented than his last, and with thick, strong arms so he could squeeze and pound on them all he wanted. I inspected everything I'd already built and mended and rebuilt as required. I received Zephar's reports from Earth. But throughout I was always thinking about the challenge the Master had set for me.

Chapter Seven

A Prince

AT a certain point it occurred to me that Zephar's reports from Earth had grown increasingly brief, and I became convinced that he wasn't spending very much time in Egypt at all, or at least not with the children of Israel. But if he missed something important, I knew the Master's punishment would fall equally on both of us.

I shifted to Earth, then searched for days before finding him, in an Egyptian's house. The Egyptian was working a potter's wheel; Zephar knelt in front of him, staring into his eyes with as much focus and intensity as if he were trying to read his mind.

"What are you doing?" I said.

Zephar was so startled that he shifted away. He returned immediately, but didn't look sheepish or embarrassed enough. "I'm practicing."

"Practicing what?"

"Possession," he said, looking back at the fallen sullenly, either because he resented the intrusion or the interruption. "Like the Master did."

"Are you insane?" I said, moving between him and the man. "The Master possessed a serpent, not a fallen."

"If it can be done with one, I believe it can be done with the other."

"It doesn't matter what you believe," I said. "You're supposed to be watching the children of Israel."

"There's no need; they've forgotten all about the Enemy. A life of luxury will do that. This work is more important."

The potter spun his wheel, smoothing out a jar-like object that might be used for baking bread or carrying water or even as a toy for a child. The concentrated look on his face held me transfixed. The purpose of the vase didn't matter to him, I knew; what mattered was that he was making it. *The Creator put so much of Himself in you,* I thought, *that you can't help but create, can you? You get so much joy out of the act. And what about me? I used to make and remake things all the time; now I do it out of necessity and to order, and don't enjoy anything about it at all. Is that because I've drifted far from the Enemy? Wasn't your whole race kicked out of the Enemy's presence; aren't you far from Him too?*

Slowly I became aware of Zephar's annoyed and impatient glow.

"You don't get to make those types of decisions," I said. "You've received orders from the Master. Get back to the children of Israel and leave this fool to his clay."

Before he could argue—or, worse, refuse to follow my orders and force me into acting against him before I was ready—I shifted back to Sheol. It didn't strike me as funny that when the Master told Zephar he had to report in to me, I couldn't have been happier, mostly because I knew it had the opposite effect on Zephar. But now I didn't want anything to do with him, and certainly didn't want to be responsible for him or his actions. I wanted to put him out of my mind, abandon him to his attempts to possess a fallen and let him deal with the consequences of disobeying the Master's orders on his own.

I hoped to see improvement, but his next report had nothing to say about the children of Israel and a lot to say about the Pharaoh of Egypt.

"Thank you, Arakiel," I said, although I didn't appreciate the eagerness with which he'd given me Zephar's report.

Arakiel didn't leave. "You're not angry? Didn't you tell him that he was supposed to leave the Egyptians alone? Now he's spending all of his time with their king, and leaving the Circumcised Ones to themselves!"

"That's between Zephar and me, isn't it?"

"But I can relay the message for you. I can talk to Sytri about taking away some of his points."

Although we spoke in a large room I'd built for myself on top of the highest castle floor—ostensibly to have a place to speak far from the wailing of the fallen (which I hardly noticed anymore, and only when I'd been away from Sheol for a while), but really so I could have those conversations without fear of being overheard—I stopped myself from telling Arakiel that when I decided to strike against Zephar, it wouldn't be with something so useless as taking away his points. *Just because a conversation can't be overheard*, I told myself, *doesn't mean it can't be repeated.*

"Give Zephar another couple of months," I said, "then ask him for an update." Before Arakiel left the room, I added as if it were an afterthought, "Oh—next time you see Belial, tell him I'd like to speak with him."

Arakiel took his time seeing Belial, or Belial took his coming to see me. Either way, I waited so long that I began to run out of patience, and considered shifting to Earth and trying to track him down myself, when Belial finally knocked on the doors to my room. "So this is where you're hiding," he said, looking around.

I closed the doors behind him. "I need your help, Belial. I need you to go to Egypt."

"And do what?"

"Find out what Zephar is up to. The Master asked him to keep an eye on the children of Israel. He isn't doing that."

Belial walked over to a shelf and picked up a small stone on which I'd scratched different things I didn't want to forget—Abraham's mantra, the words Jacob had said to Judah, other things I'd heard and thought about. "You're writing now? Like the fallen?"

Plucking the pebble away from him, I said, "What's your answer, Belial?"

"Why don't you report him to the Master?"

"Because that's what he wants me to do. He's up to something and I'd like you to find out what it is so I can figure out what to do about it."

"What's in it for me?"

"You'll be rewarded," I said, but Belial didn't look impressed. "Also—I have an idea. It's worth trying."

Belial nodded for me to go on.

"The Master possessed a serpent, right? I believe we can possess a fallen, live inside them like we're inside this room right now, maybe even control their bodies. The first angel to successfully do that will rise to the top of the ranks, don't you think?"

Belial's attitude changed instantly, and when he left, my only concern was that he'd be so eager to practice possessing a fallen that he'd forget about the task I'd given him. But he returned almost immediately.

"There was no need to worry," he said. "Zephar's doing what you want."

"How so?"

"He's been working on the pharaohs. First he made them suspicious of the children of Israel, who were becoming more numerous than the Egyptians themselves, and were better warriors. Zephar made Pharaoh turn them into slaves to break their spirit; and when that didn't work, he actually made him issue an order. Are you ready for this? He told their midwives that if a Hebrew woman gives birth to a male child, they should kill it. Isn't that clever? What is there to fear of a child of Judah if he'll never grow to be a man?"

"I know," I lied. "I gave him the idea; I just needed to be sure he was carrying it out."

After Belial left, I burned in anger at Zephar's plan. *He wants me to go to the Master and report that he's disobeying orders, so I'd look foolish when the truth was revealed.*

The next report, I thought, was meant to confuse me. Arakiel spoke of a baby who was found floating in a tiny ark by the daughter of Pharaoh, and taken up to be raised as her son.

"Why are you wasting my time with this?" I said, cutting him off.

"Zephar said this was important. The baby is the child of a Hebrew woman; she is now his nurse—hired to raise her own child, if you'll believe that."

"And?"

"He escaped the death sentence; I guess Zephar thinks that makes him worthy of attention. When the midwives refused to carry out his orders, Pharaoh turned to his people, instructing them to kill any male Hebrew babies on sight. The Egyptians were supposed to drown Hebrew babies in the river, but this baby was drawn out of the river, and not by any Egyptian but by Pharaoh's daughter herself."

"Is he from the tribe of Judah?"

Arakiel glowed an annoying color full of presumption and contempt. "Zephar said you'd ask that. No, he's from the tribe of Levi. His mother teaches him about his heritage in secret. Zephar said you wouldn't recognize the danger, but he asks you to trust him."

Unsure if Arakiel was treating me with contempt to goad me into action against Zephar, or because he saw it as weakness that I hadn't acted already, I told him to leave, and to not bother me again until Zephar had something worthwhile to report.

When Arakiel returned, almost four decades had passed on Earth.

"Zephar has left Egypt," he said, his glow of contempt stronger than ever.

"Oh?" I said, trying not to reveal my own feelings. "And why is that?"

"The child Zephar told you about? He fled from Egypt and Zephar followed him."

Not wanting to play into Arakiel's game, I struggled to remain calm. "Zephar would have told you more than that; start at the beginning."

"What more do you need to hear? Zephar has disobeyed your—" He stopped, seeing my own glow intensifying. "The child we warned you about? Moses lived in splendor in Pharaoh's house, enjoying his riches and living the life of a prince. 'Like your man Joseph,' Zephar told me to tell you, 'Moses learned the ways of the Egyptians. But like Joseph, Moses' heart was with his people.' He saw that the children of Israel were tormented by their Egyptian masters, and when he witnessed an Egyptian beating a Hebrew, he killed him. Zephar believes that Moses expected the children of Israel to declare him their savior, the one Hebrew brave enough to strike against their oppressors and who could lead them to freedom. They did no such thing—just the opposite, in fact: they spread news of the killing, all the way to Pharaoh, who ordered that Moses be arrested and executed. Moses immediately fled east. Zephar returned to Egypt only to report in, and to tell me that next time I could find him with Moses in Arabia."

As Arakiel spoke, I formulated a plan; and now that I had one, I found it easy to remain calm. "Well, don't," I said. "I've had enough of Zephar's reports."

"So that's it? He disobeys your every order, and you punish him by no longer requiring him to report to you? And what about Moses? Zephar thinks he's important, as important as Joseph or Abraham, even."

"Moses is a Levite; he isn't the one we're searching for. As for Zephar, his reports just waste my time—like you're doing now."

The nice thing about having a large floor to myself, where almost no one came to bother me (especially now that Arakiel stopped reporting in on Zephar's actions) was that I could come and go as I pleased, and not be missed.

As soon as Arakiel was gone, I shifted away myself. I arrived in Egypt and traveled east, searching carefully.

Even if Zephar hadn't been watching over the man who was watching over a flock of sheep, I think I would've recognized Moses anyway. This prince of Egypt carried Egypt with him, as if the sand around him was gold in his coffers and the sky above his own uncut diamond. He stood on a small hill surveying the sheep as if he stood on top of the tallest pyramid in Egypt, looking over the world itself. Joseph learned to wield the power of a pharaoh, but he wore it like one might wear a garment, even if it was a comfortable garment. For Moses, power poured out of him like exhaled breath and he seemed completely unconscious of it, as unaware of the power emanating from him as he was of the hair growing on his head. In that first glimpse of the man, I understood how Zephar had fallen so completely under his spell.

That night, Zephar startled me by shifting away and—afraid that he was going to the throne room behind my back, or even that he'd go looking for me in Sheol to report in directly—I followed his shift without thinking. I ended up in Egypt, with Zephar staring at me a little incredulously.

"You're spying on me?" he said.

The moonlit street was dark and nearly empty; a single figure, in the distance and walking toward us, was the only sign of life. "I need to know what's going on."

"Something big," Zephar said. "The children of Israel have turned back to the Enemy. They've smashed their idols and rejected the ways of the Egyptians; they don't worship the angels and the gods of their imagination anymore."

"You said they were done with the Enemy, Zephar."

"No—I said they were done with Him while things were good. But they remembered Him quickly when life became unbearable. When they encountered hatred and oppression everywhere they turned, they realized they had no one left but Him."

As if on cue, the figure approached; an Israelite; an old man, crippled and hunched over and hobbling along under the moonlight. As he passed through us, I heard what he was whispering—a prayer of deliverance to the Enemy.

"This one I've seen before," Zephar went on. "He walks the street and prays. He does it at night because during the day the Egyptians spit and beat on the Israelites if they talk about the Enemy, especially about the Enemy delivering them from their suffering—there's some nice irony to that, isn't there? The other children of Israel are the same; they can hardly be touched; their thoughts are always on the Enemy, begging Him to end their torment."

Zephar's words had their intended effect on me; but I resisted the urge that suddenly swept through me, to hand over the reins, to ask him what to do next. "Nothing says He will," I said, although I didn't believe it.

"Nothing except He Himself," Zephar said. "His words to Jacob are passed down to this day, as is Joseph's prophecy that the Enemy would bring them out of Egypt. That promise sustains them; otherwise they might have given up hope a long time ago."

We torment them too, I thought; *and we don't limit ourselves to the children of Israel—we torment all the sons of Adam and daughters of Eve.* If Moses was the One who would bring them freedom and peace, would he free them from just their fellow fallen oppressors or did the Enemy plan for him to attack us as well? "The seed of the woman will crush your head" was the first promise of deliverance He'd made to the fallen, wasn't it?

The thoughts ran around my head like angry, growling dogs. "Stay here," I said to Zephar, hardly able to think clearly. "I'll return to Moses. Come see me if anything happens. Understood?"

Without waiting for Zephar to answer, I shifted back to the dessert, telling myself that Moses, a Levite, couldn't be the Peacemaker Jacob had spoken of. But of course I couldn't know for certain that Moses was a son of Levi; and even if he was, I couldn't be sure that Jacob's words were accurate.

For years I studied Moses, watching him more closely than I'd watched Joseph, but never revealing myself to him for fear that he would be the One who would wage war against the Master and crush his head, and all of us with him.

His life wasn't special in any way; in fact, he seemed to have left any semblance of specialness behind him in Egypt and was now living as mundane an existence as one could imagine. He spent his time tending to sheep that weren't even his but his father-in-law's; he raised his children with his wife; he worshiped the Enemy.

After a while, the edge wore off my vigilance as Moses grew old but still didn't show any signs of interest in delivering the children of Israel from the Egyptians or from anyone else. Zephar's reports, which had filled me with so much fear when I first heard them, were now annoyingly repetitive. The Hebrews were still oppressed and still begging the Enemy to save them.

That's the problem with the Enemy, though; He's like a robber on the road, who jumps out from behind a tree just when you've lowered your guard. The Enemy did jump out to call Moses to action, and I would've missed it if not for Zephar—and in some ways, I wish I had missed it.

Perhaps in part because it wasn't comfortable to think of the angels of light, and painful to think of the Enemy, I had spent less and less time on the task He-Who-Rules had assigned to me. Mostly I ignored the spirits of the fallen dead; I knew soon they'd be taken away by the angels, to one place or the other, and I didn't like dealing with their fear or confusion. But one of the spirits wouldn't leave me alone, and through him I started to see the solution to the Master's challenge.

The spirit came rushing at me; he seemed unlike the others, who were often bewildered to find themselves without a body. He also projected a skeletal image of himself, stripped of his clothes and flesh, something I'd never seen before.

"Please," he said, in a whiny voice that made me recoil, "do you have any food?"

I tried to move away. "You're dead," I said. "You don't need food."

"Please," he said again, as if he hadn't heard me. "I'm starving. Can't you help? I'm so hungry. Please. Please."

"Look around you, fool. Eat whatever you want. Eat this dirt for all I care."

He nodded like a mad and happy dog, dropped to his knees and tried to shovel sand into his mouth but couldn't pick it up. "No, no, no," he mumbled, tears forming in his eye sockets. "Why is this happening to me? I'm so... I need... this is not fair. I'm so hungry. Doesn't anyone care? This is so unbearable... why can't I just... please, give me something to eat. Please!"

Annoyed, I tried again to walk away but he followed. Finally I said, "All right, come here, I'll give you all the food you can handle." He nodded his skeletal head again, and I grabbed hold and brought him to Sheol, dropping him in the lake of fire for someone else to fish out. What struck me as incredible, though, and what started me down the right path, was that even as I held him above the burning lake, he said to me, "Soon, right? You'll give me something to eat soon?"

Instead of shifting back to Earth, I walked around the cells I'd built for the fallen and listened carefully to their wailing. What had become for me a single mass of tormented screaming resolved into its individual components. Before, I'd only interacted with the normal-looking fallen, the ones who were aware of their situation and could be forced to labor. I'd always avoided, first, the spirits who seemed terrified of the very sight of us and were reduced to loud screaming spells whenever I or any other dark angel approached, and second, those fallen who babbled meaningless words about their life on Earth. Now I sought out the latter.

"What's wrong with you?" I said to one of them, who looked as skeletal as my drowning friend in the lake.

"Food," he said, in a voice strangely weak and hoarse, since his wailing from moments before was strong and loud enough. "Do you have any food? I want some—I can pay you."

Amused, I said, "Pay me? With what?"

"Gold!" the fallen screamed, his bony fingers grasping the bars of his cell. "I'm a rich man, can't you see that? I can give you more gold than you ever dreamed of…just give me a little something to eat! Something sweet!"

The other crazy spirits were just as amusing, and I began to catalog them in my mind. There were the starving skeletons, of course, begging for food; then the ones who begged for wine or a smoke, or other things I'd never even heard of; then the ones who begged for sex, who were the funniest of all because they often screamed at me in voices they thought were a discreet whisper.

After a while I ignored these spirits who thought they were still made of flesh, and who were tormented by the fact that they couldn't do the things they could when they did have bodies. Among the spirits who realized they were now living a different life, I found one who didn't scream or wail but sat quietly at the back of her cell. The image she projected was of an old woman, wispy-haired and wrinkled and hunch-backed.

"Is there anything I can do for you?" I said.

Even among the spirits I considered normal, most still begged to be set free from their cells, and the smarter ones asked to be set free of Sheol too. But this fallen just shook her head.

"What's wrong with you?" I said. "Don't you know where you are?"

"I'm where I'm supposed to be," she said.

"What does that mean?"

"I know I didn't live a good life," she said, moving toward the front of the cell in hobbles, as if she actually were made of deteriorating flesh and bone. "Toward the end of my life—and I died young, or maybe things would have been different for me—I started to realize... but by then it was too late... or I thought it was too late. You get used to a certain lifestyle... and you've surrounded yourself with certain people... it's like a maze, walking into it is easy but it's hard to find your way out again."

"Can't you find your way out now?" I said, and thought that I was toying with her.

"I don't think so. I pray that the One True God will set me free and allow me to serve Him in Paradise but—"

"You pray to Him?" I yelled, and in that moment my voice rang out louder than any of the wailing around me. "He allowed you to be captured! This is all His fault!"

"I knew what I was doing," she said, still speaking softly. "I made my choices. I thought I was living a good life when I gave myself everything I wanted. I ignored my conscience. In my heart, I always knew that I was doing wrong—that there would be consequences."

"You didn't know what you were doing!" I said, still yelling. "You didn't know He'd cast you from His sight to... to this place. You were tricked—other people tricked you into doing those things!"

"No one made me do anything," she said. "I could've stopped listening to them at any time, but I didn't want to. I wanted to hear how beautiful I was; I wanted their gifts; I wanted to be surrounded by pretty things. In my heart I stoked the fire of lust so that it burned higher and brighter. The more possessions I acquired, the more I desired, until I couldn't even count the things I had but refused to share any of it with anyone else. The more compliments I received, the more I wanted. If I heard ten nice things about me one day, I needed to hear eleven the next. Nothing made me happier than when men fought over me, and I did what I could to make them jealous. Such was my life, until I got what I wanted, and one day a man murdered me out of jealousy. What greater acknowledgment of my power to ignite passion could I have wanted than that?"

"You believe you deserve to be here, don't you?" I said, and a second piece of the answer fell into place. "And yet you repented—you were on the path to repentance when you died. Why didn't He send His angels for you?"

"Maybe He did," she said, "and maybe I couldn't see them. They might have stood inches in front of me, begging me to follow, but my eyes were blind to them and my ears deaf to their voices. Like I said, I made my choices in life, and my choices took me away from the light of the One True God. I spent my life learning to ignore His voice—speaking through my conscience, through my mother and my uncle, even through the poor who begged me for a piece of bread as I walked down the streets so everyone could see the fine clothes and jewelry I wore. Don't you understand? When I died, you didn't find me—I found you. My spirit moved toward yours, like a woman in the marketplace will find other women to talk to and a man other men, and children will play together."

"It wasn't my spirit you found," I said.

"You are all one spirit."

"And you're different, are you? Then why doesn't He send His angels down here to save you?"

"Maybe He will," she said, "maybe He won't. In the meantime, I pray." She returned to the back of her cell, as if she had the power to decide that the conversation was finished. Resisting the urge to order the nearest dark angel to torture her, I shifted back to Earth before my resolve wore out. In the first place, I felt that she'd helped me take the final steps along the path on which my drowning friend had started me. In the second, I didn't feel she deserved to be in Sheol—even if the Enemy did.

You call yourself merciful, I thought, hoping He could hear me. *But I've got more mercy in my heart than You. If it were in my power to do so, I'd set her free from that place—it is in Your power, and You do nothing. Just like You do nothing for these children of Israel—You brought them into that land, and did You do it so they could toil for the glory of the Egyptians and receive beatings for wages? They cry out to You day and night, but You continue to do nothing.*

My primary purpose in going back to Earth was to test out my new theory on some fallen before I took it to the Master. But in my rush to leave Sheol before doing something I might regret, I shifted to Egypt without realizing it. Zephar found me immediately, before I could shift somewhere else.

"Did you want to see me?" he said.

"Yes," I lied. "How are things going?"

"I said I would let you know right away if anything new happened here. How about Moses?"

"Same as always," I said, although in truth I didn't know.

"Should we switch?" he said, and it was only his eagerness that made me refuse immediately. Otherwise I would have welcomed the opportunity to have lots of fallen around who might die and on whom I could test out my theory—and to have Zephar's spying ears away from me at the same time. I suppose there's no sense wondering how different things might be—how much suffering I might have saved myself—if I had let Zephar go after Moses and I'd stayed with the Egyptians.

It took me a while to find Moses, who was watching over his father-in-law's sheep near the mountains at the back of the desert. He walked up the mountain called Horeb, and as I followed him I suddenly saw the Begotten and screamed in pain. Wanting desperately to flee, I forced myself to stay, to think of the High Country, to remember how I felt about the Enemy when I lived in His presence. After a while, the blinding white light faded away to reveal the mountain and a burning bush, and the pain subsided enough that I could stand to be there.

Moses approached the bush, staring at it with eyebrows drawn together. Later when I heard him talk about the experience, he said that he was amazed to see a bush burning but not burning away; on fire, but not consumed by the fire.

He came to a sudden stop, and I realized that the Enemy had spoken to him. He removed his sandals, and even then I knew the Begotten had told him he walked on holy ground and to not let a dead thing come between him and the living God.

"Allow me to hear Your voice, Oh Lord." He-Who-Rules knows I spoke these words—and like I said before, even if he didn't, what more could he do to me than he's already planning? He knows I spoke the words, but he thinks I was faking a desire I didn't feel, so that I could gather intelligence for him. The truth is the opposite; in that moment, all thoughts of the Master faded away completely. I'd forced myself to remember the High Country, and pushed past the initial pain; and now His presence didn't cause me discomfort. I wanted to hear His voice not for anything I might learn, but because I desired to hear His voice.

The Master also doesn't know what I said next. "I don't deserve to, Lord, but allow me for a while to stand in Your presence and truly remember the High Country."

"I am the God of Abraham, the God of Isaac, and the God of Jacob."

Moses stood with eyes cast down to the ground, too scared to look at the bush that burned but wasn't destroyed.

"I have seen the afflictions of My people at the hands of the Egyptians," the Enemy said. "I have heard their cries of suffering; I know their sorrow. This is why I have come down, Moses, to bring them up, out of Egypt and into a land flowing with milk and honey."

As the Lord spoke, a voice I tried to keep at a distance screamed that I wasn't in the High Country and it was pathetic and foolish to pretend that I was.

You've tricked Him into letting you hear His voice, I screamed at myself; *but what does that change? Will He let you back into His presence? He speaks to a fallen as if to a loved child. He speaks of pain and sorrow, but what about your pain and sorrow? He ignores you, and in His mercy grants you your pathetic wish to hear His voice so you can be reminded of your loss.*

The screaming got louder and the pain returned, then intensified. The bush was burning too brightly, the Enemy's voice too loud, too heavy, His words crashing into me like big waves trying to capsize a small ship.

Even as I told myself to get away before the pain overwhelmed me, the Enemy started speaking again and I realized that Moses must've asked His name.

The Enemy said, "I AM—"

"No, wait!" I yelled, and even though I was already in midshift I knew I was too late.

"—THAT I AM."

Chapter Eight

A Savior

IAM THAT I AM THAT—

"Enoch—"

I AM THAT I AM. The God of Abraham, the God of Isaac, the God of Jacob. The Self-Existent. The Unbegotten, the Begotten, the Proceeding. I AM THAT—

"Enough! Enoch, I—"

"Leave me alone! You're too painful, don't You see that? Stay away!"

"Enoch, enough of this."

Even as I screamed and begged for the voice to be silent, it dawned on me that I wasn't speaking to the Enemy. "Where am I?" I said.

"In the palace," the Master said. "In this room you built for yourself."

"I can't see anything. Why?"

"I don't know. Something has happened to you."

In the darkness, I thought I saw a shadow pass in front of me. "What was that?"

"Enoch, what did the Enemy do to you? Did you discover something?"

I AM—

"Don't start that again!" the Master yelled, knocking me to the ground.

As I lifted myself up, the darkness cleared and I saw He-Who-Rules towering over me, glowing fiery red, ready to strike me again if my next words were along the same lines.

"I'm sorry," I said, standing up slowly. "I didn't realize I was saying that."

"That's all you've been saying; no one else will come up here anymore."

"How long—" I stopped, embarrassed.

"Well? Were you about to ask how many times we came up here to see if you were making sense yet?"

"Yes."

"Too many, Enoch. Most would have abandoned you, maybe even thrown you in the lake to stop your constant mumbling of the Enemy's name. I've been patient, now I want you to—"

The door to my room was left open and Arakiel burst through the entrance. "Master!" he yelled, and went on without waiting, "Moses has struck again!"

He-Who-Rules spun around, and for the first time he didn't seem bothered by an interruption. "How? What's he done?"

"He's sent locusts everywhere into the land," Arakiel said, then looked at me for the first time. He kept his eyes on me but continued, "They're as abundant as the frogs and the insects were, and they're eating everything that wasn't destroyed by the hail."

The Master nodded, a thoughtful and frustrated expression on his face; here was a problem he couldn't yet see the solution to, I understood. "Go back to Zephar," he said. "Return immediately if these locusts convince Pharaoh to let the Circumcised Ones go out to the desert—or if they don't and Moses attacks again."

Arakiel glanced at me one more time before shifting away. The look was similar to one I'd seen on the fallen: half-horrified, half-curious.

"Moses is attacking Egypt?" I said.

The Master's angry red glow intensified and his wings spread out unconsciously. "It's the Enemy, working through him. He's already turned their river into blood so that the fish died and the Egyptians could hardly find any water to drink. He's sent them infestations of frogs, of lice, of insects. He's struck down their livestock. We don't know when his next attack will come, or what shape it will take. We don't know what to do to stop him."

"The Enemy told Moses he would free the children of Israel from Egypt," I said. I didn't voice my next thought, which was that if the Enemy had said this would happen, what chance did we have to stop it?

The Master approached, his eyes piercing into me as if he were searching out a secret I was trying to keep from him. "What else did He say? What happened to you?"

"Nothing," I said, taking a step back without meaning to. "He spoke His name, that's all. I guess it had a bad effect on me."

"Just His name?"

I thought I knew what he was getting at—why would the mere utterance affect me so greatly? "I had begged the Enemy to let me hear His voice, so I could spy on their conversation. I guess that put me in a vulnerable state—but before I could learn very much, Moses asked Him His name. I tried to shift away but—"

"Does Moses know the Enemy is triune?" the Master said, and finally I realized what he was so worried about.

"No," I said, although I didn't know for sure.

"'I am the God of Abraham, the God of Isaac, and the God of Jacob,'" the Master said, speaking each word as if he could taste its bitterness. "That's what you kept mumbling. If the Enemy is introducing Himself like that, either He's already revealed Himself as triune or He plans to soon."

"I don't know," I said, taking another step back from the Master, who was burning uncomfortably hot. "I'll go to Earth and find out."

"Go," he said. "Meet up with Zephar first. He's with Pharaoh and can fill you in on what's been happening. Abaddon is keeping watch on Moses."

In Egypt, I went straight to the palace and found Zephar hovering behind Pharaoh's throne like a fallen who paces the length of a room to wear out his anxiety. A man I presumed was Pharaoh sat on the throne itself, his head in his hands, his face scarred with various shades of red as if he'd tried to scratch off his own skin.

"Enoch!" Zephar said, catching sight of me. "Are you—?"

"I'm fine. What's happening?"

"Moses and his wooden staff is what's happening," he said. "Tell me, is it possible this man will defeat all of Egypt with a piece of wood?"

Pharaoh looked up, his forehead wrinkled with lines of worry and fear.

"Can you tell me what happened?" I said. "From the beginning?"

Zephar stopped pacing. "You didn't warn me that Moses was coming back to Egypt," he said, then paused. "But of course I learned soon enough that you weren't in any shape to be giving out warnings. He appeared here with Aaron—"

"Aaron?"

"His older brother. He speaks for him."

I couldn't help but smile. "Moses never liked to speak in public," I said, but later it occurred to me that once again the firstborn stepped aside and the glory went to the younger.

"Anyway," Zephar said, "they asked Pharaoh to let them go out to the wilderness for three days, so they could worship the Enemy."

"Moses asked for only three days? His goal is to set the children of Israel free for good."

"If that's true," Zephar said, "then he's lying. Or he's testing Pharaoh, or trying to soften him up by starting with a small request." He regained control over his annoyed glow. "Now do you want me to tell you the story, or will you keep interrupting?"

I nodded for him to go on.

O F course we refused their request without thought (Zephar said). These may be the same halls Moses ran through as a child, but that doesn't give him the right to come in here like he owns Egypt itself and make demands of the true king.

In fact, Pharaoh was so insulted by the request that he ordered the taskmasters to make the situation even worse for the Circumcised Ones. I sent word to the Master and he sent me Abaddon and others. Initially, things seemed to have gone well; Moses returned to the mountain and though Abaddon only heard his side of the conversation, it was clear he was giving up on his mission. In fact, Moses was so depressed and so despondent that Abaddon decided to return to Sheol.

Although I didn't doubt the report, I wasn't convinced we'd seen the last of Moses. I asked the angels in Egypt to meet me in the palace. But even as I spoke to them, and told them to keep watch for Moses or Aaron, the brothers walked into the room and repeated their request.

More amused than angry now, Pharaoh nodded as if he were seriously considering it, then—before I knew what he was doing—asked for a sign from their God.

"No!" I screamed in his ear, but couldn't help but notice that Aaron stepped forward immediately, as if he'd been waiting for such a demand. "Stop this," I said. "Who is their God that you should want a sign from Him?"

Aaron threw down his staff; as it hit the ground, the staff bent and hissed, and began to move around. Pharaoh and his servants fell back, scattering before the snake.

"Calm down," I said to Pharaoh. "Call your sorcerers. This is merely a trick, and they can do the same."

Pharaoh issued the order while everyone watched Aaron's serpent slither on the palace floor in a circle. When the sorcerers appeared, I ordered the angels to help them complete the spell. The sorcerers threw down their own rods, which turned into snakes as well.

"Good," I said. "Now destroy this serpent of the Enemy." Our snakes turned on it as one, but Aaron's snake devoured them all.

This worried me of course; I feared that Pharaoh would see it as a sign that the Enemy was mightier than all of us. But Pharaoh didn't care; he was pleased that his sorcerers were able to pull off the same trick as Aaron.

That became our pattern for the next signs Moses displayed of the Enemy's power, except that I'd learned from the experience with Aaron's snake. I made sure that the angels discouraged the sorcerers from attempting to reverse whatever Moses and Aaron did, and kept them and Pharaoh satisfied with simply replicating it. When Aaron took his staff and struck the river and the water turned to blood, our sorcerers did the same. When Aaron turned drops of river-water into frogs, we did the same and soon there were more leaping animals in Egypt than there were fallen. Frogs filled their streets and their homes; Egyptians were finding them in their beds and in their water jugs and cooking pots, and there was nowhere they could turn or look and not see frogs. Pharaoh was going crazy with "the croaking and the croaking," by which he meant the sound of the frogs and the complaining of his people. He ordered the sorcerers to take the frogs away, and though we had control over the ones we'd called up, we could do nothing to those belonging to Moses.

When he couldn't stand it anymore, Pharaoh told the brothers he would let the children of Israel go if Moses asked the Enemy to take away the frogs. The next day the animals started to die, and the Egyptians, hardly able to breathe from the stench, gathered their carcasses into heaps.

Pharaoh didn't let the Hebrews go, of course. Although he'd come to realize that the Enemy was real, Pharaoh saw Him as simply one more god, to be tricked or cajoled or pacified until he or she or it went away. Nevertheless, the Master was worried—he saw what the rest of us missed. The Enemy was showing Pharaoh that He wasn't only mightier than the other gods—the river-gods, and the gods with frog-shaped heads, soon the protector gods of cattle and crops—not only more mighty, but that next to Him these other gods were either powerless or imaginary.

What Aaron did with drops of water, he next did with dust throughout the land, turning it into lice. Even when the brothers sent hoards of flies throughout the land—but not into Goshen where the Hebrews lived, of course—Pharaoh relented only long enough for Moses to pray to the Enemy to take away the insects.

You have to admire a man who can withstand that kind of pressure, don't you? While our fellow angels feasted on the devastation and suffering throughout Egypt, Pharaoh deafened his ears to the cries of his people and the counsel of his advisers, and listened only to my voice.

With each new plague, Pharaoh's resolve grew stronger, because he realized that to give in to Moses' demands would make him look foolish. "You've resisted him too long to acquiesce now," I said. "If you give him what he wants, your people will ask themselves why you didn't let the children of Israel go from the first, and save them all manner of pain and loss." Again and again Pharaoh begged Moses to make the devastation stop; again and again Moses did as Pharaoh asked; again and again the king went back on his word.

"Will you still not humble yourself before the Lord?" Moses asked one day, warning Pharaoh that locusts would fill the land and eat the herbs of the field and the fruits of trees that hadn't been destroyed by the lightning and hail.

"THat can't be it," I said, looking around to double-check. "There aren't any locusts at all."

Zephar looked down at Pharaoh. "He promised to release their people if Moses and Aaron made the creatures go away."

"And will he?"

"Of course not," Zephar said. "Haven't you been listening? It just goes on like this."

"The Enemy has a plan," I said. "This ends somewhere."

Zephar looked at me quietly for a long time. "You think His plan includes an attack on us, is that it?"

"Don't you? Didn't you say the Enemy was showing the Egyptians how powerful and real He is compared to the dark angels and imaginary gods they worship?"

We never got to finish our conversation, as suddenly the flames in the room extinguished. From throughout the palace and outside came startled cries and terrified yells—a fog had descended on Egypt, a darkness that hid the sun and choked off fire.

Immediately I told Zephar to shift to Goshen. He was back in a moment. "The candles of the children of Israel are lit," he said, "but there is no light anywhere else in the land. This is the work of Moses."

"We have to put an end to this game," I said to Zephar. "Tell Pharaoh to cut Moses off; tell him not to grant the brothers any more audiences."

The darkness lasted for three days, after which Pharaoh told Moses that he would never relent and threatened to have Moses executed if he ever came back to the palace. Like Zephar, I was impressed by Pharaoh's resolve and courage; it was obvious the man was terrified of Moses and his God; everyone around him advised giving in to their demands; his country and people were all but destroyed. And yet, even though he knew these things on one level, on a deeper level he knew he was Pharaoh and Moses wasn't, and even that he was Pharaoh and that the God of Moses wasn't.

Later when he told this story, Zephar would say that Moses and Aaron shook in anger at the threat. I didn't see it that way—they didn't look angry so much as frustrated at Pharaoh's obstinacy. "Unless you repent, one final devastation awaits you," they said. "If you will not set us free, the Lord will pass through Egypt and all the firstborn will die, the firstborn of Pharaoh, of all his servants, even of the cattle."

"Your firstborn will surely not die," Zephar whispered in Pharaoh's ear.

As the brothers turned to leave the palace, I told Abaddon to forget about Moses. "The Enemy is coming. It can't be safe for us to stay in Egypt, maybe not even on Earth itself." I didn't utter my next thought, which was that maybe not even Sheol would be safe when the Enemy chose to save His people.

"He isn't interested in us," Abaddon said. "The Enemy just wants the Circumcised Ones to be free of their oppressors so they can go serve Him in the desert."

"How do you know?" I said, quickly. "Did you hear His voice?"

"No, but I heard what Moses told the elders. This is the last plague, then Pharaoh and the Egyptians will not only allow the children of Israel to leave, but they will drive them out of the land themselves."

"Moses held a meeting with the elders?" Zephar said. "What happened?"

"Nothing," Abaddon said. "He just told them how to escape the plague."

"How?" Zephar said, standing right in front of him now and somehow managing to be intimidating even though Abaddon towered over him.

From Abaddon's glow, it was obvious he recognized that he'd made a mistake by mentioning it so casually. "This is the same pattern, isn't it? A plague is visited on the Egyptians but the Circumcised Ones are left untouched."

"How?"

Abaddon flexed his wings, perhaps in an attempt to reassert himself, but he spoke quickly and in an appeasing way. "They are supposed to sacrifice a lamb, then smear its blood on their doors, on the top and on either side. When the Enemy sees the blood, He will pass over that household."

Zephar nodded, satisfied, but I said, "What else? Did you leave out any details?"

"Nothing important," Abaddon said. "They're not supposed to break any of the bones of the lamb. And it has to be a male lamb—a lamb without blemish, if that matters."

"Go," I said, speaking to Abaddon. "Warn the angels in Egypt that they are not safe here."

"We can't leave," Zephar said, but he didn't speak with much conviction.

"We aren't leaving," I said, and felt a great deal of satisfaction at the terror that crept into his glow. "You and I will stay here. Everyone else should go, to another land or to Sheol if they want. They can return once we tell them it's safe to do so."

Zephar followed Abaddon to help spread the word, and he returned later that night, our roles now reversed as I paced behind Pharaoh's throne.

"Are you sure this is a good idea?" he said.

Pharaoh and the Egyptians were a broken people, who had seen more devastation in a year than most see in a lifetime, and who were now promised another, final plague unless they repented. Perhaps influenced by their stubbornness and suffering, it was easy to reconcile myself to defiance and destruction at the hands of the Enemy, which I believed awaited us when He visited Egypt.

"It's probably a bad idea," I said. "But if something happens, we need to know."

"But what's the logic of both of us staying behind? I'm not saying it should be me who goes or you who stays. We can decide in a fair way."

"No," I said, although I didn't really care; I wanted him around simply because I saw that he didn't want to be. "No—if something happens to one of us, the other must shift to Sheol and warn the Master and the others."

We kept arguing long past all of the fallen went to bed, and we were still arguing when the sun rose and the city started to wake. Nothing had happened to us, but death had touched many of the houses in the cities of Egypt. From these homes rose screams and cries as parents discovered their children dead in their beds, and the sounds of their wailing attracted the angels from the surrounding lands. Before we could even think to send word, the angels we'd told to leave Egypt knew it was safe to return.

By the simple act of sacrificing a lamb and smearing its blood on their lintels and doorposts, the children of Israel saved themselves from death and freed themselves from bondage. The Egyptians not only let them go, but (as Moses had told the elders) they drove them out of the land, hundreds of thousands of them—children of Israel and others who wanted to leave as well. They left Egypt not only with their sheep and oxen and cows, but loaded down with silver and gold and fine clothing, as if the Egyptians had always planned to pay them for the generations of forced labor and were just waiting for the right opportunity. Moses also honored the promise the children of Israel made to Joseph over four hundred years earlier, and carried Joseph's coffin with them out of Egypt.

The other dark angels were too afraid to follow the Hebrews into the desert, and Zephar and I kept our distance as well. The Enemy was with them always, the Begotten leading the way as a pillar of cloud in daytime and a pillar of fire at night. We didn't know what He was planning for these people, but we feared the worst.

"I should return to Egypt," Zephar said. "The Master won't be happy about this; I should convince Pharaoh to come and take them back."

At the time I thought he was just saying it to get away from the sight of the cloudy pillar. I let him go but never expected to see him return so soon, let alone leading Pharaoh and his entire army in our direction. As the Hebrews reached the edge of the sea, the Egyptians raced toward them, the horsemen and charioteers throwing up clouds of sand and dust as if in defiance of the pillar of cloud.

Although I kept my distance, it was obvious that the children of Israel were panicking. Most looked like they were ready to surrender to Pharaoh and his men. *This is great*, I thought, even though bringing Pharaoh after them was Zephar's idea. I hoped that they would return to Egypt in fear and shame; after which, I felt, no power on Earth could make them uproot again.

But suddenly the Begotten moved between the Hebrew people and the Egyptian army, and Moses stood at the shoreline and raised his arms, spreading them out one to the right and one to the left. For a moment nothing happened except that Moses slumped his head and looked like a dead man, but in the next his robe fluttered in the wind. The wind picked up, stronger and stronger, creating waves—two waves, dividing the river in half, walls of air holding back the water on his right and the water on his left. The wind blew while thunder roared and lightning lit up the night sky, and in a few hours there was a path of dry ground at the bottom of the sea. Moses took the first step, and the people he'd brought out of Egypt followed.

It was due to the efforts of Zephar and the other angels that Pharaoh's army didn't rush back to Egypt at the sight and sound of the thunder and lightning that had held them captive and cowering in their homes only a few weeks before. And it was due to their efforts that the Egyptians followed into the sea, even though its water towered over them on either side.

I had stayed behind on the shore to speak with Zephar, and together we watched as Pharaoh and his army pursued the children of Israel. But all of a sudden they started to encounter difficulties: experienced drivers were steering their chariots into each other, horses went limp and collapsed, riders were being thrown to the ground as wheels fell off their chariots.

"This is the work of the Enemy," I said.

"Maybe," Zephar said.

"Tell Pharaoh to let them go for now."

"No! Their minds are full of lust for the gold and silver they'll divide among themselves when they capture the Circumcised Ones. If they give up and turn back now, we might never be able to convince them to go after the children of Israel again."

Zephar and the other dark angels swept through the army, strengthening Pharaoh and his men.

I knew what would happen next: once, the Egyptians had drowned male Hebrew babies in the river, now it would be their own young men who would drown in the sea. The waters came crashing down on the Egyptian army, throwing riders off horses and chariots. They tried to flee, swimming against strong currents and crashing waves, but already I could see their spirits rising from the water, confused and dismayed. Not one of those who pursued the Hebrews into the sea survived.

"We'll have to tell the Master," I said to Zephar, as the dark angels started to pull spirits into Sheol. "And you'll need help to drag away the rest of these fallen."

Furious that the Circumcised Ones were free, and worried about what the Enemy had planned for them, He-Who-Rules ordered me to do whatever could be done—destroy Moses, or separate him from the Enemy, or at least turn the people against him. Not daring to try the first or even the second, I instructed Zephar and the others to encourage the Hebrews in their grumbling whenever they met the slightest trouble or annoyance in the desert. And although they encountered lots of difficulties, our successes were short-lived because

Moses always turned to the Enemy, and the Enemy always worked
His wonders for them, providing for their needs in amazing ways. To
take examples from the stories Moses himself chose to preserve (and
why these stories and not others? I've always wondered): after three
days of searching the desert for water, they finally found some—but
it was too bitter to drink. On the Enemy's orders, though, Moses
took a nearby tree and placed it in the water, and the wood made
the water sweet. When they were suffering of thirst on another occasion, the Enemy instructed Moses to hit a rock with his staff, and
the people were able to drink water that flowed from the stricken
rock. When there was no more bread left in the camp, the Enemy
sent them food, including bread from the High Country itself. As if
that wasn't enough, the Enemy preserved their clothes so that in all
the decades of wandering the desert, not even the shoes on their feet
wore out.

Not knowing what else to do, and the Master demanding that we
do something, I told Zephar to inspire an army of desert dwellers to
attack the exhausted Israelites. The man named Joshua led the de-
fense, but the armies of Israel would have lost the battle if not for
Moses and the Enemy. On a hilltop looking over the fighting below,
Moses took his staff and lifted up his hands as he'd done to part the
sea. As long as he held up his arms, Joshua and his men fared well,
but when Moses grew tired and dropped his arms, the tide of battle
turned against them. Unlucky for us, Aaron and another man were
with him and saw what happened when Moses lowered his arms.
They stood on either side of him and held up his hands throughout
the day, and by nightfall Joshua and his men were victorious.

The closest we ever came to thwarting the Enemy's plan occurred
a few months later. Amid thunder and lightning, and a quaking
mountain that seemed to be on fire, the Israelites heard the voice
of the Enemy. The experience was so traumatic that they didn't want
the Enemy to speak to them any more, and they begged Moses to go
up the mountain and speak to Him on their behalf. Moses had only
been gone a few weeks when we were surprised to find that the people were already restless and, feeling renewed by this discovery, we
encouraged them in their thoughts.

Moses wasn't coming back down the mountain, we whispered in
their ears; probably he was already dead. But he was their mediator,
and without Moses, how could they worship their God? And would
this God still protect them now that Moses was gone?

Aaron ordered the people to bring him their earrings, which he melted down to make a god of gold in the shape of a calf. "This is the god that brought you out of Egypt," we whispered to the people. "Sacrifice to it, and eat and drink before your god." Aaron built an altar on which to offer the sacrifices and the people celebrated, and in their drunkenness we ignited their lust.

When Moses descended the mountain, and he and Joshua saw what was happening in the camp, he was so angry that he threw down the tablets that were in his hands, tablets on which the Enemy had written His commandments. The other angels, including Zephar, were already celebrating with the Hebrews—they felt triumphant that we'd turned the Enemy's chosen people away from Him to worship nothing more than fashioned metal—but it was only when Moses broke the tablets that I allowed myself to relax. At that point, I felt that our worries were over, that the Enemy would abandon these people, and perhaps even Moses himself.

It didn't happen that way, of course.

"Thousands have died because of what we did that day," Zephar said, when he saw how much I burned in frustration that the Enemy had forgiven the Circumcised Ones. "The Master is not upset."

"They all deserve to die!" I said. "They rebelled against Him, didn't they? All of them, this whole race of fallen people—they've been in a state of near-constant rebellion since the beginning. Why isn't He cutting them off from His presence? How is that just?"

We spent the next few years working on the people, whispering in their ears anything we thought would work: how tiring this journey must be for them; how thirsty and hungry they must feel; whether things had really been so bad in Egypt.

Although the people grumbled to our satisfaction, Moses was always there to intercede for them. Even when an infestation of poisonous snakes plagued the camp of the Israelites, and anyone who was bitten by them died, Moses turned to the Enemy and found the way to save his people. He fashioned a snake of copper and placed it on a tall pole, and anyone who was bitten and looked up at the snake lived.

Despite everything, though, within a few years I was convinced that Moses wasn't going to be a problem for us.

"I don't know," Zephar said. "The Enemy has spent a lot of time with him." Zephar had grown weary of being my messenger to He-

Who-Rules; perhaps because I was sending him to Sheol with as much bad news as I had, or with arguments and opinions I knew to be contrary to the Master's when I didn't have any bad news to share. But this time I was sure the contrary opinion was the correct one.

"Yes, He's spent time with Moses—but only to tell him stories and hand down instructions and a constitution for their new nation. None of it has anything to do with us. I need you to go tell the Master that Moses isn't the one we're looking for."

Because at the time I alone condescended to read what the fallen wrote, very few of the other angels could argue with me. They all felt it was beneath them to go to even the little effort it takes to learn one of the fallen's written languages, but I liked to read. And though the Master and the other angels couldn't understand it, they were happy to let me be the authority on the written works of the children of Israel.

It's easy to think now how different things might be for me if I'd told the Master the final truth about the books of Moses. And why didn't I? Through Zephar and Arakiel I told He-Who-Rules almost everything, starting with how much of his time Moses was spending writing. I told him how Moses wrote about Adam and Eve and even about the Master's own role in the events in Eden (I was careful to gloss over the Enemy's promise—not that it mattered by then, since everyone knew anyway but only pretended ignorance). The stories about Noah, Abraham, Isaac, Jacob, and Joseph—I told the Master how Moses was combining them all into his book, to remind this new nation of where they had come from.

I told the Master how Moses wrote about his own life, about the plagues in Egypt, about Israel's escape from captivity and all the things the Enemy had done for them. I told him exactly what the Enemy had said to Moses when they first met and He revealed His name—the things the Master had been so desperate to find out when the children of Israel still lived in bondage in Egypt.

I even told the Master how Moses had promised that the Enemy would raise up from among them a prophet like himself. "This is the one who might pose a danger to us, the one to watch," I told Zephar to tell the Master. "Not Moses, but this prophet like Moses whom the Enemy will raise up."

I left out only one thing, and I left it out under the mistaken assumption that the Master would never read these books for himself.

I left it out because I was convinced that Moses wasn't a danger, but I knew if He-Who-Rules found out this one truth, he would have immediately ordered an all-out attack on Moses. But if the Enemy had turned Egypt inside-out and upside-down, why wouldn't He do the same to us if Moses asked for His help? Moses was closer to the Enemy than any fallen before him, and I didn't know what He would do to us if we interfered with His plan for Moses.

Everyone realizes it now, of course, but at the time I alone had read his work and I alone knew the secret I carried for many and long years: Moses grasped that the Enemy was triune. The knowledge came like a shock, when I finally understood that he was aware of what he was doing when he spoke of the Enemy, of the Enemy's Angel or Messenger, and of His Spirit, and that it wasn't by mistake that he wrote of the Enemy in plural and singular forms.

The secret weighed me down like a heavy stone. Even then I knew that if the Master found out I'd been keeping the information from him, in contravention of a direct order he'd given in my own hearing, in defiance of a direct question he'd asked me, there would be no end to the punishments he would devise to torment me.

It was only when Moses died that I finally felt liberated of my burden. *What does it matter now what Moses knew or didn't know?* I thought, ignoring the witness of his knowledge he'd left behind in the belief that the Master and his angels would never read it. As if to make my liberation even sweeter, I was vindicated and Zephar embarrassed when I discovered that he'd been hedging his bets by casting doubts on my reports that Moses wasn't a danger to us.

In fact, I felt so elated and so confident, that I decided to give away information I'd been saving in case I was wrong about Moses, and needed something big to offer the Master to appease him.

"Is everything all right?" He-Who-Rules said, as soon as I shifted into the throne room. Everyone turned to look at me, glows of respect mingled with fear at the news I might bring. "Did the charge fail? Why haven't you sent Zephar? Did something happen?"

Taking a moment to enjoy the silence that was mine to break, I approached his throne before answering. "The attempt to wrestle away the spirit of Moses from the angels of the Enemy has failed, yes," I said. "As has every attempt to wrestle away any spirit that doesn't come to us of its own volition. So far. Master, before Moses distracted us from everything but himself, you gave me an order. You asked me to figure out how we can succeed at stealing spirits from the Enemy. I believe I have an answer—and that's why I came myself, and came immediately."

He-Who-Rules hissed for silence as the murmuring of the angels grew louder. When the throne room was quiet again, the Master sat back down and looked at me, his desire to project a calm demeanor betrayed by his intense and eager glow. "Well?" he said. "Tell us."

Chapter Nine

A Line of Judges

"Our problem," I said, "is that ever since we've been able to see the angels of the Enemy, we've framed everything to do with them in military terms. So when we decided to steal spirits from these angels, the first and only thing we thought of was to mount attacks. But of course—"

"What are you saying?" the Master interrupted. "That we can't compete with them on military terms?"

He had leaned forward and was staring at me, but I could tell he wasn't angry. *You're toying with me*, I thought; *trying to get me to say something in front of the other dark angels that they'd later make me regret.* At the time I believed that he played these games and set these traps for his own amusement, but I've since learned that in addition to fearing the seed of the Enemy's promise, the Master fears something else almost as much. He is constantly worried that another dark angel will lay claim to his throne and mount a rebellion against him just like he mounted a rebellion against the Enemy. Sowing discord is his way of ensuring that no one angel becomes popular enough to do so, and has too much on his mind to spare any thoughts on rebellion.

"Of course not," I said, although of course I believed, and believe now, the exact opposite. If Michael's angels defeated us before the Transformation, when we were strong and bright, how could anyone think we had a chance to defeat them in a show of force ever after? We could never compete with them on military terms, I knew; but I also knew that there were other terms, terms in which they were powerless against us.

"What I'm saying isn't that we can't compete in a fair fight," I said, "it's that the angels of the Enemy don't fight fair because they don't fight at all. They run away like cowards, taking the spirits of the fallen with them, protecting them, lifting them up toward the High Country until they reach dimensions where we can't follow."

As the murmur of agreement rippled through the room, the Master leaned back to sit comfortably in his throne again. "What is your proposal, Enoch?" he said. "How do you suggest we take the spirits from these cowards?"

"By convincing the fallen that they're better off with us than with the angels of the Enemy. Why try to wrestle away a spirit who'll come with us of its own accord?" I didn't pause to wait for an answer. "Let me give you an example. Some of these creatures have spent so much of their lives giving in to their every bodily desire that even when they are separated from their bodies, they hear the echoes of those desires and are unable to resist trying to fulfill them. At their death, we will tell them that they can have as much food, as much drink, as much sex, as much gold, even as much power as they want, if they'll only follow us to Sheol. I've seen what such a promise does to this kind of fallen—their lust consumes them so completely that they'll follow us immediately, blind and deaf to the Enemy's angels and any objections or warnings they might try to offer."

Encouraged by the Master's glow, and the approval I sensed from the other dark angels around the room, I went on, "Or take the opposite type of fallen, the kind who is more likely to follow the angels of the Enemy in the first place. They've resisted their bodily urges, they've developed control over their passions—what can we do to them? Let us go even further, brethren. Let us say these fallen have lived in service to the Enemy, obeying their conscience when they were able and repenting when they failed to do so, as even the best of them fails many times over the course of their lives. But so what? They know in their hearts that the Enemy is just, and they know that a crime must be punished, that a price needs to be paid for every sin.

"If giving the fallen a conscience wasn't a mistake, then giving the children of Israel the Law through Moses definitely was. Brethren," I said, speaking louder now and moving away from the throne to walk up and down the room, energized by the excitement that I could feel from the other angels, and even from the Master himself, "Brethren, consider Moses. Who is greater than Moses? Whose face shone with the so-called glory of the Enemy? Who else received the Law directly from the Enemy? Who was the Chosen One among a nation of Chosen Ones? We have a saying that after love, humility is the worst trait a fallen can have. But here is Moses, as humble as any fallen I've ever seen. Here is Moses, who left the palaces of Egypt because he saw the suffering of his brothers. Here is Moses, who stood before the Enemy and asked to be cut off if only his people could be forgiven—offering himself to suffer for sins he had nothing to do with! But here is Moses also, who smashed the Enemy's tablets in anger; and here is Moses, who struck a rock when the Enemy ordered him otherwise. And so Moses—the giver of the Law—was not found worthy to enter the Promised Land. If we'd caught him in time, I believe that we could have convinced even such a fallen that he didn't deserve to enter the High Country."

"How?" the Master said.

"First, we need to train angels to be gatekeepers," I said. "We can post them along the path to the High Country, from the lowest dimensions to as high as the bravest and strongest ones will go. These angels will barrage the fallen with either promises and temptations or accusations and judgments. In the first case, we will continue to do to them in death what we've always done in life, lead them step by step away from the Enemy. In the second, we will follow two lines of attack. We will shame them, reminding them that they don't deserve to be in the presence of the Enemy; or, we will scare them, asking them what they think will happen to them when they do come into His awful presence."

The Master didn't hiss for silence immediately. He looked around the room, and it seemed to me that he was noting which dark angels were cheering the loudest, which ones glowed the most excited, which ones were looking at me with admiration. Not that any of it mattered, though; when He-Who-Rules finally made his move, no one tried to defend or protect me. And how can I blame any of them when I know that I would have done the same? I too would've been happy that someone else had incurred the Master's wrath, maybe even thrilled that I was one step closer to the top—of the rankings, of an imagined hierarchy, of whatever—if only because of the elimination of another.

When he finally hissed, the Master did so quietly. The cheer of the dark angels didn't die out, but transformed into a call for points. The Master hissed again, more decisively this time.

"Yes," he said, once the throne room was quiet, "Enoch will be rewarded handsomely if his plan succeeds." He faced me. "Go back to Earth; take Abaddon with you. Show me your idea works, and I will give you enough angels to post a guard in every dimension from here to the High Country."

Because we were so successful later on, almost everyone forgets the dismal failure the idea was at first—in fact, it seems like most forgot it was an idea at first at all. This was simply how things were done, and no one spent a lot of time thinking about how it had come about or whether it could be improved.

The problem initially was that Abaddon and I couldn't keep track of the righteous spirits among the thousands of fallen that were dying as Joshua led his unstoppable army throughout Canaan.

But when we finally found and were able to follow a fallen spirit that was being guided by the angels of the Enemy, we realized that our plan contained a major flaw: the angels were ready to defend their charge, and they knew far more about him than we did. We tempted him with the pleasures and joys of Sheol; they reminded him that in life he'd always thought that the Enemy was the only true pleasure and joy. We said he was a sinner and should come with us; they reminded him of the tears of repentance he'd offered to the Enemy throughout his life.

"This won't do," I said to Abaddon, when they were gone, the fallen following the angels of light even more gladly than before. "They know too much about him. We're speaking in generalities; they're able to give him specific examples from his own life. The only way this will work is if we know each fallen as well as they do, and can overwhelm them with reminders of their every act of coldness and cruelty."

"So what do we do?"

"We need to study them; we need to watch them, take note of their actions and their words maybe."

Abaddon nodded, but in his glow I saw the question he wasn't asking. *You mean, write them down?*

I did mean write them down, but I wasn't eager to take the idea to He-Who-Rules. It wasn't enough that I wanted the Master's tempters to practice thinking about the Enemy long enough to be able to see His angels and the spirits they might be leading away, now I wanted to teach them how to read and write too.

Abaddon and I tried again with a few other fallen, but it was obvious that once a spirit was able to see—and willing to follow—the angels of the Enemy, our haphazard temptations, vague threats and lame accusations of a general disposition to sin were not going to make them abandon their guardians.

Before I could really think through how to approach the Master with my new strategy, Zephar found me and said that I was ordered back to Sheol immediately.

"Why?" I said. "What's happened?"

Zephar had started to turn away but he stopped. "The Master thinks Joshua is the One."

"He isn't," I said, and it struck me then how odd it was that this secret He-Who-Rules once guarded so carefully had become a matter of routine discussion among us. "Go back and say so."

"The Master asked for you," he said. "But if you insist—"

"No," I said. "I'll go."

Baal, Moloch, Ashtoreth and a few other angels I hadn't seen in Sheol since the first days after the Transformation stood speaking with the Master when I arrived.

Typically I approached the throne right away, confident that my business was more important than whatever the Master was currently dealing with, and also that I could handle any angel who took offense at the interruption—but this wasn't a typical sight and these weren't typical angels. Worried that stopping suddenly would look stupid—or worse, cowardly—to the other angels standing around the room, I glided in to stand beside them, as if that had been my destination all along. I picked a spot as close to the throne as possible, but Baal was whispering, and strain as I might, I couldn't make out his words.

"What's going on?" I whispered to the angel beside me.

"Enoch." The Master's booming voice echoed throughout the throne room. Every angel turned to stare at me. "Come here."

I glided away from the wall. "I—"

"How are the tests coming along, Enoch? Have you been successful? Will you be ready to capture Joshua's spirit?"

"I hope so, Master. I hope that by the time Joshua dies—"

"That time is now," He-Who-Rules said. "Baal will lead his followers in an attack against the children of Israel. Once he's dead, I want Joshua here in Sheol. Do you understand?"

"Yes," I said without hesitation, because I was certain I wouldn't have to follow through on my word.

The assaults on Joshua won't succeed, I thought. And I was equally certain that Joshua wasn't the One. *Would Moses promise that the*

Enemy will send a prophet like himself, I reasoned, *if that prophet stood three feet away?*

"You're viewing this problem from the wrong angle," I said to Baal, when we were back on Earth. "The way to defeat Joshua and his men is to work on Joshua and his men. They spent seven days walking around a city just because the Enemy told them to! As long as they have that kind of faith, they can't be defeated. But if we're able to make them doubt His word, make them hesitate about a battle for which the Enemy has promised victory—then we will be able to conquer them! In that moment we will have already conquered them, don't you see that?"

Baal wouldn't listen, and neither would Ashtoreth. They wanted to crush the armies of Israel, just like those armies had crushed their nations and killed their kings. They wanted to destroy Joshua and smash his army, just like Joshua had destroyed the temples where they were worshiped and smashed the altars where young fallen were offered to them in sacrifice.

For years I watched the many failures of Baal's strategy in silent frustration. Finally I returned to Sheol.

"Joshua is dying," I said to He-Who-Rules. "Whatever we thought we could accomplish by attacking him and his army with other fallen, we've failed. We need to concentrate on the type of thing you asked me to do with Abraham—find a way to win these fallen to our side."

The Master's glow intensified. "Joshua is dying. . . and you're here?"

"It won't work," I said, taking a step back. "Joshua is too committed to the Enemy. Abaddon and I have tried with other fallen, and if we couldn't succeed with them, we won't succeed with Joshua."

The Master's glance tracked around the throne room, and when he spoke his voice was louder than it needed to be. "Are you saying your grand idea is a failure?"

"No, it will work. . . but we have to start earlier than the moment of a fallen's death. We can't shame or scare or tempt them until we understand them. That means shadowing them throughout their lives. It also means at least trying to tempt them away from the Enemy while they're alive if we want any chance of doing so when they die. The question isn't—"

The Master was looking past me; I turned to see Zephar walking toward us. "Joshua's dead," he said. "There's no sign of his spirit."

The Master made a show of being upset at our incompetence for letting him escape, but I saw that underneath his feigned anger was genuine relief. Now that Joshua was dead and gone, the Master relaxed and was more willing to entertain my ideas. With his support, I convinced Baal and the other angels to take their vengeance on the children of Israel by working on them directly. In a short time, they found that these fallen were just as receptive to temptation as their neighbors; and soon there was no difference between the two.

Although almost everyone was pleased that we'd turned the Enemy's chosen nation away from Him, Abaddon and I discovered that such an environment actually made our task that much harder. Anyone who continued to worship the Enemy while their friends and family worshiped idols was beyond our reach; anyone who tried to live an honest and just life when their friends and family were happy to lie and cheat to get by in a world of liars and cheaters was as deaf to our temptations in death as they were in life. In fact, we didn't have our first real success until Othniel called the people back to the Enemy.

Even before that happened, though, I knew He would send someone to save the children of Israel from their oppressors, just like He'd sent Moses to deliver them from the Egyptians. He doesn't abandon the fallen to their suffering, even when they bring it on themselves, even if that suffering is exactly what they deserve. This is something the Master has never understood; He-Who-Rules tries to increase the torment of the fallen, not just for the pleasure it provides the rest of his angels, but almost as if it were an end in itself, or as if agony alone would lead the fallen away from the Enemy. Of course I'm not suggesting that we try to increase their joy or extend any pleasure to them beyond what's necessary to trap them; I am suggesting that more than one fallen has been lost to us when they found only misery at the end of the road we paved for them. The Master doesn't understand that the Enemy uses suffering to call the fallen back to Himself; he doesn't see that precisely because of their fallen nature, it's in comfort, not in misery, that they are furthest from Him.

At the time, the Master was convinced that Othniel was the One. It was like that with all of the others, too, with every ruler who came to save Israel after we'd caused them to reject and forget the Enemy, and they fell under the power of foreign tyrants. And with each ruler, the Master believed they were the One for a different reason.

I fell victim to his fears only with Othniel, who came from the tribe of Judah. But once Othniel died, I refused to entertain any more suggestions along those lines.

Ehud struck at the head, assassinating the king of Moab, the Master said; a normal man attacking a king as a sign that a normal man might attack an angel. I didn't believe it, and Ehud died.

With Deborah, the Master was convinced that she was the One because she was a woman. "Why did He not mention both parents?" he said to me, "and especially why did He mention the woman alone? He meant the seed of a woman was also a woman!" Still I didn't believe it, and Deborah died.

Gideon was the One because of his great faith. I told the Master he was wrong, and Gideon died.

Although the Master's panic reached a high pitch with Samson, I wasn't concerned for a moment in that case either.

"He isn't from the tribe of Judah," I said, repeating a conversation I'd had almost a dozen times before, the annoyance I felt at being called back to Sheol no doubt evident in my glow each time. "And the only similarity between him and Moses is that he too is sent by the Enemy to save his people from their oppressors. . . like all the others before him. He isn't the One."

The Master shook his head. "We've never seen a fallen dedicated to the Enemy in this way—consecrated to Him from birth. We've never seen a fallen with his strength. Who is to say if he can be killed?"

"He is a fallen," I said. "Of course he can be killed."

The death of a human being, especially a human being he suspected of being the One, was the Master's greatest comfort. The thought that a fallen could come along who couldn't be killed frightened He-Who-Rules to his core.

"Tempt him!" the Master said, trying to be severe but coming across as pleading and pathetic. "Get him to break the vow to the Enemy."

"No," I said, flush with confidence from my increasingly successful attempts at stealing away spirits from the angels of the Enemy. "I need to supervise our work in the dimensions toward the High Country. There's still a lot to learn. Have someone else tempt him—have Zephar tempt him."

The rumor the Master spread was that I was scared of Samson, just like Zephar and the other angels he approached with the task were too scared to get close to Samson too. The rumor was half-true: I wasn't scared of him in life, but I wasn't anxious to try to steal him away in death. Despite our successes—by that time, Abaddon had gone back to the Master, and I'd been sent a whole stable of angels to command—I was hand-picking the fallen to track through life and further choosing from those the ones we'd stop on their way to the High Country. Because we only confronted spirits I thought we had a good chance of stealing away, our success rate was high and our confidence and enjoyment of the work increased every time we brought someone to Sheol, which made us better at tempting away the next spirit. But we still weren't ready to challenge the angels of light over the spirit of anyone who had a faith like Samson's, I knew.

Before I could get too concerned about him, Samson told Delilah the secret of his strength. She shaved his head, and his enemies blinded him as literally as he'd been blinded by lust. Soon Samson was dead too.

With Samuel, things were different—and because they were different, He-Who-Rules was convinced that Samuel was the One. Not only was he a warrior who successfully lead the Israelite army against their enemies, he was a priest and a prophet who successfully lead the people back to the Enemy. I granted that Samuel had incredible success convincing the children of Israel to destroy their idols and stop worshiping false gods—but as far as I could see, year after year, that seemed to be as far as he wanted to go.

When Samuel was an old man, the children of Israel did an amazing thing. They asked Samuel to set a king over them, to rule them like kings ruled other nations.

Finally, I thought. *Finally the Enemy will abandon these people. He'll give them the king they so desperately want and give them up to his caprice and tyranny.*

"Now you'll see," I told Zephar. "The Enemy is supposed to be their Lord and King, but they want a human lord and king. Do you think He will give them one? Do you think He is in the business of concessions? Whatever He had planned for this people—including this Deliverer the Master keeps imagining has been sent to them—the Enemy will finally realize that they aren't worthy of Him."

My delight didn't survive the king's coronation. Destroying them for wanting a king was what they deserved, I thought; but giving them their king and watching them destroy themselves was also fair. Neither was part of the Enemy's plan, I saw. Samuel stood before the people and showed them their king, and said that they would be blessed if they and their king obeyed the words of the Enemy.

Zephar's glow couldn't help but betray his contempt.

"I don't get it," I said to him. "They rejected Him, they insulted Him... but He gives in and gives them a king. They abandon Him over and over, but He's there as soon as they turn back to Him. Why is He so merciful to them? Where is His justice?"

"Remember Gideon?" Zephar said. "I only just heard this story from Arakiel. The Enemy appears to him and says, 'I will save Israel by your hand.' Gideon's response is a little test—'I'm setting down some fleece on the ground,' he says. 'If you'll really save Israel by my hand, let the dew come upon this fleece but not the rest of the ground.' And the Enemy does it, jumping through the hoop Gideon holds up like a common circus animal! If I were Him and a fallen tried to test me, I'd burn him to ashes and say, 'How's that? Is that proof enough for you?'"

Zephar's purpose in telling me the story, I knew, was to show me the Enemy's complete unreasonableness and foolishness when it came to the fallen—but it had the opposite effect. I had no idea why Gideon tested the Enemy's word, or why the Enemy allowed Himself to be so tested, but I knew that once that was done, Gideon gave Him his complete trust. He sent home the largest part of his army, allowing himself to be outnumbered hundreds to one, simply because the Enemy asked him. That was His plan, I saw—not to test the fallen to prove who was good and who was evil, but to call them back to Himself, even if it meant injury to His honor and dignity.

We insist on seeing their lives from birth to death as nothing more than a cosmic test, which is why we're so annoyed by His every interference, because we regard each one as a cheat. But what I began to understand is that the Enemy doesn't see their existence as an exam, or at least not like a final exam where the student is left to themselves, to succeed or fail as their abilities enable them. He sees their earthly lives as something closer to the class before the exam, or the training a warrior undergoes before battle. Every decision they make takes them a step closer or further away from Him, shapes their character until death to be more or less like the Enemy, revealing or covering up the image of Himself He imprinted on them.

Over the course of their lives, I finally understood, He isn't testing them to see if they pass or fail; He's trying to perfect them, to bring them to a place where they will put their complete trust in Him as

Gideon had done.

But at what cost? By condescending to Gideon's test, He'd made Himself an object of ridicule to Zephar. Didn't He care?

The first effect of these thoughts was to fan my anger. *Why them and not us?* I wondered, not for the first time. Why go to all this trouble to call them back? I didn't realize that I'd have my answer very soon, or that this new king himself would provide it, or that the answer would infuriate me so much that I would throw off any last reservations I had about the mission the Master had set for us, any last hope I had in the Enemy, and dedicate myself fully to tempting the fallen away from Him.

But before that happened, the second effect of those thoughts was to cause me increased confidence in our mission. The Enemy wants to perfect the fallen, but He doesn't seem to remember that they are fallen. Adam and Eve had a choice: the Master or the Enemy, and they chose the Master. With that decision, death and corruption entered this world the Enemy had created. Whatever visions of perfection He'd had for it should have been abandoned right along with those who'd caused it to fall, but in His obstinacy He'd refused to do so. What would it have cost Him to destroy this fallen world and start again—or not start again? The Enemy had set Himself up for defeat, I realized. And perhaps for the first time since the Transformation, I believed that we would succeed in ruining His plan, because I saw that things could only end in failure for Him.

At the height of my new sense of confidence, He-Who-Rules was feeling the exact opposite. Zephar had told him how the Spirit of the Enemy had descended on the new king when Samuel anointed him with oil, and the Master was worried that after he was done throwing off their fallen oppressors, the Spirit would direct King Saul toward an attack against us. Again I was called away from my work on the spirit-temptations to help Zephar defeat a living fallen.

At first it seemed like we would have no more success moving Saul away from the Enemy than I had with Abraham. But the crown he'd only reluctantly taken up changed him; and the once-humble Saul became impatient and no more concerned with keeping the Enemy's word than he was with keeping his own, and much more concerned with appeasing his people. Our assaults were so successful that after a few years the Spirit of the Enemy left him. Despite his many military victories, Saul sat on a sad throne, teased and tormented daily by Zephar.

The Master and Zephar were delighted by his suffering, and seemed to have completely forgotten about Samuel, but I hadn't. Even though none of the angels liked to be near Samuel, I saw him as a great example of the kind of fallen we were ultimately aiming for. I asked Agares to follow him and take note of any transgressions or passions we could use against him, anything that would help us tempt him away from the angels of the Enemy, whom I was sure would come to get him at his death. In this way I learned that Samuel had traveled to Bethlehem, to the house of a man named Jesse. Although this man had seven sons, tall and strong, Samuel singled out the eighth, a young boy. Samuel poured oil on him, the same oil of anointment he'd poured on Saul to declare him the future king, and the Spirit of the Enemy descended on this boy, this shepherd named David.

At first the news disappointed me—I was more interested in information that would help me capture Samuel and people like him than in the politics of the Circumcised Ones—but it wouldn't be long before I realized its significance.

Arakiel often sought me out when I shifted back to Earth from the higher dimensions in search of more fallen to track, usually to give or receive updates, but this time I could tell that things were different.

"What's going on?" I said, thrown by Arakiel's seriousness.

"Sytri told me to find you and bring you back to Sheol as soon as possible," he said. "He didn't tell me what's happening... but I've never seen him this worried."

When I arrived in the throne room, I found it unnaturally quiet and tense. Zephar stood facing the Master, who looked past him and seemed to be staring off into other dimensions. Unwilling to break the silence, I stood beside Zephar and waited.

Eventually the Master became aware of my presence. He sat up straighter in his throne. "Zephar has found the One."

"Oh, the One," I said, waves of relief sweeping through me as I turned to face Zephar. "Is that a—is that right?" Under different circumstances, I would've been annoyed at yet another interruption, but in fact I was glad that it was simply this old and tired threat we were facing and not anything really serious.

Zephar seemed to read my thoughts. "This man is different than the others," he said, as contrite or perhaps as afraid as I'd ever seen him. "He plays the harp for Saul."

"And?"

"And the music...it reminds me of the High Country. I can't be around it."

Zephar's words washed away my relief, and with it all the contempt I'd been feeling. "Who is he?" I said.

"A young shepherd from Bethlehem," Zephar said. "A man named David."

Chapter Ten

A King

THe Master abhors the mention of David's name, but in my mind David's life is associated with a series of personal successes. It was through him that I discovered the happy surprise of where the angels of the Enemy were taking the spirits of the fallen; through him that I came to understand why the Enemy has abandoned us but lavishes attention on these creatures of matter; through him that I became convinced that there is no truly good fallen, that even among the best of them and those closest to the Enemy, as David surely was if anyone was, there exists in their hearts the capacity for great evil.

Before all of that, though, I stood in Sheol in front of the Master's throne and heard Zephar say his name—which was so shocking that I couldn't help but betray my knowledge of David. "Yes, this isn't the first I've heard of him," I said, which wasn't necessary but gave me time to decide how much I wanted to reveal. "You're right—he may be the One."

Did I believe it? I believed it enough that I was anxious to return to Earth and find out everything about David, starting with whether he came from the House of Judah.

"What makes you say that?" Zephar said. "What do you know about him?"

Before I could decide how much I wanted to say, Arakiel shifted into the throne room and approached, his glow even more feeble than the last time I saw him.

"I'm sorry," he said, speaking to the Master. "Zephar asked me to keep an eye on David and report immediately if—"

"What has he done?" the Master said, almost out of his throne.

"Challenged Goliath," Arakiel said, his glow pulsating with fear bordering on panic. "Saul is trying to talk him out of it, but—"

"Who's Goliath?" the Master said.

"A Philistine," Arakiel said. "One of their greatest warriors. He taunted the children of Israel with his booming voice, bellowed at them to choose a champion to fight him in front of the other soldiers. Saul's entire army trembled in fear of this man... except for David. He—"

"Take us there," the Master said. "Now."

Before I could fully process what He-Who-Rules was saying, Arakiel shifted. Zephar and the Master followed, and I did so more by reflex than active will or I might have waited too long and lost the trail.

Arakiel's shift brought us to a valley at daytime; the sun was high and the sky cloudless. Saul and his army were lined up on a mountain on one side of the valley, and what I presumed was the Philistine army was lined up on a mountain on the other. In the valley itself, two fallen faced each other at a distance, and they seemed like a pairing of perfect opposites.

Goliath was a soldier, or even two soldiers. He filled the air with his presence. He was tall—Goliath would've towered over even Saul— and every part of him was covered in armor, from helmet to chainmail to the coverings on his legs. As heavy as all of that metal must have been, Goliath didn't seem to feel its weight at all, and he carried his large spear and sword as if they also didn't weigh enough for him to take notice.

Opposite him was David. A boy, I remember thinking, a mere child—without armor or shield or even weapon that I could see, except for a shepherd's staff and a sling.

This is suicide, I thought, and wondered why Saul was letting him do it. The Philistines watched with as much rapt attention as did the Israelite army. It was as if a mouse had decided to fight an elephant, and everyone was so mesmerized by the audacity of the little creature that they stared with held breath, though the outcome couldn't be anything but the mouse's quick and pathetic demise under the trampling foot of the elephant.

"This boy will be killed," I said, as Goliath yelled insults at the child who presumed to challenge him with nothing more than a staff and some stones. But what amazed me is that even though the army of Saul still looked terrified, David didn't. *He believes the Enemy will save him*, I realized as I listened to his squeaks in response to the rumbles of Goliath. *He believes the Enemy will protect him from this monster.*

"The Lord does not save with sword and spear," David yelled, and as Goliath rushed at him, he pulled out a stone from his small shepherd's bag, loaded his sling, and shot.

Goliath dropped, more like a tree toppling over than a dazed elephant stumbling to the ground. It took me a moment to realize he was dead—only when I saw his spirit rise.

David ran over to the gigantic body, picked up the sword Goliath had dropped, and severed his head. At the sight, the terror that had choked Saul's army like a fog lifted from them and settled on the Philistines. They fled, and Saul's army, cheering and yelling, gave chase.

The spirit of Goliath watched his once-glorious body, dead and headless, with a look of calculation and confusion on his face, seemingly more interested in figuring out how a mere boy had defeated him than in feeling horror at his own demise.

"Come here," the Master said.

Goliath looked up. "Who are you?" he yelled, the confusion gone from his features. He sized up He-Who-Rules, as if he thought to rush him next.

"I am the king of a great kingdom," the Master said. "And I seek a great warrior."

As Goliath approached, the Master told Zephar to show him the way to Sheol. When they were gone, He-Who-Rules turned to me. "David is the One. Do you doubt that?"

"No," I said, and I didn't. Gideon's faith in the Enemy had impressed me, but remarkable as it was, Gideon was a soldier and he had his fellow soldiers around him. David's faith gave him strength and courage as he stood alone, facing a warrior who towered over him in height and strength and experience. "What do you want us to do?"

"Turn him away from the Enemy," the Master said, and though he spoke with confidence, he couldn't hide the fear he felt. "You and Zephar did it with Saul, now do it with David. When he has renounced his faith and has steeped himself in every sin, kill him."

"You'll return to Sheol?" I said, although I thought I knew the answer.

"In a while," he said.

"You're staying here?" I said. "What about David?"

The Master's glow flared in anger.

I said quickly, "I just meant you should be in Sheol where you'll be protected. It isn't safe here."

"I go where I please, Enoch. As for protection, don't forget that I have almost as many angels on Earth as I do in Sheol."

Zephar returned and the Master repeated his instructions concerning David to him before leaving us.

Our plan was to have Zephar work on Saul while I focused on David. But it turned out that Saul didn't need any work at all. The children of Israel loved David, and his popularity as a warrior far surpassed Saul's. In the hope that David would meet his death in war, Saul made him a captain in his army. The plan worked against him; David turned out to be a great leader and he and his men met success in every battle against the mighty Philistines. David's popularity grew—and with it, so did Saul's hatred and jealousy of him.

Zephar and I were just as annoyed with David. He was fighting for his life and for the lives of his men, and relying entirely on the Enemy... in such a situation, for such a person, there is little we can do.

Our frustration was reaching such a high point, no doubt fueled by fears of what the Enemy had planned for him, that when David picked up his harp to play for Saul one night, Zephar screamed at Saul to strike him with his spear. David escaped with his life, but by that point Saul became completely obsessed with taking it.

David went to the prophet Samuel for protection, and Zephar was only too happy to have me shadow them while he stayed with Saul. Samuel spent the time with David telling him stories from the history of their people. Much of what they talked about was already familiar to me, but Samuel said some things that I hadn't known, and from among those, two stories had a particular impact. The first terrified me, and forced the realization on me that our situation was more dire than we'd ever thought; but the second comforted me, and reinforced in my mind the path to victory.

The story that frightened me was about Samuel himself, or about his mother, a barren woman named Hannah who had begged the Enemy for a child. When He sent her Samuel, her heart was so full of praise that she sang a prayer to Him.

I'm convinced that the Master has read the sacred books of the Circumcised Ones, perhaps many times over, but I don't think he's ever understood the significance of these words Samuel wrote down in his records. "The Lord kills, and He makes alive," Hannah said in her song. "He brings down to Sheol, and He raises up."

Alone in a tent with the prophet that none of the dark angels liked to be around, and with the future king that I thought might be the One, those words struck me like lightning. The Master's focus was always to bring death to the fallen, to rip their spirits from their bodies. He doesn't understand physicality; and because he doesn't understand it, he fears it; and because he fears it, he wants to destroy it. He believes he can handle any spirit in the spiritual world; it's embodied spirits in a physical world that make him uncomfortable. For that reason, he only fears the fallen while they're still wrapped in matter. Not thinking to question that fundamental assumption of the Master's, I also stopped worrying about a fallen as soon as they were dead. But hearing Samuel quote his mother's words, a thousand thoughts and fears came rushing at me, all centered on the question that had never occurred to me or anyone else as far as I knew: What if the Enemy's plan was for the One to engage in battle with us not in a physical body, but in the spirit?

We weren't safe in Sheol, I started to realize. Too many fallen were aware of its existence even while they were alive, though they called it by different names and some of their descriptions were more accurate than others. Spirits were able to find Sheol all by themselves; it had always been funny to us that they didn't need to be dragged here but showed up of their own accord, drawn to it as if the cries of anguish and torment were some sort of siren song. But at that moment I stopped thinking it was funny. *If they can find us*, I thought, *why couldn't the One?*

In my panic, I almost shifted away immediately to tell the Master what I had learned. But not sure where to find him and afraid he might ask what else these two fallen said, I stayed and soon I heard the second story, the one that comforted me.

This story was about a battle with the Philistines where thousands of the Circumcised Ones died, at which point the children of Israel decided to bring the Ark of the Covenant to the battleground. With the Enemy going into battle with them, how could they lose? Although the presence of the Ark buoyed the spirits of the Israelites, and terrified the Philistines who had heard stories of what this God had done to the Egyptians, the children of Israel still lost, and this time not thousands but tens of thousands died at the hands of the Philistines.

Though there was more to the story, that was all I needed to hear to develop a conviction I hold to this day: as long as the fallen are kept from the true worship of the Enemy, as long as they try to control Him as we let them believe they control us and the gods of their imaginations, victory will be ours. That conviction inspired confidence and I vowed, as I listened to Samuel and David speak long into the night, never to fear a fallen ever again, but to focus my energy on turning them away from the Enemy.

Although I was offered plenty of opportunity for this with David, he rejected every temptation I whispered into his heart. It was so frustrating that I almost despaired of ever causing him to commit even a single act of evil.

More than once, David had the chance to kill Saul, to eliminate the man who was hunting him from city to city and into deserts. But David refused to strike against the Anointed One of the Enemy. I don't know how much Zephar had to do with it, but Saul's repentance, born from knowing David had spared his life, was quickly choked each time by his burning desire and obsession with ending David's.

"I don't understand this kind of fallen," I told Zephar the next time we met. "One moment, Pharaoh falls to his knees and says he's seen how wrong he's been; the next, he's defying Moses and his God. One moment Saul declares himself a sinner and says he repents of ever having wanted to harm David; the next, he's making plans to take his life."

"It's not a mystery," Zephar said. "They're like chariots that can't travel in a straight path, like the chariots of Pharaoh when he tried to follow Moses into the Red Sea. They're broken. The Master broke them."

"Speaking of whom, do you have any news?"

"He's back in Sheol, according to Arakiel."

"That's good," I said, but wasn't sure why I preferred to have He-Who-Rules on his throne in Sheol than roaming the Earth.

A while later, after Samuel had died and escaped the grasp of all of my angels, I found myself bored by David and anxious to tell He-Who-Rules what I had learned from Samuel about the words his mother had spoken. I shifted to Sheol and was surprised to find Zephar in the throne room, speaking to the Master.

I approached. "What's going on?"

"Saul is dead!" Zephar said. "He was struck in battle, and killed himself with his own sword rather than die by the hand of a Philistine."

"Is he here?" I said.

The Master nodded, but I noticed that a suspicious tinge had entered his glow when I arrived.

"There's more," Zephar said. "He consulted a witch. Can you believe that? This is the man who outlawed divination, the man who exiled witches and wizards."

"What did he want from her?"

"He wanted to raise Samuel's ghost," Zephar said. "He could no longer hear the Enemy's voice, and as the Philistines pressed in on him, he decided he needed some comfort from Samuel, even if he had to force it out of him."

"What happened?"

Zephar glowed with delight. "I appeared to the witch as Samuel," he said. "Scared the stupid thing half to death."

"You comforted Saul?"

"Not exactly," Zephar said, his glow intensifying. "In fact, if not for what I told him, he might still be alive."

"Zephar says your angels weren't able to capture Samuel's spirit," He-Who-Rules said.

Is that what you're upset about? I thought. "I've had to be away from my work," I said. "First because of Saul and now because of David."

"Zephar can take care of David," the Master said. He turned to face him completely. "You have done great things, Zephar; can I offer more points to one who is so far in front of the others? Bring me David as you have brought me Saul, and you will be glorified by all the angels; you will be second only to me."

Zephar snuck one look at me before he shifted away, perhaps to confirm in his own mind that I'd heard the Master's words.

"We may not want to kill David," I said.

He-Who-Rules laughed.

"I'm serious. The One may be more dangerous to us dead than alive. There's a prophecy, made by the mother of Samuel himself. Hannah said—"

"It doesn't matter what Hannah said!" I was taken aback by how angry the Master sounded. "The fallen belong to me once they're dead. Don't you understand, Enoch? I brought sin into the world, planted it like a seed; death grew, and the fruits of death are rightly mine."

I didn't argue. I wanted to, for my own safety as well as his, but I knew the Master wouldn't listen to me in his current state. "If there's nothing else, I'll return to my work on the enchantments."

"No," He-Who-Rules said. "You will stay here in Sheol. I have projects for you. Abaddon will continue to oversee the enchantments."

He gave me the projects one at a time—the first was to build more prison cells, thousands and hundreds of thousands, extending all along the lake of fire into parts of Sheol I'd never even visited. Did it ever occur to me that the Master was making me build everything he thought he'd need in the future because he was planning on doing away with me? I'd like to say that it did occur to me, and in consequence I decided to take as much time as possible with the projects, without making it look like I was purposely delaying them. The truth was that if I ever did think along those lines, I told myself that the Master had no reason to want me out of the way. I convinced myself that he was simply disappointed that despite the many successes of the enchantments, we had still let too many fallen pass through to what we assumed was the High Country. Any delay in the construction projects was because I felt that other avenues were more worthy of pursuit, even if the Master couldn't see it yet.

After receiving the first commission from He-Who-Rules, but before beginning the construction of his new cells, I decided to seek out Saul. Along the way, it occurred to me that here again the firstborn, so worthy of honor according to the Enemy and the Circumcised Ones, was being pushed aside. Saul was the first king of Israel, but already the Enemy had promised that the kingdom would be taken from Saul and given to one who was more worthy of it.

I almost didn't recognize him when I finally found Saul. Gone was the gaunt figure, half-starved from lack of sleep as much as from lack of food. Here was Saul in his prime, strong and muscular, hair straight and bright—he looked the way he'd been when Samuel poured the oil of anointment on his head. But as I approached, I saw that the haunted eyes belonged to a Saul from much later in his life, the Saul obsessed with killing David.

"Come, King of Israel," I said.

He approached, hunched over because the cell wasn't big enough for his tall body. "You!" he said, gripping the bars of his cell door. "Haven't you tormented me enough? Leave me alone!"

"That was another angel," I said, which was at least half-true. "I'm here to comfort you."

His grip on the bars relaxed and his eyes opened wide for a moment. "You're letting me go?"

"I came to tell you that the angel who led you here has set his sights on David."

Saul paused, cocked his head to one side, then seemed to understand what I was saying and he laughed. "You think you caused me to come to this place?" Again he threw back his head and laughed. "Don't credit yourself with this, devil. You led me here, but I followed. You whispered, but I listened. And the more I listened, the more deafening your whispers became—I know that now, and I knew it when I was alive. You couldn't put anything in my heart that wasn't there already; you encouraged me to cultivate the evil inside of me, and neglect the good, but don't think you brought anything new to me or forced my thoughts in a direction I didn't want them to go."

"Don't credit myself?" I said. "We brought death into the world, King of Israel. We steal spirits from under your Lord's nose; we make His work rot; we destroy where He creates. The majority of men and women would rather follow us into this place of torment than follow their Creator into a place of peace and joy. They would rather listen to us whispering than to the Lord yelling."

"Not David," Saul said, turning around and walking away from the door. "His heart is pure."

"You seem pretty sure of yourself."

"Dying brings a lot of clarity to one's thinking."

"And what clarity has it brought you for why your God rejected you, King? What did you do to deserve that?"

I turned at a loud sound, and saw a pack of dark angels approaching. When they were close, they told me that the honor of Saul's presence was being requested by Goliath. I didn't know it then, but I was witnessing the birth of the battle games, for which one of my final projects before being thrown into this dungeon was to build the battleground above the pit. Before my imprisonment, the games had evolved into epic battles where hundreds of thousands of fallen were sent to fight one another, most not even knowing which side they were fighting for, but riled up to such a point that they thought their very existence hinged on ripping apart the others limb by limb. At times I think I can still hear the cries of battle, so different from the moans of loneliness and imprisonment I'd grown used to. These were cries of pain and anguish and torment, as if the limbs they were tearing off each other were real, physical ones and not phantom limbs that would pop back into existence as soon as they forgot what had happened to them.

But before all that, the dark angels were content to watch different fallen try to gain the upper hand on Goliath, and now Goliath wanted Saul.

"What did Moses do," Saul said, as they dragged him out of his cell, "when he struck the rock the Lord asked him to speak to?"

I followed and watched the fighting for a while, amazed that even outside of their bodies the fallen still thought of themselves as embodied creatures, still tried to express themselves in physical space, still imagined they had real arms and real legs and real bodies that could feel pain. It wasn't the first time that I thought the Enemy had made a mistake when He created them both matter and spirit, because I saw that they couldn't think of themselves as anything else, even when the matter was ripped away from them.

Before long I grew bored of watching Goliath's battles. I returned to Satri and gave him the list of dark angels and the number of fallen I needed to help me build the new cells. At that time I learned that the crown had not come easily for David; at first only the House of Judah would recognize his kingship.

"But now," Satri said, "after all these years, every tribe has sworn allegiance to him. He's succeeded in uniting the kingdoms of Judah in the south and Israel in the north. As if that weren't enough, he was able to conquer the mighty fortress called Zion, and around it he builds the city of Jerusalem. I'm told the Circumcised Ones have already taken to calling it the City of David."

"And Zephar?"

"Has not been able to move him at all."

Although I tried to concentrate on building the Master's new cells, I made frequent trips to Satri to find out what was happening with David. For a long time, I wondered why I still made the effort, since each one was such a disappointment. In trip after trip, I learned that David's popularity had grown, despite consoling myself each time with the thought that at least he couldn't become more well-liked or honored. I learned that he'd expanded his kingdom ever more and was bringing peace to Israel by defeating the Philistines and all of its other enemies. My hope was that Zephar could use these successes, or at least the power David commanded, to lead him away from the Enemy. But according to Satri, David gave the credit of his victories to the Enemy; his trust in Him never swayed; and he delighted so much in His presence that when he brought the Ark of the Covenant to Jerusalem, he'd actually danced in front of the Enemy, as if he were a child or a common performer instead of the king of Israel.

It was during this time that I figured out Saul's riddle. Moses disobeyed the Enemy's instructions and struck the rock, and because of that was not found worthy to lead the people into Canaan. Moses, whom the Enemy had chosen and set apart from the rest of the fallen. Moses, whose face shone with the light from the High Country for a time. Moses, to whom much was given, and from whom much was required in return.

This is why the Enemy abandoned us, I realized. *We lived with Him in the High Country; we knew exactly what we were turning our backs on; we should have known better.*

The thought infuriated me. I'd called Him the Enemy because that's what the Master called Him; but from that moment on, I believed it fully. He had abandoned us, and I decided to abandon any hope in Him that I had left. He had closed the door to the High Country to us, and I decided that I never wanted to go back there. I decided that I'd be an enemy to the Enemy.

First, though, there was David to deal with. My rage took my lingering fear that David was the One and transformed it into mere suspicion. After giving a few more instructions to the dark angels working on the construction of the cells, I shifted to Earth, found Zephar, and told him I was there to help him defeat David. I think I did so with so much intensity and forcefulness that Zephar didn't argue, but shared with me everything he knew about David and his weaknesses. We weren't completely unsuccessful in moving David, but for years we made little significant, satisfying progress—and then he did by himself much more than we'd ever been able to get him to do.

Her name was Bathsheba, and she was the wife of Uriah, a soldier in David's army. One evening, David had gone to his roof for a quiet walk. As Zephar and I discussed what other strategy we could try, we noticed that a sudden concentration had seized him. We followed his gaze to a woman bathing on her own roof.

"Lust has entered his heart," Zephar said with delight. "You can see it in his eyes. This is how we'll defeat him."

"Wait," I said, and held Zephar back.

Remembering what Saul had said, I decided that we wouldn't do anything to David. I would later wonder if David would have recoiled from the idea if we'd tried to whisper into his ear that he should seduce Bathsheba. Would he have recognized the thought for what it was if we'd tried to force it on him?

Over the next few days, it was obvious that he was distracted. His men were waging a war, but not only was the king not there to lead them physically, his mind wasn't even on the battles. He returned to the roof a few times, and one night he finally sent his servants to bring him Bathsheba.

"This is only the beginning," I said to Zephar. We'd both seen it with plenty of fallen. Sin's greatest quality in general is that it takes the fallen further away from the Enemy; but the greatest quality of any particular sin is its reproductiveness. One sin leads to another which leads to two more; that is why no sinful thought or act, no matter how small it may seem, is without significance or importance.

Perhaps bored or worried that we weren't capitalizing on this rare sin of David's, Zephar wanted to act, but I told him to be patient and we waited. Soon Bathsheba sent word that she was pregnant, and in his panic that his transgression would be uncovered, David wrote to Joab, the commander of his army, and told him to send Uriah back to Jerusalem.

Under the pretense that he wanted to find out how the war was going, David spoke briefly with Uriah, then dismissed him. But Uriah slept in the king's home, with the servants, refusing to go back to his house, to his bed, to his beautiful wife.

David was furious when he heard this, but Uriah said, "How can I go back to my house when Joab and my fellow soldiers are still at war and don't get to sleep in their own beds or with their wives?"

Resolved to carry out his plan, that night David threw a party for Uriah and filled him with drink. But drunk as he was, Uriah refused to go back to his house.

"Uriah has to die," Zephar whispered into David's ear, and I didn't try to stop him because I could almost see the calculations already taking place in David's mind, the strategy he was forming. "There is no other way."

David sent Uriah back to Joab; and as if what he planned wasn't cruel and treacherous enough, he wrote down his instructions and sent the letter by Uriah's own hand. The king instructed Joab to put Uriah at the front of the battle, then retreat from him.

The strategy worked; his fellow soldiers, the ones he cared so much about that he refused to enjoy his wife if they couldn't enjoy theirs, fell away from him and the enemy soldiers fell on him.

Bathsheba mourned for her husband when she heard of his death, but soon she had a new husband, the father of her unborn child.

"First adultery, then murder," I said to Zephar. "Can you imagine what the Enemy will do to this king of His?"

Once again, though, the Enemy showed his fundamental unfairness. A prophet visited David and told him about a rich man with a large flock and a poor man with a single lamb, which he loved. When a traveler came to visit the rich man, he didn't want to take from his own possessions to feed the visitor, so he stole the only lamb of the poor man. As David became indignant at the rich man's injustice and lack of feeling, the prophet told David that he was indignant with himself.

David's confession was full and sincere, but so what? His life would never be the same, and his kingdom would be attacked by enemies from without and torn by civil war; Bathsheba's child would die before the week was out, but so what? How is that fit punishment for adultery and murder? The Enemy should have turned His back on David, cast him off as the failure he was—but He didn't. And if the Enemy was capricious and unfair, David's sense of justice and fairness was equally broken: even on the very day his child died, he worshiped the Enemy.

I could hardly stand to be around him anymore. Since it was obvious by now that we posed more of a threat to David than he could ever pose to us, I returned to Sheol to supervise construction. From time to time, I visited Earth to see how well the enchantments were working. Abaddon and everyone else seemed pleased with the spirits we were capturing, but I wasn't: too many fallen were still escaping our clutches.

One day I told Zephar to send word when David was nearing death, but I didn't tell him why. I'd decided that I would follow his spirit without anyone knowing, see the enchantments from his point of view, determine where we could improve our strategy to capture more of these fallen who still loved the Enemy at the end of their lives.

Of course I wasn't successful, not in capturing David anyway. But by following his spirit and the angels of light, I uncovered perhaps the greatest discovery of all, certainly the one that filled me with unending delight. I discovered where the angels of the Enemy were taking the spirits of the fallen, and it wasn't to the High Country.

Chapter Eleven

A Master Builder

O F the many disappointments I felt after the discovery that filled me with so much joy, the first was that I'd completely missed the building of the Temple; and the second was that I never met Solomon, who seemed to love making structures as much as he loved making sayings. I suppose I was glad to have skipped the fear that Solomon was the One, and especially to have missed the panic over what this house for the Enemy signified, but even still I would've liked to watch Solomon go about constructing it and his other great buildings. In particular, I would've liked to see the Temple before it was spoiled by the presence of the Enemy.

The son of David and Bathsheba, Solomon's wealth was exceeded only by his wisdom, but even his wisdom was dwarfed by his lust. At the time, I took Zephar at his word and felt grateful to him, but now I wonder how much he really had to do with turning this fallen away from the Enemy, and how much of it was actually due to Solomon's wish to appease his many wives by honoring their many gods. This suspicion isn't centered on Zephar, of course—I wonder how much real effect any of us has ever had on the fallen. I wonder if left to their own thoughts, and fears, and desires, would they do everything we try to encourage them to do anyway? Maybe the most we've done is get them to certain places sooner than they would have gotten on their own, and maybe we push them a little past the point where they would have otherwise stopped. But is that enough? Is that a sufficient reward for all of our effort—is it sufficient justification for our existence? These dark and hopeless thoughts were furthest from my mind after my discovery. I walked into the throne room and strode up to the Master, pushing aside the dark angel who stood there babbling and cutting him off mid-sentence.

"Master," I said, speaking loudly. "You once discovered the home of these fallen while they are in their bodies, a discovery that opened up endless possibilities for fun and destruction. If that was the greatest discovery, today I have made the second greatest."

"Oh?" the Master said, and in my mind's eye I see a suspicious glow on him; at the time, I was so carried away by excitement and self-satisfaction that I wasn't paying any real attention to him or anyone else, except to note and revel in the increasing amount of attention they were giving me.

"I've discovered the final home of the first fallen, Adam and Eve; the home of Abraham, Isaac, and Jacob; the home of Joseph, Moses, and David."

"What do you mean?" the Master said, as complete silence descended on the throne room. "What is this madness, Enoch? You've been to the High Country?"

"No, I haven't been to the High Country," I said, unable to contain my mirth. "But I've been to Sheol."

"Enoch—" the Master said, and finally I registered his annoyance, which tempered my exuberance.

"Forgive me," I said. "I'm very excited about what I've found out. But let me tell it from the beginning."

No one can argue that the enchantments are a great success (I began), but even so I wasn't satisfied with them, and knew that I wouldn't be satisfied until the likes of Samuel and David were here in Sheol. It occurred to me that the best way to find the flaws in our strategy was to experience things from the fallen's point of view.

When David died, I forced myself to see the angels that came to guide him—to the High Country, I thought. I followed them and watched as the Enemy's angels defended David against the charges we brought against him. Although I learned a lot through this experiment—we should organize ourselves in the dimensions according to the type of accusation or temptation, for example, to avoid useless duplication that only strengthens the enemy position—I now believe we can do away with the enchantments altogether. Still, despite everything I'd already learned, I refused to give up. Soon we were past the highest dimension where we have angels posted, but I pushed myself to keep following. Soon the light from the High Country was unbearable, but I forced myself forward. What did I expect to find? And what did I think would happen when I reached the dimensions near the High Country?

If I'd spent any time at all thinking about those questions, I would have stopped and turned back immediately. But I set every worry and concern aside and concentrated all of my energy on following David and his guarding angels. Even so, at one point the light from the High Country became blinding, and I lost them. I backtracked a shift to see if I could pick up their trail again, and realized something: I was a single dimension away from Sheol.

The thought was so stunning that I was sure I was wrong. But I shifted to Sheol and back, now wondering if I'd somehow made a bigger shift than I'd intended when I backtracked. Confused and with a thousand thoughts racing through my mind, I shifted once more to Sheol, determined to find them.

Standing along the lake of fire, on ground even my construction crews haven't yet reached, I steeled myself for what I had to do. I warped my mind, forced it to remember our days in the High Country, twisted and twisted until I thought I couldn't bear it—and then I saw something, just for a moment, just a flash.

A garden, and I saw it as if in a trick mirror. Whereas here there is a lake of fire, there they have a lake of water as blue as the clearest sky, the likes of which the Earth has never seen. Whereas here there is only gray stone, there the grass is green and thick, unlike any field the Earth has ever known. Here there is only darkness, but there the dim light from a hidden moon casts a bluish glow on the trees and the birds and—yes—the fallen. Even in that initial glimpse, I saw them—some walking around, talking; some lying on the grass, napping; some eating; some swimming. I took it in all at once, and studied the image in my mind's eye, not sure what I had seen.

Once I'd rested from the experience, I forced my mind to see the garden again, forced myself to think about the High Country in a way none of us has ever tried and to such an extent that I felt my very existence hung in jeopardy.

I saw it again, and tried to hold the sight in front of me. *What is this place?* I thought. *Where is this place? Is this where they took—*

"David, King of Israel!" I called. The image shifted and there he was. He stared back at me expectantly.

"You can see me?" I said. Before he could answer what seemed obvious, I added, "Where are you?"

"At peace," he said.

Without thought, I tried to shift toward him, to grab him and bring him back here, but no sooner had I decided to do that than I lost the image; the garden and its shimmering blue lake were gone.

My initial disappointment faded at the realization of what I'd seen and what it meant. We've worked so hard to enchant the fallen away from the Enemy, rightly feeling that they don't deserve to live in the High Country. But don't you see? They don't go there after all—and of course that seems obvious now, doesn't it? Wouldn't these feeble ghosts be burned away by the presence of the Enemy? If we who once lived there can no longer return, how could these broken creatures enter such a place? If our minds risk destruction when we force them to simply think of the High Country, and our sight is blinded by the merest hint of its light, who will lead the fallen there?

As I neared the end of my speech, I noticed that the Master, though deeply interested in what I was saying, regarded me with a surprising amount of suspicion and anger.

Believing I knew what was at the root of those feelings, I said to the angels in the throne room, "Some of you might be thinking, 'It's good that they're not in the High Country—but they don't deserve to be even in this garden.' I agree, and that is why I'm proposing that we have another chance at these fallen. If they were being carried off to the High Country, there would be no way to go after them. But they're being taken to a place right here in Sheol. If we can't turn them while they're in their bodies, and we can't enchant them away when they die, what's to stop us from capturing them afterward?" I took some steps forward and spoke so only the Master could hear me. "What's to stop us from launching a third war?"

The exhilaration I felt from the other dark angels was completely absent from the Master. As they started picking up on that fact as well, their own excitement began to fade.

"Enoch, I asked you to build me cells, not to go chasing after dead fallen."

Confused and growing a little angry myself, I said, "Construction is progressing, Master; my work is done for now. I grew tired of standing around with nothing to do but supervise." After a pause, I said, "I don't understand—you're not happy with this discovery? Didn't you say the spirits of these fallen belong to you? The Enemy has been stealing from you, but now you have a chance to get them all back."

"If the construction of the new cells isn't demanding your full attention," the Master said, "you can start repairing this building. The Enemy has a new Temple, should I be content with an old palace?"

"A Temple?" I said. "Solomon actually built it?"

He nodded, then looked past me, his way of signaling that he was moving on to other business.

Curious to see Solomon's Temple, I left the throne room and shifted to Earth. It annoyed me how much of his life David spent preparing for this one building he'd never see. Not only had he drawn up the plans for it, not only had he stored up for it gold and silver and bronze and marble and wood and all kinds of other things, but he'd waged wars with all of Israel's enemies to allow his son an uninterrupted peace during which to build the Temple.

Solomon erected it on Mount Moriah, the place where Abraham had taken Isaac to sacrifice him, the place where I'd escaped when I needed to hide from the Master, the place where I'd first seen Joseph and heard him pour out his fears to the Enemy. Later Zephar would tell me that this was also the place where Jacob had his vision of the ladder that united the High Country and the Earth, a fact which only further stoked the fears of the Master and the dark angels during the Temple's construction about what would happen when the building was completed.

My first sight of the Temple astounded me, and the more time I spent studying its walls and floors and ceilings and beams and chambers, the more appreciation I had for how much care went into its design and construction. For three years, I learned later, Solomon had prepared the wood and stone he'd need for the Temple, but as I wandered its halls in wonder, I couldn't imagine it taking less than thirty or even three hundred years.

Despite the presence of the Enemy which suffused the Temple like a suffocating fog, I might have stayed there until its destruction, admiring its architecture and dazzled by the shining gold that seemed to overlay everything. I might have been there until Nebuchadnezzar leveled it to the ground, staring perhaps until the last one was destroyed at the golden statues of the cherubim, which held me transfixed for long periods of time—except that Zephar found me not long after I arrived.

"I knew you'd come here," he said. "I tried to find you when they started construction, but you were already gone. Still—your trip was worth missing anything for, I'd say. Arakiel gave us news of your discovery."

We left the Temple so we could speak outside. Zephar told me about Solomon's reign and how he'd built the Temple and many other buildings. He told me how much the Master and others had been afraid that this son of David was the One, how they'd never encountered a fallen before who had his insight or clearness of mind. Despite everyone's fears, Zephar said, he worked on Solomon, encouraging his lust for women and for power, and through such effort managed to turn him away from the Enemy. At his death, Israel split back in half again, with Solomon's son ruling over only two tribes in the south.

"The Enemy told David that his kingdom would stand forever," Zephar said. "But look at the situation now—his kingdom has been shattered, and his grandson rules from a diminished throne over the smaller of the two fragments! The greater part of the Circumcised Ones have rebelled against the House of David and against the Enemy!"

"But he has the Temple in his kingdom," I said.

"So what?" Zephar said. "We spent so much time worrying about this building. But Solomon said it himself—is the Enemy going to come down and live on Earth, like some fallen? Of course not—this is just a building, at best a place where the fallen can go to feel the presence of their God for a little while."

I was comforted by Zephar's words and especially by his confidence, but the feeling didn't last long.

Recognizing that the Master wasn't as thrilled with my unauthorized expedition and discovery as I'd expected, to all appearances I became completely occupied with the tasks he'd set before me, supervising the construction of the new cells and designing repairs and extensions to his palace. Most of my energy, however, was devoted to the question of the third war: how to attack a garden that I wasn't sure we could even shift to, setting aside the problem that it could only be seen by those who would fill their minds with thoughts of the High Country to an extent I was sure no other dark angel would be willing to do.

Afraid of being distracted, I stopped myself from falling back into the habit of visiting Satri for news from Earth. But sooner than I would've liked, news from Earth visited me as all of Sheol buzzed with the whispers that Zephar had found the One. I tried to ignore them, but the stories were so amazing and contradictory—even over as simple a fact as the fallen's name—and grew more amazing and contradictory over time, that I could no longer rein in my curiosity or fear. Some said he was a prophet named Elijah, who could command animals to do his bidding and raise fallen from the dead, and who couldn't be killed himself. Others claimed that the prophet's name was Elisha, that he'd defeated hundreds of Baal's servants, and that his bones could bring dead fallen back to life. The image of this monster with two names, who could bring life back to dead fallen with his dead bones—even though he might not have died and maybe could not be killed—was so confusing that it was terrifying, and so terrifying that I finally ordered Arakiel to take me to Zephar. We found him in Samaria in the northern kingdom, and his glow was not primarily scared or panicked but wary and brooding.

"What's going on?" I said.

"I'm not sure," he said. "It's possible the danger has passed. But it's also possible that we've finally found the One and the danger is greater than it ever has been."

"Tell me everything," I said. "Start at the beginning."

"What's the beginning?" he said. "How much do you know?"

"Tell me about Elijah—or is it Elisha?"

IT's both (Zephar began).

From the moment I saw Elijah, I knew there was something strange and wrong about this fallen, even by the standard of most of the Enemy's prophets.

Never with the kings and queens of the Circumcised Ones did we have as much success as we were having with Ahab and Jezebel. But into their great palace walks this fallen from the wilderness—with long unkempt hair and wearing nothing but the skin of an animal and a leather belt—who starts urging them to return to the Enemy. The audacity of this unbidden guest astonished me almost as much as his courage. *At least Moses was the adopted son of Pharaoh's daughter,* I thought; *who is this Elijah? Who gave him the authority to dare to speak to the king and queen of Israel like this?* As if that measure of impudence wasn't enough, he told them that the land would suffer a great drought until he himself ordered the rain to fall again.

Like I said, I knew there was something strange about him. At first I thought he was simply crazy; but the drought came as he said it would, so I sent Agares to find him. Agares is imperturbable, or so I thought; but even he looked frightened when he returned.

"You've found Elijah?" I said.

"Living in poverty with a widow and her children," Agares said.

"Her son died; his spirit left his body. Elijah stretched out his hands to either side and placed himself on the child—once, twice, a third time. The spirit returned to the body; the child cried out."

Afraid of a confrontation between Ahab and Elijah until I understood the prophet better, I tried to persuade Ahab to forget about him. But he blamed the drought and famine on this upstart prophet who had dared to threaten the king in his own palace. Ahab sent his servants throughout the lands, destroying entire villages and cities in his efforts to find Elijah.

Finally Elijah found Ahab.

"Don't listen," I told him when Elijah asked Ahab to gather all of Israel on Mount Caramel.

"Stop listening!" I said, when Elijah by himself challenged hundreds of Ahab's prophets, pitting his God against their gods and the chief of their gods. "Ignore him!" I said, but Ahab's pride proved bigger than his sense and he chose to ignore me instead.

You won't be surprised to hear that Elijah put to shame Ahab and the almost five hundred prophets of Baal, just like Moses shamed us when Pharaoh asked for a sign from his God.

We were disappointed, of course—and yet our disappointment was superficial and tinged with relief: was this all that Elijah, and the Enemy through him, planned to do? His theatrics had turned the people and even Ahab back to the Enemy—so what? We could turn them away again. He had executed the servants of Baal—so what? There were plenty of other fallen to take their place. He had spoken of a coming drought, and it came; he signaled the end of the drought, and it ended—but all of that was temporal and earthly and had little to do with us.

Although Baal couldn't have cared less about the death of his prophets—especially once he realized he'd be able to fill in their ranks again quickly—Jezebel was a different story: in her zeal to serve him, she wanted to avenge the death of Baal's prophets with Elijah's blood.

When he ran for his life, we were content to let Elijah disappear back into the wilderness where he seemed so comfortable, not bothering to worry about this fallen since his greatest show of power didn't have a single lasting consequence for us.

The next time we saw him, Elijah had a disciple. The young man watched everything his master did and listened to every word his master spoke, and seemed oblivious to everything and everyone else.

A short while before they appeared, the king had wanted another man's vineyard to use as his personal garden, but the owner, Naboth, wouldn't sell it. This depressed Ahab, and for fun I decided to use the same trick that we'd used on David. But I knew Ahab didn't have the strength of character to go through with it, so I whispered the idea into Jezebel's ears: *in the king's name, write a letter to the important people of Naboth's city, get them to accuse him of something deserving of death, and execute him accordingly.*

Once Naboth was dead, we went down to take possession of the vineyard, only to find Elijah and his new companion waiting for us. The encounter had an unfortunately profound effect on Ahab—and on me. Elijah spoke with a confidence I couldn't yet understand. *He should still be in hiding*, I thought. Instead, he denounced both Ahab and his wife, speaking to them as if he were a judge condemning the worst of criminals and not what in reality he was, a death-sentenced prophet of a God hardly anyone believed in, speaking to the king and queen of Israel.

Having missed this encounter, Agares didn't have a problem with following Elijah when I asked him to, although I suspect he thought it wasn't worth his time. For a while, he was right; the news wasn't very interesting. Then, one day, the news was unbelievable.

"What's wrong?" I said, when I saw his glow.

"Shifted!" he said. "Elijah's shifted!"

"What? To where?" I said, even though I know, and knew, that the fallen can't shift.

Agares didn't know to where, but we went immediately to the river Jordan, where this was supposed to have happened. There we saw Elisha, the disciple of Elijah we'd first seen in the vineyard, and we heard him say that his master had been taken to the High Country.

"He may be lying," I said to Agares, whose glow had grown a sickeningly cowardly color. "Or he may be crazy. Stay with Elisha and let me know if you learn anything else."

"Where are you going?"

"I need to tell the Master what's happened," I said. "And we need to find Elijah."

The Master didn't need any convincing; he ordered Abaddon and his angels to search for Elijah throughout the dimensions leading to the High Country while I coordinated a search throughout Earth.

I'd kept Agares with Elisha to learn what we could about Elijah's whereabouts, but Elisha was proving to be a problem all his own. As if the pressure to find his master—preferably on Earth, but in the dimensions at least—wasn't enough, Agares came to see me often to tell me about the latest of Elisha's miracles. This fallen made oil multiply in vessels so that a widow on the brink of devastation could pay off her debts; in the midst of a famine, he made bread multiply in baskets so that the people wouldn't starve. He told an old woman who had been barren all her life that she would give birth to a son; and when that son died, he brought him back to life. By following his instructions to bathe in the Jordan, one man was healed of leprosy; at nothing more than his word, another man was cursed with it.

Worried as I was about Elijah, and what the Enemy planned to do with him, I was growing tired of our fruitless search for the disappearing prophet. But as I tried to convince the Master that our energy might best be spent elsewhere, Agares finally sent news that otherwise I would've welcomed: Elisha was dead.

"One less problem for you to worry about, then," He-Who-Rules said. "Now stop wasting time in Sheol. Find Elijah."

So we searched, and keep searching—it's the Master's will. But I think if Elijah could be found, we would've found him by now, a thought that actually provides me some measure of comfort. At first I wanted to prove that he hadn't escaped death or been taken to the High Country; now I'd be pleased if we never have to see him or worry about him ever again.

If the Enemy took him, He did so for a purpose. What happens if He decides to send him back?

ZEphar's story had a strange effect on me, especially some of his last words. *So we searched*, I repeated to myself, *and keep searching*.

"Elijah isn't the One," I said out loud. "I'm starting to think that maybe there isn't a One at all."

"Oh?" Zephar said, his glow bemused but also suspicious. "What makes you say that?"

"The fallen build a Temple and the Enemy fills it with His presence—but it doesn't mean anything, does it? Elijah is taken to the High Country, or wherever he was taken—but why does that matter? Don't you see the only effect any of it has ever had? I've been trying to figure out how to invade this garden where the Enemy is keeping the spirit of David and the others, but news of Elijah and Elisha interrupted me. What if everything, from Abraham to David, has had no other purpose but to distract us? What if the Enemy has kept us ineffectual by keeping us perpetually frightened?"

"To what end?" Zephar said.

My building sense of excitement started to deflate. *To what end indeed?*

"He has a plan," Zephar said. "He always has a plan."

"It sure doesn't look like a plan. He promises Abraham that he will be a blessing to all the fallen throughout the world, then the Enemy sets apart just one nation of his descendants. Why? He carefully instructs Moses on building the Ark and tells him specifically what to place inside: bread from the High Country, his brother's rod that budded with life, and the Enemy's Commandments. Why does it matter, though? He tells David that his kingdom will endure forever, but within two generations David's kingdom has been shattered."

"None of that is important," Zephar said. "The Enemy plans to send a fallen to destroy us. Finding that fallen and killing him is all that matters."

Worried that I'd spent too much time on Earth already, and trying to avoid incurring any more of the Master's displeasure or wrath, I returned to Sheol to begin working on the plans for rebuilding and extending his palace.

The door to my room was open.

"What are you doing in here?" I said, trying to keep my voice polite.

He-Who-Rules turned to face me. "I need you to build walls around Sheol. Tall, strong walls, closed off except for a single entrance near the palace. Do you understand?"

I didn't. "Are you worried that David will lead an army of the spirits of the righteous here? Because it didn't look to me—"

The Master's glow cut me off. "After you're done building the walls, restore my palace. Once that's done, come and see me—I have a special project for you." Then, with emphasis that was hardly necessary by that point, he said, "Until you're done your work here, Enoch, you're not to travel to Earth or anywhere else."

He didn't wait for my response before pushing past me and descending the stairs.

Deciding that this was a good time to demonstrate to He-Who-Rules that my obedience and loyalty could equal even Zephar's, I fo-

cused my energy on the walls the Master wanted. I built them as tall
as the tallest mountain in Sheol and as thick as the throne room's
walls. They encircled the palace and up to the furthest cell we'd built,
their boundaries curving back and extending right to the shores of
the lake of fire.

As soon as the final wall was in place, the Master issued a new
order: no angel could shift out of Sheol without passing through the
gates, and the only way in was to shift near the gates and be admitted
back in. I wonder how the dark angels have taken to this change; at
the very least, it's a limitation on a freedom they used to enjoy, and
most must see by now that the Master can keep track of their comings
and goings by way of the entrance guards.

Because the walls took so long to build, by the time they were
done a smaller team had already completed the work on the palace
and even the Master's special project.

"I want you to build a dungeon," he'd said. "Dig as deep as the
gates are tall, and make its walls just as thick."

This dungeon is a cell not for a fallen, I thought as soon as I had
a good picture of what the Master wanted, *but for an angel*. Did the
Master think of kidnapping an angel of light, I wondered, or was he
planning to imprison a dark angel?

Did it cross my mind that the prison was meant for me? I never
really thought myself that important. My leading theory was that
someone—Moloch, perhaps, or Belial—was becoming too popular among
the dark angels and the Master wanted him out of the way to spoil
any plans he might have of usurping the throne.

When the dungeon was ready, I took the Master down the stairs
and handed him the keys.

"This is excellent work, Enoch," he said as he shut the gate with
me inside and locked them.

I stared at him through the bars, much calmer than I would've
expected myself to be. "Why?" I said.

For a moment, it looked like he wasn't going to answer. Then he
said, "You failed to tell me that Moses knew the Enemy was triune."

"He didn't!" I said, perhaps a bit too forcefully.

"Moses speaks of the Enemy in the plural while emphasizing His
Oneness; he writes about the Enemy's Angel and about His Spirit;
he—"

"Maybe Moses dimly perceived that the Enemy isn't a simple entity," I said, concentrating on making my glow as sincere as possible. "Maybe he saw a tiny glimpse of the truth—but he certainly didn't fully understand what he may have guessed at!"

"I ordered you to inform me immediately if a fallen demonstrated any knowledge that the Enemy is triune; you disobeyed that order with Moses and with other prophets. You can't be trusted, Enoch. You're not fully mine; you hold a part of yourself in reserve, a part that still hopes it can return to the High Country."

"That's not true."

"It doesn't matter," the Master said, as he turned to leave.

"Wait!" I yelled, terrified of spending the rest of eternity locked up in a small cell, exiled and alone. "If you were sure of my disloyalty, you would've thrown me in the lake of fire. You're keeping me here because you think I might be of use to you."

The Master turned slowly to face me again, and I was too frightened at the time to notice that he didn't seem as upset as I should've expected.

"If the Enemy has a plan for the fallen," I said, "He would've shared it with his Chosen People. Give me access to their written works, anything that's survived. Let me read them and see if I can find some pattern or clue to shed light on what the Enemy intends. I failed you by not telling you that Moses may have known about the Enemy; let me earn my freedom by revealing to you what plans and truths the Enemy has revealed to them."

The Master's glow hadn't changed as I spoke. He still regarded me like a fallen might look at a broken tool: not very useful, perhaps, but too valuable to throw away since one day it might be repaired. "I'll think about it," he said. "But first there's the matter of your disobedience to be dealt with."

As he disappeared up the stairs, Asmodeus and Mulciber appeared in his place and began their descent toward me.

Chapter Twelve

The End

WHy didn't I try to escape? Why didn't I rush Asmodeus and Mulciber, hope to get past them and up the stairs and out of the disorienting depths of the dungeon so I could shift away? Was it because I knew that whatever punishment the Master had in mind would be doubled or tripled if I tried to evade it? Or was I paralyzed by fear, with the Master's ominous words still ringing in my mind and his infamous and well-practiced torturers heading my way?

Those thoughts gave me pause, but another held me firmly in place. The Master didn't just quietly or publicly dip or drown me in the lake of fire like he did with the other dark angels who upset him. Of one thing I was sure: the Master wanted me sane. *Whatever these two have in mind*, I thought, *it will be limited*. It's amazing how much pain one can endure when one believes there will be an end to it.

After they were done torturing me, the speed with which Asmodeus and Mulciber brought me the stones containing the holy books of the Chosen People confirmed my suspicion about the Master and what he wanted from me.

I picked up one of the stones. "How," I said, speaking slowly because residual flashes of pain were still making it hard to concentrate long enough to find my words. "How—how do I know... that—how can I be sure these are... accurate?"

Asmodeus told me that it was the angels I'd trained to write who'd made them; if the copies weren't faithful, I had no one to blame but myself.

When they were gone, I began to work my way through the stones. *The Master must have read all of these*, I thought to myself more than once. And if he went to such lengths to get me to go through them, without distractions or the possibility of telling other dark angels what I discovered (except for Asmodeus and Mulciber, who were so devoted to the Master it didn't matter what I told them) then either he'd already figured something out and wanted me to confirm it, or (as I suspected) he was frustrated by his inability to decipher the fallen's prophecies and needed me to succeed where he'd failed. After Zephar's visit, I realized my suspicion was correct. Despite my own lack of success, though, reading and re-reading the words the Circumcised Ones considered holy—including those on the new stones Asmodeus or Mulciber brought me—was enlightening on many levels. Even with the stories I was already familiar with, I learned new things. In my initial few passes through the stones, though, it was the fallen I'd never heard of, or only heard mentioned, that I found most fascinating.

Some of those stories confused me and raised questions about how much the Master is doing behind our backs. In one story, the Master asks permission of the Enemy to afflict a fallen. Was it true? Despite what he'd said about fighting for our independence, was he still subject to the Enemy? In another story, the Master is said to have argued with Michael over the body of Moses. Was it true? While we were struggling to steal his spirit, was the Master trying to take possession of his body? What would he want with Moses' body anyway?

Although those stories confused me, others made me furious—none more so than that concerning the prophet named Jonah. The Enemy instructs him to go to the capital of Assyria and tell them that the Enemy will destroy their city because of the evil committed within its borders. Jonah chooses to run away instead. For his disobedience, he is swallowed up by a great fish, but he isn't killed. Jonah survives in the creature's belly, and three days later is returned to the land when the fish spits him out. The Enemy repeats His instructions, and this time Jonah obeys. His success is unmatched; in the same day that he promises the coming judgment, the people of Nineveh repent, begin to fast, and beg for the Enemy's mercy. For reasons that even Jonah can't understand, the Enemy relents and makes a liar out of His prophet: the city is not destroyed.

That the Enemy would save Jonah despite his disobedience I could perhaps understand; Jonah was a Circumcised One, and the Enemy had work for him to do. But why save the Assyrians, I wondered; fallen who not only were not part of the Chosen People but were their very enemies?

If You want to be seen as merciful, I thought, *then show mercy to all and set aside any notions of judgment; let every creature exist without interference. But if You want to right wrongs and show Yourself the*

Protector of the weak and oppressed, then why show mercy to some and not others?

It is one of a few questions that I always returned to—why was He so long-suffering with the fallen? And where would it end? What was the plan? Did He want to judge the fallen or to forgive them?

Taken as a whole, three things struck me in particular about the works of the Circumcised Ones. The first was their increasing awareness of Sheol, of ourselves, and of their continued existence past death. Obviously we can't tempt the fallen—or possess them, as Zephar says he's taught more and more dark angels to do—without in some way revealing our presence, but I was surprised at how sure they were not only of Sheol's existence, but that their spirits survived the death of their bodies and I was puzzled by their acceptance that here the Enemy would abandon them.

The second discovery I made was also of a rising expectation among the Circumcised Ones, related to the first and in fact it's resolution. That discovery would've terrified me if torture at the hands of Asmodeus and Mulciber hadn't left me numb.

These fallen expect to be resurrected, I thought. *They're sure that the Enemy will rescue them from Sheol one day and reunite them with their bodies.*

How much of that was their own unwarranted wish-making and how much revelation from the Enemy, I didn't know. Some authors wrote in words so confident that it baffled me. Perhaps worst of all was Ezekiel, who prophesied that the Enemy would open up the graves of his Chosen People and breathe His Spirit into them so they could live again. Ezekiel even claimed to have been taken by the Enemy in a vision to a field full of dry bones and to have seen muscle and flesh and skin grow on them; after the Enemy sent His Spirit into them, this great mass of bones and flesh became living, breathing people. Or consider Isaiah or Hosea, to take two more examples: the first says that the dead shall rise from their graves with no more doubt than if he were claiming that the sun would rise the next morning, and the latter promises that the Enemy will lead His people out of Sheol and speaks as if death and Sheol were nothing. When I concentrate, though, even from down here I believe I can hear the fallen's screams of agony and despair—is that nothing?

Then there was David. While he lived, I paid very little attention to David's songs; his music was unpleasant enough that Zephar and

I always found something else to do when he played it. Reading the words of those songs, though, I realized how much of his work was about the Enemy delivering the fallen from Sheol.

Like I said, it's hard to know if this confidence is well-founded or if all of it is a pleasant fable the fallen began to tell themselves to make their deaths more tolerable. Even an author as close to the Enemy as David is confused or just wrong about what the Enemy would do for him. In one of his songs, for example, David says that the Enemy won't abandon his soul to Sheol or allow his body to experience decay, yet both of those things happened. In a similar way, Job says in one place that no one can escape from Sheol, calling it a dark land he goes to but from which he can't return, but in another place he seems to hold out hope that he will live again after he's died; and in yet another place a commentator says that Job will rise when the Enemy resurrects His people.

It was hard to know if these discoveries were worthwhile or not. At most they were interesting insights into the fallen's state of mind; but neither had anything to do with the One. Of course there were lots of promises sprinkled throughout that one day the Enemy would destroy His people's enemies—but even if that included us and not just their fellow fallen who oppressed them without end, there was nothing more to learn from those promises that we didn't already know.

The other reason I felt those two discoveries might not be important enough to mention was that although it seemed like the Circumcised Ones were going to become a powerful people, they have spent the majority of the last seven hundred years either in exile and bondage or at least under foreign rule, as they are now. It's hard for us to fear a people who can't even defend themselves against their fellow fallen.

Because I decided not to say anything to Asmodeus or Mulciber about my discoveries when they brought me new stones, and because they refused to call down anyone except the Master, and wouldn't call him down unless I had something to report that was worth his time, I had to try to piece together on my own the history of the Circumcised Ones and the context for the stories I read.

By the time of Isaiah, the northern kingdom had fallen to the Assyrians and most of its people carried off in captivity. Isaiah warned that the same would happen to the southern kingdom unless they put their trust in the Enemy. For his trouble, this prophet died a painful and humiliating death, sawn in half like a piece of logwood.

Just as Isaiah predicted, and Jeremiah after him, the southern kingdom fell. Jerusalem burned to the ground, the Temple with it, and its people were carried off into captivity by their Babylonian conquerors. Anxious to warn the Circumcised Ones not to worship the idols of their new masters, Jeremiah told them that these idols were so powerless that they couldn't even wipe the dust from their eyes when it gathered on them.

The real question, though, was how powerful was the God Jeremiah worshiped? If the point of their defeat was to punish the Circumcised Ones for their apostasy, well and good; if through oppression the Enemy was trying to call these fallen back to Himself, fine. But why allow His Temple to be destroyed? Why allow Nebuchadnezzar to stand on its ashes? Why do nothing when His name was being insulted? If the Babylonian idols were powerless, did it matter how powerful the Enemy was, if He refused to use His power?

He didn't refuse to use it in all cases, though. Because they wouldn't worship the golden idol Nebuchadnezzar declared was a god, the king threw three of the Circumcised Ones into a blazing furnace. When he looked into the fire, Nebuchadnezzar saw two things that stunned him: first, that the fire did nothing more than burn up the rope with which he'd had the fallen bound; second, that the Enemy Himself (the Begotten, of course) walked with the three men inside the fire. The king knew power when he saw it and, impressed and amazed, he pulled out the fallen and declared that he'd severely punish anyone anywhere who dared speak against their God.

That part I can understand—by saving these Circumcised Ones, the Enemy's name was honored throughout the world. But if what He wanted was for His name to be honored, why allow it to be disgraced in the first place? Why save the fallen from the fire, but do nothing to save His Temple from the same?

Because the One was supposed to be like Moses, for a moment I thought of calling down the Master and telling him that here was a parallel situation to the enslavement of the Circumcised Ones under the Egyptians, and that whoever the Enemy raised up to free them from the Babylonians would be the One we were looking for. But new stones were coming so quickly that I didn't even have time to think the thought before I learned I was wrong: the Enemy didn't raise up a deliverer to free His people, at least not from among the people themselves, and certainly not a descendant of David.

After he defeated the Babylonians, the Persian king Cyrus restored the Circumcised Ones to Jerusalem and instructed them to rebuild the Temple. When it was completed, despite what the prophet Haggai claimed as the Enemy's assurance that the glory of this second Temple would overshadow the previous one's, the very reverse was true: the second building paled in comparison to the first. I'd like to see for myself, but of course that isn't going to happen.

Receiving new stones at such a rapid pace did have its benefits, chief of which is that I never had to worry about any fallen for very long before learning that the anxiety was misplaced.

How much did the dark angels fear the Greek king Alexander, who conquered nations with a success no one had seen before? Or were they aware of, and did they believe, Daniel's prophecy that this young fallen would die just as his power reached its height and that his mighty but short-lived kingdom would be smashed into pieces.

How much did they fear Judas Maccabeus, whose family rose up in revolt when Antiochus Epiphanes tried to eradicate the worship of the Enemy among the Jews? Did they laugh when Antiochus erected the statue of Zeus within the Temple and sacrificed pigs to it? I'm sure they weren't laughing when these Jewish upstarts were victorious in one battle after another, even when they were heavily outnumbered; or when they liberated Jerusalem or when they cleansed the Temple, repaired its doors, and tore down and rebuilt the altar. I'm sure the dark angels were shocked and surprised, and maybe even terrified, at the success of the revolt.

When Zephar finally came to visit me in my cell, I received a series of shocks and surprises of my own.

The first was that the Romans—who unlike the Jews never wanted to be ruled by a king—now had not only a king, but an emperor. The second was that these allies of the Jews, who had made pacts with Judas and the rest of his family to defend each other, were now their conquerors and chief enemy. Roman soldiers occupied Jerusalem and all of Judea. The third was that I was going to be drowned in the lake of fire.

Zephar had appeared outside my cell door. For a moment I thought he had come alone, to rescue me—but immediately I noticed Mulciber's glow behind him.

"Zephar!" I said, dropping the pebble I'd been reading and rushing to the cell door. "What are you doing down here?"

"Tell me what you've learned, Enoch. Tell me everything you know about the One."

Zephar's tone was so insistent, and his glow so impatient, that I answered immediately, even though I couldn't help but feel it didn't matter—how many times had we thought we'd found the One? We were wrong in every case, and even now I guess it's possible that we're wrong about You-Know-Who.

"Beyond what we already know to look for?" I said. "It's hard to say exactly—it's not always clear which prophecies refer to the One; it's not even clear which passages are prophecies. Maybe I can return to Earth, get to know the Circumcised Ones better. Maybe they have some—"

"We don't have time for this, Enoch! Tell me something that will help me. You know something and you're hiding it."

Taken aback by the accusation, I couldn't do more than shake my head in protest. After a pause, I said, "What's his name?"

"Who?"

"This fallen you're worried is the One."

"We don't speak his name," Zephar said.

"Have the Greeks returned?" I said. "Is he leading a rebellion?"

We've always feared great military commanders, as if the ability to defeat other fallen should naturally translate into the desire or ambition to defeat us. But even as I asked Zephar the question, I thought of all the fallen who fought against their oppressors and were remarkably successful—and yet, as far as we knew, not one of them even dreamed of crushing the Master's head, during their lives or after they died.

Zephar's glow was puzzled for a moment. "The Greeks?" he said. "They are a defeated people. A Roman king rules over them and over the Jews."

It was my turn to be confused. "The Romans have a king now?"

"A king they've declared emperor."

"And this fallen has rebelled against them?"

"I wish he would; Rome is expert at stamping out rebellions. At least then we'd know the extent of his power. Maybe he does plan on leading a rebellion—but I don't think he could get very many others to fight with him. These Romans are unlike anything the Circumcised Ones have ever seen. Their empire stretches from one end of the Mediterranean to the other. They are disciplined and organized in everything they do, from building roads to inventing new tools; fair in governing their people, ruthless when fighting their enemies. They assimilate the ideas and technologies of conquered people as quickly and thoroughly as they assimilate conquered lands and cities. The patience of their leaders is exceeded only by their resolve. A Roman army never retreats in battle and, after hundreds of years of fighting, they are for the most part undefeated. Unless this fallen has a plan to stop it, Rome will rule the world.

"Yet he does nothing," Zephar continued. "He keeps to himself, spending his time in the desert. Who knows what he plans to do? Who knows what he's capable of?"

"What makes you think he's the One?"

"He glows like no fallen I've ever known; in fact, the intensity of his glow reminds me of Elijah. I've tried everything with him. This is the first time since I've perfected the technique for taking possession of the fallen that I've failed to do so. I've asked some of my best students to try—angels who are expert at possessions—and they've failed too. And it's not just that we fail—it's torture to even make the attempt."

"That's all?" I said.

Zephar's glow flared in anger. "You haven't seen him, Enoch. He has power—but he does nothing. He lives in the desert, eating honey and locusts like an animal. He's waiting for something... a sign from the Enemy, I believe." His grip on the bars of my cell door tightened. "You need to tell me what he's waiting for and how I can stop it."

"I have no idea," I said. "Are you sure he's the One? Is he a descendant of David?"

Zephar gave me a final look, full of disdain and condescension, before he turned around. "I have to get back to Earth and see what You-Know-Who is up to," he said, speaking to Mulciber. "Enoch says all of his study here hasn't revealed anything new to him. I think dipping him in the lake of fire might encourage him to share what's on his mind. Take him to the Master and see if he agrees with me."

As he shifted away, and Mulciber opened the gate to my cell door, I said, "Wait. I don't know what it is Zephar thinks I'm hiding, or why he thinks I'm hiding anything at all. Let me write down everything I know, to show the Master that I'm not keeping anything from him. It will only take a few moments."

Mulciber stepped inside my cell and watched me intently.

I picked out a smooth pebble and started writing.

At the end I'm left with the questions I've had since the beginning. Is the Enemy in control or isn't He? Did He have all of this planned from the beginning? If so, why choose me to fall with Lucifer? And what does He have planned for us now?

The answers no longer matter. The Circumcised Ones hold out hope for the One who will save them; the Master and his dark angels hold out hope that they will stop the One before he can destroy them; as for me, I don't need hope. I know that whatever He-Who-Rules has in store for me, it will destroy my mind; even with this pebble in his hand, he won't be convinced that I don't know more than I'm saying until that happens. That's one reason why I've been so honest, because I know it doesn't matter: the Master will still think I'm lying.

The thought doesn't fill me with fear. When I started writing this, part of me hoped that reading it after the Master tortured me out of my mind might help return me to sanity, since these words capture every significant experience, every interesting story, every troubling thought—everything from the moment we chose to rebel against the Enemy and fell to Sheol until I was imprisoned in this cell and read through the holy works of the Circumcised Ones in cycles whose number I stopped counting. But for that very reason I realize that I don't need these words now that I've written them down. Who needs sanity? What I will soon be given is worth so much more—an end to what seemed endless: the suspicions of the Master, the doubts of my own mind, the questions the Enemy refused to answer. The questions exist apart from me now, and they will accuse the Enemy on my behalf, while I find peace in the only way that's left to us.

Besides the questions, there is one other thing I'm left with: a thought that grants me a great measure of comfort and joy, even as I get ready to set down my pebble and tell Mulciber that I'm ready to go see the Master. It's the third realization that I had while reading the works of the Circumcised Ones.

Our great sin is that we loved ourselves more than we loved the Enemy—but will it be otherwise for the fallen? And if the answer is no—as I realize now it must be—will their ultimate fate be any different from ours?

The Enemy is a prisoner, as much as I've been a prisoner. Even if He does love the fallen, He can never express that love in a way they can understand. The heart of love is sacrifice, but what can the Enemy ever sacrifice? He created the world out of nothingness, but it didn't cost Him anything to do so. He created the fallen, but did it exhaust Him or have any affect whatsoever on His energy? His power is infinite, and for that very reason nothing He's ever done is commendable. Did He have to forgo doing something else because He was too busy creating the world or the fallen? The Circumcised Ones worship the Enemy for everything He's done for them, but what price did He pay to part the Red Sea or to send the waters crashing back on the pursuing Egyptians? One can't subtract from infinity, and the Infinite can never sacrifice any part of Himself.

They will fear and admire Him if they know anything about Him, they will honor Him if we can't help it, but they will never love Him. They will never give their hearts to Him. How could they? There is no reason to love the Enemy because nothing He has ever done has cost Him anything at all.

The Enemy's own power holds Him captive. He is like a lover who can win the mind and gratitude of his beloved, but never her heart.

Who will put their trust in a God who does good because it costs Him nothing to do either good or evil? Who will give their hearts to a God who can only offer gifts it costs Him nothing to give away? Who will love a God they can never be sure loves them?

Book Two *Substance*

Chapter One

The Son of God

Dying brings a lot of clarity to one's thinking, Saul once told me. For me, though, the clarity didn't come until after Zephar arrived in panic. Before that moment, while I stood at the edge of the lake of fire, with almost all of the devils in Hades standing around and howling for my destruction, the fear and terror clouded my mind to such an extent that I decided I'd take my chances of being found out as a liar and say something to Satan—say anything that would save me from being thrown into the fire, even if for just a little while. I didn't know what would happen when Satan finally gave the crowd what they wanted and ordered Asmodeus and Mulciber to drown me in the lake—would the pain drive me out of my mind? Would I cease to exist? I didn't know, and I had no interest in finding out.

"Wait!" I said, but it was too late—the look on Satan's face was impassable. I'd had my chance to tell him what he wanted to hear, it seemed to say.

Asmodeus and Mulciber stood next to me, ready and eager to give me the fatal push as soon as Satan gave them permission. *What are you waiting for?* I wanted to yell at Satan, but I already knew: he was waiting for the crowd's lust to reach its highest pitch.

Before that could happen, we became aware of a commotion. The devils to my right quieted down suddenly, then parted and revealed Zephar, his glow betraying more fear than I, even in that state, thought was possible for any one being to generate.

"It's Him," Zephar said, mumbling his words. "It's happened. This is it. It's Him."

Satan was beside him in an instant, gripping his arms, almost shaking him. "What's happened?" he yelled. "Is it You-Know-Who? He's the One?"

If Zephar's glow of fear and terror was scary, what happened next was worse: he cackled in long, loud, lunatic laughs. Satan struck him, but Zephar continued to howl maniacally. When he struck him again, harder this time, Zephar fell to the ground and said, "We were wrong! The One is the One. Who else? The One is the One!"

Asmodeus and Mulciber were no longer paying attention to me, and for a moment I considered taking advantage of the distraction by shifting away. But I couldn't—I needed to know what had happened.

So did Satan. He kneeled down beside him and whispered into Zephar's ear. Whatever he said worked. After a few moments, Zephar stood and seemed to have come back to himself, although his glow hadn't changed.

"I'm sorry," he said. "I—"

"Tell me what happened," Satan said. "Quickly."

W E were watching You-Know-Who (Zephar began). His name is John, for those of you who don't know.

Disciples followed John wherever he went, and great crowds gathered around him. He traveled through the wilderness of Judea claiming that the Enemy's judgment on the world was coming—but he didn't seem to want to do anything more about it, except to dip in water those people who were sorry for the sins they'd committed and were ready to turn their hearts back to the Enemy. As if that wasn't enough to make me suspect he wasn't the One—irrespective of his glow—he spoke of one mightier than himself, who would come after him, who was so much greater than John himself that John wasn't worthy to untie the straps of the sandals on this man's feet.

Not sure what to make of his statements at the time—and anxious not to send you news that John wasn't the One until I was absolutely sure—I decided to wait and watch. Before long, I saw that the words weren't just hyperbole on John's part.

One day, as he stood baptizing the fallen near the banks of the river Jordan, John looked up and froze. He was staring at a man walking on top of a hill near the horizon. John's gaze never left the man as he approached from the distance, and soon almost everyone else was staring at him too. I didn't recognize the man immediately, but after a few moments the complete absence of any glow emanating from him reminded me who he was.

"I think that's him," John said, turning to one of his disciples but almost speaking to himself. "The one I've been telling you about."

The crowd parted for the man and he stepped into the river and approached. But when his turn came, John shook his head and refused to baptize him as he'd done countless others.

"Why is he acting like this?" Abaddon asked me. "Who is this person?"

John's reluctance was transformed by whatever the fallen said to him. He nodded and baptized the man without any further hesitation, as if taking an order from a commanding officer.

I won't attempt to describe what happened when this man came out of the water. Enough perhaps to say that Abaddon is gone, as are almost all of the other dark angels who were with me; some shifted away as soon as they heard the Enemy's voice or were blinded by the appearance of the Proceeding, while others were more used to the Enemy's presence thanks to their experience with the enchantments and waited to hear what He had to say before fleeing in panic. A few turned to me and said, "Did He say that this fallen is His own son?" Half-blind and pain coursing through my body, I struggled to nod. When I finally recovered enough to be aware of my surroundings again, I found that they'd all deserted me.

I'd lost track of the man himself, but the look on John's face was enough to make me not want to seek him out or ever see him again.

"Master, what is it?" one of his disciples said.

John stared past him; the disciple grabbed him by the shoulders and repeated the question.

John allowed himself to be turned to face the disciple, but he didn't seem to see him. "The lamb of God," he said, "who takes away the sins of the world."

What could make John behave like this? I wondered. *Who was that man?*

I was worried I knew the answer. Thirty years earlier, a few angels followed some easterners who had come to Herod's palace seeking a king whose birth they said had been announced by a star. They led the angels to Bethlehem, to find a child whose distinguishing mark was that he completely lacked a glow.

We dismissed the idea that the child was the One—I went to see him myself. His mother's glow was troubling, but the child hadn't picked up any of it. Who among us would worry about a fallen with a slight glow, let alone one with no glow at all? In fact, we almost forgot about the child as soon as we saw the young John and became distracted by his incredibly powerful glow—was that the Enemy's plan all along? In the end, we did forget about the child because we assumed he was killed when Herod ordered the execution of the young males in the area.

Could the child have escaped with his life and grown to be this man? A man whom John—whose glow and dedication to the Enemy's laws have never been equaled—calls greater than himself in words I once considered exaggerated. A man whom the Enemy calls His son.

The next thought came as suddenly as the first. *What if He's not only the One—what if He's the Begotten?* Doesn't that make sense of John's words and the Enemy's declaration? What if the One we've been looking for is the One we've been hiding from?

And yet it wasn't like the time He appeared as a human being to wrestle with Jacob. This was a man, a man who was once a baby and a child; a man whose mother and father I'd seen myself. What does it mean? Has the Begotten become human? How can He be the Son of God, when he already has a human father and mother? And would the Creator really shame Himself by becoming a creature?

It's too ridiculous to be believed, isn't it?

And why? If He wishes to crush us, why not do so? Why become one of the fallen? Why hide His glow? What is His plan? What can be worth this insult to His dignity, this shaming of His name, this emptying out of Himself? What can He possibly accomplish as a human being that He can't accomplish as God?

THe clarity came to me all at once, like a fog suddenly lifting. "This is great news!" Satan said, addressing the crowd.

The final question of my first book was still fresh in my mind, bouncing around with seemingly endless passages from the scriptures. In an instant, enough pieces fell into their proper place that I finally understood.

"The Enemy plays a dangerous game, brethren," Satan went on. "If Zephar is right and He has become human, then He has become weak. He has made Himself vulnerable to us."

Frightened almost into paralysis by Zephar's story, the crowd seemed to relax by degrees as Satan spoke.

In my own mind, I heard the words of Isaiah. *For unto us a child is born, unto us a son is given*. Was this Him? Is this the Man whom Isaiah said would be called the Wonderful Counselor and the Prince of Peace? In another place, I suddenly remembered, Isaiah spoke of a sign given by God Himself: a virgin will give birth to a son, and he will be called "God with us." A human mother, then, but only an adopted human father? Had God fashioned for Himself bones and flesh from and in the body of a virgin woman?

"Nothing," Satan said, and he had the crowd completely calmed by now; "nothing we could have orchestrated ourselves could be more perfect!"

Only half of my awareness was on Satan and his devils, though. The rest of my consciousness went on thinking and remembering: when speaking of the One, the Christ, David calls him his Lord. That had always puzzled me; why would David call his own descendant his Lord... unless his descendant was the Lord Himself?

"Come with me, all of you!" Satan said. "Come watch me destroy this so-called lamb of the Enemy! Don't you see? If the Enemy has become flesh now, then we can do something we never could have done otherwise: we can kill Him."

As the crowd of devils cheered, the prophet Micah's words came back to me as well, words that suddenly made sense: a king would rise out of Bethlehem to rule over Israel, a king from the eternal past. I'd always ignored the passage as nonsense, since what kind of human being exists in the eternal past?

That God would enter the material world as a material being confused and offended Zephar; it fueled Satan's lust, and renewed and strengthened his conviction that he could actually defeat God; but the effect on me was quite different. Although I still didn't understand why He'd want to do such a thing, it was enough that He did. The idea overwhelmed me with joy at its utter ridiculousness even as I felt humbled by its humility.

"First, though," Satan said, "let us dispose of this foul creature!"

I didn't realize Satan was talking about me until Asmodeus and Mulciber turned their attention on me, smiled, and approached. I'd been thinking about another passage I'd previously dismissed too easily, more words from the songs of David. In it, David says that God is everywhere and there's no place that exists where God can't be found. I'd never believed it—*where was God in Hades?* I'd wondered.

Hands descended on me, gripped me tight. I shrugged, and Asmodeus and Mulciber fell back onto the crowd, pushing other devils to the ground.

I looked over my shoulder, stared at the burning lake.

Satan appeared beside me and grabbed my arms.

"You're worried I'm going to shift," I said, shrugging again. He landed on top of Asmodeus and Mulciber. "I'm not going to shift."

Feeling the peace that I thought only insanity would grant me, I did what must have appeared completely insane to Satan and the rest of the devils: I turned and dove into the lake of fire.

Chapter Two

The Tempted Man

HOW *many devils did Satan drown in here?* I wondered. They surrounded me on every side, some floating along in what seemed a catatonic state, others thrashing around violently as if struggling against an unseen opponent.

I tried to calm some of the screaming ones, but my voice and touch had the reverse effect; I tried to rouse the seemingly lifeless devils, but regretted it when they began to yell and curse and fight as well.

I don't understand, I thought. *The merest hint of Your Presence is pain and death to them. You gave them life, Your energy sustains their very existence from one moment to the next—but they hate You. But not only they—me too, only moments before. We twisted ourselves so much that we saw everything upside down: the source of life was death to us; the source of joy was pain; the source of existence itself was what we feared would destroy us. Is that why You limited Yourself? Is that why we couldn't stay in Heaven?*

My thoughts took a sudden turn away from the hypothetical as Satan's words came back to me. *If He has become flesh*, I thought, *then they can do what they never dreamed they could do: they can kill God.*

I swam toward the surface, rose out of the lake. The angels who'd been assembled on its shore were gone. *Did they all follow Satan to Earth? Do they disdain human flesh so much that they've stopped fearing You because You've taken humanity on Yourself?*

Without wasting any more time, I shifted to Jerusalem, and from there raced along the Jordan until I found John and his disciples sitting around a fire. Angels surrounded the group, and although I wanted to approach them and ask if they knew where I could find the Man all of the devils in Hades were now tracking down, and perhaps had already found, something held me back—fear that they would attack me on sight, perhaps, or shame at the thought of speaking, as if with equals, with angels who shined with the light from the Heaven.

Even as I stood deciding, one of the angels saw me and approached. I considered shifting away, and the way the angel looked at me made me so uncomfortable that the urge to escape became almost overpowering; but my desire to find and help the God-Man was stronger, and held me in place.

"Enoch?" His glow and voice were familiar, but before I could figure out who he was, he said, "My name is Apael. We knew each other when—"

"Yes," I said. "I remember."

He continued to stare, and his glow confused me as much as it seemed confused itself: a certain amount of worry mixed in with the joy that seemed his natural glow, but strangest (and perhaps strongest) of all was a sense of marvel. "It's good to see you, Enoch."

There was enough hesitancy in his words that I said, "I don't quite look the same as the last time we saw each other, do I?"

"You seem troubled about something."

"Is it true?" I said. "Has God become man?"

"Yes, Enoch!"

"But why? For what purpose?"

Apael approached even closer, his glow mixing with mine, his joy transferring over to such an extent that I had to fight it to keep myself focused on finding the God-Man. "To reconcile the world to Himself, Enoch! In Jesus God reaches out to the world that rejected Him; in Christ He invites those who betrayed Him back into communion with Himself. It's so wonderful we can barely contain ourselves. Already creation is responding to His call—just look at yourself."

"So Jesus is the Christ?" I said, pushing away Apael and his joy. *After all these years, and all this searching, finally I'd found the One*, I thought—but I still needed to actually find Him before Satan and the devils did. "Jesus is in trouble," I said. "Do you know where He is?"

"Of course," Apael said, confusion washing over his glow. "Don't you know? Can't you see for yourself?"

Something that had bothered me since Zephar first mentioned it rose to the surface of my thoughts: He has no glow. Why? Why would the source of light have no light of His own? *Some things are too small to see*, I thought; *but other things are too big to be noticed.* A tree stands out against the background in a painting, but who notices the background?

I looked around, hoping to catch a glimpse of whatever it was that Apael expected me to see. After a few moments, frustrated and self-conscious, I said, "It doesn't matter—can you take me to Him?"

Apael's glow was quizzical for only a moment. He cleared it in the next and nodded. I followed his shift and we ended up in the wilderness east of Jerusalem, to a scene that would've astounded me, except that I became transfixed by the figure at its center.

Jesus lay sleeping, stretched out on a piece of ground and using one of his arms as a pillow. *There He is*, I thought. The Promised One. The Christ. The Man I'd spent so long searching for and terrified of; and there He was, finally.

His glow isn't absent, I thought. It was unlike any other human being's, and even unlike the glow of the angels, but it wasn't absent—and it was wonderful. *It's a soft and subtle glow*, I thought; *the way their poets describe the sun on a hazy day*. For a long time, I'd hoped to see and experience the glow of Heaven once again, even if just briefly, but now I saw a glow that reminded me of Heaven more than any other I'd ever seen before—and the glow came from a human being! The sight and thought mesmerized me so much that I was hardly aware of what was happening around Him until Jesus stirred. If His glow had startled me moments before, the sight of His features gave me an equal shock. He looked emaciated: His face gaunt and hollow so that His eyes seemed to stick out from His head and His skin sun-burnt and leathery.

The scene that should've astounded me was this: Michael and Satan floated in the air above Jesus, Satan yelling to be allowed to speak with Jesus in private, Michael impassable but silent. Behind Michael floated equally silent angels from Heaven, while the devils behind Satan cursed and screamed as loudly as their master.

But as Jesus rose to His feet, Michael turned and made a signal to the angels, who started to retreat.

"What's happening?" I said to Apael.

"We need to leave." He grabbed me and tried to pull me away.

I shook him off. "Leave? Look at Him—He's half-dead."

"He's been fasting," Apael said. "Come on."

"I'm not scared of Satan," I said, pushing Apael away as he tried to grab me again. "Even if the rest of you are."

"Satan wishes to speak alone with Jesus, and Our Lord instructed Michael to retreat when the forty days and nights were at an end."

"I'm not leaving."

Apael tried to reach for me once more, but I avoided him and flew toward Satan, intending to grab him and shift him away from Jesus. *Whether or not He's God, I don't know*, I thought; *but He is Man, and this Man's body is weak and wasted and in no condition to stand up to the Prince of Devils.*

As I approached, Jesus turned His head to look at me. *No further*, His glance seemed to say.

I stopped.

Satan was so focused on Jesus that he didn't notice me, but some of the other devils did and soon the questions rumbled through the crowd. *Is that Enoch?* they wondered, and I noticed that some shifted away while others retreated even further than the angels from Heaven. *Didn't he perish in the lake of fire?*

I returned my attention to Jesus and Satan.

"Some of my subjects say you're the Son of God. But how can it be?" Satan looked almost human now, and the smile on his face stretched out in incredulity. "Can the Son of God be hungry? Will the Son of God die of starvation?" He glanced around at the rocky ground. "If You are who they think You are, why don't You pick up some of these stones and turn them into bread? Or is that beyond Your power?"

Although I suspected Satan was trying to trick Jesus, I didn't know how. This wasn't fruit from a tree God commanded Jesus to stay away from, I reasoned; these were stones on the ground, and this was the Son of God, and He was hungry. Why *not* turn them into food for Himself? For forty years, the children of Israel wandered the desert and grumbled, refusing to trust that the God who had provided deliverance from Pharaoh would keep providing for their well-being. For forty days, the Son of God ate nothing at all in the wilderness and, I found out later, never uttered a word of complaint. *If God's son Israel was given bread from Heaven when he grumbled out of hunger,* I thought at the time, *why shouldn't His Son Jesus happily turn stone into bread and eat, especially now that His fast was over?*

But Jesus didn't do that; instead, He said, "It is written that man shall not live by bread alone, but by every word that proceeds out of the mouth of God."

Despite His glow and Apael's conviction about who He was, His refusal filled me with disappointment and doubt. We'd been wrong before about the One, I couldn't help but think, were we wrong again?

His words seemed to have the opposite effect on Satan, though; the pretense of a human shape and form melted away as his glow intensified in anger and—almost before I realized what he was doing—Satan grabbed Jesus and shifted.

I didn't follow right away. The glance that Jesus had shot me when I first arrived—which lasted for only a moment, and was the only time He took any notice of my presence—still lingered in my memory. But the doubts over whether He was who Apael claimed and Zephar feared He was, and the desire to find out where Satan had taken Him and what was happening, overshadowed the command I thought I saw in that glance, and I decided to follow them before I lost their trace.

"Are you really the Son of God?" Satan was saying. Jesus stood at the top of the Temple in Jerusalem, looking down. Although I didn't think Satan had noticed me or was even aware of my continued existence after diving into the lake of fire, I was wrong. "Look," he said, pointing at me. "Even Your spy Enoch doubts You. Throw Yourself down if you are the Son of God. Isn't it *written*—as You say—that God's angels will catch You so that not even Your foot will touch a stone?"

Jesus didn't look at me. "Yes," He said, still staring down. "But it is also written that you shouldn't put the Lord your God to the test."

"Behold, Enoch," Satan said, turning to face me so aggressively that I stumbled backward. "Behold your God. Is this what you betrayed me for? A God who disguises Himself in human flesh; a God with no more power or faith than any other fallen, and even less than a few you and I have known."

He swung with his arm and it looked like he meant to topple Jesus off the Temple's pinnacle and send Him crashing to the ground whether He wanted to or not. But Satan shifted as soon as his arm made contact.

Ready this time, I followed immediately. Jesus stood on a high mountain, Satan behind him and covering His eyes with one hand.

"Behold the world, Son of God. Behold the wonder of Jerusalem, the beauty of Antioch, the splendor of Alexandria, the wealth of Corinth, the majesty of Rome." His voice rose in volume as he spoke and his glow grew more hungry and more lustful with every word. Perhaps it occurred to Satan that Jesus wasn't trying to stop him or cut him off, just as I noticed the same thing and wondered why. One after another, Satan spoke to Jesus of the great cities and empires of the Earth. Finally he said, "All of these kingdoms belong to me, but I am willing to give them to You. Imagine the life I offer You. You will live in the greatest palaces ever built, eat the finest food, wear robes of purple and crowns of gold. Servants will provide for Your every need; the whole world will fall down at Your feet."

He took away his hand from Jesus' eyes and walked slowly around Him. "Simply kneel down and worship me and all the kingdoms of the world will be Yours."

He placed his hand on Jesus' shoulder and they both disappeared. Mesmerized by Satan's words myself, and distracted by the fear of what would happen to me if Jesus bowed down and allied Himself to this devil who hated me as much as I'd ever known him to hate anyone, it took me a moment to realize that Satan had shifted. I followed their trace, back to the wilderness east of Jerusalem, where the angels of Heaven and the devils of Hades watched from a distance.

Satan pressed down on Jesus' shoulder, perhaps meaning to force Him to the ground.

Jesus sighed. "Go from here, Satan."

"Wait!" Satan yelled, pulling his hand away. "Listen to me! I—"

"It is written that you must worship the Lord your God," Jesus said. "And He alone."

Although I still wasn't sure that Jesus was the Son of God, my doubts about Him being the Christ disappeared when He commanded Satan to depart. He spoke with such casual but compelling authority that I had to resist the urge to leave myself. The remaining devils might have felt the same; when I turned around, I saw only angels.

"This isn't over," Satan said, snapping my attention back to him and Jesus. "This is just the beginning."

He shifted away. As soon as he was gone, Jesus fell to his knees and many of the angels rushed forward, a few carrying handfuls of water to Him.

I spotted Apael, who carried in his hands a leaf filled with honey and fish.

"Who is that Man?" I said, stopping him. "Is He God?"

Apael laughed and shook me off. "Don't you know, Enoch?" he said, speaking over his shoulder as he moved away. "Can't you see?"

I couldn't see, and I didn't know.

Whereas Adam and Eve safe and happy in the garden had succumbed to Satan's temptations, Jesus alone and hungry in the wilderness had resisted. Whereas Israel in the wilderness let us devils chase away their faith in God with doubts about His ability or desire to care for them, Jesus in the wilderness chased away Satan himself with His unwavering conviction.

But does it mean He's God? Is that what is meant by calling Him the Son of God?

Half-distracted by these thoughts, I turned to look at Jesus, not really expecting to see Him through the throng of angels singing to Him and feeding Him and giving Him water to drink. But I saw Him, His glow no longer soft or subtle, no longer the light of the sun on a hazy day. He shined with an intense white light that cut through the glow of the multitude of angels and seemed to fill half the wilderness itself.

I've never seen any human being or angel shine with that type or intensity of glow, I thought, *or any being's glow change so drastically, let alone so quickly.*

But does it mean He's God?

Chapter Three

The Lamb of God

REflecting on my thoughts at that time, I'm amazed that the question of Jesus' deity was foremost in my mind. Any doubts about whether He was the Christ had disappeared along with Satan. The doubts did leave in their place fears of what I was sure Jesus as the Christ would do next, once He'd regained His strength—but somehow those fears were secondary. Although it occurred to me that Jesus may have misinterpreted my charge against Satan as a rush against Jesus Himself, and that His glance may not have been a command but a threat that I'd be destroyed before my time if I got any closer, all other concerns melted away at the thought that God Himself had entered His Creation as a being of creation. That strange notion wouldn't loosen its grip on me long enough for any of the fears to take hold.

Instead of escaping, then, I waited and watched, though from a distance. Soon I noticed that the angels were shifting away, one by one, until Jesus was left alone. He got up and started walking across the rocky terrain, so purposeful that He looked like a general leading a mighty army, and yet I seemed to be the only one following.

Perhaps You intend to recruit an army beginning with the Baptist, I thought, when I saw where Jesus was headed. *But why recruit human beings when You already command the armies of Heaven? And why recruit an army at all—if You are God and the Son of God, can't You defeat Satan by Yourself?*

As we crested the hill, I saw John standing in the middle of the Jordan and a mass of people lined up along the shore. "Today you confess your sins and I baptize you with water," he said, calling forward the next person. "But there is One among you who will baptize with the Holy Spirit. Turn your hearts back to the Lord, for His judgment is coming, but so is His Kingdom."

Jesus stopped on the hill and watched, but suddenly John turned around, as if he sensed His presence.

179

"Behold!" he yelled, and even I was startled by the intensity with which he spoke. A sea of heads turned to look at us. "The Lamb of God! He who takes away the sin of the world!"

If the staring people were waiting for Jesus to say or do something to make sense of the Baptist's words, He disappointed them by continuing His walk down the hill, and went on toward Bethany, as if nothing had happened.

I didn't follow Him this time. *The Baptist knows something about Jesus*, I thought, and the looks of confusion and inquiry on the faces of his disciples hadn't escaped my notice.

That night, as they sat around the fire in a silence that seemed unusual for them, the disciples exchanged looks of encouragement and command and finally one of them, a man also named John, said, "Master, tell us about the Lamb of God."

The Baptist had been staring intently into the fire and he hadn't looked away as John spoke. At first, it seemed he was so lost in his own thoughts that he hadn't heard the question. But then, in a quiet and calm voice, he spoke.

"I have served my purpose," he said, his gaze still transfixed by the fire. "I believe I've done it well; I know I tried my best to prepare the way for Him. Can you believe it? The Kingdom is at hand—and the King Himself comes to usher it in; the King who is Man, the Man whom the Lord is pleased to call His Only-Begotten Son; the Son of God.

"When I was yet in the womb," he continued, finally breaking his gaze from the fire and looking around, almost as if only now aware of the disciples who surrounded him but nevertheless ignoring the confused and worried looks they shot at one another, "my parent's house was visited by my mother's niece. Her name was Mary, and she was also pregnant. My mother said that I leapt at the sound of His mother's voice. And why not? David danced in front of the Ark of the Covenant of old, wasn't it only appropriate that someone do the same before the Ark of the New Covenant?"

"Master," the same disciple said, "we don't understand any of what you're saying. Ark of the New Covenant? Son of God?"

"I have served my purpose," the Baptist repeated. "The time has come for Him to increase and for me to decrease." Until that point, the Baptist's voice was soft and quiet, the voice of one who is speaking mostly to himself; but now he looked at his disciples in turn, fixing them each with a stare that did nothing to alleviate their concern, and when he spoke again, his voice was as loud and deep as if he were on the banks of the Jordan river, preaching to a large and noisy crowd. "I've tried to prepare the way; I've tried to prepare you for what's to come. This Man will return to the Jordan—perhaps this week, perhaps later. When He does, I will point Him out and you will follow Him; you will become His disciples."

The Baptist spoke with so much confidence that it didn't occur to me to doubt the truth of his prediction, but the strength of my own conviction wasn't tested for very long: Jesus returned the next day.

I saw the light change and knew He'd arrived. The Baptist must have seen something too, because immediately I heard him say to his disciples, "There He is! The Lamb of God."

Two of those men, the young one named John who had asked most of the questions the night before and another named Andrew, approached Jesus and greeted Him, then the three men walked away from the crowd together. I followed, and listened to Jesus tell them stories from the scriptures and answer their questions about the Christ.

It was clear they believed that Jesus was this Messiah, the Anointed One, the Promised One of old, who would free them from their oppressors. I believed the same, but in viewing it from their perspective, I couldn't help but feel a thrill of excitement all over again: here He was, after all those centuries of waiting. *Everything's going to change*, I thought; *everything has changed already*. Somehow the thought didn't scare me as much as I would've expected it to.

That evening Andrew brought his brother Simon to meet Jesus. Jesus took one look at Simon (a mountain of a man) and said that from then on he'd be called Peter, the rock.

The next day, on His way to Galilee, Jesus called out to a man named Philip and told him to walk along with Him.

It seemed to me that Jesus was laying the foundation for an army, attracting disciples in every city He passed through. But for what reason? *What does the Son of God*, I wondered once more, *need with a human army?*

In his turn, Philip brought a man named Nathaniel to meet the Christ. Jesus greeted Nathaniel before they were introduced, and when the startled man asked how Jesus knew who he was, Jesus said, "Because I saw you sitting under the fig tree before Philip came to get you."

Nathaniel's eyes grew wide, but I couldn't decide if it was a look of terror or of excitement. "It's true, then! You are the Son of God and the King of Israel!"

Jesus' face broke into a grin. "Do you believe in Me because I said I saw you under the fig tree, Nathaniel? You're going to see much greater things than that!" He then told them that they would see angels from Heaven ascending and descending on the Son of Man.

Even though I didn't know what He meant at the time, a few days later two things happened that answered most of my questions about Jesus. The first was a miracle; the second was a story.

The miracle occurred at a wedding to which Jesus, His mother, and His disciples were invited. It was strange for me to watch Jesus at a party—most Jews who shone with the glow of Heaven were somber and distant creatures, as if weighed down by the pressure of maintaining their holiness and afraid of being tainted by the sins of an ungodly world. David was an exception, but even David's love of life had turned to lust eventually, and in his lust we were able to make him commit horrifying acts. Jesus' glow was pure, to say the least, but He seemed to be really enjoying Himself. He drank wine and joked with the other guests, regaling His listeners with funny stories (and not just clever and funny, but poignant and pointed stories too) and often throwing back His head and laughing heartily at the jokes others told in their turn.

Later that evening, Mary approached Jesus and pulled Him aside; to rebuke Him for drinking wine, I thought. Some servants stood behind her and waited, looking a bit bewildered. But instead of chastising Him, she said, "They've run out of wine."

He isn't drinking that much, I thought; *certainly not enough to affect the supply to the rest of the guests.*

But Jesus seemed to understand her meaning. "Why are you telling Me, dear woman?" He said. "My time hasn't come yet."

I still didn't know what Mary wanted Him to do, but it was obvious that Jesus' answer was in the negative. Undaunted, Mary turned to the servants and said, "Do as He asks."

As she walked away, Jesus looked around, then pointed at some large jars. "Fill those with water."

He watched in silence as the servants carried out the order. When they were finally done, He told them to draw out a cup and let the host taste from it.

I saw what had happened instantly: water was poured in, but wine was being taken out. In the blink of His eye, almost thirty gallons of water had turned to wine in the first jar. I looked at the second, then the next, then the rest of the jars, and confirmed what I suspected. Although Mary had been worried that the hosts were running out of wine, they now had almost two hundred gallons' worth.

I laughed.

The sound came out of me like an explosion, and startled me almost as much as the realization of what Mary had asked of Jesus. Until that moment, I didn't think of the Christ in any other terms but as the One come to destroy, the One sent to crush Satan's head and the heads of all of those who chose to align themselves with the devil. That the Christ would use His power to create was a pleasant and comforting surprise; that He was compassionate, and that His compassion extended to making more wine to avoid embarrassing the wedding party, even though it wasn't the time He'd chosen to reveal His power—was such a reversal from what I expected that, filled with unexpected mirth, and perhaps not knowing what else to do to express the joy I was feeling—I laughed. I couldn't remember the last time that had happened—since before our fall from Heaven, definitely—but it happened again shortly thereafter, when I saw the look on the servants' faces as they struggled to maintain their composure, especially when the host of the feast tasted the wine and declared it the best they'd served yet, and wondered why they'd saved the finest wine for last.

If Jesus' disciples still had lingering doubts about who the Baptist said He was, the effect of this miracle was to dispel most of them. Before that they only had the Baptist's word that there was something special about Jesus, but now they saw Him turn water into wine as casually as He might refill His glass from a pitcher.

Their excitement was infectious, and their conviction that here at last was the Christ was a feeling I shared already, but still the question of Jesus' deity gnawed at me. *Apael confirmed Zephar's suspicion that God has become man*, I thought; *but does Apael know for sure?* The Baptist called Jesus the Son of God; but I wondered what that really meant. Jesus' glow was unlike anything I'd ever seen before—and even as I had the thought, I noticed that again His glow was different than I remembered, having grown in ways I found it difficult to articulate, even to myself—and yet, I went on thinking, holy men before him had shone with the light of Heaven, if never as much or as powerfully. Jesus had turned jars of water into jars of wine, but Aaron had turned a river of water into a river of blood. He was the Christ; but was He God?

It was the disciple John who led me to the answer.

To put the question to Jesus was not something that occurred to me, and which I would have rejected if it had. The disciple named John, however, recognized something that I didn't: there was another person to whom it was natural to ask the question; another person who'd know about His origins if anyone knew.

When the wedding was over, Jesus and those with Him left Cana and traveled north toward Capernaum. John walked with Mary, a little behind the small group, and although my mind was spinning with worries about Jesus' deity, I noticed them talking. The look on Mary's face was filled with a special kind of joy that I recognized immediately. *That's the joy of a mother talking about her child*, I thought; and my next thought was that John was asking her about Jesus just as he'd asked the Baptist about Him.

I approached, and heard Mary say, "Don't think that thought hadn't crossed my mind—every day, from the moment of His conception to this morning, I awake and thank the Lord for blessing me, for choosing me from all the women that ever were or ever will be." She looked up at the sky, which was a rich blue and cloudless, and for a moment the joy drained out of her face, leaving in its place pain and sorrow. The moment passed, and she faced John again and said, smiling, "I know how blessed I am."

"I want to ask you a question," John said, who'd obviously missed the momentary look of anguish on her face, "and I want you to answer me."

Mary nodded for him to go on.

"The Master calls Him the Son of God. Do you know what he means by that? Is Jesus really the Son of the living God? How can that be?"

At first, Mary didn't seem about to respond. My desperation and eagerness for the answer to John's questions were such that I could hardly control myself from yelling at her, or even manifesting before them and demanding that she speak.

As she stared ahead, it seemed to me that Jesus looked back at her. If something passed between them, though, I didn't see it. Mary returned her gaze to John. "This isn't something I've told very many people," she said. "And it's best that you keep it to yourself for now."

John nodded, a serious look on his usually cheerful face.

"Jesus is—" She stopped. "Well, let me tell you what happened from the beginning, and you can decide for yourself."

Chapter Four

The Mother of God

WHen I turned fourteen (Mary began), the time came for me to be married. Although I resisted the idea at first—I'd grown up in the Temple, and a life dedicated to the Lord was the only life I wished for myself—it was the Lord Himself who chose for me (and for my Son, though I didn't know it at the time) a husband, a man named Joseph.

If I was reluctant about the marriage, Joseph was much more so: he was a widower with children as old as I was, and he worried what people would say when they saw us together. Like me, though, he accepted our marriage as the will of the Lord.

After we were betrothed, Gabriel (an angel of the Lord) appeared to me. He greeted me with great joy, and told me that I would give birth to a Child; a Child who would grow into a King; a King who would rule forever over a Kingdom without end.

"How can you say that I will conceive," I said, "since I am a virgin?"

"The Lord Himself will form a Body in your body and from your body," Gabriel said. "This He will do through His Holy Spirit, so that the Child you conceive will be called the Son of God. Are you astonished, Blessed Mary? Is anything impossible for God? Behold, Zacharias and Elizabeth in their old age have conceived and will give birth to a child, for their prayers have been heard. And their mighty son will turn the people back to the Lord; and in the spirit of Elijah, he will go before your Son to prepare the way for Him."

"My life is the Lord's," I said. "As He wills, so let it be done."

Although Gabriel's message left me astounded and confused, I also found in myself other and even more powerful feelings: in fact, so much joy and gratitude that I felt I might burst if I didn't share my thoughts and news with someone else. All my life I'd read the stories of our people and studied the promises of the Lord. And now, I thought in joyful wonder, had the time come when those promises, made to our fathers through the prophets, would be fulfilled? Had the time come when the Mighty One would save His people? And whom had He chosen to carry out His plan? Not the powerful, but the humble; not kings and queens, but a young girl.

I went to visit my aunt as soon as I could. When I returned home to Nazareth a few months later, delighted from my time with Elizabeth and Zacharias, the look on Joseph's face as he came to check in on me was enough to break anyone's heart. He remained silent in the face of my assurances that I'd never in my life been with any man, but I was convinced he didn't believe me; and as he left, the sorrow in his eyes threatened to haunt me and keep me entirely sleepless. Even though I knew it was within his rights to have me stoned to death as an adulteress, my only concern was hurting a man who had shown me nothing but respect and kindness. I wasn't worried for my safety or that of my Child; I knew the Lord had blessed me beyond any hope or dream of any woman, and I knew that the Lord would find a way to protect his Son and the mother who carried Him.

It turned out that Joseph himself was that way. Gabriel appeared to him in a dream and told him the truth. So much I knew by the next morning; what I found out later is that before Gabriel's visit, Joseph had resolved in his heart what to do about me. As difficult as he found it to accept the truth of what I had said, he knew the power of the Almighty and he knew that I'd made a vow of lifelong virginity, which he'd accepted at our betrothal. He spent most of that night praying and wondering what he should do, and near morning, before he dozed off into sleep from pure exhaustion, he'd decided that the wisest and most merciful course of action was to put me and my Child away quietly.

By the next morning, however, Joseph wholeheartedly accepted his responsibility as our protector. The sorrow in his face and eyes had disappeared by the time he came to tell me what had happened during the night, and it never returned—despite the pile of trouble Jesus and I brought to him. When Caesar Augustus ordered everyone to return to their towns to be counted, I don't think Joseph ever expected that he'd be a married man again or that his very young wife would be a very pregnant woman. We arrived in Bethlehem to find that all of the rooms to be let were already occupied, except for a cave that was used as a stable. It was in that cave that I gave birth to my Child.

"I'm sorry, Mary," Joseph said, as I laid down Jesus in one of the mangers. "This isn't the most glorious setting for the birth of any son, let alone this Son." Joseph walked over, looked down at the Child, then laughed. "Look at Him, lying there as if He were food to be consumed!"

I stared at my beautiful Son, who had caused me no trouble in all the months of my pregnancy, and had been born to me without pain, and who seemed to shine with the light of Heaven itself. "This is the most glorious setting, Joseph," I said, moved by an almost over-whelming love for this Child. "Because here He was born and here He lays His head."

There was no doubt in my mind that Jesus was special, of course; I knew that no other Man in the history of the world had been born of a virgin, and I hadn't forgotten Gabriel's promise that one day this Child would rule over a Kingdom without end. But when shepherds appeared at the door of our cave, and asked Joseph if a Child had been born that night, I was terrified. Joseph told them yes, and they began to sing out loudly to the Lord, glorifying Him and thanking Him for His kindness and mercy to them.

"Why are you here?" I said, placing myself between them and my Child. "Who sent you?"

One of the shepherds said, "Blessed Mother, we are here because an angel of the Lord appeared to us. We were sent by the Lord Almighty to this city, to find a Child lying in a manger, wrapped in swaddling clothes."

Another said, "The angel told us not to be afraid and that on this night the Savior of the world had been born."

A third said, "And it seemed that the field and the air were filled with angels from Heaven, and all of them were singing this song: 'Glory to God in the highest; and on Earth peace and goodwill to all people!'"

The shepherds could hardly contain their excitement, or stop star-ing at Jesus and thanking the Lord that this should come to pass in their lifetimes, but soon they began to say to one another that they must go out and tell the people of Bethlehem the good news that into their midst was born the Christ.

I didn't know what to make of all of this, or of the other visitors who came to see the Child the shepherds had told them about, or of the strange things that happened when we went to Jerusalem to present Jesus in the Temple when He was forty days old. But even stranger things happened after we returned to Bethlehem.

We were visited by men from the East, curious-looking men arrayed in clothing and jewelry the likes of which I'd never seen before. When Joseph led them into the room where Jesus and I were resting, they fell down before us. They said they had come to worship Him whose star had guided them to that place, the Great King that Daniel had prophesied would be born in that year. Immediately they rushed outside to their caravan and as they left, I couldn't help but think of one of the things that had happened in the Temple: an old and holy prophet named Simeon had taken up Jesus in his hands and said that He would be a Light to the Gentiles. And here Gentiles had traveled a great distance, following a light they said led them to the house where we were staying.

The men returned with gifts for Jesus, laying before Him gold, and frankincense, and myrrh, all the while worshiping Him with a joy that rivaled even that of the shepherds.

THe look on John's face was thoughtful and concentrated. "What happened after that?"

"We fled to Egypt," Mary said. "Joseph was told by an angel in a dream to take us there right away, because Herod sought the Child's life."

"Oh!" John said. "Didn't Herod order the slaughter of very young children in Bethlehem at one time?" Noticing the pained expression that crossed Mary's face, he said quickly, "When did you return to Nazareth?"

"Actually, we intended to return to Bethlehem. We thought we were safe once Herod died; but his son Archelaus now ruled Judea, and the Lord warned us that he was as cruel as his father. So we went to Galilee instead and settled again in Nazareth."

John nodded. "Thank you, Mary," he said. "That gives me a lot to think about." He looked up toward the larger group ahead of them; Jesus was at its center, speaking. "I should get back to them," he said. "I like hearing Jesus talk—I don't always understand Him, but I do enjoy listening to Him!"

Mary smiled and John began to walk away, but she said, almost as an afterthought, "There is another story I can tell you that you might like to hear."

"Yes, please," John said, returning and matching her pace.

"We once left Jesus behind in Jerusalem," Mary said, "after visiting the city for the Passover feast. He was only twelve at the time. We were a day's travel away before we realized what had happened; that night was one of the worst of my life, as we looked for Him throughout our caravan in a state of increasing panic. I wanted to set out right away, retrace every step we took—even in darkness where every shadow could be my Son, or an animal, or a rock, or a robber—but Joseph convinced me to wait until daybreak. We left as soon as possible, and asked everyone we encountered along the roads if they had seen a boy matching His description, but we made it all the way back to Jerusalem with no sign of Him. We searched the entire city, and finally found Him in the Temple. I stared, filled with relief and joy that He was safe, but dumfounded by the scene: He sat in the courts with the rabbis and the other students, but He seemed to be the center of the school's attention as He asked His questions and was asked questions in turn. No one seemed aware that this was a child; they spoke with Him as if with an adult."

"Were you very upset with Him?" John said, trying unsuccessfully to hide his smile.

"Relieved more than anything else, but more confused than upset, I think," Mary said. "Especially since He seemed the most confused of all of us when His father and I told Him that we'd spent three days worried about Him. Jesus couldn't understand why we were upset or how it was we didn't know exactly where to come looking for Him. 'Didn't you know that I had to be in my Father's house?' He said."

"He meant the Lord?" John said. "He calls Him Father?"

And the Lord calls Him His Beloved Son, I thought; *the Son in whom He is well-pleased. Father and Son; the Unbegotten and the Only-Begotten.* Was Jesus the second person of the Triune God, as Zephar suspected? Could Jesus really be God made flesh? At the river Jordan, John heard the voice of God and saw the Spirit of God descending like a dove on the Man he had just baptized. *The Unbegotten, the Begotten, and the Proceeding; Father, Son, and Holy Spirit.*

"Behold, the virgin shall conceive, and bear a Son, and He shall be called 'God with us.'" And here was the Virgin Mother herself, and there the Son who was God become human; the Man whose glow had somehow grown even as Mary and John had talked, so that it now extended in every direction as far as I could see, without losing any of its burning brightness of white.

Are you God? I wondered, looking at Jesus. *But how could God be born of a woman?* I returned my gaze to Mary and wondered, *How could you contain within your womb Him who cannot be contained? How could you hold the Unholdable Presence in your body and not be consumed by the fire of His glow?* And yet, I went on thinking, hadn't I myself seen God manifest Himself in a bush that burned with His glory but wasn't consumed?

More thoughts and memories and passages from scripture flashed in my mind, faster than I could keep up with them.

Mary, the Ark of the New Covenant, the sacred Tabernacle whom the Holy Spirit overshadows so she can bear Him in the flesh, the living fleece upon which God miraculously appears as the dew miraculously appeared on Gideon's fleece. Mary, the God-Bearer.

But if Jesus was God—and I no longer doubted that fact, as I'd stopped doubting that He was the Christ—Zephar's questions still remained. What was this plan that had been hinted at by the prophets of old? How long had God thought of taking humanity onto Himself? And, most important question of all: to what purpose? As Zephar had said, what could God possibly do as a human being that He couldn't do otherwise?

Zephar and Satan and the other devils stopped fearing You when they found out You'd become human, I thought. The Timeless One enters time; the Eternal One is a day-old baby; the Uncreated One is a creature of flesh and blood. God is now human—and how could something so ridiculous inspire terror? *But all of their fear came flooding back as soon as they laid eyes on You, and it washed away each one of the devils, until finally even Satan himself couldn't stand up to You.*

Here before me, I went on thinking, looking from Jesus to His mother, *is the Christ, and here the ladder Jacob saw in a dream, the living ladder that stretched to Heaven itself and that God had used to descend to Earth.* So where was Satan? Had he been scared away for good, sent scampering like a bug back to the safety he felt in his palace in Hades? Or had he retreated only long enough to regroup whichever of his devils he could, and plan a new line of attack against the God-Man? I felt I knew Satan well enough to be sure of the answer.

These thoughts would have distracted me from their conversation anyway, but Mary and John had been walking in silence, each as lost in their own thoughts as I had been in mine.

Finally John seemed to emerge from his own mind and looked at Mary, who continued to stare at the ground in front of her and didn't notice.

"You remind me of my mother."

When Mary looked up at him, he grinned with enough of his boyish charm that Mary's curious and polite smile gave way to a small laugh.

"You worry so much!" he said. "Your Son is the Christ, you know that. You heard the words from the mouth of an angel: Jesus will be a great King! Who can stand in His way? He is the Son of God! Of whom should He be afraid? Jugs of water turned into jugs of the finest wine, merely because He wanted them to! Jesus will conquer the whole world!"

Mary nodded.

"Pardon me," John said. "I'm telling you things you already know. Are you—?"

"I'm fine," she said. "If I worry, it is only as a mother. Whatever troubles come to pass, the Lord always provides us the strength to bear them." She paused to give John a reassuring smile. "Go ahead and join the others."

John thanked her again for the conversation, then ran up to the rest of the group.

Whatever dark thoughts had clouded her expression previously were now gone. Apparently taking to heart the words she'd said to John about the Lord providing a way no matter the difficulty, Mary walked on, the look of joyful tranquility that seemed to be her natural state having returned to her features.

Something bad is going to happen to Him, I thought, unable to forget the way her face had drained of every emotion except pain when she thought no one was looking. *You know better than anyone the power He commands, yet there is still something waiting for Him that you fear will be beyond His power to subdue.*

Was Mary worried about what Satan might do to her Son? I was convinced that was the case, and I was more committed than ever to thwarting the Prince of Devils any way I could.

Chapter Five

The Two Questions

BEcause I was on the lookout for Satan and his devils, I forced myself to pay more attention to the spirit world, and it didn't take long to realize that I was being followed. But it wasn't Satan or his devils who seemed to be everywhere I went, it was Apael.

Made uncomfortable by the way he looked at me, I tried to ignore him. Occasionally he disappeared for stretches of time, but he always returned.

As it was, Jesus kept my mind fully occupied and even distracted, so that I often had to force my attention back to the spirit world. The temptation to forget all about the mission I'd set for myself and simply delight in Jesus and His works was one I had to resist daily.

For a while, though, I wondered if I should be more concerned with the danger posed by His fellow men and women: Jesus didn't seem to worry about who He might upset with His actions or words, and whether those people had the power to imprison Him or even to try and kill Him.

Not long after He transformed water into wine at Cana, for example, Jesus traveled to Jerusalem to celebrate the Passover. But even as He climbed the staircase to the Temple, a change came over Him. He seemed not to hear His companions anymore; He was listening to the chaos coming from the courts: the bleating of sheep, the cooing of doves, the bellows and moos of bulls and cows, the haggling over prices and exchange rates. The smile that had sprung to His face at the sight of the gleaming marble of the Temple dropped with every step. He stormed up the last few stairs, then burst through the crowds.

"What are these animals doing here?" He yelled, picking up some cords and tying them together. "This is not a zoo!" He drove the sheep and cattle outside, then returned and commanded the startled merchants, "Take your doves out of here!"

The money changers were watching with bemusement, but Jesus

195

rushed at them too and turned over their tables, sending their Gentile and Jewish coins tinkling and bouncing on the stone floor. He roared at them, "Do you think this is a market? This is my Father's house!"

When He performed His miracle at Cana, His companions stared at Him with a reverence I found myself easily sympathizing with; now they watched Him with a decidedly different look.

The authorities arrived and said to Jesus, "Is it lawful for You to do these things? Prove to us you have the right to cleanse this Holy Temple!"

As if everything that had happened that day wasn't enough to make those with Jesus wonder if He wasn't going to get them all ridiculed or killed, He responded: destroy this Holy Temple, and in three days I will rebuild it.

Even His own followers couldn't help but look embarrassed. Was Jesus really saying that He could do in half a week what it had taken countless resources to build—armies of men moving mountains of stone, sons continuing the work their fathers had begun decades before? But Jesus' followers, at least, didn't join the others in laughing at Him. The strangers hadn't seen the power Jesus had at His disposal, though soon everyone in Jerusalem heard His name as those who received healing at His touch reported throughout the city what He'd done for them.

What I didn't understand at the time was why Jesus didn't tell those in power who He was.

They demanded to know by what right You drove away the merchants from the Temple, I thought. *Why didn't You tell them that You cleansed it because it's Your Temple?*

Such a declaration wouldn't have made a difference, I soon learned, and might even have made things much worse for Jesus—but I also learned that I could stop worrying about any harm coming to Him from His fellow human beings. That realization was a relief, especially since Herod Antipas had recently arrested the Baptist because John refused to be silent about the king's many sins, not least of which was lusting after his brother's wife and arranging for enough divorces all around so that they could be married. *The Baptist is imprisoned*, I thought when I heard the news, *by the son of the king who once executed male babies and toddlers to eliminate a Child he considered a rival to his throne. Is Jesus safe from Herod, or will the son attempt to succeed where his father had failed?*

Before I made the realization that nothing could be done to Jesus that was against His will, He passed through Samaria to return to Galilee, and there, His message was almost instantly accepted.

Exhausted from walking and the heat of the day, Jesus sat down by a well while His disciples went into the city to buy food. When a woman came to draw water, Jesus asked if He could have some for Himself. My surprise at Jesus was equaled only by her own. As far as most Jews were concerned, Samaritans were to be considered Gentiles in every respect, including in the contempt they deserved. But here a Jew was not only speaking to a woman and a Samaritan, but asking to drink from her cup. When she voiced her concerns, Jesus told her that if she realized to whom she spoke, she'd be asking to drink from His cup.

"You drink that water to quench your thirst," Jesus said to her, "but soon you will be thirsty once more. Whoever drinks the water I have to give shall never thirst again."

The woman wanted to receive the water that would quench her thirst forever, but Jesus told her to go and get her husband first.

"I'm not married," the woman said.

"You have been married, five times over," Jesus said. "But it's true—the man you're with now isn't your husband."

Her eyes grew wide before she cast her gaze to the ground. "You are a Prophet," she said.

She returned to her city and called everyone to come and hear the One who had seen into her very heart. By the time He left them, it seemed that the whole city believed that Jesus was the Christ.

When He arrived in Galilee, His popularity was already high and growing. Many recognized Him as the One they'd seen healing and doing great miracles in Jerusalem during the Passover, and were eager to see Him and hear Him speak again. In every town He visited, Jesus went to their synagogues on the Sabbath and taught, drawing ever larger crowds because of His healing power but increasingly because of the authority with which He spoke, calling them to turn their hearts and minds back to God.

But things were different in His own town, the place where He'd grown up. In Sychar of Samaria, the people declared Him the Savior of the world; in Nazareth of Galilee, they tried to kill Him. He had stood in the synagogue and, being given the scroll of the prophet Isaiah, read out the words which begin, "The Spirit of the Lord is upon

Me." Those words were familiar to me; I'd read them many times. But in hearing Jesus speak them, I realized with a shock that even they affirmed what Satan hoped God would never reveal about Himself to any man.

When He was finished reading, Jesus sat down. I was convinced He would explain to them that God is triune, and I wondered at their capacity to understand such a concept. But instead He spoke words they could easily understand, but which they refused to believe. He told them that He brought good news: in their presence was He who fulfilled these scriptures, He who brought healing, restoration, and freedom to the broken, the blind, and the captives.

Here was the Christ declaring Himself to them openly, the Christ who was raised in their town and grew up with them or their children. But for that very reason, they refused to believe that Jesus could be the Promised One. Although some were amazed at the power in His words, and others were offended that He spoke with such authority, all were taken aback.

They began to murmur among themselves how someone they'd known all their lives could say such things; and how the son of a carpenter could be so foolish and brash as to claim the title of Christ for Himself. And yet, still others said, what of the stories from the neighboring towns about how this Man could heal a sick person with a touch of His hands or expel devils from the possessed with a command from His lips?

Unable to continue teaching over their murmurs and occasional snickering, Jesus stopped. Their whispers and laughs transformed into something else at His next words. He spoke of how Elijah during the famine was sent only to a Gentile widow, though there was a great supply of widows in Israel, and of how Elisha only cleansed a Gentile leper though there were enough Israelites afflicted with the disease.

The shouts from His listeners drowned out His voice. They cried out that He should be removed from the synagogue, even that He should be stoned to death or ripped to pieces. They managed to drive Jesus outside their city, pushing and shoving Him until they came to the edge of a cliff. I watched, half-paralyzed from fear. *Have I been on the lookout for Satan and his devils*, I wondered, *preparing myself to defend Jesus against anything they could launch—when the true danger lay with mere men instead?*

But I couldn't believe that the Christ of Israel and the Son of God would allow Himself to be killed by human hands. And even as I had the thought, the mob with murder on its mind lost its resolve. Some had picked up stones along the way; those now fell harmless from their hands. Jesus had let Himself be pushed outside their city without speaking a word, but the crowd gave way as He resisted their efforts for the first time.

Although I was relieved that my confidence in Him was borne out, the incident didn't help resolve any of my confusion about Jesus.

Apael was nearby and watching, as he almost always was in those days, and I knew that he could provide insight, and maybe even answers. But afraid that he'd have questions of his own for me (*why else is he following me?* I wondered), I decided it was best to keep ignoring him and figure out Jesus on my own.

It wasn't easy. Jesus spent the next year traveling from town to town throughout Galilee, teaching in synagogues and becoming famous for His works of healing, for the stories He told, and for the answers He gave when questions were put to Him.

Because of those miraculous works, some of the Jews came to believe that He was the Promised One. And as the One whom they'd been waiting for, they expected Him to carry out their vision of the messianic mission: to liberate them from Roman rule, like Moses had liberated their fathers from the Egyptians, and to establish a kingdom for Israel and crush all of its enemies, as David had done. But far from taking up arms, Jesus spoke out against violence and told everyone who'd listen that they must show kindness and even love to their enemies, and He treated the occupying Roman soldiers and centurions with as much compassion as He did His fellow Jews. And though Jesus constantly spoke of a kingdom, it wasn't the kingdom of Israel.

As for the devils, because He'd withstood Satan in the desert, many feared He was the Threatened One, and (based on my experience with the ones I encountered) many felt that their days were numbered and consequently wanted nothing to do with Satan or Hades. But Jesus seemed only interested in confronting those devils who were torturing men and women, usually by taking possession of their bodies and causing them to do harm to themselves or others.

I couldn't understand Him or what He was doing.

He taught, but had He come to teach? He healed, but had He come to rid the sick of their infirmities? He assembled disciples, but had

He come to establish a school?

If He were only a human Christ, perhaps it would be enough for Him to reveal some of God's wisdom to people, as prophets before Him had done; perhaps it would be enough to perform miracles and call disciples to spread the message further. But in Jesus, God became human. *Why?* Zephar had wondered what God could do as a man that He couldn't do otherwise. I didn't know the answer to that question, but its reverse bothered me just as much: why did the Christ have to be God incarnate? What would the Christ need to do as God that he couldn't do as simply a man?

Despite the fact that I burned to know the answers, Jesus' teachings and stories and works of wonder filled me with irresistible joy and I couldn't help but delight in them. *And even if I don't make any progress in resolving those questions*, I thought, *at least I can defend Him from Satan or any other devil that tries to attack Him.*

In the meantime, I went with Jesus from town to town, along with a growing group of followers. Some among that crowd had heard about the wonderful things He could do and the strange but inspiring things He said, and wanted to see and hear for themselves; others wanted to be healed or had brought their sons and daughters and husbands and wives and parents to be healed by Him. Still others He had called to Himself.

On the shores of the Sea of Galilee, for example, He asked four men to follow Him, two pairs of brothers and all fisherman. Jesus watched the first pair, Simon Peter and Andrew, as they cast their nets into the lake. They waved hello when they noticed Him, and Jesus said to them, "Follow Me, and I will make you fishers of men." The second pair of brothers, James and John, were in their father Zebedee's boat, mending fishing nets, but at Jesus' word they too went with Him immediately, as if His request were an order or commandment they were only too happy to carry out.

Yet even those disciples and others whom He would single out further and make His Apostles—even those who seemed closest to Him, and went with Him everywhere, and listened to His every word—even they didn't seem to understand all of what Jesus was saying or what He represented.

The answers to my questions, of course, were in everything Jesus did and everything He said. Apael had already told me the answer to one of the questions, but I didn't understand, just as I didn't realize yet that Jesus' glow wasn't actually growing, although it seemed to me that it shone brighter with every passing day.

If Jesus' purpose is simply to call people to repentance, I thought, *simply to ask them to stop living in rebellion against themselves and their God, and to turn their hearts and minds back to Him—the Baptist had done the same, as had all the prophets before him, and Jesus didn't need to be God, and God didn't need to be human, to carry out that mission.*

Despite the amazing and wonderful things I saw Jesus do, it was in thinking about a relatively small miracle (by the lofty standards Jesus set through His other works) that I felt I saw the answer to the second of my questions, why the Christ needed to be God. The insight filled me with more delight and wonder than anything that had come before, and inspired in me so much joy that I almost decided to approach Jesus, to beg for His forgiveness, and to ask to be allowed to leave Earth and return to Heaven.

Before I could act on that impulse, though, I heard Him tell a story He'd told many times on previous occasions; but this time I believed I saw in it the answer to the first question—why God needed to become man. My suspicion would soon be confirmed by a conversation His mother had with John. *That* realization had the exact opposite effect on me.

My sense of despair was so overwhelming that I became desperate; and in that state of desperation, I gave up on two resolves which only moments before had been the strongest convictions I held: to protect Jesus with all of my power, and to keep ignoring at all costs the angel who still tormented me anytime I turned my attention to the spirit realm and saw him standing nearby, silent and watching.

Chapter Six

The Divine Savior

The nearly constant presence of Apael made it difficult to resist turning to him for answers, especially when Jesus did or said things I couldn't understand, which was often. But in addition to not wishing to hear what I believed Apael had to say to me, I became resolute in my desire to avoid him because I felt I was figuring out Jesus and His mission on my own.

More often, though, Jesus simply dazzled me so much that the sense of wonder pushed out all questions from my mind. I wasn't the only one awe-struck by Him: He amazed almost everyone, not least of which His own disciples, and perhaps Simon Peter most among them.

Peter had seen Jesus perform many miracles, and had heard of even more, but the day Jesus sat in his boat and taught the crowd that filled up the shoreline along the Sea of Galilee for as far as Jesus' voice would carry, was the beginning of Peter's growing belief that this was a Man unlike any that had ever lived before.

On that day, after teaching the crowd, Jesus told Peter to take his boat into the water and cast out his net.

"We fished all night," Peter said, looking over his shoulder at the lake. "We didn't catch a thing." He paused. "But since You say so, we'll go out again."

It was a wise decision: the fish filled up their net to the point where they feared it might break. While the others rejoiced at such a wonderful catch, Peter—who a few hours before, at Jesus' call to follow Him, had seemed prepared to go anywhere Jesus went—suddenly lost his color. He fell down on his knees before Jesus and asked Him to go away.

"Don't be afraid," Jesus said. "Haven't I already told you? From now on you will catch men."

It was in that same Sea of Galilee that the disciples saw even more evidence of Jesus' power. Exhausted from a day spent teaching and

healing more people than I could keep track of, Jesus slept in one of
the boats as He and His disciples traveled across the lake. The wind
picked up and waves began to beat against the boats. At first the
sailors were unperturbed, but the wind began to howl and the boats
started filling with water—and still Jesus slept. Panicked, wondering
if He'd sleep through their very demise, they woke Him up.

"Why are you so scared?" Jesus said. "Where is your faith?" With a
single command louder than the wind could scream or the water could
rage, He ordered both to be still, and the storm passed. When He went
back to sleep, the disciples were left in a state almost as agitated as
before, though their fear had been transformed into wonder. Who is
this, they whispered to one another, who is obeyed even by the winds
and the waves?

It was hard even for me, who knew exactly who Jesus was, to see a
man do the things Jesus did and not be continually astounded. Every
awe-inspiring miracle seemed only the prelude to a still greater one.
Even so, nothing could have prepared me (or the disciples) for what
Jesus did soon thereafter: He shared His power with the Twelve.

He had called them to Himself and told them that He was sending
them out in pairs. "Go to the lost sheep of Israel," He said, "and tell
them the good news: the Kingdom of God is at hand. Tell them to turn
their hearts back to God so they can have a part in His Kingdom. Heal
suffering where you find it; expel diseases and devils."

Jesus told them more: to use their gifts freely, because He'd given
them His power freely and because it was better to give than to receive; to not take anything with them, that their needs might be provided for by those they visited and served; and to not be afraid. His
words of warning and encouragement were so dark and ominous that
I became worried about these disciples He said He was sending out
as sheep among wolves.

Those fears were baseless, and Jesus' many exhortations to them
not to lose faith in the face of persecution on His behalf seemed at
the time like wasted breath. When Jesus sent them on their journey,
their glows were healthy, if a little faint; but when they returned,
they shone with a light that had grown stronger and deeper. They left
Jesus as fishermen and tax-collectors, but returned miracle-workers
and prophets. Each pair that caught up to Him bubbled over with
stories: at their word, a leper's skin was cleansed; at their command,
devils left the men and women they'd been tormenting; at their touch,

paralyzed limbs received new life. People suffering from all kinds of diseases were brought to them so that they could pray over them and anoint them with oil. Everywhere they went, fevers broke and pains disappeared, and people glorified God.

Jesus was filled with joy at their reports, but then some of the Baptist's disciples came with different news: John was dead, executed by Antipas at the request of his step-daughter. She had danced for him on his birthday and filled him with so much lust that he swore to give her whatever she wanted. What she wanted was what her mother wanted, and what her mother wanted was what Queen Jezebel of old desired more than anything else: the death of the prophet of God who proved a thorn in her side. But whereas she had failed to kill Elijah, this queen succeeded.

Of all the emotions I might have had, I was surprised that anger was topmost, and more surprised that the anger was directed at Jesus. *You had the power to save him*, I thought; *but instead You left him imprisoned. Even in that prison, the Baptist tried to win converts for You, sending them to ask if You were the One, so that they might hear Your answer. And how did You repay his loyalty? He watched his executioner coming to behead him.*

Did John ask why Herod had finally decided to kill him? I wondered. *If the executioner was a sadist, he may have told John the answer: "You die because a girl excited a king on his birthday, and your head is the payment she desired."*

You called John the greatest prophet that ever lived, and yet Your greatest prophet was imprisoned and killed at the requests of a vengeful queen and the whims of a lustful king.

But his life doesn't have to end that way, I thought. Jesus could easily restore John's body and raise him back to life, to die a more noble and peaceful death as an old man. Once, at the funeral of a young man—the only son of his widowed mother—Jesus' heart broke for her and He approached the corpse and said, "Young man, I say to you: get up!" The man's spirit returned to his body immediately; he sat up, and Jesus took him by the hand and gave him to his speechless mother.

Why doesn't Your heart break for John? I wondered. *And if by raising this widow's son, all the people in Judea and around Judea glorified You as a Man from God, what would they say about You if You brought back to life the great prophet himself? Wouldn't even Herod fall down on his knees and worship You?*

All of my anger burned out in the time it took me to have those thoughts. I'd been staring at Jesus, shooting the questions at Him like arrows, but now I actually registered the look on His face, the striking absence of the twinkle in His downcast eyes, the sorrow in the tightening of His lips, the deep sadness that fell on Him like darkness during a storm. My anger burned out, and there was nothing left in me but compassion—and fear. *If the Baptist's death—for so ignoble a reason—is part of God's plan,* I thought, *who was to say Jesus' death isn't part of the plan as well?*

I forced those concerns out of my head. As for the Baptist, I consoled myself with the thought that if any spirit could escape Satan's clutches, certainly it was John. *Wherever he is,* I thought, *at least I know he isn't surrounded by the devils in Hades.* How wrong I was I'd soon find out.

A growing crowd had been following Jesus from place to place; with the Baptist dead and the Twelve returning from their successful missions throughout Israel, Jesus' popularity was staggering and only increasing.

When all of His Apostles had returned to Capernaum, Jesus took them across the Sea of Galilee to get away from the crowds. But if He'd intended for His disciples to be alone for a while and rest, those crowds had a different idea: a forest of people waited for Him on the other side.

Jesus didn't send them away. Instead, He watched them with a sad look in His eyes, these people whose suffering had caused them to leave their homes and follow Him along the shoreline. *Some are here to have their bodies restored,* I thought; *others are unhurt physically but suffer just the same. All are here for You to say or do something that will end the pain and isolation that torments them.* Jesus could read the suffering that was written on their hearts and minds; I could only see their pained expressions, but even I felt sad for these creatures I'd once called "fallen," as if I or any of the other devils were any less fallen.

Over the next few hours, Jesus told them about the Kingdom of God and healed disease and pain from all the sick who were brought to Him. When evening drew near, Jesus took the Twelve and went up a mountainside. But still the mass of people didn't go home.

Jesus looked from them to His disciples. "They're hungry," He said. "Philip, do you know where we can go to buy some bread?"

"Buy bread—for all of them?" Philip spoke slowly, almost as if trying to figure out if Jesus were making a joke at his expense. "I could work an entire year and not make enough money to satisfy the hunger of so many people! Master, tell them to go away before it gets too late. There's villages around here where they can buy their own food."

"No," Jesus said. "You give them something to eat."

They will eat and have some left over, I thought. The phrase came to my mind all of a sudden, but it only took a moment to place it: Elisha quoted those words as a prophecy from God, when during a famine he fed a hundred men with twenty loaves of barley bread.

Most of the Apostles had no idea what Jesus was talking about, but Andrew, perhaps remembering the story about Elisha as well, brought Him what he could find: five loaves of barley bread and two fish.

Jesus instructed the Twelve to seat everyone on the grass. The disciples went to work immediately, dividing the people into groups of fifty, but I noticed the glances they exchanged with one another when their paths crossed. Once the people were seated, the disciples returned to stand next to Jesus and I heard Philip mumble, speaking almost to himself, "There are five thousand hungry men here, forget the women and children."

Jesus took the loaves and the fish, lifted them up, and loudly gave thanks to God. He then broke the food into pieces, which He gave to the Apostles, who distributed them to the crowd. As long as there were people who were hungry, Jesus broke off pieces and gave them to the Twelve. Everyone ate that day, and ate their full; and when they were done, Jesus told the Apostles to not let anything go to waste. They filled up a basket each with the leftovers.

What Elisha did with more food for fewer people, Jesus did with far less and for far more. Did the crowd have that thought as well? Or were they just stunned to see the bread and fish increase according to their need, as if Jesus' right hand was a field in which barley could grow and His left hand a sea in which fish could multiply? *But they've seen Jesus do miracles before,* I thought, *and perhaps even greater ones than this*. Was it rather that through this miracle Jesus gave them food to fill their bellies? Or were they thinking more nobly, of the manna their ancestors ate in the wilderness, of the manna that came from Heaven and of the Man who now gave them bread to eat after looking up to the heavens and thanking God?

Whatever their reason, a change came over them so that they began to say with great certainty what they'd only been whispering that day among themselves: here before them was the One they'd been waiting for.

Is this the day You declare Yourself King? I wondered. Certainly the people seemed ready to make the declaration for Him.

"Go back to Capernaum," Jesus said to the Twelve.

They headed down to the shore and into their boat, and Jesus told the crowd to go find shelter for the night. His words were so commanding that even I felt I had to withdraw. But much like some in the crowd, who decided to stay nearby when they saw Jesus didn't cross the lake with His disciples but rather climbed the mountainside again by Himself, I also decided to stay close. I did so even though I no longer worried about ever having to find Jesus again, because now Apael's question to me made sense. "Don't you know?" he'd asked me. "Can't you see?"

As I watched Jesus pray even from a distance, and my appreciation of the miracles He'd done that day and the lessons He'd taught made His glow appear to deepen and expand even more, I felt I could find Jesus from the other end of the universe, just by following His light. And yet, I knew, Jesus' glow hadn't grown at all; it was my own perception of Him that was growing and allowing me to see an ever-increasing portion of His true nature. The realization wasn't sudden; the knowledge seemed to have built in my mind gradually, until I saw it as the truth that explained much of what had happened before, including the look of confusion on Apael's face or my own confusion at how any glow could change so much so quickly. The answer gave birth to a different question—how much more of Jesus' glow was I yet to see?—but unlike the first, which filled me with anxiety, this was a question whose answer I was delighted to take my time in discovering.

After praying, Jesus walked down the mountain and to the lake's shore. He stared out into the darkness: the disciples were about halfway across the lake, rowing to the other side, but not making much progress because of the wind and waves that beat them back. Jesus began walking toward them.

As soon as they saw what must have seemed a dim figure floating along the water, they yelled in terror.

They think He's a ghost, I thought, but Jesus immediately said, "Don't be afraid!" Then He told them who it was who spoke to them: the I AM. In the instant when I realized Jesus was going to use His Divine Name, I flinched and steeled myself, the instinct to shift away long since buried beneath my desire to be as close to Jesus as I felt I safely could be. But the experience wasn't what I would've expected; far from crushing my mind, I felt a sense of peace, as if Jesus' command to take heart and not fear applied to me as much as it did to the disciples.

Peter's voice rang out. "Is it really you, Lord? Then—tell me to come to you!"

Although Peter often spoke before he thought, I gave him full marks for bravery.

Jesus told him to come, and Peter put one foot out of the boat and then the other. His feet rested on top of the lake as if on solid ground, waves of water washing over his sandaled toes as if he were standing on the shore.

He took a few steps, his gaze fixed on Jesus even as he seemed overwhelmed with the sense of what he was doing. At a step away from Jesus, though, the wind picked up. Peter looked down; suddenly, the expression on his face was replaced with one of panic and unmistakable terror—and even if his fellow disciples couldn't see it, they heard his cry for help.

Right away Jesus reached out His arm and held him up. "Is your faith so weak, Peter? Why did you doubt?"

As He helped him back into the boat, the storm passed. The last time He'd stilled the wind and the waves, the disciples wondered who this Man could be. Now they knew the answer and they fell down and worshiped Him.

Jesus went on healing and teaching, and as His fame grew, so did the number of sick and infirm who were brought to Him and to His disciples. Although the glow of those disciples grew stronger every day, it seemed to me (and to Jesus, if I read His frequent frustration with them correctly) that their understanding and faith still lagged.

Very little of what Jesus did or said could be understood on one level only, and that was the insight that allowed me to start seeing some of the answers to my questions. I'd wondered if He healed the sick and expelled demons out of a sense of compassion for those who were suffering; or if He performed those miracles to prove what He said about Himself was true; or if He did His great works to encourage His disciples to trust in Him and not lose heart no matter what happened, as He urged them repeatedly.

All of those were correct—but there was something else, I knew. His miracles were also signs that pointed to His divinity—but what was the explanation of why the Christ had to be divine at all?

When He needed to think something through, Jesus found a place to be alone to pray. I decided to do the same one day, and tried to block out all distractions.

Help me understand, I thought.

Jesus made sick people well again, dead people live again, and sad people happy again. He chided devils who were tormenting human beings, as a father might chide an older sibling for hurting the little brother he was supposed to be watching over.

What does it mean? I thought. *Help me understand.*

Jesus made new eyes for those who'd been born blind so they could see, and what they saw was their own Maker; He restored the ears of the deaf, and they heard the Word of God Himself; He gave voices to the mute, and they sang about what the Lord had done for them.

At Cana, He transformed water into wine; everywhere He went, he transformed sadness into joy.

But of course not everyone was filled with joy. He upset some—in particular, the Pharisees and the other scribes, the self-appointed protectors of God and interpreters of His Law—by telling those He healed that their sins were forgiven, as if He were God Himself.

Jesus upset them just as much because He healed on the day of rest. Once, when He was teaching in the synagogue, the Pharisees pointed out a man whose hand was limp and withered and asked Jesus if it was lawful to heal him on the Sabbath; but they asked the question not sincerely, but as if it were an accusation.

Jesus told the man to come to the front, then asked them questions of His own: "Is it lawful to do good on the Sabbath, or to do evil? To heal or to destroy? To save a life, or to kill?" At the word kill, the eyes of some in the crowd went wide. Jesus had seen into their hearts again, I realized; what else could their guilty looks mean? At the time, it didn't worry me at all. *Go on plotting your murder*, I thought. *In Nazareth, they couldn't even throw a single stone at Him.*

Jesus kept staring at them, His jaw clenching and unclenching.

This Man can heal you with a word, I thought; *aren't you afraid He can destroy you with a word as well?* But the Pharisees and scribes stared back at Him with resolute looks; this Man was breaking the laws they held dearest to their hearts, the laws that had caused their ancestors to be slaughtered by their enemies rather than take up arms on the Sabbath to defend themselves. It didn't matter to them where He got His power or whether He worked good or evil on the Sabbath. He wasn't supposed to work at all on the Sabbath.

Finally, Jesus shook His head, then looked back at the person standing beside Him. "Stretch out your hand," He said, His voice cracking in sadness or anger.

The man obeyed immediately; his hand was healed.

What does it mean? I thought.

Often Jesus tried to explain to the Pharisees: the Sabbath was made to serve them, not they made to serve the Sabbath! But they didn't care and it only made them want Him dead even more.

It was more than that, though—Jesus had started His work on the Sabbath. When He began His public ministry, He began in the synagogues, teaching and healing—on the Sabbath. In the beginning God created Heaven and Earth. He made the universe of dimensions and everyone in them, all the angels of spirit and the bodily creatures and the embodied spirits called human beings.

He'd made the world good—He'd made us good, I thought, and human beings. But He gave us freedom, even up to the freedom of rejecting Him. Satan was the first to do so, then and still the rest of us devils through him, then and still humans through us. And just as if a tree tried to separate itself from its roots, or a branch tried to cut itself off from the source of its own existence, creation rejected its Creator and corruption and death entered His good world.

"It all starts with a man and a woman," a delighted Satan once told us. *But it ends with a woman and a man*, I thought. For even as He banished Adam and Eve from the Garden, God knew He'd redeem the humanity that had shackled itself to sin; that He'd reconcile to Himself the creation that had rejected Him. He had a plan all along, and I now saw where it ended: with the Begotten, who was the Only-Begotten Son of the Unbegotten Father and the Only-Begotten Son of the Virgin Mother.

Thousands of years before, God chose a people by whom He'd save the whole world. He chose Abraham, and gave him a promise; chose

Moses, and gave him a Law; chose David, and gave him a kingdom. He chose prophets before and between and after them, and gave to them a mission: to bear witness to all humanity that God hadn't abandoned it, that God had a plan that would be fulfilled in the fullness of time. Finally the day came when He chose Mary, a virgin who conceived a Child by the Holy Spirit, a Child who was a creature of flesh and blood but also the Creator of flesh and blood.

For six days God created, Moses wrote; then, on the seventh day, God rested. Did Jesus begin His work on the Sabbath, I wondered, to show that His new work picked up where His old work had left off?

The implications were too much for me to think through at the time, but later I would begin to understand that the same God who created the world was recreating it—the same Father remaking the world through the same Son and the same Spirit, but this time refashioning it from the inside. The old creation He had made out of nothingness, calling it into existence through His Son and His Holy Spirit, His Word and His Breath. But for the work of new creation, the Creator entered the world as a created being, a Man named Jesus, the Immanuel whose mere presence in creation had already filled the universe with a light that had never before been seen.

Even at the time, though, I appreciated the significance of that light. It was the light of a new day, I believed, though I didn't know what that might mean. And with a certainty I couldn't explain, I knew that day was coming.

Chapter Seven

The Incarnate God

God *became a creature to restore creation. God became a creature to restore creation. God became a creature to restore creation.*

I couldn't think the thought enough, or repeat it to myself a sufficient number of times.

For wasn't I part of that creation?

I had wronged God, I knew; rejected Him to Whom I owed everything, starting with my very existence, my coming into being but also my continuing to exist and to live and to reason.

God didn't want His handiwork to go to waste, and endured all kinds of assault on His dignity and honor to avoid that outcome. So much I'd realized earlier, but I didn't understand what it might mean until I saw Him go even so far as to become human in His mission to call humanity back to Himself—rather, as I now understood it, in His mission to save them and restore His image in them. But wasn't I His handiwork too? He'd made me just like He'd made everything else; made me just like He'd made human beings.

The prophet Jonah was angry with God for sparing Nineveh, but spare it He did. The hymns were full of praises to God, whose overflow of love made Him slow to anger and quick to forgive. Didn't I see the evidence of that love myself, in the person of Jesus—in that strange act of incarnation? The God who made the universe became a baby who couldn't make up a bed to sleep in. Why? For love of the world, to save it from wasting away in corruption and death, to restore it. But what about me—wasn't I part of that created world?

And wasn't forgiveness a theme that ran through Jesus' stories and teachings like a thick cord, tying so many of them together? He told people, as often as they'd listen: if anyone asks you for forgiveness, forgive them.

My sins were greater because I should have known better. But if I asked God for forgiveness, wouldn't He grant it? Was there a limit

to His mercy? Would He say one thing and do another? Jesus hated
hypocrisy and attacked it wherever He saw it; how then could He be
a hypocrite Himself?

The scribes and Pharisees ridiculed and chastised Jesus for spending time with sinners, for entering the homes of tax-collectors and
sitting down to meals with them, for allowing prostitutes to talk to
Him and even to touch Him. And what did Jesus tell them? That it
was the sick who needed a doctor, not the healthy. That those who
felt they were right with God had no need for Him; He'd come to call
out to sinners: *turn your hearts and minds back to God*. Well, wasn't
I sick? Why shouldn't His call be for me as much as it was for anyone
else?

Wasn't I like the lost sheep in the story Jesus told, about the shepherd who leaves ninety-nine to go searching for the one that was lost?
Or the lost coin among ten that the woman tears apart her entire
house to find? Why couldn't I be that sheep that gets found and picked
up and hoisted on the Good Shepherd's shoulders? Why couldn't I be
the coin that gets put back on the necklace? If it was true that there
was more joy in Heaven over one sinner who repents than over a hundred who don't need repentance—and of course it was true, Jesus said
it—how much joy would there be over an angel of light, who had rebelled against God and become a devil—but who now returned home?

Why shouldn't I be welcomed back like the son in another of Jesus' stories, who'd rejected his father, left his home, and wasted his
inheritance on parties and prostitutes? And if I were as bad as that
son, I didn't want God to be as good as the father. I didn't want God
to see me walking along the road from a long way off, to hike up his
robes and run toward me as if He were the child and I the parent He
were rushing to. I didn't want Him to put a robe on me, or a ring on
my finger or shoes on my feet; I didn't want him to slaughter the calf
and hold a feast for me. I just wanted what the son wanted, when he
ran out of money and was starving and realized that his life would be
infinitely better if he returned to his father and pleaded to be hired
as one of the servants. I just wanted to be forgiven and to be allowed
to return to even the lowest dimension of Heaven, if only I could do so
without fear of being annihilated. I just wanted to be able to go back
to work, to sing structures and stories once more, and not because
God by Himself couldn't sing whatever He wanted into any shape He
wanted, or even call those things into being out of nothingness, but
because they brought me joy and because He and the angels of light

seemed to find some joy in my songs, too.

Those and similar thoughts were a storm in a mind; they stirred up overwhelming waves that crashed against and began to break down my fears of approaching Jesus. He would forgive me, I told myself, like He'd forgiven countless other sinners. He would forgive me, and I would be allowed to return home.

Despite this sense of confidence and joy that built up in equal measure within me, I wanted to find the right time to plead my case with Jesus. Moreover, I wanted to think through my apology, so I could explain to Him exactly why I had done what I had done: the power of Lucifer's charm over us, the hesitant step in a certain direction that felt so irreversible there seemed no way to stop and turn back, even the sense of being swept along a strong current almost as if against or beyond one's will.

As I formulated the apology in my mind, the scribes and Pharisees continued their efforts to trap Jesus into revealing Himself as a hypocrite, or tricking Him into saying or doing something that would land him in trouble with the authorities or with the great crowd that followed Him around.

Once while He taught in the Temple, for example, they dragged in front of Him a woman who was half-clothed and had obviously been beaten. She'd been caught in the very act of adultery, they said, and they wanted to know if Jesus thought they should stone her to death as the Law required. Or, another time shortly before they abandoned arguing with Him in favor of a different strategy, they said to Him, "Teacher, should we pay taxes to Caesar or not?"

Every time, Jesus' answers stunned His opponents into silence. Even the Sadducees, who unlike the Pharisees didn't believe that people would be raised bodily at the end of time, thought they had Him with a story intended to show the absurdity of men and women rising from the dead to live again; but He left them just as dumbfounded and marveling as the scribes and Pharisees. When He asked questions of His own—questions like, "Why does David call his descendant his Lord?"—they couldn't answer, although the answer stood in front of them.

I found the different reactions to Him very odd. Why did some people see His miracles, or hear His stories or teachings, or witness His cleverness or His deep compassion for the troubled and the sick, and become convinced that at the very least there was something special and powerful about Jesus; while others, seeing and hearing the same things, refused to acknowledge even the possibility that Jesus was anything but a trouble-maker and a blasphemer? In particular, there seemed to be some among the cultural elite—the scribes, the elders, the Pharisees, the chief priests—who were incapable of seeing past their own prejudices and narrow understandings of God. They once accused Him of making Himself out to be greater than Abraham, and He told them, "Before Abraham was, I AM." Hadn't He earned the right to have the claim taken with some seriousness? He raised the dead back to life, fed thousands of people with a few morsels, gave new eyes to men born blind, cleansed lepers and expelled devils. Where did His power come from, as so many wondered, if it didn't come from God? But to that segment among the Pharisees and scribes and elders none of it mattered, none of it gave them pause to wonder if what He said about Himself was true. What He said about Himself was that He was God, which infuriated them, and on that particular occasion they picked up stones to kill Him, so that Jesus had to hide and slip away from the Temple.

At first, none of their hatred of Him gave me a moment's pause; but then I heard Jesus tell a story about a man who owned a vineyard and leased it to some caretakers. When the owner sent workers to collect his portion of the harvest, the caretakers beat them and sent them back empty-handed. The vineyard's owner sent more workers, but the caretakers always treated them the same way. Finally he decided to send his own son, thinking to himself that surely they'd respect someone from his own family. But the caretakers' greed was fanned when they saw the heir himself, and they decided to not only beat but kill him.

It wasn't the first time I heard the story, but it was the first time I thought I detected something in Jesus' voice which I had never heard before: fear. No one else seemed to have picked up on it, and if my attention had waned even slightly for that one instant, I would certainly have missed it. But I'd spent years with Jesus, listening to His every word and hearing every inflection of His voice, and watching every gesture of His hands and every expression on His face. When He'd spoken of the caretakers descending on the son and heir like a pack of wolves, He'd paused. It was only for a moment, but the pause seemed involuntary and while it lasted, brief as it was, Jesus' eyes blinked more slowly than usual and there was the slightest tightening of the features of His face.

I tried to dismiss the terror that suddenly gripped me, at first by telling myself I hadn't seen what I thought I'd seen, but I knew I had; then by trying to convince myself that I'd misinterpreted the pause and the look on Jesus' face, but I knew I hadn't.

Maybe, I next told myself, Jesus saw the hatred in the hearts of some of His listeners, and that kind of burning anger—with Himself as the center and fuel—scared Him. But a Man like Jesus, I knew, didn't have to fear anything that was outside of His control—and nothing was outside of His control.

There was only one answer—He was going to be killed, and He wasn't going to do anything to stop it. *The vision of His death had perhaps flashed before His mind's eye*, I thought, *and the fear and sorrow seized Him before He forced them away and continued with His story.*

It didn't make any sense, though—why wouldn't He do something to stop or thwart them, as He'd done in Nazareth or in the Temple or anywhere else when His opponents' murderous rage overtook them?

But it did make sense. It made sense of Zephar's question. What could God do as a man that He couldn't do otherwise? He could die.

I didn't want to believe it. Didn't He realize that His death would be Satan's ultimate victory? Didn't He realize that was exactly what Satan had promised the devils of Hades, and that they would all return to him if he succeeded in killing God Himself? God chose to become an embodied spirit in Jesus—did He do so only to let Satan and His devils watch as His spirit was wrenched from His body? Would He let them drag His spirit around, maybe even to Hades itself? If He wanted to defeat them, shouldn't He do it as a creature of flesh and blood, which they feared? And if He wasn't going to defeat them, what was the point? What did it matter if He restored creation if He Himself was destroyed?

You're wrong, I told myself. *There's something you're missing. Jesus won't let Himself be killed.*

Although I repeated those words to myself frequently over the next few weeks, I noticed that I'd started keeping a greater distance from Jesus. I'd begun to regard Him with suspicion, I realized. I had thought I was starting to understand Him, I had thought that His mission on Earth was to restore creation—but I couldn't understand any mission that ended with the Christ and the Son of God as a lifeless corpse.

While Jesus was teaching one day, I saw John the Apostle speaking with Mary His mother. They stood on the side of a small hill, apart from the crowd that had formed a circle around the Teacher, and shoulder to shoulder so that they could still see and hear Him but obviously in the middle of a conversation of their own.

I approached them, and heard John say, "I don't mean any disrespect, Mary. You know that I hold you in the highest esteem—I love you as if you were my own mother. But on this point I think you're wrong."

Mary nodded, and that seemed to be the end of the conversation, which made me almost scream in frustration.

But after looking at Jesus for a while in silence, John turned to Mary. "Will you tell me again what Old Simeon said?"

Mary met his gaze. "That Jesus would be the salvation of the world, but that a sword would pierce through my soul."

John nodded but didn't say anything; he tried to project an aura of confidence, but I saw through it and Mary did too, although she smiled reassuringly at him.

A great laugh rang out from the crowd, which seemed to break the spell that had held John in its grip.

"We're getting ahead of ourselves," he said, his features clearing. "I don't believe—"

"There's something I haven't told you," Mary said.

The crowd laughed again, and Jesus laughed with them.

"Tell me," John said.

"When Jesus was born, I wrapped Him in swaddling clothes and laid Him in a manger; I had a vision when I did so. Instead of holding my Child in my arms, newly-born into this life, I held my adult Son, from whose body the life had gone out; instead of swaddling clothes, He'd been wrapped in burial clothes, and instead of a manger, He was being laid down in a tomb."

While Mary spoke, John shook his head. "You were worried about your Child," he said when she paused. "I don't know many mothers who aren't." With an upturned hand he pointed to Jesus. "Look at Him. Jesus is the Christ. He will establish His Kingdom and rule over us as King. We don't have to worry about Him or fear for His safety; we'll defeat anyone who tries to stop us; we'll call down fire from Heaven if we have to. Now—promise me that you'll put these dark thoughts out of your mind."

Mary stared at Jesus. "Whatever happens, John, I know the Lord will turn it to good in the end. I've always put my trust in Him. But you're right—a mother never stops worrying about her Child. I love Him with my whole heart, and it breaks my heart to think that anything bad will happen to Him."

He is going to be killed, I thought. *One day, the Pharisees or the scribes or the elders are going to pick up stones and He's not going to stop them, He's not going to hide—He's going to let them murder Him.*

Why? At first it was a thought in my own mind—Why?—but then it was a scream—"Why?"—and then a series of screams—"Why? Why? Why?"—that I yelled out loud.

The question threatened to overwhelm my mind, to burn away my rationality and turn me into a lunatic capable only of uttering the one syllable—Why? I tried to calm down, but the thought of God made flesh dying, especially at the hands of mere men as I was sure would happen, as if He were a normal person living a normal life rather than the source of all people and the source of all life, was so offensive that I refused to believe it could be true.

I committed to protecting You, I thought at Him although I continued to keep my distance. *I would've done anything to defend You from Satan or anyone else who threatened You. My only concern was that I could never be of service to You, but now I see that You wouldn't want my protection even if it could help You. And why not? Will You really accept to suffer and die when You don't have to? Will You really allow mere humans and devils to be able to say: "We have done the impossible—we have brought death even to God Himself"? Will You allow them that amount of power over You? And what possible good can come of Your death? There is no victory in death, for death is defeat and the ultimate defeat.*

"Why?" I yelled at Jesus again, but from my safe distance. The sense of confidence about approaching Him had collapsed under the weight of the thoughts of what I was sure was in store for Him. How could I expect Him to save me if He seemed unwilling or unable to save Himself?

For a moment, the physical world around me faded and the spirit realm came into sharp focus. My gaze fell on Apael, and without thinking about it, I yelled the questions at him: "Why? Why, Apael? Why will He let this happen?"

Chapter Eight

The Problem

APael turned to face me, but didn't speak at first. He seemed taken aback, but slowly the surprise turned to sadness, though even then it couldn't affect the joyful hue of his glow. I had gotten so close to him that some of that glow transferred over to me, and when I couldn't stand it anymore, I backed away.

"Enoch," he said. "I—" He stopped, then started again. "You—"

The pity in his voice was unbearable, the temptation to shift away almost irresistible, but I couldn't leave—not until I had my answers. "We've gone through this, Apael. I'm much changed from before, I know. I don't care about that—tell me why Jesus is going to allow these despicable creatures to murder Him!"

Confusion washed over Apael's glow. "Despicable?" he said. "How can you call them despicable when the One we love so much loves them so much, Enoch? When He loves them so much that He's become one of them?"

No longer caring how much of his glow I had to resist, I stepped closer and grabbed him by the shoulders. "Just answer my question!"

After a short pause, Apael said, "Is that it? Is that what's caused this change in you?" He pushed me away. "Go, Enoch," he said. "You've heard and seen the things the Lord has said and done—I know you have, I've seen you. If you refuse to understand His words, how can I explain them to you?"

"Seen me?" I said, laughing. "You've haunted me! You've followed my every step and watched my every move!"

Even as I spoke, though, and saw the color of his glow change, I knew I was mistaken. I'd been convinced Apael was studying me all those years, but the truth was that I'd only ever caught glimpses of him, because I'd tried as hard as I could to ignore him and the other angels of light.

"I haven't been watching you, Enoch. I did catch sight of you every once in a while, and was thrilled to see the change that had come over you. But now I see that I was wrong."

"Because I ask a question?"

"Because you'll never stop asking questions," he said. "It wasn't you I was following or watching. Since His birth, I've tried to spend as much time with Jesus as my work would allow. But once I realized you too were trying to stay close to Him, I would look for you from time to time, I would look at you and I'd be filled with joy.

"Not long ago you came up to me, desperate to know if it was true that God had become man, and I marveled at the change that had come over you. How many times before then had I seen you and wept in my glow for the angel I once knew? Your light, which was once so beautiful, had all but died out—but then, even as you frantically asked one question after another, I saw a glimmer of it again. By coming down from Heaven, God lifted the created world into Heaven. The devils felt the change, and it burned them, but you were attracted to the Light—you wanted to know more about Jesus.

"Every time I saw you," he went on, as I stood speechless, "your glow was healthier. I rejoiced that Jesus' words and actions were leading you back to Him. But now..." He paused, then started again. "When God became a man, there arose an argument among us, about whether the dark angels could be restored as well. I said that what God was doing in Jesus had limitless power to save any creature; but others said that no amount of power could turn the heart of one who once beheld the glory of God and lived in His Light, but chose to turn its back on Him. I saw you and was convinced that I was right—but I was wrong. You are a devil, Enoch, who rebelled from God at the beginning and will rebel evermore. Please, depart from me—there's nothing I can do to help you."

"Is it wrong to seek to understand?" I said, holding him back from turning away. "Is it wrong to question?"

"Of course not," Apael said. "The First Mother would have done well to question the dark angel when he told her to eat the fruit of the Tree of the Knowledge of Good and Evil; she didn't question him, and he made her break the commandment God had given her. The Blessed Mother was good to question the angel of light when he said that she would conceive and give birth to a son; she did question him, and was assured that she wouldn't have to break her vow of virginity."

"Yes!" I said. "That's why I'm asking these questions! I just want to—"

"Don't lie!" Apael said, wincing. "The Blessed Mother wanted to assure herself that Gabriel's message was from God. After that, she still didn't understand how a virgin could conceive and bear a Child; she only knew enough to put her trust in God. For whereas the First Mother disobeyed, wanting things on her terms, the Blessed Mother obeyed, accepting God's terms even if she didn't understand them."

I almost said, "I'll obey! I'll accept God's terms!" but I knew it was a lie. I didn't want to obey; I wanted my questions answered as soon as they occurred to me; I wanted God to satisfy every shifting, changing preoccupation of my mind. Everything I'd seen Jesus do and say—even the mere existence of this Creator-creature—should have been enough to make me put my trust in Him. Instead, much like the Pharisees and scribes who ignored the truth of what Jesus said, looking at it only long enough to see how they could trap Him, I was testing God daily, demanding that He explain and justify Himself to me.

"Help me obey," I said. "Please."

Apael's glow softened. "Jesus Himself has already answered your question, Enoch."

That's not possible, I almost said to him; *I've not only seen and heard but thought over and over about everything Jesus ever did and said.* It was another lie, though. I'd thought often of Jesus' miracles, because they amazed me; and just as often of His stories, because they delighted me. How often had I thought of His teachings, though? Only rarely, and even then I applied them to others and never to myself.

Jesus preached love, but I was full of hatred; compassion, but I was full of anger; humility, but I was full of pride. He spoke of a thirst and hunger for righteousness, but what did I thirst and hunger for? Only a reward of which I wasn't worthy, a life I'd once known but which I'd rejected.

"Do you want to be forgiven by your Father in Heaven?" Jesus had said. "Then forgive others."

Would I forgive Satan if he asked me, forgive him for all the anguish he'd put me through? Certainly not! And yet Jesus' message went well past that line I couldn't cross—love your enemies, He said. Love your enemies! When His listeners expressed shock at these words, Jesus said, "Everyone loves their friends and family; everyone loves those who are good to them. If you would be My follower, I give you a different rule: love your enemies. Do good to those who hate you; pray for those who hurt you; bless those who curse you."

Could I say I loved Satan, or Zephar, or any of the other devils? I couldn't; I hated them. I wanted them annihilated, and I hoped that destruction was exactly what Jesus had planned for them.

Don't judge one another, Jesus said, if you don't want to be judged. But I judged them all, the devils and the fallen humans I disliked—judged them to damnation. Yet for myself I wanted mercy and forgiveness.

One of Jesus' stories came back to me, about a Pharisee and a tax-collector. The Pharisee went to the Temple and thanked God that he was a good person, very righteous, quite holy—in every way much better than the tax-collector who stood beside him. The tax-collector, though, refused to look up to heaven but cried out, "Lord, have mercy on me a sinner!"

I'm the Pharisee, I realized, and worse than the Pharisee. At least he sincerely believed he was righteous and holy. When I'd decided to ask God for forgiveness, I first came up with explanations and excuses for what had happened in Heaven, none of which were true. And did I really think Jesus, who could see into people's hearts, would be fooled? He would know the real reasons I joined Lucifer: first, the promise of completely unfettered freedom, though I'd never considered my freedom in any way hampered until that point; second, the excitement and exhilaration I sensed in Lucifer and Moloch and the others, and from which I didn't want to be left out.

More of Jesus' teachings came back to me, one after another, and I heard them in my mind like indictments from a judge. I'd listened to Jesus speak and teach with great joy, because I never thought of His words as applying to me.

His teaching boiled down to this: love God and love your fellow creatures. Love them with everything you have, with all your heart and all your soul and all your mind and all your strength. And show that love constantly in your life, by daily forgiving those who wrong you, by daily showing compassion for others, by daily being generous with your resources to help those in need.

There is no love in me, I thought. *There is no generosity, no compassion. Only hypocrisy and jealousy and meanness.*

And even in my more sincere assessment of why I followed Lucifer in his war against God, I realized, I still viewed it as a one-time lapse in judgment. I wanted God to forgive that transgression, to wave His hands like some sorcerer and make it and its consequences disappear. But that was wrong, I now understood. It was a lie to think of that act as a mistake I'd made once in the distant past; in truth, it was a mistake I repeated daily. I'd set up a universe in my own mind where I was at the center, and every day I rejected everything and everyone else, including God, so that I could occupy my thoughts entirely with myself and my concerns.

Many of His disciples left Jesus when He said that they would have to eat His flesh and drink His blood if they wanted to have life in them. I didn't know what He meant either, but I would gladly eat flesh and drink blood if He wanted me to. What I couldn't do was go against my nature and love people I hated.

I believed God would forgive me if I asked Him to. But I also believed that it wouldn't matter—I'd be forgiven, but how long before I made the same mistake again?

How can I ever return to Heaven? I thought. Through thousands of years of selfishness and greed, even of a silly ambition that drove me to desire to collect more points than other devils in a game that was as arbitrary as it was foolish, hadn't I shaped myself into the kind of creature that could never enjoy Heaven? Darkness can't enjoy light, because it is chased away by light. And even if my glow could shine for a little while, as it had when my whole being was overwhelmed by the joy and wonder I felt because of Jesus, sooner or later my true nature would show through and the glow would die out again.

The problem wasn't with something I'd done in the distant past, I knew; and it wasn't with God not wishing to forgive that one act of rebellion. The problem was me.

Chapter Nine

The Wonder

Without realizing it, lost as I was in my own thoughts, I'd floated away from Apael. It didn't matter, though; he'd gone back to admiring Jesus and wasn't paying me any more attention.

For a moment, I considered leaving, disappearing, shifting away from Apael and the shame I felt after our conversation, and especially from Jesus and the death that awaited Him. But leave and go where? The universe was full of His light; where could I go to escape it? Not Hades, certainly. *If Satan wanted to torture me before*, I thought, *what will he do to me now that I've sided with his Enemy? And if the devils scorned me because Satan hated me, where would their contempt end if they knew that God wouldn't have me either?*

When Jesus asked the Twelve if they, too, would leave Him, after so many of the other disciples turned their backs on Him in disgust when He insisted that His flesh was really food and His blood was really drink, Peter said, "Leave You and follow whom, Lord? You have the words of eternal life."

Despite giving up on my ambition to protect Him—more than that, despite knowing what lay in store for Him—I still liked to hear Jesus talk, and His miracles still made me happy. *Perhaps that's enough for now*, I thought.

Even so, the despair that had settled on me didn't lift until I heard Jesus tell His disciples that He would soon suffer and die in Jerusalem, but that His death wouldn't be the end of the story.

His words astonished me, but they had the opposite effect on Peter. His brow furrowed and, after a pause, as if reviewing them again in his mind to make sure he'd heard correctly, he pulled Jesus away from the others. This was the Man who not long ago had asked them, "Who do you say that I am?" Peter had answered for everyone, and in front of everyone, "You are the Christ, the Son of the living God." But now the Man he had declared Christ was telling them that rather than liberate Israel from the Gentiles, the elders and chief priests of Israel

227

would reject this Christ and deliver Him to Gentiles to be killed.

When he'd pulled Him aside, Peter said, "What are you saying, Lord? These things will never happen to You!"

If Peter's view of Jesus had been shaken by Jesus' words, the reverse seemed just as true. When earlier Peter had stated who he believed Jesus to be, Jesus was delighted, and told him that this knowledge was revealed to him by none other than God Himself. Jesus told him at the time, "You are the Rock, Peter, and on this rock I will build my Church, and the powers of death won't prevail against it." But now, as Peter declared something else—that he would never allow Jesus to be delivered into the hands of men to die a violent death—Jesus drew back from him and said, "Get away from Me, Satan! Why are you trying to tempt Me?"

Still I was stunned. Peter had focused on the fact that Jesus was going to suffer and die, but he ignored the third part of what Jesus said: and on the third day, He will be raised to life.

Jesus is going to be killed, I thought. *But He's not going to stay dead. But then what's the point of dying at all?*

I didn't know, but the despair and sadness that suffocated me like a thick fog since my conversation with Apael began to lift.

It lifted much more about a week later, when Jesus went up a mountain to pray, and took with Him Peter, James, and John. As Jesus prayed, the three disciples became aware of *something*, something that soon began to overwhelm them so that it looked like they might pass out.

What's happening? I wondered. *What do they see?*

Suddenly I noticed that two men had appeared next to Jesus and were speaking with Him. The second man I didn't know, but the first I recognized instantly. *The Prince of Egypt*, I thought, *the Savior of the Israelites from the power of Pharaoh and Giver of God's Law.*

The three men spoke of Jerusalem, and what Jesus would do there, and from hints in the conversation, I figured out that the third man was the Prophet Elijah, whom the devils of Satan had searched the whole world and all the dimensions for and couldn't find.

The disciples had shaken off the stupor that threatened to sink them into a deep sleep, but as they listened to the conversation, the features of their faces fell: their joy turned to sadness, their excitement to terror, and the looks of wonder they had exchanged were now looks of worry. When it seemed that Moses and Elijah were leaving, however, Peter dashed forward and suggested that they set up three tents, one for each of the men—whether to keep Moses and Elijah from leaving, or to keep Jesus from ever going to Jerusalem and suffering and dying, I didn't know.

Before Peter could finish speaking, we were surrounded by a cloud that shined with a light as bright as Jesus' glow.

"What's happening?" I wanted to yell, but the terror froze the words in my mind. Half-panicked, I readied myself to shift away, then a voice came from the cloud, a voice that stilled me, the voice of God. "This is My Son," He said, "Whom I love, and in Whom I am well pleased. Listen to Him."

Father, I said, and didn't realize until later that it was the first time I'd called Him by that name, *consent to fill me with Your Spirit. Jesus, Son of God, help me understand why all of these horrible things must happen to You; and if it is too much for me to understand, help me only to accept it, as You accept it. All-holy Trinity, have mercy on me.*

My sense of despair was all but gone, leaving behind it only a feeling of sadness or regret whenever I thought of what was going to happen to Jesus. But even that sadness disappeared completely when He brought His friend Lazarus back to life.

Some people had come to find Jesus. "Mary and Martha send us," they said. "Your friend is sick and they want you to come see him."

"Tell Mary and Martha not to be troubled," Jesus said. "This illness won't end in Lazarus's death, but it will bring glory to God, that His Son may be glorified through it."

Although when they found Him Jesus wasn't far from Bethany, the town where the two sisters and brother lived, He didn't follow the messengers back right away. Some of His disciples said to one another, when they thought no one was listening, that as much as He loved Lazarus and his sisters, Jesus was afraid to go back into Judea, where not long before the elders and the Pharisees had tried to kill Him for saying "I am My Father are one."

But two days later, Jesus told them they were heading out. "Our friend Lazarus is sleeping," He said. "And I go to wake him up."

Lazarus is dead, I thought. *Even though Jesus said he wouldn't die.*

The disciples tried to change His mind, but when they saw He was set on going, they spoke among themselves. Some thought it was too dangerous and they should stay behind; to them, Peter said that he'd never abandon his Master, no matter the danger or the cost, even if it meant giving up his life. Thomas nodded his agreement. "Let's go, then," he said, and although his words were courageous, he couldn't stop his voice from betraying his fear. "And if we have to die with Him, so be it."

Before we were even in Bethany, one of the sisters, Martha, having heard from those who went ahead that Jesus was on His way, came out to meet Him. Her face was pale from sorrow, and her eyes red and puffy from crying, but her tears dried up at the sight of Jesus.

"Lord," she said, coming up to Him, "if you had been here, Lazarus wouldn't have died."

I was amazed. Jesus had told them through the messengers that their brother's sickness wouldn't end in death; Lazarus had died just the same, and yet their faith in Him wasn't shaken.

Martha went on: "But I know that even now, whatever you ask of God, He will grant it to you."

"Your brother will rise again," Jesus said to her.

Martha was quiet for a moment, seeming to take this answer as a rejection of her implied wish. "That is a comfort, Lord," she said. "I believe that's true—I'll see him again, at the resurrection on the final day."

"I am the resurrection and the life, Martha."

Then why will you die? I thought.

"If anyone believes in Me," Jesus continued, "they have life in them. Even if they die, they shall live. Do you believe that?"

Martha nodded. "I believe, Lord. You are the Christ, the Son of God, the One we've been waiting for."

Jesus told her to go back to Bethany and call Mary to Him.

When Mary came, it seemed the entire village was coming with her. She ran up to Jesus and fell down in front of Him, weeping. Through her crying, she said the same thing that her sister had said: if only He'd come earlier, Lazarus would still be alive.

The crowd began to wail loudly as well, lamenting the death of Lazarus. I heard some of them say to one another, "Why didn't He come when they called for Him? This Man restored strangers to health, couldn't He heal His own friend?"

I recognized some of them from Jerusalem, where they had picked up stones to kill this Man who restored strangers to health.

Jesus looked from Mary to the crowd, and something incredible began to happen: tears glistened in His eyes. For a moment, it looked like He would give way to grief too, but He regained control over His emotions and told them to take Him to the grave site.

As He followed them, Jesus wept silently.

He was brought to the place where Lazarus was buried, a cave with a large stone shutting up its mouth.

Once more Jesus fought to hold back His tears. "Take away the stone," He said.

"No, Lord," Martha said, coming up to Him and speaking softly. "It's been four days since he died; the stench will be bad by now."

Jesus said to her, "Martha—didn't I say to you, 'Have faith, and you will see the glory of God?'"

Martha turned to the men beside her and instructed them to go down to the cave and roll away the stone.

Jesus took a step forward, looked up at the sky, and prayed out loud. "Father," He said, "thank You for hearing Me. And I know You always Hear Me, but I say this so that all of these people will hear Me too, and know that You sent Me." He lowered His head and, looking at the cave, He said in a voice like thunder, "Lazarus, come out!"

Lazarus came out, a dead man walking out of his own grave, a living man wrapped in burial cloths.

The crowd of mourners shouted in wonder and fear, but Jesus' voice carried over theirs: "Go," He said, "unwrap him."

Whatever dark feelings still lingered on from my concern over Jesus' death disappeared, my despair swallowed up in the indescribable joy of the sisters and their brother, who spent most of that day holding each other and staring at one another with tears in their eyes; my sadness overwhelmed by the astonishment of the family's guests, who had come to share in the sisters' sorrow but stayed to rejoice with them, who had earlier wondered why Jesus couldn't have stopped Lazarus from dying, but who now glorified God and put their faith in His Christ; my anxiety comforted by the peace I felt in the disciples, who had feared to come into Judea with their Master, but who came anyway and saw once again that He was Master even of death, and cast it out as easily as He cast out devils.

As Jesus continued to travel and to teach and to heal, I forced myself simply to enjoy listening to His words, even though I couldn't obey them, and to delight in watching Him perform wonderful miracles, even though I knew that one day I'd have to watch Him die.

That day will come, I know. I just prayed that there was still enough time before it did for me to understand why it had to come at all.

Even when there were rumors that the chief priests and the Pharisees were plotting to kill Jesus, still I refused to worry. Even when Jesus again and again spoke to His disciples about the death He would suffer in Jerusalem, still I refused to worry. Even when He returned to Bethany and Mary poured extremely expensive perfume on His feet and wiped them with her hair, and Jesus said she did so to prepare His body for burial, still I refused to worry.

That evening I watched Him eat the meal held in His honor in Bethany, and talk and laugh with a man He'd raised from the dead; and I put out of my mind thoughts of the time when He Himself, this defeater of death, would have to die, not once imagining how close that day actually was.

Chapter Ten

The Triumph

THe next day, Jesus began walking toward Jerusalem, and sent two disciples ahead with instructions to bring Him a young donkey and its mother from a nearby village.

By the time they returned with the animals, news was spreading that the Christ approached the holy city. Many of the Jews from the neighboring villages, and also those who had come to Jerusalem from all over the world to celebrate the Passover, came out to meet Him and escort Jesus back to Jerusalem. They cheered, crying out in happy and loud voices, "Hosanna! Blessed is He who comes in the name of the Lord!" and spread whatever they had or could find on the ground before Him. Throughout they didn't cease praising God and yelling out in joy, "Blessed is the Son of David! Save us, we cry out to You! Blessed is the King of Israel!"

It was hard not to be swept along their wave of excitement. Even the gentle young donkey looked proud and excited as he carried Jesus on his back. And why not? The disciples had draped their coats over him, yells of praise and joy filled his ears, and palm branches were laid down to cushion the ground in front of his feet.

It was hard not to think of the words of the prophet Zechariah: "Behold, Jerusalem, Your King approaches; your righteous Savior comes to you, humble and riding on a donkey."

It was hard not to believe with the crowd, and maybe even the disciples, that finally Jesus would establish His Kingdom, that finally He would use His incredible power to set them free. And why not? He'd previously resisted all attempts to make Him King, had told people and devils who knew He was the Christ to say it to no one, had asked Peter and James and John to keep to themselves for the moment what had happened on the mountain when He'd spoken with Moses and Elijah. But now He no longer resisted; much more, to some Pharisees in the crowd who ordered Jesus to rebuke those who called out such praise to Him, He said, "Believe Me, if they were quiet, the very stones would start to cry out."

When His young donkey began its descent of the Mount of Olives, though, and Jesus saw Jerusalem, tears formed in His eyes and He began to sob. The city would be destroyed, He said, speaking through tears, and all of its children with it, because it was blind to peace and the One who brings peace.

The sight of Jesus sobbing sobered me up, washed away my excitement, and forced in front of me the thought that I'd tried to set out of mind for so long.

When He and His disciples returned to Bethany that evening, I stayed behind in Jerusalem, and heard many things from the Pharisees and chief priests and elders: how it seemed that the whole world was starting to believe in this blasphemer; how if they couldn't get the people under control, the Romans would come and destroy them; how Caiaphas, the High Priest himself, had said that it was better for one man to die than for all to perish.

For His part, Jesus didn't seem concerned about the plans they were making against Him. In the past, He'd avoided Jerusalem and other places in Judea because He knew they wanted Him dead, but the next day He returned, went to the Temple, and began to clear it out. He walked into the Court of Gentiles like a mighty king diving into the heat of battle and scattering all of His enemies before Him.

"What are you doing in here?" He yelled at those who were haggling over the price of animals for sacrifice. "Will you cheat even the people who've come to worship God in His Holy Temple?" He ran over to the money changers, and turned over their tables; and to the dove-merchants, and kicked over their benches; and to anyone who tried to bring something into the Temple courts to sell, Jesus was like a raging fire that sent them back or held them at bay. "It is written that My house will be called a house of prayer for all nations," He said to them, "but you have made it a den of thieves."

The next day, when again Jesus returned to the Temple to teach and heal, the chief priests and scribes were ready for Him. "You don't let people sell their merchandise here, even when we've granted them permission," one of them said. And another said, "You let the people cry out 'Hosanna!' to You!" And a third, "The people question us because of You!"

Finally one of the chief priests quieted them down, and turned to Jesus. "We want to know by what authority You do all of this."

"I will ask you a question first," Jesus said. "And if you answer Me, then I will answer you."

"Ask," they said.

"By what authority did John baptize, by the authority of men or by the authority of Heaven?"

No one among them dared to speak out loud; instead, they whispered to one another, "If we say, 'From men,' the people will hate us; but if we say 'From Heaven,' He'll ask us why, in that case, we didn't believe him." Finally they looked up at Jesus, who stood waiting, and told Him that they didn't know.

"Then I also won't answer you," Jesus said.

He didn't stop there, though. He told parables, old ones and new ones.

He spoke to them of two sons, one who said that he would absolutely do everything His father asked but did none of it, and another who outright refused His father's commands to his face but then had a change of heart and did them anyway. When Jesus asked which son obeyed, and they answered Him that it was the one who eventually did as their father had asked, Jesus said, "Yes. And for that reason tax collectors and prostitutes enter the Kingdom of God before you."

He told them the parable that first convinced me He was going to die, the story of the wicked caretakers who killed the owner's son. From the sneering looks they shot at Him, it was obvious that they believed Jesus intended this story of greedy, murderous men to be another attack on them.

He asked if they'd read in the scriptures about the stone that the builders rejected, which became the chief cornerstone.

He told them that the Kingdom would be taken from them and given to others, people who would produce fruit for God.

Jesus' popularity with the crowds was immense, so that it often seemed as though the whole city came to the Temple to hear Him speak every morning, listening in awe or bursting out with praise at the words that came out of His mouth.

In voices just as loud, however, the scribes tried to trap Him with questions from scripture, but His answers left them speechless; and thinking they were being cunning, the Pharisees tried to trick Him, but His cleverness left them dumbfounded.

Jesus said to the crowds in the Temple, "Don't think I say to you, ignore the scribes and Pharisees. They sit in the seat of Moses, so you should listen to them and obey. But do what they tell you to do—don't do what they do, because they love to preach on the law, but hate to practice it. Whatever they do practice, it's so people can see them and honor them. They are hypocrites, white-washed tombs that look good on the outside but are full of rot on the inside; serpents that stand at the gates of the Kingdom of God, not going in themselves and not allowing others to enter either."

I wanted to beg Jesus to stop saying these things, as it only infuriated His enemies even more and fortified their resolve to silence Him just like His words silenced them anytime they tried to argue with Him. And because they had no answers for His answers, they had turned to the last refuge of the defeated but stubborn and desperate, the ultimate reply to an irksome opponent that would silence them forever.

How many times I wanted to warn Jesus, I can't say. How I resisted the urge to go to Him and beg Him to leave Jerusalem, or at least demand that He explain to me why He had to die, I don't know. But I held my peace and watched what would happen, and whenever Jesus and His disciples retired to Bethany for the night, I stayed behind in Jerusalem to see what the chief priests and Pharisees were planning against Him.

On the fourth day, Judas the Iscariot stayed behind as well.

Of the Twelve, I liked Judas the least. To feed a multitude, Jesus was happy to multiply fish in His hands, but for Himself and His disciples He depended on the charity of His followers and admirers. That part I didn't have a problem with—as Jesus said, the worker is worthy of his wages—but what I couldn't understand was how Jesus, who could see into the hearts of men, was willing to put a man like Judas in charge of their money. *You see everything else*, I wanted to say to Him; *don't You see the lust this man has for silver and gold? Don't You know that he steals for himself money that these people give for You and Your disciples and for the poor?* Much of Jesus' support came from women whom He had healed of diseases or devils but who were risking their reputations, their marriages, and even their lives by following and providing for Him. *Don't you care what happens to their money?*

Judas had pulled his cloak over his head, as if the darkness of the night wasn't enough cover to hide what he planned to do. He went straight to the chief priests, walking quickly, his gaze fixed on the road in front of him, not daring to look up at anyone along the way.

"You're one of His followers," they said, when he removed his hood. "What do you want?"

"Not what I want," he said, speaking softly. "You want Jesus. And you want to take Him when He's alone. No crowds to rise up against you. If I say I can give Him to you—what are you willing to give me?"

Before answering Judas, the chief priests looked at one another.

"This Jesus of Nazareth will be the destruction of our nation if He isn't stopped," one of them finally said. Another said, "Come back and tell us when we can take Him quietly, and we will give you as much as thirty pieces of silver."

Judas' hands stopped trembling. He nodded, looking at each of them in turn but not really seeming to see them, then pulled the hood over his head again and left.

Before I could follow, a sound pierced my mind, a humorless laughter I knew very well but which I'd hoped never to hear again.

I brought the spirit realm into focus and saw him, although he looked different than I remembered. Where was the fiery glow that had terrified me for so long? All I saw now was feeble and pathetic, more like a shadow than anything that could be called light. Suddenly I remembered that that's how Satan had looked when we'd first fallen from Heaven and he'd crawled out of the lake of fire.

"Old friend," Satan said, not guessing at the thoughts going through my mind. "Isn't this delightful? One of His own will betray Him!" The hissing in his voice made his words almost indecipherable. "One of the Twelve—and only the first, if I have my way."

"Nothing happens that He doesn't allow," I said, weakly.

"He will die, Enoch," Satan said, his glow heating up. "I will make sure of it. And what do you think will happen to your Jesus then? What do you think will happen to you?"

I shifted away without answering.

That night Jesus watched Judas return to Bethany, and I could see from the look in His eyes that He knew what Judas had done to Him in Jerusalem.

On the evening of the next day, Jesus was having supper with the Twelve. It wasn't a night like any other; not only did Jesus' words have a greater sense of urgency as He spoke to them again of His suffering and death, and even told them that they too would experience persecution because of His name, but earlier that night Jesus had gotten up, put a towel around His waist, and filled a basin with water. He'd carried it to one disciple after another, bending over like a slave so He could wash their feet.

When He kneeled in front of Judas, and took the dirty betrayer's foot in His hands, plunged it in the water and wiped it clean, I wanted to yell. I heard a sound then, but I didn't know if it was Satan laughing or just my imagination, and I didn't want to find out.

As embarrassing as I felt it was to see Jesus humble himself like that, it wasn't the worst insult to His dignity I witnessed that night, nor was it the strangest thing He did.

He took bread and said that it was His body, broken for the forgiveness of sins; He took a cup of wine and said that it was His blood of the new covenant, shed for the forgiveness of sins. Even though He'd alienated many of His disciples before by saying, "My body is truly food and My blood is truly drink," He didn't distance Himself from the words but went even further. "Take and eat," He said to His disciples, "this is My body" and "Take and drink, this is My blood."

Satan howled with laughter, and I could no longer pretend that it was only my imagination.

Do You give thanks for Your own death, Lord? I thought. *Even as Your enemy ridicules You?*

While they were eating, Jesus looked sad and pensive. Finally He told the disciples what was on His mind: one of them would betray Him. They shook their heads, and they all denied it vehemently, even Judas, but Jesus looked at him again in that piercing way He had that made people feel like He was seeing into their hearts.

"You think I'll betray You?" Judas said, whispering.

"The words came out of your own mouth," Jesus whispered back. Then, in a normal voice, He told him, "Do what you're going to do, but do it quickly."

Judas got up; the rest of the disciples watched him leave with curious but unconcerned looks on their faces.

Without pausing to think, I started to follow Judas.

Satan appeared in front of me. "What are you planning, Enoch?" he said, smiling. "Do you think you can change his mind? It's already made up. Your Jesus shouldn't make promises He can't keep; it has a way of disappointing people."

Jesus said to the remaining disciples, "This is the new command I give you: love one another as I have loved you."

"Go ahead and chase after my Judas," Satan was saying. "See if you can stop what your own Master has already accepted."

"He is God," I said. "You can't kill—"

"He is human!" Satan yelled, and I had the sense that this wasn't the first or the hundredth time that the objection had been raised with him. He paused, and when he spoke again, he had regained control over himself. "He is human, and I will bring about His death just as surely as I brought about the death of the very first of these fallen."

I know, I thought.

Satan waited for me to respond, and when he saw I wouldn't, his smile grew even wider. "The only reason you continue to enjoy your freedom is so you can be free to watch this Man die, which will only be the beginning of His suffering. You'll see this through to the end, because you're a coward. If you had the strength to turn your back on this so-called Son of God, you would've done it by now."

He shifted suddenly and, with only enough time for a glance back at Jesus, I followed. He brought me to the room I'd built for myself atop the palace in Hades.

"It's not too late, though," he said. The hissing had disappeared from his voice. "Haven't I always offered you forgiveness and fellowship in the past, Enoch? I offer them to you again."

I shook my head. "I want to go back to Heaven. Don't you?"

"No," Satan said, and I knew he meant it. "Never. How can I, being free, ever submit to God's rule again? Don't you see what you've become? You've been following a Man; you've been putting your faith in a fallen. It doesn't have to be that way. You can follow me."

"No," I said. "Never again."

"Then things are about to get much worse for you," he said, and shifted.

I followed immediately; once I arrived, though, I felt that I could've guessed the destination on my own.

We stood outside the Temple in Jerusalem. Judas spoke with the chief priests and elders, no one bothering to whisper. They held torches and lanterns, which spread a flickering light over them and over the band of soldiers and the group of Temple guards who stood waiting.

"You're sure He'll be there?" one of the elders said to Judas.

"Don't worry." Whatever nervousness he had displayed before was gone. "I'll take you to the very spot."

"And how will we know—"

"I'll go up to Him and greet Him," Judas said. "Arrest the one I kiss. Are we ready?"

They were ready, and they headed out, Judas at the front. He led the large crowd to a garden at the Mount of Olives, and then to a clearing, where Jesus and some of His disciples stood watching the crowd approach.

Jesus did not look good. His hair was matted down on His forehead; His face glistened in the moonlight, with tears and sweat; His tired eyes were red but His lips pale and bloodless.

If I'm going to act, I thought, *I have to act now.*

I looked for Satan, and saw him standing by Judas, his glow full of as much satisfaction and delight as I could remember seeing in him.

At a signal from their commander, the guards grabbed Jesus.

Now! I screamed at myself.

Before I could do anything, though, something metallic flashed in the moonlight, there was a yell of rage and, in a different voice, a cry of surprise and pain.

Strike now, I thought, *while Satan's distracted!*

"Enough!" The word froze me in place, even though Jesus hadn't addressed it to me. He made Peter put his sword away, then walked over to one of the men that had come to arrest Him. That man held the side of his head; blood poured through his fingers. Jesus gently forced the man's arm down, then touched his head, and when He pulled away His hand, the ear was as whole as it had ever been. Immediately, the man's face had cleared of all signs of pain, though not of surprise. He stared at Jesus in amazement.

Jesus turned to the rest of the crowd, His gaze seeming to pick out the chief priests and elders. "Why do you come to Me in the middle of the night," He said, "swords and clubs in your hands? Wasn't I with you, every day in the Temple courts? Why didn't you arrest Me then?"

The commander ordered the arrest of everyone with Jesus. Watching them flee in fear, I remembered what Jesus had said when He'd quoted further words from the prophet Zechariah: "Strike the Shepherd and scatter the sheep."

Left alone, Jesus stood silent as the guards bound Him like a dangerous criminal, and didn't protest when they led Him out of the garden like a captive animal.

I don't understand, I thought. *How can You allow this?*

How could He allow Himself to be dragged around, I wondered, eventually to the house of the High Priest, where a crowd of chief priests and Pharisees and elders had assembled to hear testimony against Jesus.

How could the Judge of all creation allow Himself to be judged? How could it be His plan to stand and hear a series of witnesses say half-truths and outright lies about Him, each one contradicting the other?

How could He allow Himself to be spat upon, hit, slapped, insulted, declared a blasphemer and worthy of execution, all because He said the truth, that He is the Christ and the Son of God?

How, finally, could He stand to look at Peter, when He knew that His friend and Apostle had just warmed his hands over a fire in the courtyard and denied having ever known Him, let alone being a disciple of His, and not only once but three times, all exactly as Jesus had predicted?

The Creator of life deserves to die, this council of creatures decided. They brought Him to the Roman governor so He could be crucified, telling Pilate that Jesus taught rebellion against Caesar, saying no one should pay taxes to the Romans and that He Himself was King.

Pilate tried to send Jesus to Herod, but when Herod realized that this celebrated miracle-worker refused to provide any entertainment, he sent Him back.

The governor then tried to dissuade the crowd of chief priests and scribes and elders and their supporters, saying he'd found nothing worthy of death in Jesus or His actions, but they yelled at him, "We want Him crucified!" and "He deserves death, He is the enemy of our king, Caesar!" and "Any friend of His is an enemy of Caesar's!"

Next Pilate tried to set Jesus free as part of the Feast, and then tried to satisfy the crowd by ordering Jesus to be flogged: struck with whips so that the leather striped His skin, and the pieces of metal and bones tore it off, as if a hungry animal were biting into His flesh and feasting on it. So much blood poured out of Him that I wondered that Jesus still had more to give. Because they were laughing and bowing in front of Him as King of the Jews, the Roman soldiers also took thorns, twisted them into a crown, and forced it onto His head so that more blood ran into His swollen eyes.

It didn't change the crowd's mind, though, and in fact may have had the opposite effect than Pilate intended. The sight of the bruised and bleeding Man who had called Himself Christ and Son of God, but who had spent the night and morning being beaten and spit upon and ridiculed and whose face hardly looked human anymore, only convinced them that they were right when they decided that He couldn't be who He said He was. They wanted another prisoner released; they wanted Jesus crucified.

Pilate watched the crowd with a resigned look in his eyes, and I knew what he was going to do even before he gave the order. Their anger and hatred of Jesus was so strong that nothing he said or did could touch their hearts, and their rage-filled, murderous voices were so loud and incendiary that their words struck fear in him as much as they frustrated him.

Pilate knows that Jesus is innocent, I thought, *but he's still going to have Him killed rather than risk a riot.*

"I wash my hands of this Man's blood," he said, and I wanted to strangle him for the cowardice and complacency of a conscience that didn't recoil from torturing an innocent Man, but even went so far as to place a sentence of death on Him.

Pilate turned to his soldiers. "Do as they wish," he said. "Crucify their King."

The crowd cheered, and I shuddered at the sight of Jews delighting in the execution of one of their own at the hands of the oppressors they despised, of humanity cheering the death of their own Creator.

I don't understand! I wanted to yell. *Why do You allow this?*

When the soldiers put a cross on Jesus, however, and led Him through the city and out of the city, and up the hill to the place where He would be crucified, with a shock of recognition and realization I remembered a sight from thousands of years before, and I began to understand—not why this was happening to Him, but what I was supposed to do about it.

Chapter Eleven

The Victory

BEfore *King David conquered Jerusalem and made it his capital*, I thought, as I watched Jesus drag His cross through its dusty streets, *a man was called by God and given a promise and then a test. He was told to travel to this place and to sacrifice his beloved child, his son of promise.*

Almost two thousand years earlier, I'd watched that son walk up the mountain in obedience to his father, carrying himself the wood on which he would be sacrificed. Abraham had told his son what at the time I took to be a lie, that God Himself would provide a lamb. *And yet here is that Lamb*, I thought, *bruised and bleeding, the wood of Its sacrifice weighing It down.*

"Behold the Lamb of God," the Baptist had said, "who takes away the sins of the world."

Why hadn't those words meant anything to me before? Why hadn't I connected them to the words of Isaiah, written hundreds of years earlier, about the Lamb who would be led to the slaughter, the Man who would take on Himself humanity's sins, the Righteous One whose bruises would heal the world?

Satan and Cain couldn't understand what Abel was doing, I remembered, when he offered to God the life of an innocent lamb. To be truthful, none of us understood the point of all the sacrifices, why the blood of countless animals was poured out on the altar and enough grain to feed the populations of the world a hundred times over burned up. *The point was to point to You, wasn't it?* I thought, looking at Him. Nor could we understand why God's people had to give up the best of what they had, but that answer now seemed as obvious as the first.

The Lamb of God, I went on thinking, *who said more than once, "My body is truly food and My blood is truly drink."* The Passover Lamb slaughtered so that the people of God could eat His flesh and place His blood on their lips, the doors of their bodies.

Before Aaron was priest, Melchizedek was priest; and before Saul was king, Melchizedek was king. A thousand years before Jesus was born, another king, David, wrote down these words of the Lord: "You are a priest forever according to the order of Melchizedek." And two thousand years before Christ, Melchizedek the Priest-King offered to God a sacrifice of bread and wine.

More passages and scenes from scripture returned to me, and I saw them in a new light, the light of Christ, and I finally understood them.

What was once lost through disobedience in the Garden of Eden was regained through obedience in the Garden of Gethsemane.

Out of one tree humanity through Adam had plucked the fruit of sin and corruption; out of the tree of the cross, I was certain, humanity through Christ would pluck the fruit of redemption and restoration. The first was the Tree of the Knowledge of Good and Evil, which brought death, but the second was the Tree of Life, which would bring everlasting life to anyone who ate of its fruit, as Jesus Himself had said.

Isaac rode a donkey for three days, not knowing that he was supposed to be sacrificed when he reached his destination. Jesus rode a donkey to the same place, but He knew exactly what awaited Him in Jerusalem. "For three days you've been dead, Isaac," Abraham told his son, "but today the Lord has brought you back to life." *Jesus is going to die,* I thought; *but He isn't going to stay dead.*

Joseph was sold for silver by his own brothers; Jesus was sold for silver by one of His Twelve. Joseph was handed over to foreigners and bound and led away, and so had Jesus been, only the night before.

But that wasn't the end of the story, of course, and even as I watched Jesus cough blood and almost collapse, I knew it wasn't the end of His story either. "From the depths of the dungeons I was lifted up to the right hand of the king," Joseph once told me, "and people all over the world are saved from starvation because I was sold into slavery."

Before then, though, Joseph interpreted the dreams of two of his fellow prisoners, Pharaoh's baker and his butler. The first dreamt of bread, the other of wine; the first meant death, the other meant a release from imprisonment and a restoration in as many days—in three days. The Son of Man, Jesus had said, will be handed over to be killed, but He will rise again on the third day.

The chief priests, the elders, the Pharisees, and the scribes thought they were being clever: if they stoned Jesus to death, He might be remembered and revered as a martyr, and might have been just as problematic for them in death as He had been in life. But who would continue to honor the name of a Man who'd been executed by Roman crucifixion? The shame would force even His greatest supporters to distance themselves from Him. *Isn't their thinking reasonable?* I thought. *Isn't their strategy wise?* Hadn't Peter—Peter, mighty Apostle; Peter, who had told Jesus he'd follow Him anywhere, even unto death—on the very night he made that promise, even before Jesus was handed over to the Romans, hadn't Peter denied so much as knowing his Master?

Their thinking was reasonable and their strategy was wise indeed. But they should have remembered the words of Isaiah on what God does to the wisdom of the wise and those who take council in secret and work in the dark.

Because it was in death by crucifixion that Jesus would carry the wood of His sacrifice up the mountain, as Isaac had done. It was in crucifixion that He would be lifted up and all who looked at him would have to look up at Him, as if in worship. It was in crucifixion that His arms would be stretched out to either end of the cross beam so that even as He died He would hold His arms open in welcome to the whole world.

It was with outstretched arms that He could clear the way to salvation, just as Moses had stretched out his hands to part the Red Sea; and it was with outstretched arms that He could conquer, just as his army had conquered because Moses stretched out his arms.

Words and images from scripture continued to flash in my mind like shooting stars lighting up the night sky. Here was the meaning of the rock Moses had struck with his staff, from which water had flowed to quench the thirst of the Israelites; here the meaning of the bitter water made sweet when Moses dipped a tree into it; and here was the copper snake placed on a stick, so that whoever was bitten and looked up at it would survive, as Jesus Himself had said.

And, of course, I thought of the words that had terrified Satan since the beginning. For who else was the seed of the woman except the One born of a Virgin Mother? *Delight in His crucifixion while you can, Satan,* I thought. *You've bruised His heel, but He will crush your head.* Because Jesus was indeed the Passover Lamb, but the story didn't end there. After the Passover came the Exodus, when the people of God were led to freedom from the tyrant's rule.

While I had these thoughts, Satan didn't cease from jeering and laughing. Sometimes he'd scream in Jesus' ears and sometimes in mine, alternating between us when he saw he wasn't getting anywhere with either one.

"Do you see, Enoch?" he said at one point, when Jesus fell on His way to Golgotha. "This so-called Son of God isn't strong enough to carry His cross by Himself, but needs the help of another!"

Lost in thoughts that delighted me as much as Jesus' suffering delighted Satan, I hardly heard what he was saying.

Did God have this planned all along? That was the question that had tortured me since the beginning, but now I could answer it at last: Yes! Most gloriously: Yes!

There was a time when I could think that humanity would never be sure of God's love. There was a time when I could think that there was no real reason to love God, because nothing He'd ever done had ever cost Him anything. There was a time when I could think that God chose good because it was easy for Him to do so.

That time had passed, I knew. Out of love, God came down from Heaven to live with human beings as a human being; the Invisible became visible, the Ineffable became a Man with a name, an object for the senses. And as I watched Jesus prepare to give His life to buy back that which was always His but which had enslaved itself to another, I knew I could never think any of those thoughts again.

Satan's maniacal shrieking forced itself on my attention. "He's asking God to forgive them!" he said, speaking in between flashes of laughter. "Forgive the people who are executing Him!"

Satan continued to hurl more insults at Him, as did the two others who were crucified with Jesus, one on each side, and as did the chief priests, and the scribes, and the elders who yelled at Him that if only He could come down from the cross, then they would believe in Him. Some people pointed at the sign above His head and laughed. "You, King of the Jews!" they said. "You helped so many, can't You help Yourself?" Others wondered how a Man who claimed He had the power to destroy the Temple and rebuild it in three days couldn't do anything to save Himself. And still others asked why, if He were truly the Son of God, wasn't His Father rescuing Him from death?

I ignored Satan and all of the others. *God is God,* I thought. *He has a plan. And I want to be part of it.*

"If you want to be My follower," Jesus told His listeners, "you must deny yourself, take up your cross daily, and follow Me."

Yes, Lord.

Satan stopped laughing. Something had happened between Jesus and one of the thieves.

Jesus turned His head and for a moment, the pain disappeared from His face and He smiled. "I tell you the truth," He said to the man crucified next to him, "today You will be with Me in Paradise."

Satan opened his mouth to speak again, but then something else happened: darkness filled the sky, the sun setting at noon, and the light of day growing dark over the land, as the prophet Amos had written.

Panic flashed through Satan's glow for only a second. "Save Yourself," he said, shifting to float beside Jesus and whispering in His ear. "You say You have a special relationship with God. I've seen you work wonders; I've seen the power You possess. You raised a person back to life who'd been dead for four days; you healed the eyes of men born blind. Can't You do anything for Yourself? Can't You do what they're asking You to do? Is this what Your life has amounted to, death on a cross like a criminal and between criminals? Is this what Your mission from God turned into? Save Yourself, Christ!"

Jesus ignored him. He looked down from the cross and called out to His mother, the widow He would soon leave childless, and to John, the Apostle whom He loved. "Woman," He said, speaking with difficulty, "this is your son." And then to John: "This is your mother."

Finally I turned my full attention on Satan. "You want me to rebel against Him and follow you?" I yelled. "I did it once, because I allowed myself to forget the first thing we knew about Him. God is love. Out of love He made us from nothingness; out of love He gave us freedom, even the freedom to reject Him. But now I see in front of my own eyes the extent of that love, a love that extends to death itself, even death on a cross. How can I ever forget that? How can I ever turn my back on Him again?"

My gaze returned to Jesus, but as I looked at Him, beaten and bruised and bleeding, struggling to breathe and speak, the sorrow that had built up inside of me since His arrest slowly hardened into rage. I looked again at Satan, who had reverted to insulting Jesus when he saw his temptations weren't working.

"This is your fault," I yelled at him. "His death wouldn't have been necessary if you hadn't led us in rebellion against Him, and then humanity after us." I paused, realizing that once again I was trying to deflect responsibility from myself. "Not your fault alone; we willingly followed you, or you could have had no power over any of us, just like you have no power over Him."

Satan approached, the heat of his glow burning me. "Wait a minute," he said, pointing over his shoulder at Jesus. "Isn't that how you know God loves you?"

"You are a devil to your core," I said.

Satan began to respond, I steeled myself for an attack, when from Jesus a great cry broke out:

"My God, My God," He said. "Why have You forsaken Me?"

"You see?" Satan said, hissing in delight, but I recognized that Jesus was quoting one of David's psalms, and I remembered its words. "Your God has abandoned His so-called Son!"

I ignored him and kept watching Jesus, and soon I saw something that I'd never seen a human being do before. When He was ready to die, Jesus put His head down on His chest and gave up His spirit.

"Now!" Satan yelled, his voice like the roar from a lion.

Someone grabbed me from behind and shifted. Before the world around me disappeared, I saw that devils had descended on Jesus' spirit as well. Moloch grabbed His right hand, Baal His left; Beelzebub held His feet together. I didn't struggle, because I saw that Jesus wasn't resisting them or even looking at them; I felt that He was looking at me. On His face was an expression of joy and peace; He had the same twinkle in His eyes as when He'd told His disciples only the night before, "In the world you will experience trouble; but be of good cheer, I have overcome the world."

I was brought to Hades, just outside the entrance gates. Everything was the same as I remembered, except for one major difference.

"Go ahead and burn me." The pained voice came from the devil holding me, and I recognized him as Zephar, but didn't know what he was talking about. "Is that really the best you can do?"

"Aren't you going to threaten to drown me in the lake of fire?" I said, looking at where it used to be but where now I saw a lake of water. A man stood on its shore and cried out to the crowd in front of him, and even if I hadn't recognized the figure, I would've recognized the voice.

"Repent!" the Baptist cried out, "for the Kingdom of God is at hand!"

Zephar held me in his grip, though it seemed to cause him more pain than it was causing me. "Are you afraid to approach him?" I said, looking at the army of devils that waited inside the gates but away from the lake. "Has it been like this since John's arrival in Hades?"

Even if he intended on answering, Zephar never got the chance.

"Behold!" the Baptist cried out, in a voice even louder than before, "the Lamb of God!"

It was hard to behold anything else. The devils had shifted Jesus next to me, but it wouldn't have mattered if they'd shifted Him as far as the furthest cell: in that dark place, His glow was like the light from an exploding star.

Moloch, Baal, and Beelzebub held onto Him as long as they could, which wasn't very long. The pain quickly overwhelmed their resolve and they let go. Satan had shifted into Hades inside the gates, at the head of his army near the palace, and now the three devils who'd held Jesus and the one who'd held me shifted away from us and reappeared beside their master. Their glows betrayed their confusion and anger and fear, a strange mixture of fury tempered by a hesitant dread.

The devils had brought Jesus outside the gates, I was certain, through careful instruction from a cautious Satan. Now the Prince of Devils forced himself to stare at Jesus, and seemed to wait to see what He would do.

Jesus walked up to the gates. In a voice louder than the crack of thunder or the roar of lions, He said: "Lift up your heads, O gates; and be lifted up, you ancient doors; that the King of glory shall enter."

The gates began to shake at His first word, as if they, too, trembled at His approach; the gates as tall as mountains and thick as the palace's thickest walls; the gates I'd designed and which the devils had built. Before Jesus finished speaking, they began to fall in sections, so that from all around us came the sound of creaking and crumbling and rock crashing on rock.

Jesus stepped onto the broken gates.

"Stop Him!" Satan yelled, but none of his devils had the strength to listen, let alone obey. They had fallen to their knees, and were trying to shield their eyes from His glow with their hands and their arms, and some were even trying to bury their heads in the rocky ground.

Satan yelled more orders, but his words were tinged with an increasing shrillness. He thought he had captured the Son of God and was realizing too late that the Son of God had captured him. The moment he'd believed would be his greatest victory turned out to be his ultimate defeat. He'd brought about the death of the Son of Man, but in doing so, without knowing it, he'd been bringing about his own undoing.

Fighting back the pain, Satan forced himself to his knees, then pushed himself up. He grabbed Asmodeus and Mulciber, the devils nearest him, and launched them at the approaching figure Whose glow was blinding and torturing them, but Whose light couldn't be escaped anywhere in Hades. Satan retreated, picking up more devils, two at a time, and throwing them at Jesus before moving on to the next pair. Finally he looked back and saw that none of the devils had budged from where they'd landed, but lay whimpering and curled up before the Light that walked past them as if they weren't even there. Satan stopped moving. He seemed to push away the pain by sheer willpower and to draw on every ounce of energy he had left. Suddenly, he let out a deafening roar of fury and made a rush at Jesus, traveling so quickly that he looked like a flash of lightning.

Jesus lifted His right hand. With His fingers, He cut the air in front of Him vertically and then crossed that line with a horizontal one. Satan fell back and recoiled, hissing as he scampered away.

John and his followers approached Jesus and, one after another, dropped to their knees and bowed their heads to Him. Jesus made the sign of the cross over them.

Together Jesus and the crowd returned to the lake. When He reached the shore, Jesus raised His hand over the water and a third time made the sign of the cross. Immediately a geyser erupted from the middle of the lake, the mighty fountain sending down torrents of rain.

To the devils, to judge from their screams, the rush of water was a river of fire that burned them and threatened to drown them in unbelievable pain. To John and his listeners, to judge from their cheers of "Hosanna!" the water was a blanket of warm light, chasing away the cold and darkness of Hades.

To me, it was something else. I watched the water splash against the walls of Satan's palace, breaking apart the structure I'd built and rebuilt, tumbling rocks on top of stones, and sweeping everything away. I watched Satan's throne crack and disappear along the current. More waves crashed into the prisons I'd built, tearing them down, by the hundreds and by the thousands, washing them away, erasing any sign that they'd ever existed.

"Hosanna!" I cried, my voice joining that of the others. "Hallelujah!"

Water crashed onto the battleground, shattering it, and the overflowing lake filled the pit into which the devils often threw the fallen spirits to see them try to climb out.

As the cells that held them captive were destroyed, some of the prisoners were swept along the river, screaming that they were being burned alive, while others didn't seem to move with the current. These were left standing where they were, but they dropped to their knees and scooped the water into their mouths. When they looked up and shouted in joy, I knew what they were saying even if I couldn't hear them over the sounds of screaming devils and tumbling stone and crashing water. They were saying what the rest of us were saying, if in their own language and in their own way.

As I watched the water flood Hades and destroy everything I'd built there, I heard a loud and familiar voice: "Listen, all of you! I am Jesus of Nazareth, the Christ, the Son of God. He who believes in me, though he dies, yet shall he live. Follow Me!"

Yes, Lord, I thought. Before I could move, though, something caught my eye: a loose pebble resting on the ground near me, not moving with the water. I reached down to pick it up, and saw that words were written on it. I began to read and, with a shock, recognized the text. *This is the book I wrote when I was in the dungeon,* I thought.

When I looked up again, men and women were standing next to Jesus at the lakeshore. Some I recognized because of my familiarity with them during their lives—Abraham, Isaac, Jacob, Joseph, Moses, David, even the robber whom Jesus had promised Paradise. An ancient-looking man and woman stood to either side of Him.

The third war, I thought. *But it isn't what we expected—it isn't the devils doing the invading.*

Jesus took the hands of the elderly couple and said, one more time, "Follow Me." The old man and woman took the hands of those standing next to them, and those in turn took the hands of others. The chain of spirits stretched as far as I could see, all along the shoreline and far past any cell I'd ever built.

I wanted to join them, but I didn't move. I looked back down at the pebble. *This is the book I wrote, but that isn't my handwriting.*

Someone grabbed my other hand; a woman. "I remember you," she said.

At first I didn't recognize her, but I looked closer. "Yes, I remember you too," I said, in awe. The last time I saw her, she'd looked out at me from behind prison bars and her hair was like thin straw, her back was bent, and wrinkles pulled down her face with the weight of sorrow. Now she stood straight, and her hair was long and white, and the wrinkles around her eyes and mouth were marks of joy.

"Aren't you coming?" she said.

"I remember you," I said again. "I used you to accuse God of lacking mercy. In my mind I was more merciful than Him, and yet I did nothing for you, nothing to ease your suffering or pain, nothing except insult God for not doing anything to help you."

"That doesn't matter anymore," she said, looking back at Jesus and all of those who had linked hands with Him. "Aren't you coming?"

Aren't you going to Heaven, Enoch?

"I can't," I said. "I can't leave."

The woman nodded. After a moment, she turned around and ran back to join the others.

Once more I looked down at the pebble in my hand. When I looked up again, Jesus and everyone with Him was gone.

Chapter Twelve

The Eighth Day

THis *is how it ends*, I thought, but I was wrong. It wasn't the end yet, though it was the end of Hades.

Before Satan and his devils brought Jesus to that dark and cold place, Hades was their abode. As much as they loved the Earth, that was only their playground. Eventually they all came home, to where the spirits they'd stolen paid them their dues, where the pain-filled sounds of the screaming fallen delighted them, where the suffering was so palatable and abundant that they could devour as much of it as they wanted but still have more before them. Even the lake, which to them was a lake of fire because it was a reminder of the Source of their existence and so a reminder that they weren't self-existent, even that they used to torture one another and the fallen.

But Hades was their abode no longer. The lake had erupted, as if it too wanted to honor the One who came to liberate all who desired freedom, raising its arms in praise of Him who conquered death by His death. Zechariah was right—by the blood of His covenant, He'd freed the prisoners from the pit without water. But He'd done even more than that: He'd filled the pit with water; He'd replaced the dark with His light and the cold with His presence.

After Jesus and the others were gone, I scanned Hades. Most of the spirits were difficult to tell apart, though. They were a writhing mass, an undulating creature floating in the lake, twisting and thrashing about as each devil tried to get away from the others.

A few had found their way to higher ground, where they could escape the touch of the water, though not the blinding light. Their mournful groaning was as loud as the horrible screeches of pain from those still caught in the water.

Satan wasn't among either group as far as I could see, and neither was the devil I was looking for.

Before I could begin my search in earnest, though, Apael found me. "Why are you still here, Enoch?" he said. "You've been following

Him for so long, and this is the time you choose to stop?"

"I can't leave Hades."

"Why not?" he said, smiling.

"I'm looking for someone."

"Who?"

"A devil," I said. "A devil who isn't experiencing the flood of water as a burning fire."

"Why?" Apael said, the peace and gladness in his voice drowning out the screaming of the devils.

"Because he doesn't deserve to be here, that's why."

"Where do you think 'here' is, Enoch?" he said, looking around.

I didn't say anything.

"This is the realm of the dead," Apael said. "Hades swallowed up all of those who died before Christ. But it had to spit them out, because Jesus embittered it."

"I don't understand," I said.

"No one is here who doesn't choose to be," Apael said. "So why do you choose to be?"

"Where am I supposed to go?" I said. "Am I supposed to follow Jesus and the others to Heaven? I don't even know if He'll let me into Heaven!"

"You still don't understand, Enoch. Jesus isn't in Heaven. Come and see."

"He went to Earth to rise again, like He said."

"Yes, but not like you think. Come and see."

"No," I said, wanting to be left alone to continue my search for the devil who copied my book. I paused for a long moment. "What do you mean, 'but not like I think'?"

Apael laughed. "Come and see."

He shifted, and I followed.

We arrived in a garden; a figure stood in front of us. One look at Jesus and I understood why Apael hadn't tried to explain it to me himself.

"The Lord kills, and He makes alive," Hannah once sang. "He brings down to Hades, and He raises up."

The Lord raised up Jesus, I saw. The disembodied spirit that had descended into Hades and flooded it with His light had been reunited with the body that had suffered and died on the cross.

"Do you understand now?" Apael said. "Do you see?"

Jesus was looking directly at me. I approached, and bowed down in front of Him.

"Enoch," He said, and it was His voice, the same voice that I'd listened to for so long, the voice that expelled devils and healed diseases, the voice that spoke the stories that delighted me and the teachings that condemned me.

"Yes," I said, rising. "Here I am."

"Follow Me."

I looked over my shoulder; Apael was gone. Not far from us, a band of armed men stood guard in front of a large stone closing up the mouth of a cave. The sun peeked over the horizon.

"No, Lord," I said, not meeting His gaze. "I can't follow You. I want to, but I can't. I'm not worthy, Lord."

The ground quaked; I looked around again. Apael was rolling away the stone blocking the cave.

"Enoch," Jesus said. "I never asked you to want to love your enemies, or to want to do good to those who hate you. I only asked you to do so."

Startled, I looked into His eyes. With a few words, He'd collapsed the gates I'd built up inside my mind and heart, just as with a few words He'd collapsed the gates I'd built up in Hades.

After a few moments, Jesus pointed at the cave. "While My Apostles and the other disciples cower in fear behind locked doors," He said, "those blessed women you see over there come at this early hour to anoint My body, because they don't understand what I said to them. But I will go show Myself to them, that they may believe that I am risen from among the dead. I will send them as Apostles to the Apostles, to preach to them the good news that they will hear and see first."

"Will they recognize You?" I said.

"I will help their understanding," Jesus said. "My brothers won't believe their reports, however. Many won't believe that I am risen until they see Me for themselves; some, not until they touch the holes where the nails were driven into My hands or the wound where the spear pierced My side."

"You're not angry with them for needing to see You for themselves?"

"No," Jesus said. "But blessed are those who haven't seen and yet believe."

I kept staring at Him, marveling at what I saw. The Lord had raised Jesus up indeed, but not like He'd raised up Lazarus or anyone else in the history of the world. They would all die again, but Jesus never would.

It wasn't something I'd ever seen before, or even something I'd imagined could exist, but I understood right away that this must have been what God intended for humanity from the beginning. I'd always assumed that the mark of the physical world was corruptibility. But there was nothing corruptible about Jesus; His body was physical, a body of flesh and blood, but it was now a solid body. It was the same body that had been crucified and died, but also different: as if the first was the shadow and this the substance.

"Will You establish Your Kingdom at this time, Lord?"

"I will establish my Church at this time," He said. "After I have returned to My Father, He will send the Helper and Comforter to My Apostles, as I promised them. Clothed in His power, they will go to all of Judea and all of Samaria, and to the whole world, to tell everyone the news of salvation, to preach to Jews and Gentiles, to men and women, to rich and poor, and to free and slave."

As Jesus spoke, I was reminded of the words of the prophets Joel and Jeremiah. His Spirit would be poured out on all flesh and the good news would be proclaimed, the first had written. And the second: God would establish a new covenant with His people; He would write His law on their hearts, and He would forgive their sins. That was the good news, I saw: the old covenant based on the Law had been fulfilled by Christ, and by His blood God had established the long-promised new covenant, a covenant as superior to the old one as Abel was superior to Cain, or Isaac to Ishmael, or Jacob to Esau, or Ephraim to Manasseh, or David to Saul, or even Jesus to Israel.

"I think I understand," I said, and then blurted out: "And what of me, Lord?" Jesus didn't respond immediately, but it was too late to take back my words and I pressed on, asking the question that I'd wanted to ask Him for so long, the question whose answer had haunted me for thousands of years: "Will I be allowed to return to Heaven?"

"Whenever you wish, Enoch," He said. "But I have lots of work for you to do on Earth." He looked at me, and a smile overtook His face. "You think this is a punishment, but that is because you don't yet understand. You will see amazing things, Enoch—I will raise up great saints in My name, men and women who will live according to My word, men and women who will account suffering and death as nothing compared to the joy they will find in Me, men and women who will speak Truth even if they stand alone against the whole world—and they will prevail. I will send you to protect and strengthen some of them, but your services to them will pale next to their services to you."

He was right, of course. At the time, though, I simply nodded without understanding. "Lord, there is something else. I wrote a book once and a devil in Hades copied it in his own hand. He may still be down there."

"Ask him about it," Jesus said, and behind Him I finally noticed a dark shadow crawling along the ground in between some shrubs. "Then come and find Me."

Jesus walked away, toward the cave whose mouth now stood open, and I approached the devil crawling on the ground.

"Satan," I said.

He looked up at me, his glow faint but still full of anger and hatred. "You've changed, Enoch. You were strong and resolute once. You wanted freedom from Him as much as I did. But you lived too long in their changeable realm; you allowed yourself to be influenced by these despicable creatures."

"Yes!" I said. "Don't you see? Salvation has come to humanity from the Jews, but to the rest of creation from humanity. Don't be unchanging, Satan, but allow yourself to be changed by them too!"

"Why?" Satan said, rising in front of me. "So I can bow down to Him like you did? I saw you—bowing down to a Man."

"Yes!" I said, again. "That's exactly what you need to do."

"Never."

I took a step closer, but he recoiled from me. "Can't you see that you've been defeated, Satan? Your back is broken, and nothing awaits you now but the everlasting fire—unless you turn to Him and ask for healing."

He hissed. "You are a slave, Enoch, and want to make me a slave like you."

"You're wrong. I want you to be free."

"I will never be a slave!" he said. "I will never bow down to Him!"

"But how can the work Jesus accomplished not melt your obstinacy?" I said. "All people were under a sentence of death, but Christ remitted it; He blotted out its words with His blood. They were imprisoned by the fear of death, which made them greedy and selfish and avaricious, but Christ set them free, trampling down death by His death. They were cursed, but Jesus took the sins of the world on Himself, that they might be blessed by His wounds. All of them were transgressors, every one unrighteous, except for Him. They all deserved to die, but He who was without sin died in their place, that they could live with God."

"Enough!" Satan yelled. "Everything you say—all of it strengthens my resolve to oppose Him, fuels my hatred for the unworthy fallen for whom He did all these things, deepens my desire to separate them from Him and make them suffer." He paused, and drew closer to me though I saw it pained him. "You can help me, Enoch. Help me oppose Him. You would be my chief angel, and under your authority I would put Zephar and all the others."

"This is pathetic," I said. "If you won't repent yourself, at least tell me who copied my book in Hades."

Confusion washed over Satan's glow for only a moment, but it was quickly replaced by rage. He looked at me as if he wanted to say something, but he thought better of it and shifted.

Without pausing, I followed him to Hades.

"Asmodeus!" Satan was yelling, shifting from one screaming or whimpering devil to another until he found him.

Hunched over the tip of a rock that extended just above the water, Asmodeus collapsed even more into himself at Satan's call. Satan whispered in his ear.

Asmodeus stopped crying long enough to laugh. "Do you think I care?" he said. "What more can you do to me?"

I turned away from them. "Listen to me, all of you!" I yelled out. "You're terrified—you think we've lost. We have! Everything is lost; God has conquered us in His Christ. We are thoroughly defeated, Hades is laid waste, salvation has come to humanity and all of our work is undone. Our greatest weapons were shattered on the Cross of Christ. Anyone who believes in Him will not fear the enemy that Jesus has conquered, and without death and the fear of death, what power will we have over them?"

Satan hissed, louder and louder and with so much insistence that the devils finally stopped screaming for the moment. "Lies!" he said. "He speaks lies! We aren't defeated—we've won! The Enemy doesn't realize what He's done! When the fallen rejected Him in times past, He could forgive them: what they did, they did out of ignorance. But now He has lived among them, and died, and risen again. When they reject Him now—and they will, of course, and we'll be there to make sure of it—what excuse can He make for them?"

Some of the devils cheered; their strength seemed to have returned. It was a wonder to behold—as much as they still suffered in that illumined place, their pain was manageable so long as they could focus on the suffering of others.

"We helped them turn away from the invisible God," Satan went on. "Do you think it is beyond our power to turn them away from the God made visible? Foolish angels, our task is even easier now! They will doubt that Jesus is God at all, for how can the Invisible become visible, or the Creator become a creation? As we've done in the past, so we'll do in the future. We'll make them doubt everything about God: His goodness, His commandments, even His very existence. Sin will run rampant and rule their lives, as it always has. Our strategy won't change—but their penalty will. By showing Himself to them, God has made their rejection that much worse. This is what God has done for us in His Christ, brethren."

Amid their cheering, I raised my arms. "Look around at what God has done in His Christ—where are all the spirits you stole? Why are all of you still shielding your eyes? Why do you cheer Satan one moment and scream out in pain the next?"

Satan ignored me. "Those fallen who refuse to doubt His existence will be our favorites. We will allow them to confess Him with their words and deny Him with their deeds. They will feel self-satisfied for the convictions they profess and turn a blind eye to the lives they lead."

As he spoke, more devils crawled out of the water and onto the tops of rocks, so that they could better hear him.

"By now you must see the truth!" I said. "Satan has told you from the beginning that there is a way to win against God, but that's impossible. You can't win apart from Him, because He is the only goal and His grace the only trophy."

Led by Satan, the devils shouted me down.

"You can accept God's love," I said, becoming frustrated with them, "or you can have His fury. You can consent to His mercy, or endure His wrath. Repent and be saved, or continue in rebellion and suffer."

Satan shouted me down again, then went on as if I'd never spoken. "We will teach the fallen what we already know: that the only authentic life is a life of freedom, which can only be lived by rejecting the One who wishes to rule them. But all the while we will be making them slaves to sin and to ourselves. And what more can He do? He has already offered to them His body and His blood—can He offer it to them again and again?"

The devils laughed.

"In Christ," Satan went on, "God has done everything He can to win them back to Himself. But with your help, brethren, we will show Him that it wasn't enough. He can do no more than what He's done—but it still isn't enough."

I tried to say more, but it was obvious the devils only had ears for Satan.

Back on Earth, I followed Jesus' glow to the shores of the Sea of Galilee. The sun was starting to rise. Jesus stood in front of a fire of coals on which bread and fish were cooking, staring out at some fishermen in a boat in the middle of the lake. Apael stood next to Him.

I approached, but Jesus turned away from me. Going down to the lakeshore, He called out to the fishermen: "Children, have you any food?"

"Apael," I said, "I've just returned from Hades."

"Then cast your net on the right side of the boat," Jesus called out, "and you'll find some!"

To my surprise, the joy in Apael's glow never dimmed as I told him what had happened with Satan and the devils.

"I don't understand," I said. "Why didn't He destroy them?"

"Destroy that which He made?" Apael said, shock undulating throughout his glow.

I turned my head at the sound of splashing water; one of the fisherman had jumped into the lake and was swimming to shore.

"But nothing's changed!" I said, turning back to Apael and trying to control my voice. "God became Man; He died; He rose from the dead. Shouldn't that change everything?"

"It has."

"It hasn't! Satan might be paralyzed and weaponless, but he is still free; he still plans ways to corrupt humanity and turn them away from God."

"Did they attack you?"

It was Peter, I now saw—the fisherman who'd jumped into the lake. He rose out of the water, dripping wet, and stared at Jesus in awe and wonder, and as if he wanted to ask Him a question to which he already knew the answer. The other disciples reached the shore in the boat, tugging behind them a net full of fish.

"What?" I said, distracted.

"Did the devils attack you?"

"No."

Apael's smile widened. "Isn't that strange? I've read your book too, Enoch. It wasn't only one copy that was made. Satan ordered them all destroyed, he just didn't find them all. So why didn't the devils attack you this time? Why didn't Satan command them to attack you? Why didn't he attack you himself?"

Peter ran to the boat and dragged onto the shore the net bursting with fish.

Jesus told the disciples to gather around the fire.

"I don't know," I said.

"I'll tell you, then," Apael said. "They're afraid of you. Because they're afraid of Jesus, and because you belong to Him."

I was quiet for a long time, listening to the conversation of the disciples and their Master as they ate breakfast. Finally, when it looked like they were finishing up, I turned to Apael and said, "What about the others? What will happen to those left in Hades?"

"The Cross will conquer the whole world," he said. "The Cross will conquer everything but one."

"Simon, son of Jonah," Jesus said, speaking softly and fixing Peter with His gaze, "do you love Me more than these?"

"Yes, Lord," Peter said, smiling. "You know how much I care about You."

"Feed My lambs," Jesus said.

"The free choice of free creatures," I said to Apael.

He nodded. "Everyone must choose. Christ is the dividing line."

Jesus asked Peter a second time if he loved Him, and a second time Peter said how much he cared about Him; Jesus said, "Tend My sheep." A third time Jesus asked Peter if he cared about Him and, eyes downcast, Peter told Him that he did, and a third time Jesus said, "Feed My sheep."

"Do you see?" Apael said, his joy and excitement contagious. "Peter denied Him three times over one fire, but Jesus restored him three times over another. So it is with anyone who seeks welcome from Him; for whoever asks will receive, as He said."

Over the next few weeks, I followed Jesus as He visited His Apostles and disciples and helped them understand what He had done for the world from the very beginning, and prepared them to receive His Spirit. I followed Jesus and thought about what Apael had said.

More than one copy was made. What could it mean, except that even as Satan filled their ears with lies, some devils still felt the pull to Truth? Questions require answers, but no one had answers that would satisfy—for only One is the answer.

I have to write another book, I thought. I didn't know if any of the other devils would ever turn back to God, but I was certain that it was God's will that they do so. I had to write that book, I knew: a book to complete the first, the form to the shadow. But also I knew I had to wait. Jesus had told me to follow Him; there was work for me to do, He said. I even heard what out of kindness He didn't put into words—how could I teach others when I didn't understand myself?

But, little by little, I was starting to understand.

When He gathered His disciples on the Mount of Olives shortly after His resurrection, Jesus said to them, "All authority in Heaven and Earth has been given to Me." I looked at Apael, but I thought I knew what He meant—what was always His in His divinity was now also His in His humanity.

For it was a created human being who rose to Heaven that day; a creature of flesh and blood who sat down at the right hand of the Father.

Did we fear flesh because we didn't understand it? And did we hate matter because it's so transitory? It was only because we didn't understand. I once thought that Jesus was working to restore that which humanity had lost in Eden, but Jesus only began with restoration. Eden wasn't a destination, it was a path to somewhere else, a path to Someone else. Jesus set them along that path again, and cleared the way of all dangers. His purpose was to create them anew, for the Risen Christ was something new, something the physical world had never contained before: an incorruptible physical body, a breathing, living human being who will never again taste death, an embodied spirit who will live forever as an embodied spirit.

Where does that path end? This is the truth you've heard many times now, but have never understood: God became man so that man could become God.

Not long after Jesus set His Church in motion at Pentecost, a man named Stephen, a Christian full of the Holy Spirit, was brought to trial in front of a council of Jews on charges of blasphemy. Stephen refused to deny his Lord, however, but tried to show them how everything in the Law and in the Prophets was fulfilled in Him, and how their hardness of heart caused them to persecute Jesus just as their ancestors had persecuted His prophets and resisted His Spirit from the very beginning.

"Enoch," Jesus said, when the Jews, full of rage at Stephen's words, began calling for his death.

"Here I am," I said.

"That is him," Jesus said, and I knew I was finally ready to begin working. But Jesus wasn't indicating Stephen; He looked at one of the Jews dragging Stephen outside Jerusalem.

I nodded, not asking the question that sprang to mind: *You want me to destroy that man?* For a moment, I was convinced that this was how Jesus would use me: as a defeater of humans, tempting them to death as I had done before, the only difference being that now I would work on those opposed to Him rather than those opposed to Satan.

"Enoch," Jesus said, "I want you to protect him."

Why I was sent to protect a man who held the clothes of the witnesses against Stephen's blasphemy, a Pharisee who looked on with an approving smile as those witnesses threw stones at Stephen until he died, a Jew who snickered when the dying Stephen, falling to his knees, looked up at the sky and said, "Lord Jesus, don't hold this sin against them"—I didn't know. And what I was supposed to protect him from, I wasn't sure.

But I followed the Pharisee who, in his zeal to serve the Lord, and persecute the Christians he believed were insulting the God of his fathers, went to the High Priest to receive the authority to arrest followers of Christ.

I didn't understand, but that didn't matter. I trusted the One who sent me; I trusted that something would happen that would help me understand what I was supposed to do.

For the moment, it was enough to know what I did know.

Humanity's fall began with a man and a woman, but it ended with a woman and a Man. The first Adam and the first Eve brought death and corruption into the world; the second Eve and the second Adam brought salvation and incorruption

The first Ark held within it the manna, the Law, and the rod that budded with life; the second Ark held within her womb Christ Himself, who was the true bread from Heaven, who fulfilled the Law, and whose Cross was life-giving.

The first Moses had to die before God's work of salvation could be accomplished, and so did the second Moses. For Jesus indeed rested His body in the grave on the Sabbath, the seventh day. But when He rose again, it wasn't only on the first day of a new week, a day like any other that would restart the cycle of weeks—it was to a day that had never been seen before. He rose on the morning of the eighth day, the resurrection day, the day of new creation.

It is a day that will never end, a day that will be light to those who love Him and darkness to those who hate Him.

The sun is yet on the horizon, but sometime soon (no one knows the hour), the Son will be made manifest. When that happens—when God withholds Himself no longer, but reveals Himself fully in His creation, when God becomes the all in all—He will also reveal the choice that each one of us has made.

For Jesus came to the world lowly and humble, as humble as a baby crying in a crib; but He will return in His proper glory. He came riding on a donkey, but He will return riding on the clouds of heaven. He came to be judged and to die, but He will return to judge the world and grant life everlasting to all who believe in Him.

Creation is being remade. One day all will live in His presence—some, joyfully in the new Heaven and the new Earth, glorifying Him always; others, experiencing His glory as the torment of everlasting fire.

That terrifies you, I know—because you believe that God won't forgive you. But don't you see the lesson Christ came to teach? God will not only allow you to return to Him, He desires it with all His heart.

It isn't as difficult as you think—His yoke is easy and His burden light.

He stands and calls out to you with the words that He called out to His Apostles and disciples, the words that He called out to me, the words that He calls out to all, now and forever: "Follow Me."

Father John VS the Zombies:
Book One of the Father John Trilogy

It happened very fast. Within weeks, isolated news reports of people acting in strange and often violent ways became frequent and widespread. Terrifying videos were uploaded to the internet in shocking numbers from across the globe. Chaotic images of societies in rapid decline.

Then—everything went dark. No electricity, no internet, no broadcasts on the emergency radio station.

Now—howling, angry, bloodied creatures claw to get into Johnny Salibi's house, where he lives with his wife and young daughter.

But Johnny and his family are safe. He's boarded up the windows. The door is locked and secure. They will ride things out until the government can get things under control again. They're safe. . .

. . . except that they're not.

Johnny must try to protect his wife and daughter in a world suddenly turned apocalyptic. But things will not go according to plan. Johnny will learn that the zombie plague is not what he or anyone else thought it was. He will learn that the government is not in any position to rescue them. And he will also learn that an unlikely group of survivors might hold the key not only to survival, but to salvation.

Combining elements of zombie fiction, apocalyptic literature, and spiritual thrillers, this is the gripping tale of a man whose faith in God is put to the test with life and death—and even greater—consequences.

Visit www.ootersplace.com/FatherJohn for more information.

ALSO BY THE AUTHOR

Available in paperback and ebook formats.

Bishop John VS the Antichrist:
Book Two of the Father John Trilogy

Beset by violent nightmares and feeling abandoned by the God whose presence he'd felt so keenly only a short while ago, Father John Salibi is distracted, irritable, and completely devoid of spiritual power.

But then he meets an enigmatic old man who tells him that all will be well. In contrast to John, the old man commands staggering power: he travels great distances in moments, he multiplies food in his hands; and he performs wonderful miracles of healing in a world desperately in need of healing. The old man even claims to have defeated the antichrist, the mysterious figure haunting John's dreams and whose activity in the world allowed the plague John had once thought of, in his ignorance, as the "zombie apocalypse." Is the old man real, or a figment of John's troubled imagination? If real, where does his power come from—from God or from somewhere else?

A story of good and evil, of faith and love, of defeat and death and resurrection, and of the one thing necessary.

In this epic sequel to *Father John VS the Zombies*, the story of the end of the world continues…

Visit www.ootersplace.com/BishopJohn for more information.

ALSO BY THE AUTHOR

Available in paperback and ebook formats.

Ooter's Place and Other Stories of Fear, Faith, and Love

Why doesn't God do something to stop the evil and suffering in the world? Some people who call themselves the "Atheists Against God" think they know the answer. And they know what they're going to do about it, too.

A hired gun—who doesn't use a gun and won't be hired by just anyone—realizes that his profession is killing him, but finds it hard to quit. Until he discovers that his talent has more uses than he ever dreamed possible.

A young boy learns that his best friend is an alien. But does that mean they have to stop being friends?

Meet interesting, complex characters; explore worlds both strange and all-too-familiar; and discover the answer to thought-provoking mysteries in this collection of 13 short stories by Karl El-Koura. Twelve of these short tales were previously published in magazines between 1998 and 2010, while the bonus story is exclusive to this collection.

Spanning a wide range of genres (including science fiction, fantasy, horror, detective fiction, military fiction, and superhero fiction) and a wide range of lengths (from the shortest story at 250 words to the longest at 7500 words), *Ooter's Place and Other Stories of Fear, Faith, and Love* is an eclectic collection. Join the author as he introduces you to stories both light and dark, fun and serious, always entertaining.

Visit <u>www.ootersplace.com/OotersPlace</u> for more information.

ALSO BY THE AUTHOR

The Lost Stories:
A Series of Cosmic Adventures

These are the adventures of James Kollins: greedy, petty, selfish captain of the galactic warship *DeVille*; a man obsessed with the holodrama *Captain Courageous and the Women Who Love Him*; a man completely unforgiving of his much-maligned first officer. A man who has just met the Creator of the universe, though he doesn't quite realize it yet, and whose life is about to change in ways he never dreamed possible, though he doesn't quite know it yet.

Find out what happens when an overgrown child in charge of a large military ship, and sadly lacking a conscience and possessed of a strange sense of humor, comes into contact with God Himself, who isn't above playing a few tricks of His own.

You'll be plunged into interstellar war and ultramodern espionage, witness textbook-poor diplomacy and longstanding family feuds, and even encounter a seemingly evil empire of cute babies.

It's a safe bet you'll laugh while reading this book; a virtual lock you'll crack a smile or twenty; and inconceivable that you won't groan and shake your head on a regular basis. In the tradition of Isaac Asimov's pun-in-cheek "feghoots," each of these twelve short-shorts ends in a play on words and phrases that will leave you wondering what's wrong with the author.

Part loving Star Trek ~~parody~~ homage, part spiritual journey, *The Lost Stories* is a series of cosmic and comic adventures that is silly, fun, and also demonstrates the power of God working in the life of even the most self-obsessed warship captain you've ever met.

Visit www.ootersplace.com/TheLostStories for more information.

www.ingramcontent.com/pod-product-compliance
Lightning Source LLC
Chambersburg PA
CBHW052036240626
47153CB00006B/2105